# The Edge of Nothing

## The Lex Chronicles, Book 1

*A Legends of Arameth Novel*

# Crystal Crawford

Edited by Christy Freeman
**Cover design by Jason Crawford/Fierce, Inc.**

*To the one who dreams bigger than I ever could*

and to Jason,
*for believing in me enough to defend the time and space I needed to write.*

# Table of Contents

# ARAMETH

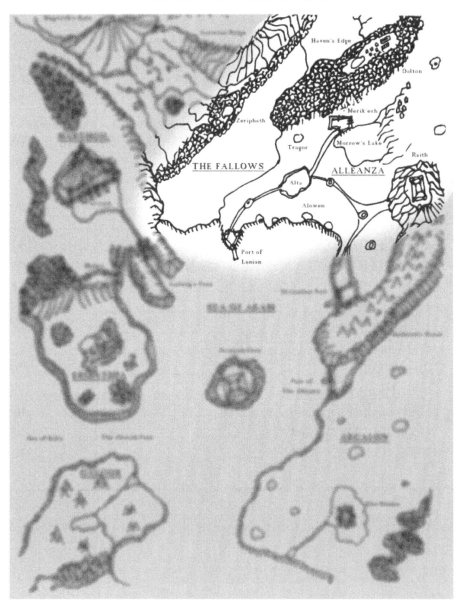

*They said no man could ever cross the Aracthea and survive.*
*The desert Aracthea, with its barren sands hot enough to melt the soles off a man's feet.*
*Aracthea, with its mile-long stretch of searing rock, the bubbling pits of lava surrounded by a sea of sand. Aracthea, the wasteland.*
*They called it Death's Snare.*
*There was a story once, long ago, that mothers told their children, about a man so brave and so full of hope that he crossed the Aracthea barefoot in one day. One night, one particular mother told this story to her son for the very first time.*
*"How could hope keep a man's skin from melting?" the son asked.*
*"It didn't," the mother said. "The man crossed the Aracthea, but when he reached the other side, his feet were melted away and his legs were blackened stubs. Yet he didn't care, because what awaited him on the other side was all that mattered to him."*
*"What was waiting for him there?" the boy asked.*
*"Victory," said his mother, "and then death."*

– Fable of Raith'il
Recorded in *Book of the Ancients,*
Arayear 5 p.A.;
Original reported missing from Arcalon Hall of Records,
Arayear 52 p.A.;
Copied to Arcalon Archives via Historian Memory Consensus,
Arayear 53 p.A.

# PROLOGUE

The rider leaned forward, legs tense against his horse's sides as her hooves tore through the desert. He had been riding for days, though he could no longer remember why. Sand caked his short beard, making him ache for a shave. He shook his head and more sand sifted down from his hair. Sand coated his eyelids, his lips, even the inside of his mouth. He rode bareback, holding onto the horse's mane. His horse's white coat was darkened with sand, and more flew up around them with every step. He clenched his jaw, feeling sand crunch between his teeth, and turned his head to spit. No spit would come; his mouth was completely dry. He leaned forward, urging his horse to go faster.

The horse stumbled beneath him and he murmured to her, but she had already regained her footing. He wished he could let her stop and rest, but they were almost out of time... he just couldn't remember for what. They could not afford to slow down, that much he knew, but the reason danced just out of grasp. What had brought them to this wasteland? He could not remember, but he knew they must keep going. No matter what happened, they must not stop. The horse seemed to read this thought, surging forward to make up for the few seconds she lost when she faltered.

In the back of his mind, a memory whispered – *The Fallows* – a stretch of barren desert that took three days to cross at its narrowest point, even by the fastest horse and rider. And that was if the rider's luck held, if he missed the sand pits that caved in without warning, and the vipers, and the mirages that lured men to slow deaths in the burning sun. This information came to him from a distance, like remnants of an oft-told bedtime story. Even remembering that much felt like drawing up a heavy pail from a deep well; the memories resisted lifting. The details of the past few days refused to rise at all, slipping away even as he tried to grasp them, but he couldn't shake the feeling that as they raced across The Fallows, death was only a step behind.

The sun sank down, first slowly then quickening. The air took on a chill. Still they rode. They were out of water, out of food, parched and sunburned and on the brink of collapse. His horse's breaths grew ragged, and the heat from her body rose up to him through her skin, surrounding him in a hot, dry cloud. They had both ceased sweating long ago. Deep in his mind he knew that was a bad sign – there was no fluid left in them. He lifted a calloused hand from the horse's mane and reached to pat her neck. He and the horse had a deep history. He could not remember it, but the memories were not as important as the knowing of it. He could read her like an old friend, and he could tell she was weakening, the last of her energy draining into the sand beneath them. Her gallop became strained, hooves laboring in the sand. He tensed his knees and leaned forward, placing a hand on her hot skin, feeling his heat mix with hers. *Only a little further, Mare,* he thought, noticing that he had somehow remembered her name, though nothing else. Her faltering gait grew a little steadier under his touch. He shifted, steadying himself with his knees to stroke her neck again. His hand was inches from her sand-crusted coat when something caught his eye in the distance. There was a line of black ahead, as if someone had drawn across the desert with black chalk. He raised his free hand to shade his eyes from the last rays of the setting sun. It wasn't a black line; it was a row of trees – the edge of a forest, growing closer by the moment. Wherever it was they were going, they were almost there.

The world tilted then righted itself again, and he was staring at a girl. The desert was gone, his horse was gone; there was nothing but grass and trees and sky and the girl... and him. The world had gone still. He ran one hand across his face, feeling the chafe of days-old stubble. He spoke and his voice scraped like flint; the words dissolved into the air before he could place them. The girl was not looking at him but past him, at something beyond. Wisps of blonde hair rested on either side of her eyes, framing them. Recognition hit him, along with a wave of longing. *I know her*, he thought. Excitement sang in his veins. He could not remember who she was, but he knew she mattered. He reached for her. Her eyes snapped toward him and widened in surprise. Her lips parted, as though about to speak–

She vanished. The world went black. He was falling into nothingness.

# THE EDGE OF NOTHING

He had a flash of awareness – he was dreaming. Again. It was not the first time he'd had these dreams. These same scenes, the horse and rider, the girl – they haunted him, pulling him in and then tossing him back out before he ever discovered their meaning.

He was slipping toward wakefulness when he realized he didn't remember anything of his waking life, either. Panic rushed in at him and he flailed in the darkness, afraid he was falling into yet another dream, uncertain what was real. Something in him stirred, a memory, then slid away. In its wake was a surge of familiarity: he had done this before. His fall accelerated and in the darkness a presence neared, a surface rising up to meet him as he hurtled downward. He steeled himself, preparing for impact.

# CHAPTER 1

**2017**

*Lex*

Lex groaned, stirring in his chair. Pain spread through his body, greeting him as he blinked his eyes open. Even his eyelids hurt.

"Look who's awake," a voice spat.

Lex blinked again, struggling to focus his blurry vision. Sour breath filled his nostrils as the man towering over him leaned down, inches from Lex's face.

"Not so fierce *now*, are you?" the man sneered.

Lex began to push the man out of his face, only to realize his arms were bound behind him. No wonder his shoulders hurt, his arms and legs were both tied tight to the chair. *How long have I been sitting like this?* he wondered. "Where am I?" he asked, surprised by how rough his own voice sounded.

The man circled Lex's chair, taking him in. "You don't look so tough. You don't look much more than a boy." He shoved Lex's head, and the chair tipped precariously before righting itself back onto the packed-dirt floor with a thud. Lex felt the back of the chair give under the impact. "How old are you, eighteen? Stupid kid."

*Seventeen,* Lex felt his mind respond. Now that he was waking up more, anxiety crept in. He had no memory of how he got here, of this man, of any of it. Even trying to think of his own life, he was coming up blank, a realization he shoved down so as not to panic. He knew his age, at least; he hadn't lost all his memories. But his frustration grew as he strained to remember more with no success. His memories, whatever they were, felt trapped behind a barrier.

Lex eyed the man. He was large and muscled, and the tanned skin on his face and neck looked tough as leather. He wore dark brown trousers, boots, and a dingy tunic – work clothes. His face was faintly lined with the early creases of age, laugh lines edging his eyes. Lex couldn't imagine this man laughing. He was scowling, fuming, his raw, jagged energy chafing the air.

Seeing Lex study him, the man crossed his arms over his chest, revealing forearms covered in thick, reddish hair that matched the curly tuft atop his head. The man looked like he could rip a tree up from the roots and barely break a sweat.

Lex glanced down at his own body. The dirty tunic and plain brown trousers he wore hung upon lines of taut muscle. He was strong, too, but in the lean way of a wolf – nothing that could match the bear-strength of the man before him. Lex's muscles instinctively tensed beneath his restraints, but trying to fight this man was a bad idea. Besides, being tied to a chair would hardly make it a fair struggle. Lex considered asking the man how he had gotten there, but since the man seemed likely to murder him at the slightest provocation, Lex swallowed his questions and remained silent – for now.

He chanced a look around at the space as the man circled again, passing behind him. They were in a small room with a dirt floor, wood-panel walls that leaked thin strips of light, no windows, and one door. Metal tools like those used for farming hung from large, wooden pegs on one wall. *A storage shed*, Lex thought. A lantern swayed from a hook on the ceiling above them, its dim light shifting the shadows from wall to wall as it swung. A wheelbarrow filled with something dark sat in one corner, but the rest of the space looked empty, except for the man and Lex's chair.

Lex strained his mind, trying again to place the sequence of events that brought him there. His thoughts felt disjointed, flashes of color and emotion. He couldn't focus them into anything that made sense. *I must have been hit on the head,* he thought, but the concern that elicited was swallowed by a more immediate threat. There were footsteps and voices outside the door.

The man moved back in front of Lex. "Now the real fun starts," he said, and his smile sent a chill down Lex's spine.

The door slammed open and sunlight poured into the room, along with a half-dozen men. *Farmers,* Lex realized. They wore work trousers and boots caked with mud, and even in the dim room, Lex could see they were all tanned and muscled from labor in the sun. They were the type of people Lex might think of as decent, working folk, if they weren't studying him like a pack of hyenas who spotted prey. They hung back, making a loose semi-circle in front of the open door. Other than the man who had shoved Lex earlier, none of them seemed to want to get close to him. Maybe they didn't see him as prey, Lex thought; maybe he was a caged predator.

Fear surged through Lex again as he realized he truly didn't know why he was here, or even whether he was the victim or a perpetrator. Had he done something to anger these people? He couldn't remember anything before waking up in this room. His memories were only glimpses, flashing and fading so quickly he couldn't make them out. He tried to focus the memories, to seize one of them, but they slipped away as though he were trying to grasp oil. Panic swelled within him. He could remember nothing about his past, other than an awareness of his name and the general sense he felt about himself. He didn't think he would have hurt anyone or done anything to justify being trapped here, but how could he say for sure if he didn't even know who he was? That thought scared him more than the crowd of men staring him down, but he swallowed his fear and forced himself to meet their eyes.

Most of the men looked to be between their thirties and fifties in age, and their faces displayed varying degrees of uncertainty, fear, and anger. The man who shoved Lex stood in the front of the group, surlier than the rest. In the back stood a teenage boy, dirty and tanned like the rest but without their accumulation of muscle. The boy avoided looking at Lex, hiding behind the cluster of men. One other man stood off to the side, different than the rest. He was clean, well-shaven, and meticulously dressed in fine trousers and a spotless, white tunic. A startling shock of thick, black hair topped his narrow head, combed neatly to one side. His boots looked barely walked in, and his face betrayed no emotion beyond a slight air of skepticism.

Lex decided the man in the clean tunic must be in charge. The eyes of all the others kept sneaking glances in his direction, as though waiting for him to make the first move; he controlled the group with the nonchalant presence of someone who felt confident enough in his authority to have no need of asserting it.

Lex cleared his throat, and some of the men shifted nervously. He focused his eyes on the man with the black hair. "Why am I here?" Lex asked, taking care this time to control his voice so it wouldn't sound weak or frightened.

Surprise sparked in the man's eyes at Lex's decision to address him over any of the others, but he said nothing. He looked back at Lex silently, studying him.

The man who had shoved Lex earlier stepped forward. "You know why you're here, you filth."

Whatever Lex had done, it was clearly very bad. Unless he was innocent. It was unsettling not knowing for sure. Lex was beginning to worry, but something inside of him stirred, a steel-smooth whisper like a sword blade unsheathing. *You've gotten out of worse than this*, it purred. *You have this under control.* Lex let its calm confidence spread through him, warming the chill of his fear. He focused his eyes on the man before him. "No, I don't," he said. "Why don't you explain it to me?"

The crack of the man's hand against Lex's mouth rang through the air. Lex shook his head, his vision blurring. Warm liquid filled his mouth and he turned his head, spitting on the dirt beneath him. *Blood.*

The man raised a hand to strike again.

"Enough," a voice cut through the room.

Lex spat once more and lifted his face toward the sound.

The rest of the group shuffled aside as the man with the black hair strode forward. He knelt, narrowing his eyes as he studied Lex's face.

Lex returned his stare.

"You really don't remember, do you?" the man whispered, low enough that Lex wasn't sure anyone else heard him.

The man stood and turned back to the rest of the group. "This is a waste of time," he said, with the finality of a verdict.

The other men fidgeted, scuffed their feet, ran hands through their hair, scratched their faces. No one met the black-haired man's eyes. The man who had struck Lex sank back into the crowd as though trying to melt away.

Lex glanced between the group and the black-haired man. As he tried to puzzle out exactly what this all meant, the teenage boy slipped out from behind the group and stared at him, his face a mask of awe. Lex met the boy's eyes, trying to decipher his expression.

A large, calloused hand shot out from the group and grabbed the boy by the neck, yanking him behind the other men. The farmer who had grabbed the boy turned backward. "Stay out of this," he grunted, shaking the boy before releasing him.

"But he looks just like him," the boy whispered, his voice rising to near-panic. "Don't you see it?"

The other men in the group shuffled, still under scrutiny of the black-haired man's stare.

"Hush, boy," growled the farmer, shoving the boy behind him.

The black-haired man's gaze swept over the group again and they stiffened.

"Go," the black-haired man said, and the men and boy rushed out through the open door as though the building had caught fire.

When the sound of their fleeing footsteps died down, the black-haired man turned back to Lex. "Now," he drawled, "what do we do about you?" He stepped back and worried his lip with his teeth, studying Lex as though he were an interesting problem.

Lex opened his mouth to ask what in the world was going on, but a boom from outside interrupted him, rattling the walls of the shed.

The black-haired man snapped his head up, his nose pointing toward the ceiling like a dog sniffing the air. He spun and walked out the door.

Lex waited a few breaths, expecting the man to return. When he didn't, Lex realized this was his chance. Lex had felt the back of his chair splinter when the farmer shoved him, so now he threw his weight from side to side, rocking the chair until it tipped. Lex slammed sideways into the floor. Pain shot through his ribs but he ignored it, jerking his shoulders forward against the weakened chair. The wood cracked free of the base and Lex slipped out, stumbling to his feet as the ropes fell from his arms and torso. His fingers fumbled on the knots that held his feet to the chair's legs but they weren't well-tied – apparently these farmers were not experts in the business of kidnapping and restraint – and he was free in a matter of moments. He rushed to the wall of the shed, flattening himself against it, and peered out through the open doorway.

The door opened onto a small village, an assortment of wood-frame shops and houses connected by foot-worn pathways. Beyond the small cluster of buildings lay farmland, a patchwork of crop rows and grassy meadows. The village was set in a valley, the farmland sloping up and outward around it. Steep rises of forest rimmed the area in the distance, boxing in the valley on all four sides. Nothing was visible beyond the trees.

The village's dusty streets were in chaos. Sheep scurried between the buildings, people skirting around them as they rushed down the pathways, many carrying large bundles in their arms. Half of the families seemed to be rushing from building to building, and the other half were dashing out into the farmland. A man darted past, carrying a baby in one arm and a chicken in the other. A woman ran behind him, gripping a bundle against her chest. She seemed to be struggling under its weight, shifting it against her as she ran. The family cut between two buildings, startling a stray bunch of chickens. The birds exploded into a flurry of flapping and clucking. The couple kept running, trampling rows of seedling crops as they fled into the nearest field.

Lex glanced around, but the men who held him captive were nowhere in sight. He stepped outward to get a better look. The shed was on the edge of the assortment of buildings, with nothing but farmland behind it. The crops were still young and wouldn't provide much cover; if he tried to escape across the field, he would be exposed. But no one was paying much attention to him at the moment – they were too busy with their own chaos.

Lex made a run for it.

He was a few rows into the field – and feeling a bit guilty, even in his flight, for trampling the village's crops – when he saw a flash of movement to his left. He glanced over. A teenage girl fled parallel to him, no more than ten feet away. They were both moving too quickly for him to see details, and the girl didn't seem to notice him. But she was definitely close enough to raise the alarm if she recognized him as the escaped captive. He veered away from her, but before he had put much distance between them, a scream sliced the air. He turned his head back, then stumbled to a stop.

A large, winged creature thumped to the ground before the girl, arching toward her. It was dull grey, as large as a horse but with a narrow-muscled, lizardlike body with four long, claw-fingered limbs. It held its veined, bat-like wings outspread as it stood upright on its hind legs, casting a shadow over the girl in the sunlit field.

The girl scrambled backward, tripped and fell onto her bottom, then scurried crablike on her hands and feet, trying to escape. The creature stepped forward, shifting its shadow over the girl once more. It almost seemed to bring the darkness with it, as though the shadow were emanating from within rather than simply being cast by it. Lex felt a chill creep down his spine as the creature leaned over the girl, opening its gaping jaws to reveal sharp, yellowed fangs.

Lex felt himself reaching for a weapon at his side, though there was nothing there. Did he usually carry a weapon? He couldn't remember.

Angry shouts burst out from the village and Lex turned, tearing his eyes from the girl. The farmers were rushing in his direction – at him or at the creature, he couldn't be certain. He tensed, torn between fleeing and helping the girl. The farmers could be coming to the girl's rescue, or they could be coming for him. But they would certainly help the girl, once they saw she was in danger, and Lex couldn't risk being re-captured. He spun toward the rise of trees; with the men still a way off, he would have a good head start. Even if they had recognized him, once he hit the woods he might be able to escape.

The girl screamed again. Lex turned back. The creature had her pinned to the ground, its clawed forelegs on her chest as it hovered over her. But the men were approaching. If he helped the girl, he would put himself directly in their path; he would be caught for sure. He considered leaving the girl – surely the farmers would help her – but the creature leaned close to her face, so close that the girl squeezed her eyes shut and cried out in terror. It would have her gutted before the farmers could even reach her.

Wishing again that he had a weapon – any weapon – Lex rushed forward, hurling himself at the creature. He had only an instant to catch the surprise in the creature's eyes before he slammed into it. Lex knocked the creature off balance, its sinewy muscles and scaled flesh writhing against him as they both tumbled to the ground.

They rolled to a stop a few feet from the girl. Lex had landed on his back, and as he braced himself for the creature's backlash, he felt something cold and hard on the ground beside him. He grasped it – a farming spade – and scrambled to his feet. As the creature leapt for him, Lex thrust the spade upward with all his strength, driving its bladed end into the creature's belly.

The creature let out an ear-splitting screech, then stumbled backward on its hind legs and collapsed to the ground, twitching.

Lex watched only long enough to be sure it wasn't getting back up before spinning to the girl. "Are you alright?" he asked. A leaden chill settled over him as he realized he had just thrown himself at a horse-sized, freakish lizard-bat.

The girl staggered to her feet, then doubled over with one hand pressed to her chest. She was dressed more like a farmer than a lady, in trousers and boots now muddy from her struggle with the creature. The creature's claws had shredded the front of her dark tunic, revealing a simple white shirt beneath, but she seemed to be unharmed. Her slim body trembled as she took ragged breaths, and her hazelnut hair tumbled down around her face, concealing it.

Lex pulled back, knowing she must be terrified, and gave her a moment to gain her bearings.

The stampede of footsteps and angry yells grew closer, shocking Lex back into focus. He turned to flee, hoping the girl would be alright, but as he spun her hand grabbed his arm. Her touch was like a shock against his skin. She turned her face up to him. She was startlingly beautiful, with large, ice-blue eyes rimmed with dark lashes.

The world tilted. Lex was standing in a field, ice-blue eyes staring down at him from the horizon. The girl's lips parted as though to speak–

Lex shook his head, the world righting itself as the vision vanished. He was still there, in the middle of the rows of barely-grown, now-trampled crops. The girl stared at him wordlessly, breathing heavily and trembling. A look of concern entered her eyes as she noticed his distress. Lex gaped at her, his pulse racing for more than one reason. He struggled to fit the pieces together. *Was that a memory? Do I know this girl?*

The angry shouts and footsteps suddenly seemed much closer. *The farmers.* They were almost upon him, close enough to see him clearly.

"You!" one of them shouted. "Stop!"

Lex had wasted too much time, any hope of a head start now gone. His mind raced through his options. Be caught and beg for mercy? Stay and hope they were grateful he helped the girl? Try to run? The men were strong, but Lex might be faster. The last option won. Lex's boots dug into the dirt as he turned toward the distant trees. As he moved, his eyes caught on the body of the creature – it was gone. In its place was a man, blood blossoming across the front of his stark-white tunic. A shock of neatly-combed black hair topped his ashen face.

Lex's throat went dry. He spun, pulling his arm from the girl's grasp.

"Wait!" the girl called out behind him.

Lex focused on the line of trees and ran.

# CHAPTER 2

L ex woke the next day, aching and shivering, and groaned as he peeled his body from the cold ground. He shoved aside the branches that concealed him and crawled out from his hiding place. He was kneeling in a small clearing. Skinny-limbed trees towered above him, and dappled sunlight filtered down through a criss-cross of spindly branches. Lex took a few breaths and rolled his neck, awareness seeping in as he fully wakened. *The farmers.* He jumped to his feet, ignoring his body's protests. Lex's nerves were so strained it took him a few seconds to realize he was no longer in immediate danger. Everything was quiet. Lex finally relaxed as the events of the night clicked back into place.

He had made it to the edge of the trees and darted into the dense forest with the farmers close behind. He didn't have time to make any sort of plan; he simply threw an arm up to protect his face from slapping branches and tore through the forest. Lex had been correct that he was faster than the men, but they were still only a few steps behind him – until his brain finally kicked in. Running panicked was leaving the men a clear, noisy path of broken branches to follow. His only advantages were his speed and his lean frame, but his speed was leaving too obvious a trail. It was dark in the forest. If he slowed down and moved quietly, he might have a chance at melting into the shadows. Lex forced himself to stop moving forward, and slipped sideways into the darkness between the trees. He crept farther into the forest, keeping as much distance as possible from the men without drawing attention to himself. The men were determined, but as they moved deeper into the shadows, their unease grew and they began to argue over which way he had gone. Lex tuned them out, focusing instead on becoming one of the forest's many shadows. After what seemed like hours of Lex slipping between the trees just out of the farmers' sight, they gave up. Their voices faded into the distance as they backtracked toward the valley. In the wake of their parting, bone-deep exhaustion claimed Lex and he crawled into the nearest cluster of overgrowth, concealing himself beneath the branches of some short, shrubby plants. He was asleep within moments.

Now that he was awake and finally had time to think, images flooded in at him – the creature, pinning the girl to the ground. Its horrid shriek as he stabbed it. The girl's slim body quivering in shock, her blue eyes wide with fear. The jolt of terror as he turned back to see the creature had transformed into the man from the shed. *Did I kill a person?* The thought sickened Lex, but at remembering the girl's terror he wondered if maybe it was worth it, even if he did. Whatever that thing was, it had been trying to kill her. He had saved her life. But what *was* it, why did the body look human, who were those farmers, and why were they after him? Why had they tied him up in the shed? What in the world was going on? And then a lingering thought he couldn't quite shake: *Why can't I remember anything?*

Lex stood still and concentrated on taking deep, slow breaths, then rotated to take in his surroundings. Now that it was daytime and he wasn't being chased, the woods seemed peaceful. The ground was a mix of grass and light brown dirt, and there were small clusters of shrubs and other plants growing around the bases of the trees. There was sunlight above the clearing, but dew still rested on the leaves of the plants so it couldn't be too far into the day. In the distance he could hear the chatter of various birds, and a slight breeze ruffled the trees above him. All in all, it was a pleasant place to be, except he still had no clue where he was. He swallowed down a lump pushing its way up his throat. "We'll figure this out," he said aloud, feeling better talking as though he wasn't quite so alone.

He considered finding his way out of the woods to ask for help, but since he was a hunted man – for whatever he did at first and now, perhaps, for murder – there was no way he could go back to the village below. He doubted they would give him a chance to explain himself. But maybe there was another village nearby, one where the people might be willing to listen and help.

There was a rustle in the trees and Lex tensed, turning to face the sound. It was too subtle a noise to be the whole group of farmers returning, but it might be one of them coming alone to finish the hunt. Lex couldn't see very far beyond the clearing. The trees were so dense that everything beyond the open space was bathed in shadow, even in the daytime. He lowered himself into a crouch, ready to run or to defend himself.

Another rustle came from the branches behind him. Lex spun around. Whatever it was, it was moving, slinking almost soundlessly through the trees. The rustle grew closer. Lex again ached for a weapon but readied himself to jump at the man anyway; he was tired of running. His calves tensed in anticipation and he narrowed his eyes, trying to see into the trees. A large shadow shifted among them, a dark mass moving toward him. He remembered how the creature from earlier seemed to bring shadow with it, and his pulse quickened. Was it another creature, come to seek revenge for the one Lex killed? Lex abandoned his plan to fight and took a step back, eyes sweeping the clearing for the best direction to run.

The shadow emerged, stepping out into the light. Lex froze. It wasn't one of those creatures; it was a large, black panther. Its yellow eyes fixed on him with a predatory gleam.

Panic flooded Lex's veins. The creature was lithe, muscled, built for the chase. There was no way he could outrun it. It took one silent step toward him and Lex's pulse hammered, his mind racing with options but landing on nothing helpful.

Another noise came from behind him, this one clumsy, more of a crash than a rustle. Something was plowing toward him through the trees. Lex flicked his eyes back to the panther; it had crept another step forward while he was distracted. Lex stepped backward, hearing whatever was behind him continue its rush forward as the panther eased toward him yet another step. He was closed in. Lex gritted his teeth, knowing whatever was behind him was almost there, but unwilling to take his eyes off the panther.

The thing slammed into him from behind, and Lex tumbled face-first into the dirt. Whatever had hit him stumbled and fell as well, landing behind him. Lex curled his knees into his chest, bracing himself for the panther's leap, but to his shock the panther backed up, turned, and darted back into the shadows. Lex knew what this meant – the thing behind him must have been frightening enough to scare even the panther away. He swallowed hard, then pushed up onto his knees and turned to face the monster.

The girl's large, blue eyes stared back at him. Dirt smeared one side of her face as she crouched inches from him, still wearing the torn clothes from the day before, her brown hair darkened with a layer of dust. "Was that a *panther*? I've never seen one of those here before," she said. She stood, reaching a hand down toward Lex. Black dirt caked her fingernails.

After a moment, Lex extended his arm, unsure whether she wanted to shake his hand or help him up. Lex startled at how warm her hand was as it grasped his; there was a strange undercurrent to it, like an electric hum. He started to pull back, but she tightened her grip and threw her weight back against his, pulling him to his feet.

She dropped her hand once he was standing, and looked up at him. She was several inches shorter than Lex, and the dappled sunlight speckled her face as it tipped upward. She raised a dirty hand, shading her eyes, and smiled. "I'm Amelia," she said, extending the hand not over her eyes.

Lex was so focused on her eyes it took him a few moments to realize that this time she was trying to shake his hand. "Lex," he said after a few awkward beats, and reached out to clasp her hand. At the touch of her, a jolt sizzled up his arm. He dropped her hand and stepped back, his heart racing.

Amelia's eyebrows narrowed for a moment but then she shrugged, the expression slipping away. "So," she said, drawing the word out. "A panther. That was... interesting?" She ended the statement like a question.

There were so many things Lex wanted to ask that he didn't know where to start. He settled on, "Where are we?"

Amelia tilted her head. "Somewhere in Haven's Edge, I think. I mean, I've never been this far in before, but I'm pretty sure this is still part of the same forest. You were kind of hard to find, actually." Her lips quirked up into a half-smile. "I didn't know there were panthers out here, though. That's... new." She glanced around as though expecting the panther to reappear at any moment, and for all Lex knew, it might.

"Are there not many panthers around here?" Lex asked, his own eyes also scanning the trees.

Amelia placed her hands on her hips, turning to glance at the trees behind them. "None, that I've seen. I'm not sure where that one came from."

Lex wasn't sure if that was good news or bad news. At least the woods weren't crawling with panthers, but what if the panther was there for *him*? He knew he was being paranoid, but then again, everyone else seemed to be after him so maybe it wasn't that crazy.

Amelia noticed his discomfort, and filled the emptiness with a gentle laugh. "Anyway," she said, "we survived. So that's a win, right?" She gave Lex a smile that made his heart skip a little. "And by the way, thank you." She tucked a piece of dusty hair behind her ear. "For earlier. You saved my life."

The hair escaped and swung down in front of her face again, and Lex itched to reach out and tuck it back behind her ear. He shoved his hands in his pockets instead, thinking of the sizzle he felt the first time he touched her. He tore his eyes from Amelia's, turned his gaze down and shifted his feet in the dirt. "Of course," he said, "I couldn't *not* help."

There was a flash of something deep in his mind, a voice rising. *I couldn't not help,* it pleaded. He had heard that phrase before... or maybe he was the one who had said it. He froze, trying to focus, but the memory slipped away.

"Are you alright?" Amelia asked, her brows drawn together in worry.

Lex shook his head. "Yeah," he said. He hated not even knowing his own past. He felt confused, weak, vulnerable. The anxiety of it still simmered inside him, but when he forced himself to meet Amelia's eyes, her look of concern loosened the knot in his chest a bit. "Really, I'm okay." *For now. But for how long*? Until he figured out what was happening, who he even was, how could he really know whether he was safe or okay?

Amelia smiled at him again, and he returned it with a smile that was only partly forced. There was something about Amelia that felt familiar, comforting. Aside from that, she also seemed remarkably calm, given what she had been through in the past twenty-four hours, at least the parts Lex had witnessed. Who knew what else she might have been through. Was she so calm because stuff like this happened to her all the time? Could she know something that might help any of the past day make even a little bit of sense? Lex's curiosity stirred.

"So you're from the village?" he asked.

She shook her head. "Me? No. I'm from Alta."

The name meant nothing to Lex. "Is that far from here?" he asked.

She tilted her head again, a smile playing on her lips. "Don't get out much, do you?"

Lex faltered, unsure how much to reveal. "No... not really," he said.

"Hm," Amelia murmured, her mouth curling into a half-smile again. "That's a shame." She stepped toward him.

Lex felt heat rush to his face as his pulse quickened. "So... what brought you here? To the village, I mean?" He stepped backward, putting distance between them despite his sudden desire not to.

Amelia stopped, letting him keep the space he'd put between them. Amusement glinted in her eyes as she studied him. "Oh, the usual... spy stuff, murder, massive governmental conspiracies."

Lex gaped. "Really?"

Amelia tipped her face up as her bright laugh rang through the clearing. "No, of course not," she said, meeting his eyes again. "Do I look like a spy to you?"

Lex examined her face, the clever spark in her eyes, her confident stance, and thought back to how she tracked him through the woods and how the panther fled at her presence. "Maybe," he said, beginning to think it wasn't so unlikely.

Amelia laughed again. "I was just here to get a few things from the village," she said. "Or I *was*, until everything went crazy."

"What exactly happened back there?" Lex asked. His heart sped at the chance to finally get some answers, but he still didn't know what he should disclose, so he chose his words carefully. "I was in a building, then... boom. When I came out, it was total chaos."

"I was hoping you could tell me. I mean, this is your village, right?" Amelia said. "Why were those farmers after you? Did you kill one of their cows or something?"

Lex ran a hand through his short hair, masking his disappointment. "No. I mean, I don't think so."

"You don't *think* so?"

Lex looked at her, those blue eyes locked on his, and felt he could trust her. He wanted to trust her. He took a breath, then said, "I can't remember."

Amelia didn't catch the weight of his statement. "Oh yeah," she joked. "I'm sure I've killed lots of cows and just not noticed it." She stopped, her eyes scanning his face. "Wait," she said, and Lex could almost see the thoughts turning behind her eyes. "You can't remember *what*?"

Lex squeezed his eyes shut for a moment, weighing his options. She could be working with *them* – the assortment of farmers and a panther who all seemed to be after him – but that didn't really make sense. Why would the farmers have turned back and sent her after him alone, and why would the panther have run away? She could really be a spy, or after him in some other way, but... no. He had seen for himself how she fled from the village, how the creature attacked her, and how the farmers passed right over her to come after him instead. He was just being paranoid. Besides, he had to trust *someone*. There could be more people after him, more wild animals and traps around every bend, and he wouldn't know until it was too late. He didn't have enough information to survive on his own.

He opened his eyes to find Amelia studying him, and the concern on her face was enough to make the choice for him. "All of it," he said. "Any of it. I don't remember anything."

Amelia stepped toward him. "Really?" she asked, and her tone was sober, all joking gone.

"Really," Lex said, not bothering to conceal his despair anymore. For all he knew this could be a huge mistake, but he wanted so badly to trust her.

She placed a hand on his arm, and energy pulsed through Lex at the contact. This time, he didn't pull away. He looked down at her hand on his skin, her fingers delicate despite the dirt inhabiting her fingernails. Her touch sizzled through his veins.

Lex turned to look at her, their faces inches apart.

"Let me help you," she said.

Lex didn't have it in him to say no.

"SO YOU REALLY REMEMBER nothing other than those glimpses?" Amelia asked.

They sat in the forest clearing, backs against a tree, shoulders pressed together for warmth. Night had begun to creep in over them, but they couldn't build a fire – even if they had the skills and materials, it might attract too much attention. The clearing was like a world of its own, an open circle rimmed by trees and lit with moonlight. They were hungry and thirsty, but Amelia had produced a canteen of water and some kind of protein squares from a small sack Lex hadn't even noticed she was carrying on her back, and they had decided that would get them through until morning. Neither of them was eager to venture into the forest in the dark. They would shelter in the clearing for one more night, then face the outer world tomorrow.

Lex had been talking for what seemed like hours, giving Amelia the details of the past couple of days. She asked few questions, mostly listening. It had initially made Lex uncomfortable. He had thought it odd for her to be so quiet, since she had seemed so full of questions before. But with her eager nods and her gaze fixed on him, eventually he realized she was being quiet out of sincere interest. She really wanted to hear what had happened to him. It had been far easier for Lex to continue talking after that. He told her about waking up in the shed, the farmers, not understanding why they were holding him captive, the explosion, his escape – she had let out a soft *oh* when she realized what he had risked to stop and help her – all the way up to when she found him in the clearing. He left nothing out, not even his own confusion, not even the admission that he didn't even know who he was, beyond a name and age and a few scattered memories. It had been a relief to tell someone, to feel not quite so alone.

"I really don't," Lex answered her. They both stared frontward, side by side, keeping watch on the circle of trees. He was beginning to get used to the ever-present hum of her energy after sitting so close to her for the past few hours. It was like electricity constantly pulsed through her, though she didn't seem to notice it and he hadn't yet worked up the courage to ask about it.

Amelia was silent a moment, then shifted beside him, pressing her shoulder more firmly into his. He knew she had only pressed into him because she was cold – he could hear her teeth chattering – but he couldn't help his pulse quickening a bit at the contact.

THE WORLD TILTED. HE was in a clearing again, but a different one. A campfire crackled in the center, casting shadows across the tents that ringed it. Voices chattered from inside one of the tents, then laughter. Beside him was someone warm and familiar, her soft hair spilling onto his shoulder as she leaned against him. The flames of the firelight cast their spell upon its strands, shifting the color from blonde to orange and back again as the flames flickered. Her scent was intoxicating. A blanket hung around their shoulders, linking them together. The girl shivered against him and a surge of feelings flooded through him – concern, fondness, longing. He scooted toward her, letting his entire arm and side make contact with hers, hoping his closeness would warm her. She looked up at him, blue eyes reflecting the light of the fire.

LEX BLINKED. BLUE EYES stared up at him, but the fire and tents were gone.

"Lex?" a voice asked, anxiety edging it. "Lex, what's wrong?"

*Amelia.* She knelt in front of him, her face filled with concern.

Lex shook his head. What had just happened? Had he and Amelia traveled to a different moment, somehow? A different place? But no, it hadn't been Amelia. The face was similar, but not exactly the same. And the hair was different, blonde where Amelia's was brown. He had been transported again, witnessing someone else's moment. Was it happening in real time or showing the future, like some kind of psychic vision? Or was it a memory? He was certain the girl was not Amelia. But those eyes... there was so much likeness in their eyes.

Lex squeezed his own eyes shut, trying to process the vision – memory, dream, whatever it was – before it faded. The images were already slipping from him, but the emotions were as crisp as if they were his own. Whoever that girl had been beside him, the guy in the vision had felt strongly about her... but he had also felt cautious, afraid for her to see how much he cared. He had been in love with her, but she didn't know.

"Lex," a soft voice pleaded, almost a whisper. "Please, talk to me. What did you see?"

Lex opened his eyes. Amelia had pieced things together; she knew he had seen another *glimpse*, as she called them. He wanted to tell her what he had seen, but the feelings were still so strong he couldn't put them into words.

Amelia watched him for a moment, then sighed. "It's alright," she said, placing a hand on his face. "Tomorrow we'll head to Alta; there are people there who might be able to help you get some answers."

Lex leaned into Amelia's hand, the feel of her touch mingling with the fading memories of the touch of the other girl. *She thinks I didn't want to tell her what I saw*, Lex realized, and in a way he didn't. What he had seen felt private, like he had witnessed someone at their most vulnerable. What was happening to him? Whose life was he glimpsing? Or if these were *his* memories, then who and where was that other girl?

Amelia's words finally sank in – head to Alta tomorrow. Yes, that was a good idea. Maybe her family or someone in Alta would be able to explain what was happening to him. "Okay," Lex said. "Tomorrow we go to Alta."

Amelia nodded, then dropped her hand from his face and scooted back against the tree, pressing her shoulder against Lex's once more. She shivered.

Lex fought down a wave of emotion triggered by her movement, a flood of feelings he wasn't even certain were his own.

"Will you hold me?" Amelia asked suddenly.

Lex turned to her, surprised.

"Not like that," she said, raising an eyebrow at him.

What had she read on his face?

"Just for warmth?" She gestured to his arms as if asking him to embrace her.

Lex swallowed. "Yeah, sure," he said. "For warmth."

She leaned into him, pulling his arms around her like a blanket. "There," she said.

The feel of her against him sent sparks zinging through Lex's veins. Whatever the energy was when they touched, it seemed to only go one way; Amelia gave no sign she felt it. She adjusted his arms around her, and any remaining thoughts of the other girl slipped away from Lex as the solidity of the present enfolded him.

Amelia tipped her head back, looking up at him. "That's better, isn't it?"

He could feel the warmth of her body all along his. "Yeah," he said. "That's better."

"Good," she smiled, then squirmed and tucked her head beneath his chin, curling against him like a kitten.

*Who is this girl?* Lex thought. He realized suddenly he still knew very little about her; they had spent the whole time talking about him. He looked down to ask her about Alta, the village she said she came from.

24

## THE EDGE OF NOTHING

She was already asleep, breathing softly into his chest.

# CHAPTER 3

Lex woke to the chatter of birds in the trees. The sun filtered down through the branches above him and the sky had a faint orange tint, as though not quite done with sunrise. When the memories of the previous day and night settled upon him, he startled upright. Amelia was gone.

There was no sign of her in the clearing, and other than the birds, no sounds of anything moving nearby. Lex's first thought was that Amelia had betrayed him and gone to get the farmers, but he pushed it back, ashamed for assuming the worst. She could be lost or in danger. He stood and turned in a slow circle, double-checking the clearing for footprints or a sign of where she had gone.

"Looking for something?"

Lex jumped and spun around. *Amelia*. "Where did you come from?" he asked. He should have heard the noise of her shoving through the branches.

Amelia tilted her head, the half-smile on her lips once more. "A bit jumpy?" she asked.

"Where were you?" Lex shouted, but caught himself halfway through the statement, lowering his voice. He hadn't meant to yell at her; his nerves were getting the best of him. She didn't move away, exactly, but something about her presence pulled back. *I've upset her*, Lex realized, feeling immediate guilt.

"I was in the woods," Amelia said, a bit defensively. "You know, doing what everyone has to do in the morning?"

*She was using the bathroom.* Or whatever you called it when your "bathroom" was the woods. Now he felt like a jerk. He hadn't heard her walking up, that was all. He must have been more distracted than he had realized. Lex inhaled and exhaled once. "Right," he said, feeling his face go hot. "Sorry."

Amelia relaxed. "Whatever," she said brightly. "So, back to Alta, right?"

"About that," Lex said, steadying his voice. "I wanted to ask you some things before we go. Just so I know what to expect."

Amelia flopped to the ground, crossing her legs in front of her. "Sure," she said. "Go for it." She looked up at him expectantly.

Her agreeability surprised Lex, but he sank down to sit across from her. *But what to ask?* He started with something easy. "How far is it from here to Alta? How long will it take?"

Amelia looked to the side, thinking. "Two days, maybe? It took me three days to walk here, but I stopped a few times on the way."

"You walked for three whole *days?*"

Amelia shrugged. "Yeah, but not without stopping. Like I said, I didn't come straight here."

Lex looked at Amelia, seeing her in a new light. She didn't look like someone who would travel cross-country on foot. But maybe she was; he hardly knew her. In any case, Lex didn't like the idea of walking two whole days, with or without stopping. "Is there a faster way? Like a shortcut, or something we could ride?"

"You mean like a horse?" Amelia asked.

"Yeah, I guess," Lex said, unsure what resources were available. "Is that how you usually get places?"

Amelia narrowed her eyes. "Usually? No. But around here it's probably your best bet. I saw some horses in a little pasture back toward the valley."

Lex tensed. He couldn't go back toward the village. The men would be looking for him.

"Not that valley," Amelia said quickly. "Haven's Edge – where we are, I mean – is like a thin strip of forest. The village you came from is on one side, but if we keep pushing through that way," she gestured to the far side of the clearing, "we'll come out into another valley. That's where I saw the horses. It's on the way to Alta."

"I don't have any money," Lex said. "You don't mean *steal* horses, do you?"

Amelia mumbled something that almost sounded like *not this time.*

"What?" Lex asked.

"I have money," Amelia said, offering him an innocent smile.

Lex relaxed. "Okay," he said. Then something occurred to him. "You had to come through Haven's Edge to get to my village? I mean, the village where I first saw you?"

"The village is called Dalton," she said. "It's still weird that you don't know where you came from."

*Imagine how weird it is for me*, Lex thought. "Okay, Dalton," he said. "You came through Haven's Edge alone to get there?"

Amelia shrugged again. "It's not a big deal," she said. "Other than that panther, there's nothing much in here. Usually there's not even that."

At the mention of the panther, Lex felt his skin prickle. He glanced around the clearing again, just to be sure.

Amelia kept talking. "There's a little path, if you look for it. I mean, the people of Dalton have to get in and out somehow, right?"

Lex thought back to the village and the people fleeing outward across the farmland. "What do you think happened down there?" he asked.

Amelia hesitated, just for a moment. Then she said, "I have no idea, and I don't want to go back to check. But I'm sure word has gotten to other villages by now. And there's a larger city at Morrow's Lake. Merik'esh, I think the sign said. I went around it on my way here, but it's on the way to Alta and I think it's a trading hub for merchants or something. Maybe we can ask there. Someone should know what happened."

Alta, a two- or three-day walk away. Less, if they could ride horses. But first they had to *get* the horses. Lex felt his stomach growl. "How far is this pasture with horses?" he asked. His body ached from the strain of the day before and from sleeping on the ground, and he knew they would need fresh water and food before the day was up.

"Maybe half a day?" Amelia said. "Give or take."

Lex stifled a groan. "Right," he said, feeling his muscles complain as he stood. "Then let's get going." He offered her his hand.

She took it, and Lex did his best not to react as the hum of her touch moved through his veins again. *Does she really not feel it?* In a moment of rashness, he decided to ask her. After all, if they would be traveling together, there needed to be a certain level of trust, right? Currently, his many questions were getting in the way of that trust. There was something going on with her that both intrigued him and made him wary. He met her eyes as he pulled her to her feet, and opened his mouth to ask–

Amelia's eyes went wide. Before Lex could ask why, the ground beneath them rattled. A strengthening quake spread through the forest floor, raining loose leaves and twigs down on them. The earth below them began to fracture, dry cracks appearing in its surface. The ground heaved like a massive inhale and they both stumbled, Lex catching Amelia as she tripped. His fingertips buzzed at the touch but he ignored it.

The quaking eased almost as soon as it began, fading away into a dull rumble. The birds – which had gone quiet a moment before the tremor, Lex realized – squawked and scattered into the sky in all directions. The rumble stopped, and the forest fell silent. The ground beneath was still but bulged upward from the quake, with shallow fissures webbing its surface.

Lex steadied Amelia as she regained her footing, then stepped back to meet her eyes. "What was that?" he asked.

She didn't answer. She was staring at something behind him.

The world tilted. He was staring up into large, blue eyes, but the girl was not looking at him; she was looking past him, at something beyond–

"Lex? Lex!" Amelia's voice pierced like a needle of fear.

Lex shook his head. His thoughts felt blurry. "What? What is it?"

She grabbed his shoulders, and a gasp escaped him as current jolted through his chest. She shook him. "Lex!" she shouted again.

He blinked. "What?" he murmured, feeling far away.

She pulled at his arm. "Run!"

He snapped into focus. *Run?* He glanced behind him, where her wide eyes were looking.

One whole side of the forest was rolling toward them, ground and trees rushing higher and closer by the moment like a tsunami of land.

He spun back to Amelia, grabbed her hand, and ran.

The deep breath the forest had taken was now in exhale. The ground rolled like a tidal wave behind them, adding everything in its path to the growing surge. Lex and Amelia ran as quickly as they could, but it wasn't fast enough. The ground-wave was gaining on them.

Suddenly Amelia tugged Lex to the left, making him stumble. "We have to get out of the forest," she shouted. "This way!" She darted down a path Lex hadn't noticed, a narrow rut worn into the ground between lines of trees.

Lex followed. Her detour had taken them out of the direct path of the swell, but he could still hear the crash of trees toppling, too close for comfort. The forest floor beneath their hurried steps trembled with the strain of what was happening behind them. Amelia gripped Lex's hand so tightly his fingers went numb, and the buzz of her touch through his veins nearly overwhelmed him. He could barely focus on where he was running.

Lex heard a loud crack and looked back; the trees they had just passed snapped in two and toppled downward, collapsing the path they'd come through. "How much farther?" Lex yelled, realizing they couldn't outrun this much longer.

But there was no need for Amelia to answer. As soon as Lex turned forward again he saw it – the end of the trees ahead, grassy green hills visible beyond their branches, rolling into farmland in the distance. Everything looked still and calm out on the hills. An unpleasant remembrance of the last farmland Lex encountered twinged in his mind, but he pushed it down. There were bigger problems to worry about at the moment. Like surviving a forest tsunami.

The earth heaved and surged behind them, toppling Lex and Amelia across the last few yards of the forest. They rolled out through the trees and down the hill a bit before righting themselves. Lex jumped up, preparing to run again, but everything on the hill had gone still. The forest was eerily quiet – or what was left of it. Uprooted trees and rutted earth spread outward in all directions. Beyond the wreckage, Lex could see the drop-off where the rise of what was once the forest dipped off into the valley toward Dalton. He shivered. "What the heck?" he whispered.

Amelia appeared at his side, brushing at the grass stains that now accompanied the dirt and tears on her clothes. "Well, that was exciting," she said.

Lex raised an eyebrow at her. That wasn't the word he would have used.

She looked around. "Aha," she said. "There." She pointed downhill, beyond the expanse of grass, to a patch of farmland with a barn and fencing.

Horses grazed in the fenced area, oblivious to what had happened on the hilltop. "See? I told you there were horses."

Lex paused. There were so many things wrong with what just happened, he couldn't even process them, and she was already on to the horses? Her nonchalance was beginning to put him on edge, but he felt the need to play along, to pretend he was as unfazed as she was. "Yeah, look at that. Horses." As his brain restabilized from the shock, his thoughts cleared a bit. "From how you described things, I thought they'd be much farther," he said. "You said half a day, but we barely even ran for ten minutes."

Amelia shrugged. "Well, I think I came the long way around before," she said. "Besides, that weird forest-quake thing might have made us cover more distance than we realized."

This didn't quite make sense to Lex, but few things did lately. He shoved down the edge of anxiety prickling in his chest. "Okay," he said.

Amelia smiled and grabbed for his hand but Lex avoided the contact, pretending to scratch his head as he looked past her at the barn below them. He just didn't feel like being touched at the moment. *How is she so calm?* he wondered. It was beginning to unnerve him.

If Amelia noticed his avoidance, she didn't show it. "Let's go get a horse, and then we're off to Alta," she declared, and marched downhill.

*What is wrong with this girl? Why is she not freaking out?*

Lex started to ask exactly that, but was interrupted by the sound of hoofbeats. Lex turned to see a horse and rider galloping uphill toward them, the horse's mane and coat gleaming white in the sun–

The world tilted. He was astride a horse as she galloped full-on through a desert, sand flying up in all directions. He looked down, seeing his fingers tangled in her white mane, grains of yellow sand darkening her once-white coat beneath him–

Lex refocused in time to see the man dismounting. The man draped the reins over the pommel, his attention on the horse for the moment as he patted the side of its neck.

Lex had a sudden urge to approach the horse, but instead took a moment to study the man. He was handsome, with hair so dark brown it was almost black and startling, leaf-green eyes. He was muscular beneath his simple tunic and pants, and freshly-shaven. He appeared a few years older than Lex, maybe in his early twenties. From the corner of his eye, Lex noticed Amelia's posture straighten as her gaze swept over the stranger. Lex fought back a twinge of jealousy. Why should he care? He barely knew the girl. But he felt it just the same.

The stranger turned toward them, his eyes landing on Amelia first. He gave his head a quick shake, then smiled. The head-shake was so fast Lex almost wondered if he imagined it. *Had the sight of Amelia surprised him?* It was hard to tell, since now the man grinned warmly, any traces of shock wiped clear. "Everyone okay?" the man said, and his voice was friendly. "I thought I heard a–"

His eyes widened as they landed on Lex, and he stopped talking completely. There was a breath of awkward silence.

*What is going on?* Lex wondered. *Does he know me?*

But if the man did, he said nothing of it. His eyes were focused once again on the hilltop behind them. "What in the world happened up there?" he asked, gesturing toward what used to be the forest.

Amelia stepped forward, her smile a little bigger than usual. "We have no idea," she said. "The forest just... collapsed."

"*Tsunamied* is more like it," Lex mumbled, and though he was certain Amelia heard him, she pretended not to.

"Thank goodness you found us," she said, her tone dripping syrup. "We were nearly killed up there!"

Lex was more than a little disturbed. Had she been so obviously flirtatious with him? He thought back to when she asked him to hold her in the forest, and felt suddenly deflated. Disappointment and jealousy battled in his chest. *Get a grip*, he scolded himself. *You just met the girl; it's not like you're together.* So then why did seeing her flirt with the man feel so much like a betrayal?

Amelia continued talking, but Lex found it slightly nauseating to watch her bat her lashes at the stranger, so he turned his attention to the horse. The horse had been standing stone-still since the stranger dismounted, and now it tilted its head, focusing one large, steady eye on Lex. He stepped toward it, reaching out a hand.

The horse reared up, eyes wild, its forelegs scraping the air. The stranger spun toward it, grabbing the reins. "Easy, Mare," he soothed. "Easy." He placed his hand on her side and she settled back to the ground, huffing.

Lex's heart raced. *Mare.* Why did that seem so—

Memories flooded in at him. Thick-tongued thirst, sand-crusted teeth, the bone-deep ache of exhaustion. He took another step toward the horse.

"I wouldn't do that," the man said, his grip tight on the reins as the horse danced backward. "She's particular about strangers. Give her some room?"

The way he said it, not quite meeting Lex's eyes, did not escape Lex's attention. But Lex obeyed, taking a few steps back. *What was going on here?*

The man seemed to sense Lex's question. He stepped forward, offering his hand. "I'm Acarius," he said. "That's my horse ranch down below."

Lex accepted Acarius' handshake, relieved at the lack of any strange sensations. After Amelia's electric touch and the way the horse reacted, Lex had been starting to wonder if something was wrong with the living creatures in this place – or with him. "I'm Lex," he said.

Amelia bounced up next to them, refusing to be ignored. "Amelia," she said, shooting her hand out.

Acarius gripped it briefly, then let go and turned back to Lex. Amelia sank back, seeming disgruntled by his polite disinterest.

Lex glanced down the hill to the field and horses beneath. He wouldn't exactly call the place a *ranch*; it was more like a barn and a bunch of grass. "You own a ranch?" he asked anyway. "You seem young to own a business."

Acarius smiled. "It's sort of a family business. Or it was," he answered. A shadow of something passed over his face, then vanished. "Anyway, you two look like you could use..."

He paused, and Lex realized how many things they must look like they could use. They were filthy, famished, banged up – and they probably smelled.

Acarius shifted his phrasing. "We've got food and hot water for baths, and we can probably even find a change of clothes for each of you." His eyes swept over Lex. "You could wear some of mine."

"What about Amelia?" Lex asked.

"*We?*" Amelia asked at the same time.

Acarius smiled. "My sisters live here, too. Five of them." He turned to Amelia. "I'm sure one of them has something that will fit you."

Amelia smiled brightly. "Sisters. Great," she said, placing her hand on Acarius' arm. "Thank you so much!"

Acarius grimaced slightly. *Does he feel something when Amelia touches him, too?* Lex wondered. If so, it wasn't the warm, intoxicating hum Lex felt when she touched him. Whatever Acarius was feeling, he seemed not to like it.

Amelia didn't notice. She left her hand on his arm and grinned up at him. With the way she was looking at Acarius, Lex wouldn't have been surprised if she had stepped right up and leaned her head on his shoulder.

*What is with this girl?* Lex wondered again. The jealousy and betrayal he knew he had no right to feel mixed with a twinge of embarrassment, for her sake. Had he really almost fallen for such clumsy flirtation? After just meeting her? He must have really been off his game. *If I even have a game,* he thought. For all he knew, he might fall for strange girls he just met all the time.

But deeper than the embarrassment and discomfort at watching her flirtations, deeper than the jealousy that she had moved on to a new target, something else stirred. In the wake of realizing her kindness to him might have been manipulation, he felt... a loss, a small, dark pocket of sadness worming deeper into his gut. He had really been starting to–

The world tilted. He was standing in a crowded hallway. A girl draped herself on his shoulder, her fingers playing with the hair on the back of his head. He looked down at the girl's blonde hair, then nudged her face up toward his with one hand, eager to see her blue eyes – it wasn't her. It was some other blonde-haired girl, green-eyed, staring up at him. Something in him recoiled but he fought it and smiled back, not wanting to be rude.

A murmur from behind caught his attention. Across the hallway, revealed by the whispering crowd that had parted like the Red Sea, she stood. Her blue eyes were fixed on him, wide with shock. He ached at the pain on her face and stepped toward her. She looked younger, he realized suddenly, different than in his other visions. He glanced around. Everyone in the hallway was also young, just barely into puberty. Was he young himself? He looked down, thinking...maybe. He was slimmer than in the other visions, leaner. He focused back on the girl. She was beginning to seem panicked, looking for a path to escape the crowd of witnesses to their mute exchange. He stepped toward her but she flicked her glance toward a boy to his left; he was their same age, tall, with blonde hair yellower than hers, lemon-like. *Steve*, his mind whispered, and he knew Steve was a friend, someone he trusted, but something felt off, a tension he hadn't anticipated. The girl broke her eye contact with Steve and shoved through the crowd, rushing down the hallway. As she left, Steve turned to him, a *What now?* expression on his face. It carried an edge of judgment.

He stood there feeling empty and guilty as Steve walked away. *What had he done?* He had the sense it hadn't been intentional, that he had somehow been used. Suddenly he felt a desperate need to find the blue-eyed girl and explain. He glanced down to see the girl on his shoulder smiling up at him, smug. He shoved her from his shoulder, his eyes scanning the hallway for the blue-eyed girl. She was gone.

A voice brought Lex back. He opened his eyes. Amelia eyed him warily, Acarius standing just behind her. "Is everything alright? That one was a long–"

"I'm fine," Lex grunted, cutting her off. The glimpses made him feel disoriented, unsure of his own mind, and the last thing he needed was to look weak and pitiable in front of both Amelia and this stranger.

Acarius studied Lex, and for a moment Lex expected him to question. Instead, Acarius changed the subject.

"Let's head down to the ranch and get you both cleaned up and fed," he said. He turned to grab the horse's reins, Amelia's hand sliding off his arm as he pulled away from her. He tugged the reins gently. "Come, Mare," he said.

Lex felt a small flicker of gratitude to Acarius for not prying. Maybe this guy wasn't so bad, though he seemed to have Amelia in a tizzy. Her scowl told Lex she wasn't pleased with being disregarded by Acarius, but she kept her thoughts to herself.

Acarius walked Mare down the hill, clearly expecting Lex and Amelia to follow. Amelia, not yet giving up, hurried to walk beside him. Lex quickened his steps and fell in pace with them, but on the other side of the horse. He made sure to give Mare space, keeping about an arm's length between them, but still she turned and snapped her teeth at him the instant he neared.

"Easy, Mare," Acarius scolded. He turned to Lex. "I'm sorry. She's not usually like this." He glared at the horse as though reprimanding her.

"She really doesn't like me," Lex responded.

Acarius took a quick, forced breath. "Like I said, she's particular about strangers."

Being both *not usually like this* and *particular about strangers* didn't quite make sense, but Lex thought better of pointing this out. The stranger was probably just being kind, trying to keep Lex from feeling bad about the horse disliking him. Animals just disliked people sometimes, he had seen –

The world tilted. He stood in an open garage, sunlight spilling in through the upraised door. The garage was mostly empty, but a large oil-spot on the concrete floor marked a car's typical residence.

He held a box pressed tightly to his chest, and it was... squirming? Something *in* it was, anyway... and giving off a low, menacing growl.

A door on the wall burst open – it must lead into the house, he realized – and he looked up. It was the girl. Her blue eyes were bright with excitement, her delicate lips spread into a grin.

"Let me see!" She rushed toward him and reached for the box.

He pulled back. "Careful," he heard himself say. "I think it's got rabies or something."

The girl hesitated, her hand lingering inches from the box. She raised one eyebrow. "Really?"

"It was going crazy all the way here. It sounds like it's about to rip the box apart from the inside."

The girl took a breath. "Okay, set it down gently."

He placed the box on the ground then halted, wanting to move back but not wanting to leave the girl exposed to whatever was in the box. He settled for stepping around the box and placing himself next to her, close enough to block whatever came out of the box if he needed to.

She knelt down and slowly lifted the lid.

A crazed ball of orange fur barreled out, snarling. It was a cat, though in its current state it hardly looked like one. Chunks were missing from its matted fur as though pulled out from the roots, revealing oozing sores. One leg was bent at an odd angle. It bristled, turned its filthy face up at them, and let out a rumbling yowl, followed by a hiss.

He reached for it, trying to put himself between it and the girl. It lunged at him, lashing his hand with needle-claws. "Ouch!" he yelled, pulling back. He threw a hand in front of the girl, who leaned forward despite the creature's apparent madness. "Careful," he gasped.

The girl gently moved his hand aside, reaching for the creature. "There," she said, making the word sound like a song.

The cat paused, its eyes locking onto her, then it... melted. The tension fell right out of it and it leaned its head into her hand, rubbing against her. It was even purring.

He stared. "What the–"

The girl lifted the cat to her chest, stroking it. "You poor thing," she cooed. Her eyes sparked with amusement as she turned to him. "Rabies? Really?"

He shook his head. He should have known. There had never been an animal that hadn't melted in her presence.

She smiled at him and sent his heart racing. "Thanks for bringing him here," she told him. "He looks half dead. He's lucky you spotted him."–

Lex came to, panting. As his vision refocused, he realized he was on his back... on the ground. *What is happening to me?* The visions seemed to be getting worse.

Acarius was in his face suddenly, hands on his shoulders, nearly shaking him. "What did you see?" he asked, urgent. The horse paced sideways behind him.

Lex blinked and sat up. "What?" His mind was racing. He couldn't think, could hardly breathe, and Acarius was making it worse. "Get out of my face," Lex grunted, shoving him.

Acarius toppled backward.

Lex stood up, feeling only vague regret at having knocked Acarius down. He hadn't meant to, but he needed space, and the man was acting crazy. Besides, Acarius had asked "What did you see?" *How had he known?*

Lex stood, swaying as his head swam. Acarius also rose to his feet, facing Lex.

Amelia stepped up, glancing between them.

Lex felt his body tense, readying for a confrontation.

Acarius deflated suddenly and took a step backward. The horse behind him went still. "I'm sorry," he said. "I just..." He shook his head. "It's nothing. The world's gone mad, is all. There have been a lot of strange things happening around here, lately."

"That's an understatement," Amelia said. "But hey, we're still alive, right?" She glanced around, smiling. Her face fell when they didn't join her.

Acarius extended his hand to Lex. "You okay?" he asked.

Lex hesitated. There were a lot of things about Acarius which didn't make sense, but the man *was* trying to be nice. He shook Acarius' hand. "I'm fine," he said. He started to pull his hand away, but felt Acarius press something into his palm within the handshake. Lex opened his mouth to comment, but Acarius met his eyes with a glare that said *don't*. Lex slid his hand from Acarius' and slipped the cool, hard object into his pants pocket. He got the feeling Acarius meant for him to look at it later... without Amelia.

Acarius stepped back, casual again. "Let's get you two to the ranch, then," he said. He grabbed Mare's reins and led her down the hill, not waiting to see if they followed.

Amelia fell into step beside Lex as they trailed Acarius down the hill. "More glimpses. Are you okay?" she whispered, leaning her head toward him.

Lex turned to look at her. "Didn't think you'd care. Aren't you all about the Hot Horseman now?"

The hurt on Amelia's face startled Lex, and for a moment the edges of reality blurred, Amelia's face overlaid with the blue-eyed girl's from the hallway.

Reality snapped back in almost instantly, but Amelia was already looking away, staring forward as they walked. Regret surged in. He hadn't thought Amelia cared about him, not after her display with Acarius, but her face... *Did I miss something*? Lex wondered.

As though she could hear his thoughts, Amelia turned to him. "Not everything is what it seems. I'd have thought you, of all people, would realize that."

The pain in her eyes left Lex speechless. He stood still for a moment, stunned, as Amelia jogged ahead to catch Acarius.

The ranch surprised Lex; there was more to it than he thought. Next to the barn, concealed by it from where he'd been standing on the hilltop, was an array of smaller buildings: a supply shed, a couple of small stables, and two wood-frame houses. The houses were small but well-tended, with a little garden between them and flowered vines suspended from pots around the eaves of each porch. One house was slightly larger than the other, almost like a main house and a guest house. Acarius led Lex and Amelia up to the larger house.

"Wait here," Acarius said, stopping them at the steps to the porch. "I'll go let the girls know you're here."

*The five sisters,* Lex remembered. He didn't really want more uncomfortable interactions with strangers, but it seemed he didn't have much choice.

The door closed behind Acarius and Lex could hear him saying something inside. There was a flurry of movement, footsteps and what sounded like chairs scraping. Then Acarius came back out. "They're getting baths ready for you," he said.

The door flew open and two girls in simple cloth dresses rushed down the steps. They were both in their teens, pretty, with flowing, dark brown hair the same shade as Acarius'. But neither of them had his leaf-green eyes. Their gazes lingered on Lex as they sped past, heading for the house next door. Lex felt Amelia stir beside him. *Was she jealous? That would be ironic.*

"This house belongs to my sisters," Acarius said. "Amelia, you can go in. They're running you a hot bath inside. Lex, you can head to my house." He nodded toward the smaller house. "Anna and Sasha should have your bath ready by the time you get there."

Lex froze. He hadn't seen the floorplan of these houses, but he was really hoping it wasn't an open one. The thought of bathing with those two girls watching was unsettling.

Amelia seemed to have the same thought. "Um, are they – I mean – will there be, like, privacy?"

Acarius laughed. "It's a small house, but don't worry; we don't bathe in the living room. You'll have privacy." He walked down the steps.

"Where are you going?" Amelia called out.

Acarius turned back. "I have some things I need to tend to," he said.

Across the yard Mare stomped, as though declaring she was one of those things.

Acarius continued. "Get washed up. I told the girls to put robes out for each of you; we're still working on finding you some spare clothes. You can wear the robes if you finish up before we've found you something else. After you bathe, the girls will take your dirty clothes and do what they can." He glanced at Amelia's shredded tunic, and the dirt-stained white shirt beneath it. "Emily's pretty good at mending."

Sitting around in a robe with a bunch of strangers, trusting that they would bring him something else to wear after they confiscated his only clothes? Lex suddenly thought maybe he'd prefer to stay in the dirty ones.

"Don't worry," Acarius chuckled as he noticed Lex's expression. "We should have some spare clothes ready soon." He headed off toward Mare. "Food should be ready by the time you're all cleaned up and dressed," he called out behind him. "Liz's pot roast is the best!"

Lex glanced at Amelia. She really did look filthy, leaves and twigs tangled in the strands of her dirty hair, her clothes torn and stained. He imagined he looked the same. "See you in a few minutes, I guess," he sighed.

Amelia shrugged, then headed up the stairs to the porch. Lex turned toward the smaller house, hearing the door of the first house open and close behind him as Amelia went inside. He swallowed and headed for the other house's front door.

The doorknob turned easily, and the door swung inward to reveal a small living area, the sitting room, dining room, and kitchen all sharing one open space. A large fireplace took up most of one wall, a fire crackling despite the warm day outside. Kerosene lanterns speckled the space with glowing globes, some hanging and some on shelves or tables. The place had a sole-occupant vibe, everything scaled small – a two-chaired table, a couch that was more of a loveseat, a minimal kitchen with a small gas stove and a washbasin and a few hanging pots and pans. To the back was a short hallway, leading into shadow. Lex headed for it, figuring the bath must be down that way.

He had just reached the edge of the hallway – there were two doors leading off it, one on each side – when the left-hand door flew open. One of the sisters stumbled out, seeming startled to see him. "Oh!" she said. "You're already here. Well, come in, then." She disappeared back inside the room.

Lex followed her. A clawfoot tub stood to one side of the small room, taking up most of it. There was a washstand and what looked like some sort of toilet contraption over to the other side. A large, white towel and fluffy, white bathrobe hung from hooks within reach of the tub. Curls of steam twisted upward from the hot water. A skylight poured sun downward, lighting the whole room.

The girl – he still didn't know which sister she was – eyed him for a moment. "There's soap on the edge of the tub," she said, her gaze sliding over him. "Do you need anything?"

Lex felt an unwanted blush creep to his face. "No," he said quickly. "I'm good."

The girl narrowed her eyes playfully, and smiled. "Okay then," she said. "See you in a bit." She left, shutting the door behind her.

Lex peeled out of his dirty clothes and dropped them in a pile on the floor, then leaned over the tub. He halted at his reflection. The face staring back at him was familiar, but not like it should be, not as a person looking at himself. It felt more like looking at a photograph of someone he knew well. He studied his face, realizing it was the first time he'd seen himself since – well, since whatever happened to him that took his memories. *I'm good-looking*, he thought with satisfaction. There was a layer of thick stubble on his face – he rather liked the look of it – and he was noticeably dirty. But he had short, thick brown hair that spiked up in the front, messy in a way that almost looked intentional. His eyes were blue – much darker blue than the girl in his visions – beneath dark lashes. His lips were full but not too full, and the line of his jaw was angular, masculine. He did look young – *What are you, eighteen?... Seventeen*, the memories surfaced – but there was also a look of age about him, like – he searched for the word – *maturity*. Like he had been through some hard stuff and carried wisdom beyond his years. All in all, he was rather pleased with himself. He thought of Acarius, and felt mild triumph at knowing he could give the Hot Horseman a run for his money. Not that it was a competition, of course.

Lex stepped into the tub, watching his reflection ripple away, and eased himself into the water. Heat flooded over him, stinging then soothing. He sighed, feeling his aching muscles uncoil. He knew he couldn't take too long. One of those girls or Acarius could come barging in any minute – he wasn't sure which would be worse – but the water felt so good he allowed himself a moment to enjoy it. He leaned his head back against the rim of the tub and closed his eyes.

Something banged from the living area. Lex lurched up, then grabbed the soap and furiously began bathing. He wasn't sure who was out there or if they would walk in on him, but he didn't intend to sit there naked long enough to find out. He scrubbed as much dirt off as he could in one quick pass, dunked himself under the water to rinse, then stood and reached for a towel.

Lex was one leg out of the tub, in the process of drying his other leg, when the door flew open. He flung the towel the rest of the way around himself, pulling it tight just in time to cover himself from the waist down before someone rushed in.

It was Amelia. She was panting and her cheeks were flushed. Her hair dangled wet around her face and a fluffy, white robe had swallowed her body, pulled tight around her waist with a blue sash. Her skin still looked damp, as though she had jumped straight out of the tub and run here. The scent of bath oils and fragrant soap drifted off her. She was barefoot, and the dirt from outside had re-soiled her wet feet, the only part of her which wasn't soapy-clean. Behind her, Lex could see a track of muddy footprints trailing out into the hall.

Lex blinked, pulling the towel tighter around his waist. "Everything... okay?" he asked.

Her eyes slid over him, lingering on his bare chest. "Oh, I'm fine," she said, her tone flat. "What about you?"

Lex was growing more uncomfortable by the minute, confusion and tension replacing the panic he had felt at her entrance. She was clearly upset about something. "What *about* me?" he asked.

Her eyes narrowed.

Lex stepped forward, almost dropping his towel but recovering it just in time. "What's *with* you?" he asked. "You're acting crazy." He didn't know her well; maybe she was always like this – erratic, unpredictable, a pendulum of emotion. From the little he did know of her, she was certainly unusual. But her behavior since they had encountered Acarius seemed strange, even for her, and it was beginning to annoy him.

She sighed and her shoulders sagged. "I'm sorry," she said, looking at the floor. "I just ..." She stopped.

Lex's heart sped. There was so much about her that reminded him of the girl from his vision, especially with her current expression. But it wasn't just that. Amelia seemed truly bothered by something. Lex felt a twinge of concern. "Amelia," he asked, making his voice gentle. "What is it?"

She crossed her arms. "This is all so new for me," she said, still looking at the floor.

Lex looked back at her. She turned her face away so he could only see her profile, half of her expression. "What is?" he asked.

"This," she said, gesturing wide with her hands. She turned her face back to him. "All of this. You, me, this place, *them*... it's a lot to take in."

Lex rolled her words around in his mind. He felt the same way, but then he had no idea what this place even was. This was her home, wasn't it? Or close enough. She lived only a few days' walk from here, in Alta. And she talked of the village and the forest like she knew the area and had been here before. Yes, there was strange stuff happening, but if anyone should be overwhelmed, it was him. He didn't even know how he had gotten here. He thought through the past couple days. She had been attacked by the creature and was with him in the forest when the tsunami hit, but she hadn't seemed very bothered by those things earlier. Why was she so upset now? Was this about something else?

Lex felt a tingle of curiosity again. This was his chance to ask about her, to find out more. But he would have to do it gently; if he pushed too hard, she might close off again. He decided to go with honesty. "I don't understand," he said.

Her eyes narrowed.

"But I want to," he said. "Please, help me understand."

Her face relaxed. She exhaled. "It's just that you seem... and I know you're not, you can't be, but still it feels..."

Her statements were broken, not making sense. "What?" Lex asked.

Amelia sighed, then flopped down right there on the ground, the bottom of her bathrobe settling into a pool of fluff around her. She crossed her arms again.

Lex tightened one hand on the towel around his waist, then grabbed the robe off the hook near the tub, awkwardly sliding into it using his free arm. When the robe was on him he turned back toward the wall, letting the towel drop to the floor as he tied the robe closed with the attached sash. He turned back to Amelia.

She eyed the dropped towel with a raised eyebrow. "Anyway..." she said.

Lex carefully lowered himself to the floor in front of her, ensuring he was fully covered as he did so, and keeping an appropriate distance between them.

Amelia continued. "There was this guy," she said. "I... thought I loved him. But he was just using me."

The expression on her face brought another flash of the blue-eyed girl Lex saw in the hallway. He swallowed.

"Anyway, you don't need all the details. The point is that you remind me of him. Sometimes. And I know it's crazy, but it makes me feel connected to you somehow." She let out a short, harsh laugh. "I know it's not real. It's stupid." She looked up and shrugged. "But I like you. And I *want* you to like me, but then I feel scared. I don't want to be hurt again, which is crazy since–" She looked down, then tucked the robe around her legs and pulled them to her chest. "It's dumb."

Lex's mind reeled. *She feels a connection, too.* It didn't seem exactly the same as what he felt toward her, and he knew she wasn't the girl in the visions, but it seemed too much to be a coincidence. *What am I saying, then? That it's fate?* That would be crazy, he knew that. Yet here she was, this girl he felt tied to despite having met her the day before. And now she was hurting, visibly retreating into herself in a mound of fluffy robes. But...

"What about Acarius?" Lex hated himself for asking it the moment it left his mouth, but it just came out.

Amelia looked up. "He's hot, I won't deny that," she shrugged. "But I was mostly trying to make you jealous."

Lex's heart sped. "Why?"

Amelia sighed. "You just seemed to be pulling away, I guess. I mean, not that we were close; we just met, I know that." She stopped, glancing at the ground again. "But at first, I thought maybe there was something..." She sighed again. "But then the next day, you seemed so guarded, like you didn't really want me around. It was stupid, I know, but I hoped seeing another guy notice me would make you interested in me again, like you seemed to be at first."

Lex thought back. He *had* pulled away, in a sense, but only because there was so much he still didn't know about her, and about himself. After he had told her about his memory loss, he wondered whether it had been a mistake, whether he could truly trust her. But now...

Amelia bit her lip. "It didn't work, anyway," she said. "He wasn't into me at all." She flopped her face down onto her robe-covered knees.

*It was working, just not on Acarius.*

Looking at her curled up before him, Lex felt irresistibly drawn to her. He couldn't quite separate out how much of what he was feeling was really about Amelia and how much was left over from his visions of the other girl, but right then he didn't care. He scooted toward Amelia. "Then he's stupider than I thought," he said.

Amelia turned her face up, and her eyes were surprised. "Really?" she asked.

Lex felt the hum of her energy course through his fingers as he tucked some strands of wet hair behind her ear. "Really," he said. *Even her hair is electric,* he noticed.

The door opened. Amelia jumped back, her robe nearly gapping open before she caught it.

One of the sisters raised an eyebrow at the two of them sitting in robes on the floor, then glanced off, uncomfortable. "I've got your clothes," she said.

Lex hurried to his feet, holding his robe with one hand as the girl shoved a bundle of clothes into his arms.

The girl turned to Amelia. "Yours are waiting for you in the other house." She left.

Amelia stood, straightening her robe. She met Lex's eyes. "See you in a bit?" she asked.

"Of course," Lex answered.

She left, shutting the door gently behind her.

Lex set the clean bundle of clothes on the floor. He gathered up his dirty ones, expecting one of the sisters would want to collect them. As he set them in a pile beside the door, something fell out, pinging metallic as it hit the floor. *The thing Acarius gave me,* Lex realized. He knelt and picked it up. It was a pendant, crescent-shaped and made of dull-silver metal etched with symbols and shapes. It hung on a black cord, as though meant to be a necklace. Something stirred deep inside Lex as he looked at it, but he couldn't quite grasp the recognition and it slipped away as quickly as it came.

Lex tucked the pendant into his fist and reached for the clean clothes. The sister – whichever one she was – had brought him what must have been some of Acarius' stuff. Lex slipped the tunic over his head. It fit him well, and he felt pleased yet again that he was muscular enough to fill the Hot Horseman's clothes. He shook his head at himself. Acarius seemed nice, for the most part, and it wasn't Acarius' fault that Amelia had tried to use him to make Lex jealous. In fact, Acarius had given every sign he wasn't interested. Lex told himself he really should stop thinking of the guy as competition, and go easier on him. He bent down, reaching for the pants. As he lifted them, a bit of white paper fluttered out. Lex picked it up, turning it over.

There were words on the other side, written in rolling script.

*Don't trust her. She isn't who you think.*

# CHAPTER 4

Lex exited the house to find Amelia waiting for him. She was stuffed into some kind of long-skirted peasant dress, and clearly unhappy about it.

"It's pink," she said with a scowl.

Lex fought back a smirk. "It suits you."

Her scowl deepened.

Lex examined her face, her eyebrows scrunched together over her ice-blue eyes, her perfect lips pursed in frustration, her still-damp hair drying into messy, brown waves about her face. He could feel the note in his pocket, weighing at him despite being made of paper. It said not to trust her, warned him to keep his distance. But Amelia's gaze upon him spoke the opposite, urging him to brush her soft hair away from her eyes. What was he thinking? He barely knew her, and right now he needed to confront her, to get answers. He mentally shook himself. *Focus.* He felt balanced on a crazy knife-edge, his pull toward her at odds with reason.

Amelia's expression was guarded, but Lex could see something vulnerable behind that. He didn't know much about her past, but her story about having her heart broken had seemed genuine. Lex thought back to the creature's attack; the farmers hadn't even seemed to care she was in danger. They ran right past her to pursue Lex, even after seeing her assaulted by the creature. *Maybe she just needs to be able to trust someone,* Lex thought. Deep down he found it hard to believe there was anything truly bad in her. She was wild and emotional and sometimes flippant – and she did seem to be hiding something, her answers about her past always in veiled snippets – but that didn't mean she was untrustworthy. Everyone had secrets.

Yet the note nagged at him, drawing all the gaps in his knowledge about Amelia into focus. Why did the men run past her? Why had the creature attacked her? How did she find him in the woods that night? Why did the panther run from her? Had she really just gone to relieve herself when he woke up, or had she disappeared for some other reason? Why did she resemble the girl in his visions? It seemed like such a coincidence for Lex and Amelia both to feel such a connection to one another, unless... maybe that was a lie, too, an attempt to manipulate him. How would he even know? The tsunami in the forest, his missing memories, being captured and tied up... how did he know she wasn't involved with some of that? Maybe with all of it.

He studied her face again and his heart sped. Though he knew he had every reason not to trust her, that charming fake-scowl was pulling him in, all other thoughts tangling on thoughts of her. *Is she doing that on purpose, too, somehow?* He wondered. How would he know if she were?

Amelia was still holding the scowl, but now an edge of self-consciousness crept in behind it, her eyebrows rising. "Why are you staring at me like that?" she asked.

Lex *had* been staring at her for an awkwardly-long time. He felt his face go red as he ran a shaky hand through his hair. He let his eyes roam her face; she looked as uncomfortable as he was. He considered confronting her about the note then and there, but then her lower lip trembled, just for a second. She got control of it almost instantly, smoothing her face back into one of stone.

Lex's heart squeezed, and he shoved thoughts of confronting her to the side. He could do it later. If he demanded answers now, she might feel like he was accusing her of something... and what if she was innocent? He owed her the benefit of the doubt for being there for him so far; he needed answers, and she had offered to help him find them. Besides, there was something connecting Amelia and his visions, and he still needed to figure out what.

He would have to find a way to be friendly without truly opening himself up to her. He would be wary, but polite. But keeping her close for now was just good strategy. Could he help it if part of him felt glad for having a reason to stay near her? *I'm really going to have to work on that*, he thought. His heart seemed to have a mind of its own.

*Besides, Acarius obviously knows something.* Lex could try getting answers that way. He was tired of feeling like he was in the dark, left out of some big secret.

"You're still staring at me," Amelia said. "I swear, if you're thinking of making some joke about this dress..."

Lex's heart gave a little skip at the uncertainty on her face. She looked vulnerable and uncertain, insecure about what he was thinking of her. Maybe it was the dress... she did seem self-conscious about it. Honestly, it looked good on her, though the murderous glare on her face spoiled the effect a bit. He smiled at her. "It's really not so bad," he said. "It's a nice dress."

She lowered her eyebrows again. "Then why don't *you* try wearing it?"

The laugh escaped Lex before he could stifle it.

"I hate dresses," Amelia groaned, but she relaxed. Her lips twitched up at the corners as she nearly smiled back at Lex but fought it, still wanting to act mad.

The door of the other house swung open and they both turned toward the sound.

Acarius stepped out onto the porch. "Dinner's ready," he called, eyeing them, then slipped back into the house.

Lex had been uncertain how to proceed with the conversation *and* he was starving, so he was doubly thankful for Acarius' distraction. Lex looked at Amelia again. He hoped he hadn't made her too suspicious that something had changed. If she *was* up to something, revealing too much too soon could be a dangerous mistake. For now, they could be two friendly acquaintances who both needed to eat, couldn't they?

"Food?" he asked. He threw the question out in a casual tone, hoping it sounded natural.

Amelia's faux-scowl melted into a smile and she nodded.

Lex's tension eased a bit – she didn't seem to be suspicious. Yet that bothered him, too, as though he was somehow betraying her. They walked toward the other house.

"I could eat a horse," Amelia sighed as they reached the porch.

As they breached the steps, Mare poked her head around the far edge of the house, where she had been grazing.

Amelia glanced at Mare. "Sorry," she said. She turned back to Lex. "Does that horse weird you out as much as she does me?"

Lex looked at Mare, who stared directly back at him. Memories of her kicking and biting at him on the hill blurred with the white horse of his visions. "I... sort of," he said, his thoughts whirling.

Mare stared at him for one beat longer before turning her nose back to the grass.

Lex and Amelia climbed the rest of the stairs to the front door, which had been left ajar for them.

"I hope they made something good," Amelia said, entering the house.

Lex followed behind her.

Enticing aromas filled the room, making Lex's mouth water. He closed the door behind them and glanced around the space. It was almost an exact replica of Acarius' house, only larger and with more furniture, intended for a full family. The front room where they stood was open, divided into a living area and dining area. Lex noticed the dining table was already arranged with plates and silverware, and some mismatched chairs seemed to have been added to the rest, probably for him and Amelia. Beyond the dining area was a wall, unlike the open floorplan of Acarius' house. A doorway was propped open, revealing part of a kitchen. On the left stretched a hallway with closed doors leading off both sides, and on the right-hand wall of the house was what appeared to be a door to the outside. Lex stepped further into the room, the smells from the kitchen luring him inward.

"It was my parents' house."

Lex jumped, startled by Acarius appearing behind him. From the corner of his eye, Lex saw Amelia jump as he did, and she turned to face Acarius alongside him.

"Was?" Amelia asked, taking Lex's hand.

Lex's fingers closed around Amelia's instinctively. *Pulling away quickly would be rude,* he reasoned. He didn't want to offend her... or make her suspicious. *If she isn't trying to kill me, maybe we can even be friends.*

*Get it together,* he berated himself. After a moment more, he pulled his hand away. The coldness of the air hit his bare hand, contrasting her warm touch. He stuffed his hand in his pocket.

Amelia let her hand fall back to her side, not seeming bothered.

Lex had been so preoccupied during the lull in conversation that he'd almost forgotten what Amelia had asked, until Acarius finally answered: "They're dead."

The phrase thumped to the floor like a boulder, stunning Lex and Amelia into silence. Lex could feel Amelia's energy pulsing beside him, the air around her growing warmer... or was he imagining it?

"I'm sorry," Lex said after a moment, meeting Acarius' eyes.

Acarius glanced at Amelia before turning his eyes back to Lex. "It happened a long time ago. But thanks," he said. He headed toward the kitchen.

Doors flew open all up and down the hallway, and a flood of sisters rushed out from their rooms.

"You're back!" one of them said, tackling Acarius midway to the kitchen and throwing her arms around him.

Acarius placed his hand on the girl's brown hair as she smiled up at him. He returned her smile, then peeled her arms away and turned her toward Lex and Amelia, presenting her. "This is Emily," he said. "She's the second-oldest of my sisters."

The girl nodded her head in their direction.

*Second-oldest*, thought Lex. She did look slightly older than the two who had prepared his bath, but Lex could hardly keep track of all these sisters. He wondered briefly about his own background, whether he had any siblings–

There was a flash of something in his mind, the feel of a small hand clasped in his. It was tiny, pudgy, a fraction the size of his own. Lex tried to grasp at the image, to see it more clearly, but it vanished.

"You alright?" Amelia asked, looking up at him.

"Yeah," he said, swallowing. "I'm good."

Lex looked back toward Acarius. There was a row of sisters now, trailing beside Emily as though waiting for Acarius to introduce them. All lined up like this, Lex could definitely see the family resemblance. They all had the same olive skin, the same dark brown hair – though varying in lengths – the same slim figure, and the same thick, black eyelashes. Their eye colors differed – various shades of hazel and brown – and they had small differences in some of their features, but their bone structures were similar and they were all in the teenage-range and all ridiculously attractive. Acarius blended right in with the good looks of the rest of them; they looked like a family of models. They clearly had a quality gene-pool.

Amelia tensed beside Lex as though reading his thoughts. *Does she feel threatened by these girls?* Lex wondered. She didn't need to. Lex noticed their attractiveness in a detached way, just an observation. It was nothing like the pull he felt toward Amelia, a pull he seemed always to be fighting. Even now, he battled the urge to take Amelia's hand to reassure her. He didn't; he knew he needed to maintain boundaries. But he did still want to be nice to Amelia, for her to see him as a friend. Besides, she could be really unpredictable, and her being jealous of some imagined attraction Lex had toward the sisters would probably not end well for *anybody*. He turned and gave Amelia a small smile, hoping it would reassure her. Amelia relaxed beneath his gaze, and Lex turned back toward Acarius, only then wondering if Amelia's discomfort may have been for a totally different reason.

"Megan is the oldest," Acarius said, pointing at the girl on the end. "Except for me, of course. And you've already met Anna and Sasha." He gestured to the two girls next to Emily, the ones who had run past Lex on the way to start his bath.

Lex still didn't know which one was Anna and which one was Sasha, but it seemed they thought he should, so he didn't ask. He mentally tallied the sisters. *Four.* Hadn't Acarius said there were five?

As if on cue, a voice sounded from the kitchen. "Coming through with hot food! And don't you make me drop it; I worked hard on this!"

The line of siblings parted as a figure slid through the doorway, still facing away from them as she navigated a tray of food through the opening.

Lex's breath caught. He could only see the back of her head, but she had not-quite-wavy blonde hair, as though it was meant to be straight but had rebelled, hair exactly like–

The girl turned. It wasn't her. The face was wrong, nothing like the one in Lex's visions, and this girl's eyes were a deep brown, not light blue. She was just as beautiful as the other sisters, and looked quite a bit like them, but her blonde hair somehow emphasized her features differently, distinguishing her from the others.

Acarius rushed to relieve the girl of the food-laden tray. "This is Liz," he said, nodding toward her as he carried the tray to the dining table. "She's my middle sister." He set the food down, then turned back. "Come on, everyone. Let's eat."

Lex's heart was still pounding from the shock of Liz's hair, and he couldn't help but wonder how there came to be one stark blonde in a family of brunettes. Amelia seemed to notice something was off with Lex and glanced up at him. He gave her a shaky smile. She raised her eyebrow but took his hand again, and warmth surged through him. He didn't pull away.

"Come on," she whispered, tugging him toward the table.

The sisters had filled in most of the seats, leaving two chairs open near one end of the table. Amelia slid into the one on the side, giving Lex the one at the foot of the table... or maybe it was the head; he wasn't sure. Lex took the seat opposite Acarius, who was already at the table's other end, watching him. The thought of Acarius staring at him across the table for the entire meal made Lex feel rather awkward. He broke eye contact and looked down, fidgeting with his empty plate.

One of the brown-haired sisters – Lex still couldn't keep track which was which, even after the introductions – took small platters of food from the larger tray and passed them down the table. The smells tortured Lex as he waited for the food to reach him. The platters held slices of pot roast, baked ham, some kind of roasted vegetable, warm bread that seemed homemade, and an odd kind of jelly-dessert layered with slivers of a fruit Lex didn't recognize. He piled his plate with a bit of each as the platters reached him, noticing that no one was eating yet. Lex's stomach pinched in hunger as the fragrance of his own plate drifted up to him, and his fingers twitched to his fork. He didn't want to seem rude, though, so he waited, watching for a signal that he could begin eating.

When all the platters had returned to the center of the table, the sisters and Acarius silently bent over their plates and started eating. Lex happily followed their cue and Amelia did the same. Everything was delicious, even the things Lex didn't recognize. Acarius was right about Liz being an excellent cook.

While they ate, Acarius and his sisters discussed the day, sharing info on horses that needed extra grooming, which crops from their small garden were thriving or faltering, whether Emily had managed to mend Acarius' torn riding pants (she had), and what needed to be picked up from the market on their next trip to town. Lex was struck by how easily the conversation flowed between the siblings. He felt like an outsider, as though he'd walked into someone else's private moment. Which, he supposed, he had. Lex and Amelia ate in silence, directing most of their attention to their plates.

Eventually, Acarius turned to them. His eyes fell on Lex. "There are some things we need to discuss," he said.

Lex set his fork down, his blood running cold. His thoughts jumped to the note hidden in his pocket, and to the pendant which currently resided against his chest beneath Acarius' borrowed tunic. Lex glanced around the table, and none of the sisters would meet his eyes. *Which one of them wrote the note?* Lex wondered. *Or was it Acarius?* The pendant was its own mystery, so familiar, though Lex still couldn't remember why. He resisted the urge to finger the pendant, not wanting to draw attention to it, his thoughts going back to the note. Surely Acarius didn't mean to confront him about Amelia, right here in front of everyone...

"We're on a bit of a time crunch, I'm afraid," Acarius continued. "Ordinarily I'd invite you to stay here and rest as long as you need, but I have horses to transport to Merik'esh by tomorrow and since that's where you were headed, it would be best if you both just come with me when I go."

Lex paused. "Actually, we didn't say where we were headed," he said slowly.

Acarius tapped a finger on the table. "Oh. I just assumed. There really isn't much else around here other than Dalton, and after what happened to the forest, I didn't expect you'd want to head back that way. Did you need to go somewhere else?"

The words came out so smoothly Lex almost believed it really had been a lucky guess. Almost. "No," he said, not taking his eyes off Acarius. "You were right."

One of the sisters – *maybe Megan?* – cut in. "That's lucky," she said with a smile. "It'll be perfect, then. Aren't you taking two cart-horses down to that merchant from Lanian?" she asked Acarius. "They can each ride one, and you can take Mare."

Acarius nodded. "Yes, it really is perfect timing. The horses will be much easier to transport with riders. Leading them behind Mare and I would have slowed us down. Lex and Amelia will need new horses if they travel beyond Merik'esh, of course, since the other two are spoken for, but I'm sure there are some available in the city. Yes, that will work." He smiled at his sister and she returned it. He looked back to Lex and Amelia. "You don't mind riding separately rather than sharing a horse, do you? It would really help me out."

"Not at all," Amelia said, smiling back at him. "I like horses."

Lex wasn't sure whether Acarius asked if they minded riding separately because he thought Lex and Amelia might want to ride together, or if Acarius had expected one of them to want to ride with him. In no version of his plans had Lex imagined riding double with Acarius, that was for sure. Sensations of the desert, of a horse's hot skin beneath him, whispered at the edges of Lex's awareness. "Sure," he said. "I can ride alone." *At least I think so.*

Acarius smiled at them both. "Great," he said. "Then we'll head out soon. I just need to get some things ready." He grabbed his plate and rose, heading for the kitchen.

Lex watched Acarius leave the table, realizing this might be his only chance to get Acarius alone before the three of them were on the road. He needed answers, and he wanted to get the confrontation out of the way before locking himself into spending a whole day or more with the guy. He pushed his chair back and stood. "I'll help clear the plates," he said, grabbing his own.

The sisters looked surprised. "You don't have to do that," one of them said. "You're our guest."

"It's no problem," Lex mumbled. He grabbed Amelia's plate too, for good measure, and she stared up at him with wide eyes that seemed to say *What's going on?* and *Don't leave me alone with them* at the same time. Lex mouthed a quick *sorry* to her, then hurried after Acarius, who had already disappeared into the kitchen.

"So, thanks for the food," Lex heard Amelia saying from the table behind him. The voice of one of the sisters began to answer, but as Lex slipped through the door the sound faded, replaced by noises of the kitchen.

A pot of something simmered on the stove, its bubbling hiss filling the air with a spicy fragrance. Lex looked around. It was a much larger kitchen than the one in Acarius' house, with a wood stove and a wide array of pots and pans of various sizes hanging from hooks on the wall. There was an icebox over to one side, almost like a deep chest freezer. Lex wondered if it was simply an insulated cooler or if something powered it. He had yet to see any electricity or plugs in this place. Suddenly he wondered how he thought to look for plugs, and whether he had them where he was from. It was a strange feeling, not knowing his own past, and for a moment it threw him off. But he was in the kitchen for a reason. He shook off his question and refocused on the room before him. Large, curtainless windows spanned the wall opposite the door, giving a view of the hills beyond the ranch. In front of the windows, Acarius stood before a large washbasin filled with soapy water. He lowered his plate into the washbasin and turned around, startling as he saw Lex.

"Oh," he said, his voice betraying his surprise at being followed. He noticed the plates in Lex's hands. "Here, let me take those."

Lex handed over the plates, his mouth going dry. How did someone begin a conversation like this? He sort of liked Acarius, or at least felt a kind of gratitude toward him. He seemed like a generous person, and Lex didn't want to appear unthankful or combative. Lex also hated the thought of revealing just how clueless he was, even about his own life, but it was likely to come up in the conversation once he admitted how little he knew about Amelia, the pendant, or anything else. He hated feeling so helpless. But he needed answers, so what choice did he have? He decided just to go for it. "So, I found a note in my pants earlier," he said.

Acarius turned, hand frozen midway to dropping the plates in the sink. "What?" he asked.

"I mean, your pants. That I borrowed," Lex said. He gestured to his legs. "These pants. And not in them, really, more like *on* them." *I'm making it worse,* Lex thought, heat flooding to his face.

Acarius raised an eyebrow. "Okay," he drawled. He lowered the plates into the soapy water and then turned, drying his hands on a nearby towel. "And the note said what, exactly?"

Though Lex wasn't thrilled with his awkward opening, *this* was the part he was really dreading. Would Acarius deny it and pretend he knew nothing about what was going on? Or would he admit to leaving the note and reveal dark secrets about Amelia? Lex wasn't sure which would be worse. "It said not to trust Amelia." He spit out the words before he could change his mind.

Acarius' eyes widened, then focused on Lex with an eagle gaze. This was not something Lex had expected; Acarius had looked genuinely surprised. He took one step toward Lex, his posture stiff. "When did you find this note? Where?"

Lex instinctively took a step backward, bumping into part of the kitchen counter. His anxiety flared at the aggression in Acarius' posture, igniting his desire to run, yet at the same time, something deep within him stirred. Something the opposite of flight. Lex straightened, standing tall. "It was inside the folded clothes one of your sisters brought me," he said. "Why? What does it mean? Didn't you know about it?"

Acarius' gaze flicked to the open kitchen door, where his sisters could be heard still chatting at the table, then back to Lex. "No," he said. "I didn't know about it; I didn't leave it, and I'm not sure who did." He turned back toward the sink. "But I wouldn't let it bother you," he said with a sudden lightness. "Probably just one of the girls trying to mess with you." He grabbed a cloth off the edge of the basin and buried his hands in the suds, scrubbing at the plates.

Lex's thoughts spun. *Why does everyone here act like they're hiding something?* He stepped forward, unwilling to let this go. "Then what about the pendant?" he asked. "Are you going to pretend you didn't give me that, too?"

"Of course not," Acarius said, turning. "We were both there. Why would I deny it? Whatever you might think, I'm not your enemy."

*But someone is.* Lex could feel the meaning hanging behind Acarius' statement. Lex swept his eyes over Acarius, evaluating him. Acarius seemed nice enough, kind, and his sisters clearly adored him. He had helped Lex and Amelia when they had nothing and nowhere to go. But... like everyone and everything else, Lex knew nothing about him. *I'm so tired of being ignorant,* Lex seethed. Frustration roiled within him, a distant, churning fury. He pushed it down. "The pendant," he said again, withdrawing it from beneath his tunic. His voice came out hard, cold. "What does it mean?"

Acarius sighed and his shoulders slumped a bit. "It's something I've had for a long time," he said. "Think of it as a good luck charm. I thought it might help you." He paused. "It used to be my mother's."

"Oh," Lex said. A wave of pity swept over his anger and suspicion. "Then I can't–"

Acarius grabbed Lex's hand partway through pulling the necklace off to return it. "No," he said quietly, not quite meeting Lex's eyes. "I want you to have it. Please."

Something in his expression made Lex slide the leather cord back around his neck and tuck it back into his tunic. "Thanks," he said. He scanned Acarius' face. There had been a look there, for a moment, which Lex couldn't interpret. But now it was gone.

Acarius stepped backward. "I should finish up the dishes," he said, "so that we can get ready to go. Will you go grab the rest of the plates?" His demeanor was suddenly casual, back to the neighborly horse rancher.

Lex was halfway back to the dining room before he realized Acarius had intentionally sent him away to distract him. The sisters hushed as they noticed Lex's approach, all five glancing at him. *What is going on with these people?* Lex wondered. Amelia sat stiffly at the end of the table, looking uncomfortable. Anger simmered in Lex's chest. *Did they say something to her?* Lex had suspected from the time of their arrival that Amelia and the sisters didn't quite approve of each other, but was something more going on? Lex felt a familiar awakening, something belly-deep unfurling with a low growl. He turned back toward the kitchen, determined to get some answers from Acarius, whether he liked it or not.

He had barely made it two steps when Acarius barrelled out from the kitchen, nearly slamming into him. His eyes were wild. "We have to go. Now!" he yelled.

The sisters erupted in a flurry of scooting chairs, footsteps racing in all directions, cabinets and bedroom doors being slammed or flung open. Outside, Mare gave a shrill whinny.

Amelia was the only one still sitting, eyes wide, staring at Acarius. "What?" she said dreamily, as though in shock.

Lex turned back to Acarius, heart pounding. "What's going on?" he demanded.

But Acarius was pushing past him, toward Amelia. He grabbed her arm, hauled her to her feet, and shoved her none-too-gently toward Lex. "We have to go," he said again, heading for the front door.

Lex followed, anxiety invading him as Acarius flung the front door open. "Go where?" Lex spit out. "Why?" He stopped and Amelia bumped into him, sending a jolt through him.

But Lex's attention was on Acarius, who had just slammed the front door shut again and spun around, his face alive with panic.

"It's too late," Acarius said, his back pressed to the front door. "They're here."

# CHAPTER 5

"Who's here?" Lex demanded, stepping toward Acarius. "What's going on?"

A sister rushed in from the kitchen. "What about Mare?" she asked, looking at Acarius. Her voice trembled.

"She'll be fine." Acarius was pale, his eyes scanning the room. "Side door?"

"Already blocked," she answered.

Outside, Mare whinnied.

"Back window?" Acarius asked.

"Blocked too."

"How many?"

"At least twenty and more on the way," she said.

"Megan!" One of the other sisters called from the hallway.

"Coming," she called out. She glanced at Lex, then back to Acarius. "The front's the only way."

Acarius nodded. "Get them ready," he said.

Megan took a deep breath. "Please be careful," she said.

Acarius smiled. "Aren't I always?"

"Megan!" the voice from the hall called.

The girl rushed to Acarius and threw her arms around him.

"Megan!" another voice shouted, sounding panicked.

"You know what to do," Acarius said, placing his hand on her face.

Megan nodded, then raced off toward the hallway.

"What's happening?" Lex demanded again.

Acarius turned to him. "Give me a minute," he said.

Amelia placed her hand on Lex's arm. "What's going on?" she asked. "Who's coming?"

Lex felt a tremor in her touch, a high-frequency vibration.

63

"Let me think," Acarius answered. He squeezed his eyes shut for a moment.

Lex and Amelia waited, unsure what else to do.

Acarius' eyes snapped open. "Get down!" he yelled, launching himself at them.

All three tumbled to the floor as the room exploded around them.

Lex coughed and sat up, blinking through the dust in the air. His lungs burned. He was still in Acarius' living room, debris filtering down from a large hole in the roof above him. The edges of the hole were smoldering, sending out flutters of ash. The frame of the house was intact, but Lex sat in the epicenter of a large, charred circle which spread outward across the whole front room. Anything within that circle's radius was either singed, destroyed, or covered in ash from the damaged roof. Lex moved his arms and legs, checking for injuries. He was sore and his skin felt hot and dry, like he had been too close to a fire, but otherwise he was unharmed. *What happened?* Lex wondered, looking around the room. Where were Acarius and Amelia and the sisters?

"He's still in there."

"Get him!"

Lex leapt to his feet at the sound of voices outside. He glanced around. Should he run? Hide? He wasn't sure; he didn't even understand what was happening.

He jumped as a hand grabbed his shoulder from behind.

"This way," Acarius hissed.

Lex followed him down the hallway and into the last room on the left.

"What's going on?" Lex whispered. "Where's Amelia?"

"Shh." Acarius signaled Lex to kneel down just inside the room, then eased the door to the room shut and knelt beside him. "They're coming," he whispered.

Lex couldn't take it anymore. "Who's coming? Tell me something!" The words hissed out more loudly than he'd intended.

Acarius glared at him. "The men from Dalton. They must have tracked you here. Now hush, before you get us killed." He crept across the room and inched the curtains open to look outside.

Lex sank back against the wall. The burnt, destroyed house; the men outside – it was all because of *him*? "Why are they after me?" he whispered. "What did I do to them?"

Acarius turned, his face solemn. "I don't know," he said. He paused as though he might say more, but then turned back toward the window.

Lex moved toward him in a crouch. "What about Amelia? Your sisters? Are they safe?"

"My sisters are fine; they know how to handle themselves," Acarius answered, not moving from the window.

Lex felt a cold sliver of dread worm through his stomach. "And Amelia?" he asked. She had been standing right beside him when the explosion happened, but he had seen no sign of her when he woke up.

Acarius turned toward him. "I don't know," he said. "When I woke up from the blast, she was gone."

Lex thought back to what happened. "You jumped at us," he said, "a moment before the explosion. You yelled 'Get down.' How did you know?"

Acarius ran one hand across his forehead and sighed. When he lowered his hand, his forehead was smudged with sweaty soot. "I can –"

The glass of the window exploded inward, showering Lex and Acarius with shards.

"Go. Go!" Acarius shouted, shoving Lex toward the door.

Blood ran into Lex's eyes and his arm stung where a piece of glass had sliced him, but he obeyed, rushing for the door to the hallway. As he pulled it open, he glanced back to see a boulder had been thrown through the window. Acarius was a step behind him, grimacing as though in pain.

"Go!" Acarius urged again, pushing Lex forward.

Lex pulled open the door and rushed out into the hallway, where he collided with someone.

"This way," Amelia said, grabbing his arm.

Buzzing heat flooded through him, making the cut on his arm and forehead throb. "Amelia?" Lex asked. "Where were– "

"The back's clear," Amelia urged. "Let's go." She pulled him down the hallway and toward the kitchen.

The scene in the kitchen stopped Lex at the doorway. The window was completely busted out, jagged remnants of glass edging its frame. Glass

65

fragments covered the entire floor, sparkling beneath the pool of soapy water and broken dishes from the tipped-over washbasin. The rest of the kitchen looked as though it had been ransacked – food spilling out of the overturned icebox, pots and pans scattered around the room, cabinet doors standing open with the contents strewn across the shelves, counters, and floor.

"What happened?" Lex asked. Had looters overtaken the house? It looked like it had been robbed, or... maybe not looters; maybe people looking for something specific. But why, and how had it happened so quickly? *How long was I unconscious?* he wondered.

"I'll explain later," Amelia said, pulling at his arm. The glass on the floor crunched beneath her boots as water soaked their leather. "We have to go now."

Lex looked at Amelia and again at the room, trying to process everything. "Where were you?" he asked.

Acarius slid into the room behind Lex, his steps hardly making a sound. His eyes locked on Amelia with laser-focus. "Yes, Amelia, where were you?" he asked again. His tone sliced the air like a knife.

Amelia went pale. "I came to and you were both still unconscious." The words came in a rush. "I checked you; you were both okay – still breathing – but you wouldn't wake up. I came in here to look for something to wake you – smelling salts or something, I don't know. I sort of made a mess with the cabinets." She tucked her hair behind her ear, revealing a bloody gash on the side of her face.

Lex rushed forward. "You're hurt," he said, tipping her face up toward him. The gash ran from her jawline up to her cheekbone. It was shallow, but still trickling blood.

Amelia removed Lex's hand from her face. "I'm fine," she said. "Just a cut from the glass. I was in here when the– "

Acarius stepped toward her. "What did you do?" he asked.

Amelia held up her hands in a plea. "The cabinet mess is my fault, but the rest of this wasn't me, I swear. I was right in the middle of searching when the window just exploded in, and that's when I saw a whole group of people outside running past, toward the front of the house."

"And you just stayed here, after seeing people run past? Why didn't you try again to wake us, or try to find my sisters for help?" Acarius' words slid out with icy fury.

*What is going on?* Lex wondered again. "That's enough," he said to Acarius, his voice firm. "She's scared, just like we are."

"Then why didn't she at least hide?" Acarius said. "We wake up, frantic to find a way out of here, and she's just hanging out in the kitchen with the window busted open, yet no one came in after her? They broke in the window, like they did to us," he gestured at a large rock in the pool of water and glass which Lex hadn't noticed at first, "but they didn't try to come in, they just left her completely alone. Don't you find that odd?"

Lex needed answers, too, but he could feel Amelia's energy spiking beside him, and he couldn't stand Acarius railing at Amelia as though this was all her fault. It wasn't. Was it? Either way, Amelia deserved a chance to explain herself. Lex stepped between them. "Let her explain," he said to Acarius. He turned to Amelia. "What happened? Tell all of it this time."

Amelia continued, her voice trembling. "After the window exploded, I came out into the living room and you were both gone, so I went to look for you. That's when you came out. I knew the window was busted out in here and with those people running to the front, I thought we might have a chance to get out this way, so I pulled you in here. That's it; I promise. That's all I know." She stopped and looked at Lex. "You believe me, don't you?"

*Do I?* He wasn't sure. So many pieces were still missing; none of this made sense.

Suddenly Acarius' legs buckled and he grabbed at the counter for support. He reached up to the back of his head; his hand came away covered in blood.

"You're hurt," Amelia said. She rushed forward. "Kneel down."

Acarius paused a moment, eyeing her, then crouched down, unable to kneel because of the glass and water covering the floor. "The rock clipped me as it came through the bedroom window," he said, looking at the floor as Amelia examined the back of his head. "It hurt, but I thought I was fine."

"How bad is it?" Lex asked.

Amelia sighed. "I'm not a medic, but it looks pretty bad. It's only bleeding a little, but if I had to guess I'd say he also has a concussion." She grabbed a kitchen towel from an open cabinet, smoothed her hand over it to be sure no glass had landed on it, then balled it up and pressed it to the back of Acarius' head. He winced. "Do you have any bandages?" she asked Acarius. "I thought I saw some earlier."

"Top left cabinet," he said.

Amelia moved to get them.

"Concussion? What does that mean?" Lex asked.

"It means I need to be careful for a while," Acarius said. He was holding the towel to his head with his own hand now, and blood was slowly soaking through the cloth.

Amelia stepped behind him, unrolling a strip of cloth bandage. She took the bloody towel from Acarius and used the bandage to secure a pad of gauze to Acarius' wound.

"He probably shouldn't sleep," Amelia said. "At least for a day or so, until we're sure he's okay." She severed the end of the cloth bandage with a kitchen knife, tucking in the end so it held tightly around Acarius' head. "Looks like the bleeding has slowed. Sorry for making it so tight, but the pressure will help. We'll have to clean out the wound as soon as we have time."

"I know." Acarius rose to his feet, then turned to Amelia. "Thanks," he said.

"You're welcome," she answered.

There was an awkward silence, then Acarius burst into motion, grabbing bandages and other supplies from the cabinets and tossing them into a sack he'd pulled from the counter. "We've wasted far too much time; it's a marvel they haven't burst through the doors yet. We need to get out of here while we still can." He moved cautiously, as though the world was still a bit unsteady for him, and Lex resisted the urge to tell Acarius to sit down and rest, because he knew he was right.

"I still don't understand what's happening," Lex said. "You said it's the men from Dalton—"

At this, Amelia's eyes widened.

"But why are they after me?" Lex continued. "What do they want?"

"I don't have a full answer to that, but I'll explain what I can later, when we're safe. For now, we need to focus on getting out of here." Acarius slid the straps of the sack over his shoulders, then pushed the tipped washbasin to the side and stepped up to the window, peering out. "There's no one back here," he said. "It doesn't make sense."

"Maybe they think they have us cornered in the front of the house?" Lex asked.

"Maybe," Acarius said. He didn't look convinced.

"It could be a trap," Amelia suggested.

"Probably," Acarius responded. "But do we have a choice?"

"Could we just talk to them?" Lex asked. "Maybe it's a misunderstanding."

Amelia let out a harsh laugh. "They tied you up, chased you through the woods, and came after you here, all over some misunderstanding?"

"Maybe they have me confused with someone," Lex said. "One of them said I looked just like–"

"I've heard about the Daltoners. These men are dangerous," Acarius interrupted. "Trust me; they are not open to talking. Not in their current state. You can try diplomacy all you want, after we're somewhere safe. Send a messenger or something. For now, believe me, we need to get away." He glanced out the window again, then looked back at Lex and Amelia. "And yes, this is probably a trap, but right now it's our only option. Do either of you have any better ideas?"

Lex sighed. "You don't happen to have a secret tunnel or something, do you?"

Acarius met his eyes. "We weren't planning to build that until next week." He wrapped a kitchen towel around his hand, using it to knock loose the bits of glass still attached to the window frame.

Lex laughed, only to wonder if Acarius was serious. "Where did you say your sisters are?" he asked suddenly. "Shouldn't they be leaving with us?"

"They're already gone," Acarius said, then flung himself through the open window.

After a moment, his head came back into view. "Come on," he hissed.

Lex swung one leg up onto the window frame and pushed himself over the edge, landing in a crouch on the grass. He glanced around. There was no one in sight. In fact, everything outside was completely quiet.

Amelia scrambled out after them, toppling onto the ground. "What are we–"

Acarius shushed her whispers with a gesture, then waved for Lex and Amelia to come with him. He crept toward the end of the house, keeping his body low. Lex and Amelia followed.

"Got you!" A large man leapt out from around the corner of the house, tackling Acarius. "They're here, boys!" he shouted.

Two more men scurried out on their bellies from beneath the house's raised foundation and lunged for Lex and Amelia's ankles, knocking them off balance. Lex's back slammed hard into the ground. He gasped for breath, struggling to see over the man pinning him to the ground.

Amelia screamed and something inside Lex burst to life. He jerked an arm free and drove his elbow upward into his attacker's nose, then leapt to his feet as the man staggered backward.

"You broke my nose!" the man yelled.

Lex ignored him, lunging at the man atop Amelia. He wrestled his arm around the man's throat, planted his feet to steady his weight, and squeezed. "Get off of her," he growled.

The man's eyes bulged, his face beginning to turn colors. He released Amelia, grabbing at Lex's arm.

Amelia hurried to her feet and stumbled a few steps backward. She was breathing heavy and her hair stuck out in wild disarray around her head.

"Are you okay?" Lex asked, still compressing the man's throat. The man was beginning to slump against him.

Amelia stared with wide eyes at the man in Lex's grasp. "Yes, I think so," she said.

A voice called from the side. "Let him go."

"Not likely," Lex said, turning his head. "Why would I–"

He stopped. The man who had spoken had Acarius in a hold similar to Lex's, but with a sword pressed to Acarius' throat. The man whose nose Lex had bloodied stood beside them, leaning against the side of the house.

"Let him go," the man said again, tightening his arm so that Acarius struggled to breathe.

Acarius' stare seemed to be trying to tell Lex something, but he couldn't interpret it.

"Fine," Lex said, releasing his hold.

The man sank to his knees, gasping as the color of his face returned to normal. He stood and hurried toward the other men.

Amelia stepped toward Lex, and when none of the men stopped her, rushed the rest of the way to him. She planted herself beside him, glancing between him and the men who had Acarius. "Lex," she whispered, "What do we do?"

Lex wondered that himself. Should he negotiate? Try to reason with them? Maybe he could convince them they had the wrong person. Acarius had said not to try talking to them, but if he could just–

Lex's thoughts were interrupted by a shift in Acarius' face. Acarius' eyes fluttered closed and he sagged slightly beneath the man's grasp. *Oh no*, Lex thought. With Acarius' concussion, maybe he was falling unconscious? They had to get him out of–

Acarius exploded into motion, his eyes snapping open the same instant his elbow slammed into the ribs of the man holding him. The man staggered backward, dropping the sword, which Acarius snatched up instantly with near-inhuman speed. It happened almost as a blur, but the tides had turned – Acarius backed the man against the side of the house, the tip of the sword pressed into the man's throat.

The two other men stepped toward Acarius.

"Don't," the man croaked, waving his friends back. "He'll kill me."

"Smart choice," Acarius said. "Now, what are you– "

He was interrupted by yet another voice. "I thought I said not to start the party without us," it said.

Lex turned. Dozens of men appeared from both sides of the house, circling them. One man walked forward, and Lex's blood turned to ice. It was the farmer from the shed, the one who had questioned and struck him. He headed straight for Lex.

"Demon filth," he hissed, then spat in Lex's face.

Fury boiled within Lex, but something deeper whispered *Wait*. It wasn't the right moment. He calmly wiped the spit from his face, then dried his hand on his pants. "You're a lot braver when your boss isn't around to tell you what to do," he said. Images of the man on the ground, blood pluming from his chest, surged up, and Lex felt suddenly ill. He pushed the memories back, focusing on the man in front of him.

The man's face turned red, and he grabbed Lex by the shirt collar. "You stupid–"

"Uncle, don't," a voice yelled.

Lex looked to the side. It was the teenage boy from the shed.

"Don't," he pleaded again. "You've seen what he can do."

"Hush, boy," the farmer growled. "You know I don't believe all those superstitions. Besides, look at him. Does he look dangerous to you?" He leaned his face into Lex's. "You will pay for what you did to our village," he growled. "I'll see to that myself."

Panic clawed in Lex's chest against a backdrop of fury and confusion. He had so many questions, and he would like nothing more than to teach this man a lesson, but right now they were outnumbered, and Acarius was injured. Right now, they needed to escape.

The men shoved Acarius into the middle of the circle with Lex and Amelia.

Lex glanced around, trying to formulate a plan. The men were pointing weapons – an assortment of knives, swords, and some kind of sharpened shovels – at them from all directions. They were surrounded.

Lex glanced at Acarius, hoping he had a plan, but his eyes were focused off in the distance. He was probably struggling to stay conscious, Lex thought. He looked to Amelia but she seemed dazed, too, her eyes wide and glassy. He could feel waves of hot energy rolling off her. He glanced around again. There had to be something they could–

Lex barely had time to register the sound of hooves before Mare burst through the circle, knocking men in all directions. She reared and spun, her hooves impacting men's heads and chests with sickening cracks as she made her way toward Acarius.

Acarius grabbed a sword from the ground and tossed it to Lex, who surprised himself by catching it.

"Cover them," Acarius yelled. He pulled Amelia toward him and shoved her upward onto Mare's back, then slid the sack of supplies off his back and wedged it in Amelia's lap. The men were staggering to their feet now, many of them injured but looking angry. Mare pranced nervously, seeing the men move toward them.

"I can't," Lex shouted. "I don't know how."

"You can and you do," Acarius said, pulling his own sword from the grasp of an unconscious farmer on the ground near them.

Acarius waited a moment, as though expecting Lex to do something. When Lex didn't, Acarius sighed. "Fine, I'll do it." He charged forward, slicing at the men who closed in on Mare.

Amelia still seemed dazed, but she clung to Mare's mane and tightened her legs, hanging on.

Acarius kicked a man in the face then spun, elbowing another in the jaw. The second man fell onto the first. Acarius had cleared a small break in the circle, but the others were rushing in. Acarius nodded at Mare and she took off, barreling through the men who didn't move out of her path.

Acarius fell back, taking his place beside Lex.

Lex spun slowly, the sword heavy in his grasp. The men had reformed into a circle, and were inching in toward him and Acarius. Most of them looked furious, except for the teenage boy, who hung back looking terrified.

"Step aside, Acarius," one of the men said.

Lex snapped his head toward Acarius. *They know his name?*

Acarius didn't look surprised. "You know I won't," he answered.

The circle stopped its inward progress and the man who had assaulted Lex in the shed stepped forward to face Acarius. "He destroyed half our village. He killed dozens of our people. *Children*, even. He deserves to die." He glared at Lex.

Lex's heart slammed against his chest. *I did what?* "No," he pleaded. "Please, I would never do that. You have the wrong person."

"Shut up, demon," the man growled. He turned back to Acarius. "We respect you, Halben, but if you get in our way, we won't spare you."

"I wouldn't expect you to," Acarius said, tightening his grip on his sword.

"And the girl?" the man spat. "Are you willing to die to protect her, too?"

Lex tensed. "What does Amelia have to do with this?"

"She's not who you think," Acarius said to the man calmly. "You obviously didn't look closely enough."

"A trick," the man said. "Appearances can easily be disguised."

"No trick," Acarius said. "She's a stranger. She has nothing to do with this fight."

The man laughed. "Strangers here are never innocent. We both know that."

Lex was completely confused, but on one point he was certain – Amelia didn't deserve to die for anything he had done. "The girl goes free," he said, stepping forward. "And that's the end of it."

Acarius glanced at him, an eyebrow raised, then turned back to the man. "Those are our terms, then," he said. "The girl stays out of it, but we'll fulfill our end of the deal."

The circle of men around them shifted, drawing their weapons.

Lex turned to Acarius. "Wait, what deal?" he asked.

Acarius raised both eyebrows this time, then spoke slowly, as though explaining to a child. "They let her go, we fight to the death for our freedom... what exactly did *you* think we were negotiating?"

"What?" Lex sputtered. "No, wait, I–"

"Trust me," Acarius murmured, just low enough for Lex to make out.

Lex shut his mouth.

"I'll make sure you get an honorable burial, Halben," he said to Acarius. "And you..." He turned to Lex. "My daughter was among the dead. She was only twelve." He took a shaky breath. "You are going to pay her suffering back, with interest."

Lex opened his mouth, but the words stuck in his throat. He wanted to apologize, to commiserate the man's loss, but... how could he when they believed *he* was the one who caused it? He would never have killed a child; he was certain of that. "I didn't kill anybody," he said again. "You have the wrong person."

"Men," the farmer called out, "soak yourselves in their blood."

With a roar, the ring of men charged inward.

# THE EDGE OF NOTHING

# CHAPTER 6

Lex squeezed the sword hilt so hard his fingers turned white as the burly farmer raced toward him. Lex had no idea how to fight, but if he was about to die at this man's hands, he intended to make him work for it. Lex shifted sideways, readying to strike when the farmer got close enough.

The world tilted. He spun. His sword sliced in a graceful arc, drops of blood flinging outward in its wake. The man before him dropped, his throat slit open. Another took his place immediately. The enemy seemed endless, surging in from all directions. He jabbed, the new enemy impaling on his sword mid-charge, then pulled the sword free again and turned as he swept his blade through the stomach of another one. "How are you holding up over there?" he yelled.

A young man with leaf-green eyes casually elbowed an attacker in the face as he turned toward him. "Me? Oh, I'm doing great," he said.

*Acarius.* Younger, but it was him.

"Don't mind me," a voice wheezed. "I don't need any help." An old man struggled a few feet away beneath the collapsed body of an enemy.

*Nigel,* his mind whispered. "Crazy old man," he heard himself say as he jabbed his sword's hilt into the jaw of an enemy, knocking him unconscious.

Acarius laughed, glancing at the old man. "You managed to down one. Imagine that." Acarius kicked an approaching enemy in the chest, then reached to help the old man stand.

It was suddenly quiet. Bodies littered the ground around the three of them, all either dead, unconscious, or injured and moaning.

Relief bubbled inside him, but he knew not to give in to it – there would be more coming, and soon.

Nigel staggered as he stepped around the bodies of the enemy. "Mocking an old man, eh? I see you still haven't learned proper manners." Nigel bent to retrieve a knife from the ground, then straightened with a groan and slid it into his belt. A shaggy white beard hung past Nigel's knobby knees, which protruded from the bottom of a brown cloth tunic. A tan rope-sash held the baggy tunic to the old man's bony body. Nigel moved slowly as though frail, with one hand on the small of his hunched back. Thin hair stuck out in all directions from his head like white, wiry antennae, and his face was wrinkled and red, as if chapped by the wind or sunburned. Makeshift sandals of leather and rope covered the old man's feet, which were caked with mud...and blood. Frail or not, Nigel looked slightly unhinged.

He felt a shiver of caution as Nigel's hawkish eyes focused on him. The old man was definitely more than he seemed.

A teenage girl darted up, and he felt his heart squeeze as her ice-blue eyes fixed on him. Blood matted her blonde hair. "They're coming," she said.

"Good," Nigel said, shaking a dying man's hand off his sandalled foot. "Let's end this."

Lex blinked back into the present, panting. The smell of blood from the vision still filled his nostrils. He looked around, trying to get his bearings, and gasped. The smell wasn't from the vision. It was from the ground. Two dozen bodies splayed out, the soil swallowing their blood. Every one of them was dead.

Lex turned to find Acarius watching him.

"What happened?" Lex asked. "I blacked out, and..." His gaze caught on the teenage boy from earlier, his expression terrified even in death. Lex squeezed his eyes shut as bile rose up in his throat. He took a shaky breath, then forced his eyes back open. "Sometimes I have these visions, like I'm somewhere else. I know it was a terrible time for me to have one. I'm sorry." He glanced around again, his throat tightening. "How did you take them all by yourself?

"I didn't," Acarius said, stepping toward him. He moved slowly, as though trying not to spook a wild animal. "You did."

Lex blinked. "What? No."

Acarius looked around, his attention suddenly captured by something in the distance Lex could neither see nor hear. "We'll talk about it later," Acarius said. "More might be coming; we need to get out of here." He turned, then stumbled and crumpled to the ground with his hands pressed to his head.

Lex dropped his sword and rushed to Acarius.

"My head," Acarius groaned.

"What can I do?" Lex asked. "Tell me how to help."

"The bag," Acarius said. "There's medicine."

Lex stood, looking around. *Amelia took the bag.* There was no sign of her or Mare, and all the horses from the field were gone as well. As Lex knelt back down, his eyes caught on the sword he had dropped. It was covered in blood. *Did I really kill all those people?* He shook his head, forcing back another wave of nausea. "The bag's gone," he said to Acarius. "Mare–"

Before he had finished her name she appeared, galloping over the top of a hill on the far side of the field. As she neared, Lex could see her more clearly – Amelia was not with her.

Mare trotted to a stop, prancing. The sack wasn't on her; Amelia probably had it. Lex looked at Mare. Would she be willing to let him ride? Maybe she could take Lex and Acarius to Amelia, or at least carry them somewhere they could get help.

"Acarius," Lex said, "come on, let's get you onto Mare." He looked down. Acarius was unconscious.

Mare whinnied and nosed Acarius.

"He's hurt," Lex said, realizing only after he said it that he was talking to a horse. It almost felt normal.

Mare bent her front legs and knelt.

*She's trying to help me get him on her back,* Lex realized. He tucked his arms under Acarius' armpits. It took him a few moments, but Lex managed to lift Acarius over his shoulder and then hoist him somewhat-carefully onto Mare. She straightened and Lex adjusted Acarius, straddling Acarius' legs over Mare's body and leaning his torso onto her neck. If Acarius wasn't so slumped, it would almost look like he was taking a casual ride. But Lex knew Acarius would start to slide off if Mare moved too quickly, and Lex had nothing with which to secure him.

Lex glanced at Mare and wondered again if she would let him ride her. Her dislike for him seemed to have abated, or at least she'd set it aside for the moment, since she wasn't trying to bite him. Whether she could sense the urgency of the situation or she'd simply warmed up to him, he was glad for the change. He heaved himself onto Mare's back and reached around

Acarius, grasping her mane. He kicked at her sides, but she didn't move. Was there a command or something?

Inside him, something whispered *Ride*. Lex paused. Surely it wasn't that simple. "Ride, Mare," he said aloud, and Mare shot forward like an arrow. Lex was nearly thrown backward as Acarius slid against him, but Lex's grip on Mare's mane held them both in place. He shifted forward, tightening his hold, and rode.

Amelia came into sight as soon as they crested the hill, all traces of her previous disorientation gone. She jumped up from the grass and ran toward them. "What's wrong?" she asked, seeing Acarius slumped on Mare's neck.

"His head," Lex said, sliding to the ground. "He grabbed it like he was in pain and then just passed out."

Amelia helped Lex lower Acarius to the grass.

"Do you have the bag?" Lex asked. "Acarius said there was some kind of medicine in there he needed."

"No," Amelia answered. "I mean, yes, I have the bag, but... I looked in it while I was waiting. There's nothing in there but food, bandages, and a bunch of weird herbal liquids. Nothing that would fix this." She knelt beside Acarius and pushed his hair back from his forehead, then gently lifted one of his eyelids. "He's out. I mean, really out." She looked at Lex. "I don't know what to do."

Lex turned to her. "You seemed to know about concussions before. Isn't there something we can try?"

Amelia slid the bag from her back and began rummaging through it. "I've heard a few things about concussions, what to watch out for. I know some first aid. But like I said, I'm not a medic." She pulled out a few bottles from the bag and set them on the ground. "I don't even know what any of these are beyond that they're herbs of some kind. One of them might be something that could help him, I guess, but I have no idea what they do."

Lex grabbed one of the amber bottles, turning it over. A dark liquid sloshed inside. "Can't we try one?"

"Without knowing what it is, we could make things worse," she said. "But I've heard people aren't supposed to sleep if they have a concussion, so if that's what's wrong, then we need to wake him up."

Lex unstoppered another small bottle and raised it to his nose... and gagged. "What about this one?" he said, handing the bottle to Amelia. "This smell would wake the dead."

Amelia sniffed it, then closed it carefully. "Maybe," she said, "or it could be poison."

Lex wiped his hands on his tunic. "Seriously?"

"I mean, maybe... I just don't know." Amelia sank to the ground, dropping her head in her hands. "I don't know what to do."

Lex paced, his hands gesturing wildly. "There has to be something we can do or someone who could help. What about your family? You said they live in Alta, right? Would they know how to help him?"

Amelia looked up, her face miserable. "No," she said softly. "I never said that."

Lex stopped pacing and turned. "Yes, you did," he said. "In the woods, when I first met you."

"No, I didn't," she said again. "I never said I have family there. I said I was *from* there."

Lex paused. "So... you're from Alta but your family isn't?"

Amelia sighed. "I'm not exactly from Alta, either."

"What?" Lex said. "Then why did you say you were?"

"It's complicated," Amelia said.

Lex felt anger stirring in his stomach. "Why would you lie to me about where you're from?"

"I didn't think it mattered," she said.

Lex blinked. How could it not matter that she lied to him? *And how many other things had she lied about?*

"Listen," Amelia said, "it's not like–"

A groan interrupted her as Acarius pushed himself up to sitting. "Ugh," he said. "My head feels terrible."

Lex dropped to the ground beside him. "Are you okay?"

"I think so," Acarius answered. Mare nosed him, shifting from the spot where she'd planted herself when they'd arrived. Acarius braced against Mare's body and pulled himself to his feet. "A bit dizzy, and my head feels like someone left a knife in it, but I'll live." He turned to Lex. "Wait... there's not really a knife sticking out of my head, is there?"

Lex shook his head. Acarius looked strangely pale. "No, but you don't look well." He grabbed the bag from the ground, avoiding looking at Amelia – he would have to process that conversation later. For now, Acarius needed him. He held the bag out. "We didn't know which medicine to give you."

Acarius shook his head. "It's the brown one that smells terrible," he said. "But it's only a pain-killer. It will help, but it won't heal me." He paused, leaning against Mare. "I think I really just need food and rest. I lost blood and overexerted myself. When those men charged us, I really thought we–"

"The men charged you?" Amelia interrupted. "What happened?"

"Nothing you need to worry about," Acarius said. "After all, *we're all still alive*. Isn't that what you said after the forest collapsed?"

Amelia fell silent.

Lex did too, but for a different reason. Acarius had told him *he'd* killed all those men. Was that even possible? Lex barely even knew how to hold a sword.

Acarius continued, and Lex noticed his breathing sounded a bit strained. "I have friends in Merik'esh," he said. "We can find a safe place to eat and rest. And there is also a healer there. She might be able to help speed my recovery a bit." The way he said it felt odd to Lex, as though Acarius was avoiding saying something, but Lex shrugged it off, thinking the strangeness in Acarius' tone could just be from not feeling well.

Lex wanted to ask more about what happened while he was in his apparently-murderous trance, but he was a little afraid to bring it up, afraid of what he might learn about himself. Lex's blood turned cold as he realized something – if he'd gone into a murderous trance this time, how did he know he hadn't done it before? Or that he wouldn't do it again? What if next time, it was his friends he killed? He felt frozen to the ground.

"Lex?" Acarius was looking at him, concerned.

"I– just–" Lex couldn't quite form words. He took a breath. "All those men. Was it really..."

"You? Yes," Acarius answered. "And I'm thankful for it. If you hadn't jumped in when you did, we'd be dead for sure. With my head the way it is, I was barely holding my own against the farmer who charged me, much less the more-than-twenty others."

Lex didn't know whether to feel proud or sick; at the moment he felt a little of both. "I really don't remember," he said. "I don't even know how I–"

"What are you talking about?" Amelia interrupted again. "What happened after I left?"

Acarius talked over her questions. "Lex, you fought like a warrior. If you feel unpracticed with a sword, it's your mind holding you back, not your skill."

Lex tried to process this. "When you tossed me the sword at first," he said, "I said I couldn't fight, and you said, 'You can and you will.'" He paused, meeting Acarius' eyes. "How did you know?"

"I can't pretend to know everything about you or your past, but you're more than you think, that much I do know," Acarius answered.

Lex still didn't understand. "But how did you know I could fight?"

"I could see it in the way you moved," Acarius said. "You've been trained; it's obvious."

*To everyone but me, apparently*, Lex thought. It was frustrating to constantly find new reasons to feel like an outsider to his own life.

Acarius squeezed his eyes shut and grunted. When he opened his eyes again a moment later, a fog of pain lingered in them. "I need to get to Merik'esh before my head gets so bad I can't hold myself up on the horse, plus there could be more men coming," he said. "We need to get riding."

Lex had to agree that Acarius needed medical attention and he wasn't eager to encounter any more rampaging farmers. He paused, looking around. "But how? We only have one horse."

Acarius put his fingers in his mouth and let out a sharp, brief whistle.

"What–" Lex stopped as the sound of hooves approached from beyond the hill. Within moments, two horses were galloping toward them, one chestnut with a reddish-brown mane, and one a solid, sleek black. "How..." he began to ask.

"They're trained to run out toward the woods if there's ever an attack," he said, "and to come back in pairs when I call." The horses slowed to a stop beside Mare, and Acarius walked toward them.

Lex raised an eyebrow. "Do you get attacked often, then?"

"Not usually by people," Acarius answered, adjusting the saddles the horses already wore.

Lex blinked. "What does that mean?"

"We've had problems with large animals bothering the horses," Acarius answered, his fingers deftly adjusting the straps along one horse's side. "Being attacked by a mob of farmers today was a first."

"Large animals," Lex repeated. "You mean like panthers?"

Acarius froze, his fingers falling from the saddle. He turned. "Did you see a panther?"

"A huge one," Amelia interjected. "It was about to kill him when I found him in the woods."

Acarius looked confused. "She attacked you?" he asked Lex.

Lex thought for a moment. "No, it didn't, but I'm sure it was about to." He paused. "Wait...*she*?"

Acarius waved his hand, dismissing the question. "It's usually the females who hunt." He stepped forward, eager. "When did you see this panther?"

"Not long ago," Lex said. "The night before the forest erupted and we met you."

The sun was beginning to set now, but it had only been that same morning that he and Amelia had tumbled out of the collapsing forest and into Acarius' ranch. It was strange to think it hadn't even been a full two days. Waking up in the shed felt like a lifetime ago.

Acarius shook his head. "It doesn't make sense."

"What does, around here?" Amelia laughed.

"What about it doesn't make sense?" Lex asked, ignoring Amelia's joke.

"We just don't really get panthers around here," Acarius said. He turned, beginning to adjust the saddle on the chestnut horse. "Something must have brought one out this way; it's not their normal territory."

"That doesn't sound good," Lex said.

Acarius turned. "It's not," he said. "And so, what, the panther just came after you and you fought it off?"

"No," Lex said. "Actually, when Amelia showed up, the panther turned and ran away." He was realizing anew how strange that sounded, and it stirred uncomfortable feelings toward Amelia. What was she hiding? So many things about her didn't make sense.

Acarius glanced at Amelia. "I see," he said. "Probably felt spooked by there being more than one of you. Panthers can be finicky hunters."

There was something strange behind his eyes, something which hinted he wasn't telling the full story.

Amelia fidgeted, and Lex felt a surge of suspicion rise. Later, he'd have to sit down and demand some real answers from Amelia. So much of her story just didn't match up. But Lex would save his questions for Amelia for later. Right now, Acarius was distracted by adjusting the saddles and was finally opening up to him, and Lex wanted to get answers while he could. "What about your sisters?" he asked. "We were attacked so quickly, but somehow they got out. How?" *And why didn't we just go with them?* he wanted to add, but he refrained.

Acarius shrugged. "We had an escape plan," he said. "The girls slipped out just before the explosion. We'd prepared supplies and a plan for how they would get out, and a safe place for them to go. Ideally, the rest of us would have been just behind them, but the explosion upset that part of the plan. Still, they know to wait there until I meet up with them."

"You sure seem to be a family of planners," Amelia deadpanned.

Acarius looked at her. "Yeah," he said simply.

"But how did you know we would be attacked?" Lex asked. He was still struggling to make sense of all of it.

"We didn't," Acarius said. "But we knew it was a possibility."

"Because of being so close to Dalton?" Lex was beginning to wonder if Dalton was just a town of murderous, psychotic farmers. After all, they'd accused him of killing a large number of their townspeople *and* of being a demon, both of which he was sure weren't true. At least, mostly sure.

"No," Acarius said. "Because of you."

"What?" Lex asked. He hadn't expected that answer, but something in him had known that it wasn't arbitrary the farmers had come after him. He couldn't remember his past, but others certainly seemed to, and from all signs it was an unpleasant one. He swallowed. "Why? We just met this morning. How could you know I would be a threat to you? Did we meet before? Why is everyone after me? What did I do?" Once he got started, the questions just poured out. And there was one more he didn't ask, that he was afraid to ask: *Who am I?*

"I don't actually know exactly what you did, but I can tell you what the farmers *think* and why they're after you," Acarius said.

"What?" Lex's heart was suddenly racing.

"They think you're a demon in service to the evil goddess, Ardis, and that you used your demon powers to blow up half their town and murder a bunch of their people."

Lex blinked. "What? That's crazy. I'm not..." He paused. He didn't really know his past, but he was fairly certain he wasn't demonic. "I'm not," he stated again.

Acarius rolled his eyes. "Of course you're not. Do you think I'd risk my life to save a murderous demon? Believe me, I have better things to do." He turned and stuffed the sack into one of the saddlebags. "There," he said, giving the brown horse a pat. "Ready to go."

"Wait," Lex said. "I still don't understand. What do you know about me? About my past? How did you know I'd come here?"

Acarius looked at him. "We didn't," he said. "But when we heard what happened in Dalton, we hoped you'd head this way, so that we could help you. We didn't believe you did the things they claimed."

Lex's head was spinning. "And you know about my past? About who I am? Did we... know each other?"

Acarius gave him a sad look. "Not exactly," he said. "I knew what happened in Dalton, because some of the people who fled the town came through this valley. I knew the farmers would come after you once they heard you were here, but I'd hoped we'd be on our way to Merik'esh before that happened. But more than that... I can't really say."

Acarius looked sincere, but something in the back of Lex's mind nagged at him, an inkling of untruth somewhere in Acarius' story which he couldn't place. He set it aside, wanting to think it over more carefully before saying anything. Instead, he asked, "Earlier, I asked you how you knew things were about to explode. You started to answer, but we got interrupted. How did you know?"

Acarius smiled. "That's an easy one," he said. "I was born with extra-sensitive ears, and I can hear several decibels higher and lower than most humans."

"I don't get it," Lex said. "How did that help you know something was about to explode?"

Acarius handed Amelia the reins of the chestnut horse and swung himself onto Mare's back. He was moving more smoothly now, as though his head had eased off, but there was still a cloud of pain behind his eyes. He shrugged. "I could hear the static electricity ramping up in the air, getting shriller. It's sort of hard to explain, but it happened fast and once I noticed it, it was too late to do anything about it other than yell for you to duck." His eyes shifted to Amelia for a moment before turning back forward.

*Did he think Amelia had something to do with the explosion?* Lex thought. Was it possible? Maybe Amelia really *was* working with the farmers, and had set a bomb to sabotage their escape. He pushed the thought aside. It was true Amelia had lied to him, but assuming she was some kind of enemy spy was crazy. *Wasn't it?* Maybe Amelia's "I'm a spy" joke was one of the few honest things she'd said to him. The thought made a shiver run down his spine.

Lex set thoughts of Amelia aside. Acarius was talking, and Lex knew this was his chance to find out more about himself. Acarius *had* to know something about Lex, or his visions – after all, he'd been *in* the last vision Lex had. Together they'd slaughtered dozens of the enemy – dozens of *people* – without even a second thought. Just as he'd done himself, while the vision controlled him. Lex needed answers. He wasn't sure he would like what he might learn about himself, but he had to ask. "Did we know each other... before? When I was in my vision, I saw you. We were fighting together."

Acarius' face went very still, and he paused a moment before answering. "No," he said. "Your vision must have been wrong. We've never met before you showed up on the hill above my ranch." His words were measured, as though chosen carefully.

Lex was certain it had been Acarius in the vision, but he decided not to argue that point. He took a different angle. "But then why help us so much?" Lex asked. "Why risk your life for me? And what" –he pulled the pendant out from beneath his tunic– "about this?"

Acarius kept his gaze steady, not giving away any emotions. "There are bigger things at play here than you, Lex. Besides, I told you; the pendant was for good luck. You seemed to need it."

Lex wasn't satisfied. There was something Acarius wasn't telling him, he was sure of it. "You know something," he insisted. "You knew I could fight, even when I didn't believe it. I'm *still* not sure I believe it. And you knew the men were coming for us. You knew everything, and you tried to protect me. Why? Who am I to you?" He was pleading now, desperate to understand something, anything, about his past. "What do you know about me?"

Acarius listened, unreactive. After a moment, he asked, "This vision you had... what exactly did you see?"

Lex described the vision – the battle, a younger Acarius, the old man... the girl. Lex glanced uncomfortably at Amelia while describing the last part. He wondered if the strong feelings about the girl which permeated his visions were coming through in his voice, though he tried not to let them. He didn't want to make Amelia jealous.

Amelia wandered back over to the horses, but was clearly listening to them even while pretending not to be. Lex was almost disappointed that Amelia showed no reaction to the mention of the girl, then immediately got upset at himself for caring. But his internal debate was interrupted by the fact that Acarius *did* react.

"Her name is Jana," he said, his eyes wide. He shook his head, as though in disbelief. "I remember that day. We took down over a hundred of them before the menagerie arrived."

"The menagerie?" Amelia moved back toward them.

"It wasn't an actual menagerie, that's just what we called the reinforcements because they–" He stopped. "It doesn't matter," he said, speaking more quickly now, his whole body turned toward Lex. "What else have you seen?"

Lex summarized the visions he'd had so far, leaving nothing out.

Acarius listened intently, then fell silent for a few moments. Finally, he spoke. "I thought you were him, at first. You are so much like... but you aren't; I knew that as soon as you spoke. But these visions, what do they..." He trailed off.

"What are you saying?" Lex asked, impatient now. "Who did you think I was?"

Acarius muttered to himself in a language Lex didn't understand, as though thinking out loud. Then he stopped, his eyes snapping back toward Lex. "You have his memories," he said, his eyes wide with wonder. "Somehow, you're inhabiting them, as if you're there."

"Whose memories?" Lex demanded, his temper mounting. "Tell me what you know!"

Acarius shook his head. "You were not there that day, my friend. The day of the battle. It was only myself, Jana, Nigel, and Marcus."

"Marcus?" Lex asked. He had seen the others in his vision, but there had been no other person, only Acarius, Jana, Nigel, and... himself. He stopped, realization dawning at the same time dread sank in. He was so close to having answers, but did he truly want to know? He swallowed. "Who is Marcus?"

Acarius paused, as though deciding what to say. "Your brother," he said finally. "I knew your brother. He was my best friend."

Lex didn't know what to say. He had a brother. A *brother*. The vision of himself holding a small hand rose to memory. "A younger brother?" he asked, trying to make sense of everything. "How old?"

Acarius shook his head. "Not younger. Older." He paused, and something shifted subtly in his expression as he swept his eyes over Lex. "By at least seven years."

Lex's mind was spinning. If his brother was older, then whose hand was he – *Wait*, he reminded himself. *Those are* his *memories I'm seeing*. So then the smaller hand must have been Lex's, and he was seeing himself holding it through his brother's eyes. The visions just got more and more confusing. "If these are really my brother's experiences, how am I seeing them?" he asked. "I don't understand."

"I don't really understand, either," Acarius answered. "But it's the only thing that makes sense. *He* was the one there with us that day, not you. The visions you've had, they're things he has done, people he knew, places he's been. Somehow, you're seeing his memories."

Lex was frustrated not to understand more of what was happening to him, but at least he finally had a clue to who he was. "Tell me about myself," he said. "You're close to my brother; you know my family, right?"

"Yes, but– " Acarius said.

Lex continued talking, excited now. "Then tell me about *me*. I don't remember anything before waking up in Dalton, tied to a chair with those farmers. How did I get there? What happened to me? How do I know how to fight?"

Acarius shook his head again. "I don't know the answer to any of those," he said.

Lex halted, confused. "You said my brother was your best friend. You have to know *something* about me."

"No," Acarius said, meeting Lex's stare with a sad look. "Marcus was estranged from his family. They didn't speak. But I knew Marcus very well. We lived together, travelled together, fought together. He saved my life... more than once. Jana, the girl in the visions, she and Marcus were in love. She meant everything to him, for a time."

Lex felt the flood of emotions connected to Jana wash over him yet again. So they were his brother's feelings. That explained that much of his visions, at least. Whoever Jana was, his brother had truly loved her; he could feel it. It was bizarre to feel so strongly what his brother felt, yet have no memories or feelings of the brother himself. What had happened to Lex's *own* memories? How could he remember someone else's past but not his own? He turned back to Acarius, suddenly hesitant. Something in the way Acarius had answered his last question made Lex afraid to ask the next part, yet he had to. "And me? What do you know about me? You must know something."

Acarius sighed. "Until a day ago, I didn't even know you existed."

Lex turned away, stunned. How was that possible? Why would Marcus have never mentioned him? Was he such an embarrassment to the family that they pretended he didn't exist? It didn't make sense. *Unless I really am a murderer.* The thought chilled him at the same time everything in him rejected it. He didn't believe he was that kind of person. He *couldn't* be. "Then how do you even know I'm his brother?" he asked.

"You must be," Acarius said. "You look exactly like him. You have his memories, even some of his mannerisms. I can't begin to explain the memories, but being his brother is the only thing that even remotely makes sense, right?" Acarius placed a hand on Lex's shoulder. "I'm sorry I don't know more. When I heard the Daltoners had captured someone who matched Marcus' description and heard what they were saying about him – about you – I knew you'd be in danger, but I couldn't believe it was truly Marcus they'd captured. I needed to see for myself. I was just leaving the ranch for Dalton when the forest-tsunami, as you called it, happened... then it stopped and you tumbled down my hill. You do look like him, exactly like he did when we first met."

Lex felt as lost as ever. He knew something about his family now, about who he probably was, but it only made him more confused. If he really was Marcus' brother, why hadn't Marcus told Acarius about him? How had Lex come to be in Dalton, captured by farmers, all alone? Where was the rest of his family? And why did the Daltoners think he was a murderer? He needed answers, *now*. And he finally knew who to get them from. He turned to Acarius. "Where is my brother?" he said, his voice firm. "I want to talk to him."

"You can't," Acarius said. "He's dead."

Lex felt the weight of that reality settle on him. He had only just discovered he had a family, and now– "What happened to him?" he asked.

"He died in battle," Acarius said softly.

Lex began to ask more, but Acarius stopped him. "I know you have questions, but I don't know how much longer I have before my head gets worse again. I don't want you having to carry me into the city, for more reasons than one. And besides, when the farmers don't return, more from Dalton are sure to come looking for them... and us. I'll explain more later, I promise, but for now, we need to go."

"Okay," Lex said, swallowing his impatience to know more. "Then let's go." He knew Acarius was right; his answers would have to wait. Maybe they'd have a chance to talk once they were on the way to Merik'esh.

"We're heading that way," Acarius said, pointing past the hills before them. "There's a dirt road of sorts on the other side of the hills, and once we're on that, it's a pretty straight shot to Merik'esh."

"Will we make it before dark?" Lex asked. The sun was rapidly setting.

"No," Acarius said, "but I'd like to put some distance between us and the ranch before night hits, then we'll stop and rest. We can ride the rest of the way in the morning."

Lex neared the black horse and grabbed its lead. When the horse didn't protest, he slid his foot into the stirrup. Before mounting, he glanced at Amelia. She was just standing near the brown horse, lost in thought.

"Amelia?" he asked. "You coming?"

Amelia stepped toward him, her eyes pleading. "Lex," she said, reaching out a hand.

Lex met her gaze with a steely one. He almost felt bad as he saw her face fall in response, but he knew now he couldn't fully trust her. She lied, she disappeared frequently, and during the fight she spaced out right when they were about to be attacked. He'd assumed she was in shock, but what if she'd simply been unwilling to harm the Daltoners, because she was one of them? How had she found him that night in the woods, anyway? For all he knew, she could be trying to delay their escape so more farmers could reach them. He was beginning to think whoever left him that note had good reason to be suspicious. "We can talk later," Lex said. "Didn't you hear Acarius? We need to get away from the ranch."

He turned his horse after Acarius and Mare, who were already moving ahead.

After a moment, Amelia mounted and directed her horse beside him. "I'm sorry I lied to you," she said. "But I don't get why you're so upset. It's not like people usually just go around spouting their life stories to people they just met."

Lex was so sick of people making excuses, of them acting like it was normal to lie and speak in half-truths. And it wasn't just Amelia, it was Acarius, too. He wanted to trust Acarius, but everything the man said seemed to hide something unspoken. Acarius' explanations had given Lex more questions than answers, and he still couldn't shake the feeling Acarius wasn't being totally honest with him. And Amelia... Lex had wanted so badly to believe she was good, but now he wondered if that hadn't been entirely the rational part of him speaking. He could feel her presence tugging at something deep inside him, even now, beneath his anger. The fact that she had so much pull over him made him even angrier.

"Ride," Lex grunted to his horse. He kicked, urging his horse away from Amelia, and his horse gradually increased speed until they had pulled past even Mare and Acarius. Acarius had pointed, and Lex was so sick of following blindly. *They can follow me, for a change*, he thought. He leaned forward into a gallop, letting the wind envelop him.

# CHAPTER 7

After a few minutes, Lex saw the road Acarius had mentioned sprawling out before them. He steered his horse onto it, hearing Acarius and Amelia do the same in the distance behind him. They rode.

When night had fully settled in, Lex slowed his horse to a stop and let the other horses catch up to him. They rode in silence together until Acarius pointed out a small pond on one side of the road. They dismounted and led the horses near the pond to drink, then settled on the ground nearby. Acarius unpacked some food from the bag and handed a bit to each of them. They ate in silence, a heavy tension between the three of them. Acarius removed some blankets from the saddlebags and passed them out.

When Lex finished his food, he turned away from the others and curled up on the ground, drawing his blanket over him. He knew he was being unfriendly, but he didn't feel like talking. As he rode, Lex had only grown more upset with the half-truths Acarius and Amelia had both been feeding him. He didn't trust either of them, but since Acarius seemed to want him alive, at least Lex didn't have to worry about being killed in his sleep. Probably. Lex rolled over, pulling the blanket around himself more tightly. The ground was hard and the air was chill but the blanket helped, and his body was exhausted. Even with his mind racing, he was soon asleep.

Lex woke early the next morning to the sound of Acarius re-packing the horses. Lex stood and stretched. "Got room for one more blanket?" he asked, holding out the blanket he'd slept under.

Acarius turned and smiled. "Sure." He took the blanket and stuffed it into a saddle bag.

He looked better than the day before, Lex noticed. The pain in his expression had lessened. And yet, dark circles ringed beneath his eyes and he moved with a weariness.

"Are you alright?" Lex asked.

Acarius nodded. "Just tired," he said. "My head actually feels a little better."

"Didn't you rest?"

Acarius shook his head. "Couldn't. Concussion, remember?"

"You stayed awake all night?" Guilt washed over Lex as he thought of how quickly he'd fallen asleep, too upset to even talk to the others.

Acarius shrugged. "It's no big deal. Someone had to keep watch, anyway."

Lex felt a new round of shame that he hadn't thought of *that* before falling asleep, either. In the light of day – and in the light of Acarius' continued commitment to protecting and helping him, for some reason he still didn't understand – his anger toward Acarius had abated. Sure, Acarius gave guarded answers, but at least he did answer some of Lex's questions and so far he hadn't lied... that Lex knew, anyway. Acarius kept risking himself to help others, which made it hard to be mad at him.

Amelia was another story.

On the ground behind them she stirred, hearing their conversation. She yawned. "Is it time to go?"

Her brown waves had grown crazier during her sleep, but still Lex felt his heart contract as she blinked and stretched, her mouth scrunching up into a sleepy frown. They'd been through an explosion, run for their lives, slept on the ground all night, and the pink dress she still wore was so dirty it was barely pink anymore, yet she somehow made the dirt and crazy hair look beautiful. *She's a liar*, he reminded himself. *And maybe a spy.* He looked away.

A hot buzz shot up his arm and he jumped.

"Hey," Amelia said. She was right beside him, her hand on his wrist. "Are we okay?"

Lex pulled his arm out of reach. "I don't think we are," he said.

She blinked. "Oh," she said, stepping backward.

Something painful twisted in Lex's chest. "Let's talk later, okay?" he sighed. *After I've had time to think.* Thinking with her staring at him was almost impossible.

"Okay," she said. She turned and walked toward Acarius, handing him her blanket.

Acarius shoved the last few things back into the saddlebags. "Everyone ready?" he asked, turning toward them. "We've still got a few hours to ride before we reach Merik'esh."

If he noticed the tension between Lex and Amelia, he didn't show it. Lex wondered if he'd overheard their conversation.

Amelia climbed onto the brown horse. "Ready," she said. The usual lightness in her tone was gone.

Lex felt another wave of guilt, though he knew it wasn't really his fault. She had brought his distrust upon herself. So then why did he feel so terrible? He avoided looking at Amelia, breathing through the pressure in his chest. "Yeah, sure," he said. "I'm ready." He approached the black horse and mounted.

"Great," Acarius said. He swung up onto Mare's back, and she shook her mane out and sidestepped, eager to ride. "Let's go, then," Acarius called out.

Mare lurched forward, not even waiting for a command. She headed for the road.

Amelia urged her horse forward to catch up and then turned onto the road, too, settling into stride just beside Acarius and Mare. "So what's my horse's name?" Lex heard her asking Acarius. Her voice sounded bright again, though it seemed a bit forced.

Acarius' answer faded beneath the sound of the horses' hooves as they moved ahead down the dirt road.

"Ride," Lex murmured to his horse. The black horse surged forward, but as soon as it closed the gap Lex pulled back on the reins, falling in step a horse-length behind the others. It was going to be a few hours' ride, but he didn't plan to spend it making conversation. He needed to think.

THE LATE AFTERNOON sun shimmered on Morrow's Lake, nearly blinding Lex as Merik'esh spread out before them in the distance. It was a sprawling waterfront city – or more of a town, really. It wasn't huge, but it was certainly larger than Dalton had been. Merik'esh framed the edge of the lake in a semi-circle, open on the lakeside but surrounded by a stone-and-mortar wall on all other sides. Lex slowed his horse to a stop and raised a hand to shield his eyes. He could just barely make out a large, wooden gate in the stone wall, facing their direction. The lake spread out to the left of the city, and a dock stretched out toward the lake's middle. A few flat-bottomed boats floated out in its center, with men, barely visible from this distance, sitting inside them. *Probably fisherman*, Lex thought. Other than the boats, he couldn't see any activity; the city's wall blocked everything else from view.

Lex tensed as the hoofbeats of Amelia's and Acarius' horses grew closer behind him. Lex had pulled in front and ridden at least a few yards ahead of them for the past few hours, following the road and avoiding conversation. As he rode, he thought back through the earlier conversations and only grew more upset. Neither Acarius nor Amelia had been upfront or honest with Lex, not even from the start. One of them had lied to him and the other was clearly hiding something. And here he was, clueless and completely at their mercy for what to do next. He felt like a fool.

Amelia and Acarius seemed to sense his desire to be alone; they hadn't even tried to catch up. At one point, Lex even had to reprimand himself for feeling a twinge of jealousy as he heard a murmur of conversation float up toward him from behind. After all, *he* was the one who'd pulled away, so it shouldn't bother him if they talked without him. But since when were Acarius and Amelia so friendly?

As the horses slowed to a stop behind him, he heard conversational tones once more, though he couldn't make out what was said, followed by laughter. *At least* someone *is having a good time*, he thought, then instantly berated himself for being childish. Why shouldn't they laugh? They were traveling together, bonding... this was a good thing. A day ago, Lex would have been glad to see Acarius and Amelia acting as though they were friends. Now it made him want to hit something. It was a little jealousy, but it was also more than that – a day ago, he hadn't yet known Amelia had lied to him, or seen Acarius clearly tell half-truths about something as important as Lex's own past. A day ago, he had been starting to think they were both his friends. Now, they were bonding while he realized he barely even knew them at all.

Acarius halted Mare beside Lex. "Let's head in," he said.

Lex glanced over in time to see Acarius' face as he led Mare past him and took the lead. It was pale and coated with a sheen of sweat. It was warm outside, but not that warm. *He must be in pain again*, Lex thought. No wonder he seemed in a hurry to get inside the city. Lex fell in behind Acarius, hoping if there were any secrets to getting through the gates or any guards to appease, Acarius would take care of it.

Amelia pulled her horse up beside Lex. "So," she said. "We're here." Her voice lingered on the last word.

"Clearly," Lex said.

Amelia sighed. "How long are you going to be mad at me?"

Lex turned toward her. "How long are you going to not be the person you said you were?"

Amelia's expression was as though he had slapped her.

Lex felt a pang of regret. But then, *she* was the one who had lied to him, so why should he feel sorry for her? He met her eyes, feeling a strange mix of anger and embarrassment – was he being childish?

Amelia's whole face went suddenly blank. "Fine," she said. "I won't bother you again." She urged her horse into motion.

As he watched her settle into pace beside Acarius, Lex wondered if he'd been too harsh... but then again, maybe the problem was that he'd been too soft before. His lack of memories left him vulnerable, and with at least one group of people out to kill him, he couldn't afford to be sentimental or gullible. Even with the gaps in his knowledge of his past and present, his glimpses and instincts had guided him well; they had saved both his and Acarius' lives. The glimpses might be coming from his brother, somehow, but the fighting instincts... those were ingrained in Lex; Acarius had known that even from how Lex moved. Though Lex knew little about himself, right now *himself* seemed to be the only person he could trust. Sometimes Lex could feel the edges of his past whispering to him – in the itch for a weapon against the panther, the split-second reactions in battle – though he couldn't control when or how it surfaced, his body had knowledge Lex didn't. He just hoped it was enough to keep him alive.

The gates of Merik'esh swung open as they neared, the hinges groaning beneath the weight of the heavy, wooden doors. The doors were as thick as Lex's shoulders were wide, and seemed solid. Two guards stood just inside the gates, armed with spears and clothed in simple armor – a brass chest-guard over chain mail, shin guards, and an open-faced helmet. They nodded to

Acarius as he entered, and all three of them rode into the city, their horses' hooves clacking against the cobblestones.

Lex's curiosity was beginning to outweigh his desire to remain aloof when Amelia voiced his own question.

"Why did they let us in so easily?" she asked.

"My parents were merchants; my family is known in most of the towns and cities in this area," Acarius responded.

"Oh," Amelia said with surprise. "I thought they were horse ranchers."

"They were both," Acarius said. He gave her a quick smile before turning his horse away. "If you don't mind, I need to find the healer."

"I'll come with you," Amelia said.

Acarius shook his head. "It will probably take some time. The inn is just up ahead; go on and stable the horses – the innkeeper will show you where – then get yourself something to eat and rest for a bit." He handed her a money pouch. "I'll meet you there once I'm feeling better."

He turned Mare down a side path, leaving Amelia and her horse standing in the street.

She turned to Lex. "To the inn, then?"

*What choice do I have*? Lex thought. He had no money of his own, and he was starving. He was truly beginning to hate being so reliant on other people. He sighed. "Sure. Let's go." He dismounted, and Amelia did the same.

The inn was not easy to find. They roamed the streets near where Acarius had pointed for quite some time, feeling as though they were going in circles, before stumbling across a building with a huge, wooden sign hanging above the doorway, *Aracthea Inn* etched into it. Lex wondered briefly why it wasn't called *Merik'esh Inn*, after the town, but his thoughts were broken by the approach of a man from the alley beside the inn. Lex glanced down it, wary of an ambush, but no one else was there. The alley dead-ended at a sturdy-looking wooden structure containing several open-air stalls, a few of which already housed horses. The smell of fresh hay and new pine boards drifted toward Lex. Everything in this city seemed surprisingly clean; even the cobblestones were free of grime.

"Rest your horses?" the man asked. "Food and stable for the night; fair prices." The man's bushy mustache tipped up in a smile to reveal white but very crooked teeth.

Lex suspected *fair prices* were rather relative to this man; he eyed Lex and Amelia as though sizing them up.

Amelia was already opening the pouch. "How much?" she asked, her fingers digging into the coins.

Lex tensed. He might not want to talk to Amelia right now, but he couldn't stand by and see her taken advantage of. She was too trusting.

The man's eyes focused on Amelia's hand, still buried in the pouch. "Ten alleans," he said. "That will cover both horses until the morning."

Lex couldn't be sure, but from the man's expression he suspected the price was anything but fair. He was just about to say something when a shrill voice interrupted.

"Don't you pay him any more than two alleans per horse!" An old woman hobbled over, her cane swinging violently between quick steps. She was squat and bulbous, with short, sturdy legs.

She reminded Lex a little of a walking mushroom.

"Shame on you, Maxim." The woman jabbed her finger upward into the air anew with each word. "I *know* your mother taught you better, I was there to see it! Now take your money and go care for these kids' horses." She snatched the coin pouch from Amelia and pressed it against her chest as she dug into it with gnarled fingers, then shoved some coins into the man's hand.

He hurried toward the stable, horses in tow.

The old woman handed the pouch back to Amelia, and Lex felt suddenly exposed as her eyes raked over the both of them.

"Poor, naïve things," the woman said. "Follow me, before you get swindled out of every coin." She hobbled toward the inn door, then turned back. "Come on now, don't waste time," she scolded.

Lex and Amelia scurried to catch up.

The inside of the inn was filled with body heat and chatter from the tables of patrons scattered around the room. Hanging lanterns illuminated the whole space, reflecting off polished oak tables and giving everything a golden glow. The air smelled vaguely like meat. To the left, a bar stretched the length of one wall, some patrons seated on stools before it. Beyond the bar, a narrow staircase stretched upward through a doorway. The man behind the bar was busy washing glasses, his unkempt beard hanging nearly to the apron around his waist. The man's tunic sleeves were torn off, revealing muscular arms. Lex glanced around; there were still several empty tables, but even so, the place was fairly crowded. It made him uncomfortable.

The old woman led them further inside, and shut the door behind them.

"Thank you for your help, ma'am," Amelia said. "I'm not familiar with Merik'esh prices."

The old woman gave her a warm smile. "Don't worry, honey. That's why I stopped to help. Now sit, and I'll have some food and hot tea brought out to you. You look exhausted." She bustled away and began chattering at the man behind the counter.

Lex noticed for the first time that Amelia did look rather worn out. Faint shadows hung beneath her eyes and her skin looked the slightest bit yellow – but maybe that was the lighting.

Amelia took a seat at an empty table, and gestured to the chair across from her. She smiled. "Join me?"

Lex shook his head. "I think I just need some time alone."

Amelia's smile vanished. "Okay," she said. She fixed her gaze on the opposite side of the room.

Lex made his way to a table back against the wall, far enough from Amelia not to risk conversation, but keeping her in his line of sight. He didn't trust Amelia, but he trusted the people of this town even less. Amelia's youth and wide, innocent eyes clearly made people think her an easy target, and they wouldn't exactly be wrong.

As Lex took his seat, he noticed a group of older men already eyeing Amelia from a table against the opposite wall. The interest in their gaze spoke of a desire for more than just her money. Lex felt something whisper deep inside him and he welcomed it. He wasn't sure if he would ever be able to consider Amelia a friend again after realizing so much about her was a lie, but the thought of her being harmed twisted in his gut like a knife. He turned his chair so he had a clear view of both Amelia and the men. The whisper stirred, a hot breath across his nerves. The skin on the back of his neck prickled.

Lex was so focused on the men across the room that he jumped when a hand plopped a glass mug down on the table.

"You're a skittish one." The old woman chuckled as she followed up the mug with a steaming plate of some kind of stew and rice. "Eat," she said.

"Both of you are too skinny." She hobbled off toward Amelia's table, not waiting for a reply.

Lex lifted the fork from the plate and poked at the stew while turning his gaze back to the men. They were huddled over a board game in the center of the table, no longer looking in Amelia's direction. Lex relaxed, and shoved a forkful of the rice and stew into his mouth – then spat it out immediately as it burned his tongue. He took a sip of the drink – which was also hot. Lex set the mug down, breathing with open mouth to cool his tongue. Amelia glanced over at him and then away again. He was sure she was fighting a smirk.

Lex blew on the second bite for a few seconds and had it almost to his mouth when a man strode past him, heading straight for Amelia. Lex froze, watching. The man seemed a few years older than Lex, maybe close to Acarius' age, and he moved with confidence. He had a square jaw and dark brown eyes, and his light brown hair was carefully trimmed and combed, as was his facial hair. He wore a simple tunic and trousers but they were good quality, and very clean. There was a towel thrown over his shoulder. *Is he the bar-hand?* Lex wondered. *What does he want with Amelia?*

The man plopped down in the chair across from her – the chair she had offered Lex – and leaned across the table. Lex couldn't hear what was said over the distance and the chatter of the room, but Amelia smiled. She set down her fork and her posture visibly straightened. She leaned in toward the man, and as she did, a lock of her hair swung forward into her face. The man reached up, tucking it behind her ear.

Lex's chest constricted with a jealousy he knew he didn't have a right to feel.

Suddenly a young woman appeared at the table, about the same age as the man. She was pretty, with green eyes and auburn hair tied back in a loose braid. She pulled a chair over and sat next to the man, giving Amelia a smile. A few words passed between them that Lex couldn't hear – was the woman angry with Amelia for flirting with her husband? – but no, Amelia was still smiling, seeming at ease with the conversation. *Maybe the guy is the woman's brother*, Lex thought. But then the man leaned over toward the auburn-haired woman and kissed her. *Oh.*

Some more conversation passed between them, then all three stood. Amelia followed the couple a few tables over to the right, where the three of them were greeted by more smiling faces. The five people already at the table shifted, making room for the newcomers. Amelia sat, happily shaking the hand of the man beside her when he offered. He was middle-aged and partly balding, but he gave off a warm, fatherly air. Another woman from across the table leaned in, engaging Amelia in animated conversation, her hands moving wildly like hummingbirds. Amelia nodded and smiled back. She said something, and the table burst into laughter. Amelia beamed as those around the table nodded their agreement with whatever she had said.

"It's lonely on the outside, isn't it?"

Lex turned to see the old woman easing herself down into a chair beside him. The chair creaked under her weight as she wiggled, getting comfortable. She leaned back, draping one wrinkled hand across her lap. Lex suddenly realized – she only had one arm. The loose cloak she wore around her shoulders had hidden that fact before, or maybe he just hadn't looked that closely.

The woman leaned towards him, so close to Lex's face he had to resist the urge to lean back. "How long have you had a thing for the girl?" she asked.

Lex blinked. "What?"

The old woman waved a hand, nearly hitting him in the nose. "It's obvious; don't deny it. How long?"

"I've only known her a couple days," Lex said. "And I don't have a thing for her."

The old woman narrowed her eyes.

"Really," Lex said. "She's a liar; she can't be trusted."

The woman settled her girth back into her seat. Lex took a deep breath, feeling less claustrophobic.

"I see," the woman said.

Lex resisted the urge to explain himself. He didn't know this woman; he didn't know any of these people, not even Amelia, really. He didn't owe them anything. He glanced down. *Well, except the cost of the food.* Which he needed Amelia to pay...with Acarius' money. Lex sighed.

Amelia's laugh rang out from across the room and Lex glanced over, unable to help himself. Amelia looked happy. Really happy. How was she so able to open up to a bunch of strangers and instantly make friends, while he was brooding here in a corner? Maybe she was lying to all of them. That thought gave him a bit of comfort. At least he wouldn't be the only one.

The group at Amelia's table rose and walked toward the stairs at the back of the inn. Amelia followed, caught up in conversation with a motherly-looking redhead.

Lex tensed. He knew nothing about these people. How was Amelia going with them so easily? More importantly, why were these people so interested in a girl they just met? Lex pushed back his chair.

A cold, clammy hand pressed his, stopping him. "Not everyone in the world is untrustworthy," she said. "Some people do have good intentions."

"And some people lie," Lex said, pulling his hand from hers. "Now if you'll excuse me, I need to make sure my friend is safe." *I guess I do still consider her a friend,* he thought. That surprised him. But she had helped him escape death more than once, and he supposed that had a way of bonding people. It didn't make up for the lies.

Lex pushed past the old woman, wanting to catch the end of Amelia's group before they disappeared up the stairs.

"I know who you are."

Lex froze. He turned back to find the old woman watching him with steely eyes.

"You've lost yourself," she said. "I can give some of it back to you."

Lex slid back around the table and into his chair. "What do you know?"

"You," she said, leaning toward him. "I know *you.*"

# CHAPTER 8

"How do you know me?" Lex asked. His voice sounded steadier than he felt.

"We've met before," she said. "You're Marcus, hero of Alleanza. Are you not?"

Lex's heart sank. "No," he said. "Marcus was my brother. He was the hero."

The old woman leaned back. "That so."

Lex wasn't sure if that had been a statement or a question. "Yes. I'm not Marcus. I'm Lex, his brother."

The old woman wrinkled her nose. "Marcus never said anything about having a brother."

"So I'm told," Lex said.

Lex jumped as the old woman's wrinkled hand slapped the table.

"Be gone with it then, I say," she declared.

"Be gone with what?" Lex asked.

"Your jealousy over that girl." She shrugged. "Those are good people, the owner of this inn and his wife. He noticed the cut on Amelia's face and offered to take her back to his family's apartment behind the inn to have his wife clean it. The others were his wife's aunt and parents. There is nobody in that family to give you competition. The innkeeper is handsome, but he's already married." She winked at Lex.

Lex felt his face go red. Was he that obvious? But at least that explained why the man pushed Amelia's hair back from her face; he had been looking at the gash on her cheek... a gash Lex had totally forgotten about, being so absorbed in his own problems. It had probably been hurting her since Acarius' house and he hadn't even checked on her, he'd just demanded she help him with Acarius, then grilled her with questions. Curse his self-centeredness – he was still mad at Amelia, but now he felt he might not have been entirely fair. She had lied, but when she'd made an effort to talk to him about her reasons, he'd pushed her away. When she got back, he'd have to at least give her a chance to explain. Maybe he would even apologize. Maybe.

The old woman's stare was making Lex uncomfortable. "I thought we were talking about my brother," he said.

The woman gave a curt nod. "Be gone with that, too."

"With what?" Lex asked again.

"His memory. He wasn't as much of a hero as they say, anyway. By the end, he was so stuck in the past it destroyed everyone around him."

Anger stirred within Lex. He had never known his brother, but he had felt his memories – his courage, his love. "My brother was a good man," he said, meeting the old woman's eyes. "He was a hero."

"I never said he wasn't," the old woman said. She stood. "Mistakes and goodness aren't incompatible. But living in his memories will destroy you, too. Now eat your stew. It's getting cold." She hobbled away.

Lex fought the urge to go after her. Half of him thought she might be the wisest person he'd met so far, and the other half thought she might be crazy. She was already at the bar, wagging her finger at the barkeep about something. If she really had known Marcus, she was his best chance at answers. He headed for the bar.

A scream stabbed the air, coming from somewhere above. *Amelia.* Lex dashed for the stairs.

The old woman stepped out in front of him.

"I thought you said they had good intentions!" Lex shouted, shoving past her.

"They do," she called after him. "But I can't say that for the rest of what's up there!"

Her voice trailed after him; he was already halfway up the narrow staircase. The stairway was only one flight, and ended in a small landing with one closed door. Lex burst through the door, realizing instantly that he had no weapons – the sword Acarius had loaned him was still strapped into the pack on his horse. However many people waited beyond the door, he would have to fight them unarmed.

The room was empty, illuminated by moonlight from a single window. Had night come so quickly? The room was bare, wooden floors and blank, wood-paneled walls. A small door which looked like it perhaps led to a closet stood in the back wall. It was the only possible path besides backward, so Lex rushed forward and swung the door open. More stairs, this time leading down. He could see only the top two steps; the rest descended into darkness. Lex left the top door open – he hoped it wouldn't close on its own – and moved forward into the blackness.

He made his way down by feel, one hand on the wall and reaching carefully with each foot before shifting to the next step. After about ten steps, he hit a landing. The ground felt hard beneath his boots, like concrete rather than the wood of the stairs. He felt around with his hands. The walls also felt like concrete, and on both sides they ended in corners just within his reach. He was in a narrow corridor, and he'd hit a dead end. He slid his hands centerward along the wall he now knew was in front of him and encountered wood – a door. He groped for the handle, took a breath, and eased it open.

The odor hit him before the door was fully open. He recognized that smell – blood. He flung the door open, and squinted against the yellow light of lanterns.

The blood was everywhere, a red lake spanning the small room. The bodies seemed to float in it. A lantern swayed, hung from a large metal hook protruding from a wooden support beam in the center of the room. Everything above it was shadows, but the yellow glow of the candle moved with the lantern's swing, flitting across the lake of blood beneath it like a disembodied spirit. Lex forced himself to look at the faces of the dead. There were nearly a dozen of them, and he recognized most of them. They were the people who had been at the table with Amelia. They were all eerily pale – judging from the amount of blood, they'd been bled dry – and turned flat onto their backs, their arms and legs perfectly straight and their empty gazes fixed upward. Lex held his breath as he glanced around the room, then exhaled. Amelia wasn't among them. *Where is she?* Lex thought. The metallic smell of the blood was smothering him. He pressed his arm to his mouth and nose to suppress a gag. *Who did this?*

A strange noise snatched Lex's attention. It sounded like a grunt... was one of these people still alive? He looked down, his eyes scanning the bodies.

*There it was again. It sounded like it came from* – he turned his face up, just in time to see a monster leaping down on him from the rafters.

It slammed him to the ground. Lex drove his head upward, ramming his forehead into the creature's face. It pulled upward and moaned, face covered in blood. It seemed dazed, and Lex tried to scoot out from under it, but its legs were still planted on top of him, holding him in place. The creature's weight compressed his chest, making it a struggle to breathe; he was beginning to feel dizzy. Lex forced his mind to focus against the closing fog, glancing around for anything within reach he could use as a weapon. There was nothing, except bodies and the warm blood soaking through his tunic and pants. He looked up – the creature's leap had bent the lantern's hook and wedged it against the rafter, so that some of its light spread outward. Lex froze. Amelia was above him, tied hands-and-feet and tucked into the corner of the rafters. The lower half of her face was covered with a tight cloth, but her wide blue eyes found Lex. They were wild with fear. She tried to scream again, the sound muffled by the cloth across her mouth – the grunts he had heard. She struggled, trying to pry her hands loose from her feet, and teetered, nearly tipping off the rafters. She squeezed her eyes shut and tipped her head back against the beams which held her. Even from the floor, Lex could see her chest heaving with panicked breaths.

Lex could barely breathe and he couldn't even begin to guess what was going on, but relief washed over him. *She's alive.* Then panic swept in. *We have to get out of here.*

The creature was recovering now. It tipped its face down to Lex, and a trickle of burgundy blood slithered from a slit nostril to the creature's chin as it stared at him. This was the same type of creature from the field. Its face was unnatural, lizardlike but flattened and distorted, as though something had gone wrong in its making. It was heavier than its wiry frame suggested, and its claws were digging into Lex's ribs as it leaned on him. There was an intelligence in its dark eyes, almost humanlike.

Lex shoved against the creature, but it only leaned down further. It pressed Lex's head to the floor with a clawed hand, and Lex felt the blood of the dead seep up around the back of his neck and into his hair, the metallic smell flooding into his nose. He gagged.

The creature hissed – a sound like a snake but throatier – and closed its sharp fingers around Lex's jaw, tipping his chin upward. Lex could only breathe in short gasps as the creature's weight crushed his lungs. His throat was completely exposed, and it occurred to him suddenly that this might be how he died – bled out by a lizard creature with a terrified girl watching above him. Dark shadows crept in from the edges of Lex's vision. He struggled, but the lack of oxygen left him weak; he could barely move his arms. What would happen to Amelia, when he was gone? Would anyone else come to save her?

The creature snapped its wings open, blocking Lex's view of the rafters and Amelia. "Lexxxxxxxxxx," it hissed, leaning down to his face. Lex felt his eyes sinking shut as the creature folded its wings back in and leaned closer against him. He could feel its breath against his throat.

Had it said his name, or had he imagined it? He was so close to unconsciousness he couldn't be certain, but he couldn't die here. Not like this. He tried to force his eyes open, but they were heavy as lead. His body felt numb, as though frozen.

The creature slammed its full weight into him, knocking the last remaining breath from his chest. Pain exploded through his lungs and Lex's eyes flung open as his brain screamed for oxygen.

Suddenly, the creature shifted its weight against him and then rolled off.

Lex gasped heaving breaths and felt heat flood through him as his lungs refilled. He glanced around wildly, waiting for the creature's next assault.

It didn't come. Lex closed his eyes and lay still for a moment. He was still rather dizzy, and he didn't know why the creature wasn't attacking. Perhaps it thought him unconscious. He took a few quick breaths, readying himself to fling upward and take the creature by surprise.

Then he heard a grunt. *Amelia*. He looked up to the rafters to be sure she was okay – she wasn't there.

The grunt came again – from the floor beside him.

Lex abandoned his plan for a surprise attack and pushed himself upward. Amelia was curled atop the creature, her hands and feet still tied. The creature sprawled unconscious beneath her, its clawed limbs spreading the now-drying blood into a demented snow angel.

Lex rushed to her, pulling her off the creature, though he almost wished he hadn't when she splashed into the pool of blood, unable to catch her fall due to her restraints. Lex pulled her upright. Blood coated one whole side of her face. "Are you alright?" He rushed to remove the cloth across her mouth and then began untying her feet and hands.

"We have to go," she said. "We have to go."

"I know," Lex said. "Just let me untie you."

"We have to go," she said again. She shook her head. "We have to go." Her eyes were wide and wild.

*She must be in shock*, Lex thought. The ropes fell from her wrists and ankles. "Can you walk?" he asked. He tugged her hands, pulling her upward.

She stood, though shakily. "We have to go," she said again.

Lex agreed, but her repetition was a bit unnerving. He pulled her toward the door he'd come in through.

Behind him, the creature's claws scraped the wood floor. It was waking up.

Lex shoved Amelia toward the door. "Go. *Go.*"

She staggered toward the doorway, almost through it, but the creature was faster. It leapt for them and Lex spun, putting Amelia behind him. She stopped, half in the doorway. Lex braced himself as the creature lunged for him.

It reached around him. In just the moment it took Lex to realize it was going for Amelia, it had already grasped her arm. It yanked her toward itself, then kicked out a clawed foot and knocked Lex through the doorway. As he toppled backwards into the steps, he saw it leap upward for the rafters, dragging Amelia behind it like a rag doll. The creak and crash of breaking wood sounded as Lex scrambled to his feet and back into the room, but he was too late – the creature had burst through the ceiling and into the night, taking Amelia with it.

Lex tore up the steps, through the empty room he'd first seen, and back down the other set of stairs. He barreled into the inn. "We need help," he shouted. "There's been an attack!"

Dozens of stunned faces turned to him, interrupted from their dinners and card games. A dark-skinned woman with long, black hair stood and rushed toward him. She wore leather pants and boots, and a thin, fitted leather tunic – she looked like some kind of forest warrior. "What happened?" she asked. Her dark eyes focused on his face. "Marcus?" she asked, her voice sounding almost in awe.

*Why does everyone think I'm Marcus?* Annoyance rose in Lex, immediately drowned by more urgent things. "A monster," Lex said. "It killed a bunch of people and took Amelia." Lex grabbed the woman's arm and pulled her toward the stairs. "You have to help me." He looked around the room. No one else was moving. "What's wrong with you?" he said, not caring if he was rude. "There's been an attack!"

The inn's patrons turned back to their plates and card games.

Lex stood, stunned.

"Is the monster still here?" the woman asked.

"No," Lex said. "But it took my friend."

Lex saw the woman's jaw muscle twitch. "Let's go," she said, pushing him toward the steps. "Show me where it happened."

The woman stood in the doorway, staring at the congealed blood covering the floor. The bodies poked up from it, not unlike the fruit in red gelatin Lex had eaten at Acarius' house. The thought made Lex's stomach turn.

"Aiacs," the woman said.

"What?"

"It was an Aaic. They are demon creatures, unnatural. They relish blood."

"So it killed all these people, just to drink their blood?"

"They do not consume the blood; they just enjoy the smell and sight of it. It brings them pleasure."

Lex shivered. "Then this was... what? Some kind of game for it?"

The woman turned to him, and the light from the lantern glinted off her dark eyes. "No. They enjoy blood, but they do not kill solely for pleasure. They are too clever for that."

"Then why?" Lex asked, his eyes raking across the dead. They were already beginning to turn a grey-violet, the hue of death. "Why did it take Amelia?"

"You mean why didn't it kill her like the others?"

Lex nodded.

"I don't know," the woman answered. "But I believe she is the answer to why it killed all these people."

"What?" Lex was fighting to stay focused, his mind jumping to images of Amelia, bled out in a dark alley, a barn, the stables. Where would the creature take her, and how long would it keep her alive?

"Amelia is the answer," the woman said. "These creatures kill only with purpose. You say it took her unharmed. These people were with her, yes?"

"Yes."

"Then it killed them to take her. That is the most logical answer."

"But why?" None of this made sense to Lex.

The woman shrugged. "Does it matter? Either way, it has her. Your attention would be better focused on getting her back."

Lex resisted the urge to snap back with sarcasm. "I am," he said, holding his voice even. "That's why I want to understand what's going on."

Quick footsteps thumped from the stairway above. Lex spun toward the door and glanced around. Was there anything he could use for a weapon? From the corner of his eye, he noticed the woman had turned sideways into a partial crouch, as though ready to leap at whoever entered.

Acarius burst through the doorway. "Lex?" he said. His eyes took in the bodies, the blood. He paled and reached for the sword at his waist. "What happened?" Then his gaze hit the woman. His arms dropped and his whole body went stiff. "Lytira?"

The woman straightened from her crouch, and her hands opened and closed at her waist as though grasping the air. "Acarius," she said. From the look on her face, he had been the last thing she expected to come through the door.

Lex glanced between them. The sudden tension in the room was suffocating. *What was going on with these two*? But Lex had bigger things on his mind. He turned to Acarius. "It was one of the creatures, like from the farm. It took Amelia."

Acarius focused on Lex. "Then we need to go. Now."

*The same thing Amelia had said.* "We can't leave without Amelia," Lex insisted.

"You can't save anyone if you're dead," Acarius said. "If you stay here, that's exactly what you'll be." He turned for the door. "Come on." His heavy steps thundered up the stairs.

*Dead*. Lex's eyes flicked to the corpses. "What's going on?" he called after Acarius, but he was already gone.

Lex started to follow, but the woman's slender hand grabbed his arm.

Her warm fingers pressed into his flesh with surprising strength. "You did not say Acarius Frost was with you," she said.

Lex turned to her. "I didn't know I needed to. He went to the healer's when we reached the city, and Amelia and I came here." He paused. "How do you know each other?"

"It doesn't matter," she said. "But you were foolish to leave his side. Why did you not stay with him?"

Lex chafed. "I said he went to the healer's. Besides, I didn't know we were in danger." It wasn't exactly true; Lex *had* sensed something wasn't quite right in the inn, though the creature had not been a part of that. Still, the men watching Amelia, the overly-friendly people – Lex had felt something bad coming, he just hadn't been able to identify it. Guilt swept over him. He still wasn't sure those other things had anything to do with this creature, but he should never have let Amelia go upstairs alone. He had gotten distracted by the old woman and the chance to learn about his past, but he should have been protecting Amelia. He should have trusted his instincts.

"Stay with Acarius from now on," the woman said, letting go of his arm. Her fingernails left purpling divets in his skin. "Do not leave his side."

"Why?" Lex said, turning on her. "Do I look that helpless?" The creature was following him, for some reason, and he'd stopped it before. He could have done it again, if he'd been here. If he'd stayed with Amelia.

Lytira studied his face. "So it's true; you are not Marcus. I had heard the others call you Lex, but I still thought" – she paused – "No, I can see it now. There are differences. But Acarius is the last living hero of Alleanza, the one who rode beside Marcus himself. Do you not know of his power?"

Fury surged up within Lex like a geyser. "No, I don't," he spat. And from the way she was talking, he was beginning to be glad he *wasn't* Marcus. What good had Marcus been as a hero if she thought he needed a sidekick like Acarius to survive?

"I see," the woman said. "And yet you ride with him."

"I didn't have much choice," Lex said.

"Then fortune smiled on you. For your own sake, do not leave his side." She turned and walked up the stairs.

Lex sighed. He was growing tired of others telling him what he should do. He felt like a fool, relying on strangers to inform him on his own life. Would he ever get to the end of all the unknowns?

"Lex," Acarius called out. "Hurry."

Lex's boots squelched free from the blood-coated floor as he turned for the steps. When he reached the common room, Acarius was already at the inn's front door.

"Mare and the horses are ready," he said. "Let's go."

Lytira followed them out. "I'm coming with you."

"I assumed you would. Here," Acarius said, handing her the lead of the black horse.

She eyed him silently for a moment. "I do not ride."

"Tonight you do," Acarius said.

Lytira tensed, and for a moment Lex thought she might strike Acarius. But then she huffed and launched herself onto the horse with surprising grace.

Acarius ignored her silent fuming and turned to Lex. "Mount," he said. "We need to go. Now."

Lex clambered onto the brown horse and followed behind Mare as Acarius led the way back through the open courtyard which housed the inn and toward the city's gates. Lytira fell in behind them. Lex glanced back at her, thinking she was keeping her distance out of anger, but she no longer looked upset. She rode with alertness, her eyes taking in all sides of the courtyard as they passed through. She wasn't moping; she was watching their backs. Who was this woman?

The guards swung the gates outward as the riders reached them. Acarius and Mare took the lead, and one of the guards nodded to him as he passed through. "Mr. Frost."

Lex turned to Lytira, who was close behind him. "Why does everyone here keep calling him Frost? I thought Acarius' last name was Halben."

Lytira stared at him for a moment. "Where did you hear that?" she asked.

"One of the farmers called him that when they attacked us," Lex said.

Lytira shook her head. "It means half-breed. Do not let Acarius hear you call him that. He is not fond of the term."

"He didn't seem upset when the farmer said it."

"Then he was hiding it well. Trust me, it is a sore spot for him."

Lex reasoned that being called a *mutt*, essentially, wouldn't sit well with most people. It must be some kind of slang for a low-born person or something. Or maybe it was some kind of racial slur. He almost didn't press it further, but he was curious. He turned back to Lytira. "Half-breed of what?" he asked. "Why do they call him that?"

"That's something you will have to ask him."

They were through the gates now, and the guards swung them shut with a bang. Acarius spun Mare to face Lex.

"It won't be long until they notice we're gone. We need to put distance between us and the city."

"Until who notices?" Lex asked.

Acarius stared at him. "The people who are trying to kill you."

"What? But I thought the creature– "

Acarius shook his head. "The creature was only part of it. I came to the inn to find you because I overheard some men talking in the street– from Dalton. They've rallied part of the city against you. They're here to take revenge for their fallen kin. I didn't know about the creature until I found you."

Lex thought back to the men at the table on the far wall of the inn. So they *had* been watching Amelia – and him, too.

"We can head to Alowen," Lytira said.

Acarius turned to her in surprise. "They will kill him on sight, and probably me, too." He paused. "Perhaps even you."

Lex saw the muscle in her jaw twitch again.

"A lot has happened since you've been away," she said. "Things are different now."

"You mean *you're* different," Acarius said, his face lighting with realization. "You've become one of them."

"Yes," she said, her voice firm. "But they have changed as well. I would not have joined them otherwise. Besides, what choice do we have?"

"Plenty. We could head to the Port of Lanian–"

""They'll be watching the roads that way for certain. We'd never make it that far. It is not only farmers, remember? They have help."

"You mean the Aiacs," Lex interjected. *The creatures were working with the farmers. Of course– that was why they didn't bother to help Amelia that day in the field. The creature was on their side.* What that meant about the farmers in the big picture, Lex wasn't sure, but it couldn't be a good thing. "They have Amelia," Lex said. "They'll hurt her because of me. We need to go back."

"The Daltoners are here to kill *you*," Acarius said. "And there are many of them, all throughout the city. We need to leave."

Lex was beginning to wonder if there would ever be a day where someone *wasn't* out to kill him.

"Alowen is our best option," Lytira said.

Acarius snapped his gaze to her and shook his head. "I don't like it."

"The idea, or the fact that I'm right?" she asked.

Acarius raised an eyebrow, then shrugged. "Both, actually." He turned to Lex. "Going to Alowen is dangerous, but if we're lucky, they'll be willing to help us. When we have enough support, we can come back for Amelia. But right now we have to keep you safe– you're the one they're after. As long as you're free, they'll keep her as bait. But going back in there on our own is a suicide mission, and if you die, they'll kill her for sure."

"Are you sure they won't hurt her?"

Lytira moved her horse toward him. "Acarius is right," she said. "They're after you. They know they can use her to draw you in."

Lex sighed. He didn't like the plan at all, but as Lytira had said, what choice did they have? "How far is it to Alowen?"

"Only one hour," Lytira said.

*An hour.* Two hours once they made the return trip. It wasn't that long; Lex would just have to hope Amelia was okay until they got back to rescue her, with backup. "Fine," he said. "Lead the way." But if anything went wrong, he was coming back for her– reinforcements or not.

Lytira pulled her horse into the lead and Acarius fell in behind Lex. They were flanking him again, protecting him. Lex couldn't decide whether to feel grateful or insulted that they thought him so helpless.

As they rode farther from the city, a fog settled across the land. The moonlight cut through it, giving the smoke an eerie white glow. Even with the moon's light, Lex couldn't see more than a few feet in front of him through the fog. He could see the back of Lytira's horse, and he could still hear Mare's hooves behind him, so he focused on following Lytira. As he rode, he let his thoughts drift back to the inn, replaying the night's events – Amelia inviting him to sit and him refusing; the men watching from the table; the friendly people, now soaking in their own blood in the back room of the inn; the strange old, one-armed woman. As Lex replayed his conversation with her in his mind, he realized that when she spoke of Marcus not being the hero he was claimed to be, she had said, "by the end." She had known Marcus was dead. So then why did she pretend to think Lex was Marcus? The old woman's statements were making less sense the more he thought about them. *Who was she?* He realized suddenly he didn't even know her name; he hadn't thought to ask.

He called to Acarius over the sound of the horses' gallops and slowed his horse. Acarius pulled up to ride beside him. "What is it?" he asked.

Lex described the old woman, and how she'd kept Amelia from being swindled by the stableman. "She said some things to me about Amelia, and how I shouldn't focus on the past." He was too embarrassed to admit the woman had opened the conversation by chastising him for being jealous over Amelia.

"It had to be Zenora," Acarius said. "She's the healer of Merik'esh. She's the one who helped my head."

Lex glanced over. He'd nearly forgotten about Acarius' head, in all the chaos, but Acarius really did look better. "But wait," Lex said. "How could she be the healer who helped you? She was already at the stables when we got there."

Acarius shrugged. "She wrapped my head with herbs and told me to lie down, then left. I thought she just wanted me to rest in quiet, but I guess she must have headed down to the inn. She lives near it."

Lex supposed there had been a slight delay where that could be possible. "The woman I talked to seemed crazy," he said.

Acarius laughed. "It was definitely Zenora, then. She's not crazy, but she is known for being a bit... strange. But she's a gifted healer. And she has a way of knowing things. Whatever she said to you, she was probably right."

*About which part?* Lex thought. But he said nothing; he'd have to process this new information about the old woman later. The fog was clearing to reveal a spiked-log fence towering a few yards ahead of them and spreading off into the fog in both directions.

In front of the fence stood a half-dozen archers with their arrows aimed directly at Lex.

# CHAPTER 9

L ex froze in the saddle, afraid to make any movement which might provoke the archers. Acarius and Lytira brought their horses to a halt beside his.

"What is the meaning of this?" Acarius said. His voice seemed to bounce around in the fog.

Lex eyed the archers. They were men of various ages, but all dark-skinned and dark-haired like Lytira, and all staring at him like hawks eyeing prey. They wore matching thin-leather breeches and tunics, fitted in a way that highlighted their lean, muscular frames. Their tunics were sleeveless, revealing muscular arms pulled taut in resistance to their bows.

Lytira eased her horse forward. "Lower your weapons," she said. Her tone carried a slight note of humor, as though she had caught a friend pulling a prank on her. "There's no need for this."

One of the men in the middle glanced at her. He straightened slightly, but his arrow never moved from its focus on Lex. "He is not welcome here," he stated. His eyes slid back to Lex.

Lytira stiffened, and a tense silence settled over the night air.

*What did I do this time?* Lex wondered. *Does* everyone *hate me?*

"How dare you–" Acarius spoke out, grabbing his reins as though to move forward, but Lytira whipped her head to the side and silenced him with a glare. Acarius stopped mid-sentence and gave her a subtle nod. He focused his eyes forward and shifted astride his horse.

Lytira turned back toward the archers. "We don't have time for this," she said. "Open the gates."

The archer to the left glanced at the man who had spoken first, then to Lytira. "I am sorry, Rahmanasha Lytira, but we cannot allow him entry." He glanced at Lex then back to Lytira, and bowed his head slightly, as though in respect.

*Rahmanasha? What did that mean?* Lex cut his eyes to Lytira, afraid to fully look away from the archers.

Lytira sat straight-backed on her horse, her chin lifted slightly, looking as regal as a princess. How had he not noticed her demeanor before? She was clearly high-born, from the way she carried herself. But back at the inn she had seemed fierce, unafraid of the horrors the Aiacs had left behind, and intensely focused, like a huntress tracking game. *Who is this woman*? Lex wondered.

Lytira turned back toward the man who had first spoken. "This is not a game, Maharan. We are under attack. Our pursuers are likely on their way this very moment." Her voice was cold. "Open the gates."

"You brought them *here?*" An archer on the right spoke, wide-eyed, his voice betraying alarm.

Lytira shifted on her horse, suddenly looking uncomfortable. "I had no choice," she said. Her voice was still regal but Lex could hear a slight waver in it. "You know I would not have come otherwise. We need asylum. The Aiac–"

She had barely spoken the last word when Maharan spun his bow toward Lytira, his eyes wild with anger. He spat on the ground. "How dare you bring them here?" His voice was like a dagger slicing through the foggy night. "You have betrayed us."

Lytira's voice was urgent now. "No," she said. "No, I would never–" She stopped, letting out a rush of breath. "Look at him!" She gestured to her right, where Lex and Acarius' horses stood.

Her eyes were still on the archers, and Lex wasn't sure if *him* meant himself or Acarius. The archers glanced over, their eyes sliding across both men before returning back to her.

"You see what is at stake," Lytira continued. "Open the gates, before it is too late!" She paused.

Lex could see her argument was having little effect. The archers glared between the three of them, as though uncertain which of them to aim their arrows toward.

"Take us to Baram," Lytira said, her voice quaking slightly. "I will explain everything. But please, you must let us in."

A sharp whoosh sliced the night and the archer to the far left dropped like dead weight as an arrow pierced clean through one of his eyes and out through the back of skull.

"They're here!" Lytira shouted. "Let us in!"

The archers pointed their arrows out into the night, their eyes searching wildly, but nothing was visible beyond a few feet through the dense fog.

Another arrow sailed by, lodging itself in one of the tall logs of the fence.

The archers glanced at one another, their faces panicked. Maharan shook his head as though arguing with himself, then turned around, pulling at a length of rope between two of the logs. The gates – which had blended in as though part of a seamless log fence – began to creak outward. "Come, hurry," he disappeared behind the fence as he climbed down, then reemerged, waving them in. The other archers moved around them, still scanning the night for the source of the arrows.

Something sped past Lex's ear, just barely missing him. It struck the archer who had called Lytira *Ramanasha* in the chest, knocking him backward onto the ground. He stared up at Lex with a look of shock, taking a ragged breath as blood bubbled out of his wound and spread across his chest.

The world tilted. He sat on a floral rug in a dimly-lit room, a bluish glow from the blank screen of the television casting shadows on the large, floral-patterned couch behind them. He glanced over. The girl, Jana, was beside him. She looked young; maybe 12 or 13. He looked down at his own body – he was young, too, he supposed. His legs and torso were lean, not yet filled out. *Gangly.* Had his brother, the warrior hero, really been this scrawny? But Lex had seen from other glimpses that he didn't stay that way.

"Isn't it supposed to be doing something by now?" he heard himself say.

Jana nodded. "Yeah. Maybe something isn't hooked up right. Hold on." She set down a grey controller she was holding, careful not to yank the cord that attached it to the bulky, metallic box. *A video game.* An edge of curiosity crept into his awareness. The metallic box didn't look like an ordinary console to him, but then he didn't have a lot of experience with video games. Something about it nagged at him, though. He sat in the bluish glow of the television, watching as Jana crossed her legs in front of her, then squinted at the instruction manual in the dim light.

He leaned to the side and pulled the chain of the lamp on a nearby end-table. Golden light illuminated the room. Jana turned to him and smiled. "Thanks," she said, then buried her face back in the manual. She was biting her lower lip, as she always did when she was concentrating, and as she craned her neck forward, a piece of blonde hair slid loose from her ponytail and swung down around her face.

*Where are we? When is this? Why this glimpse? Why now?*

He felt himself reach out to brush her hair behind her ear, moving on impulse, but he caught himself – or Marcus, the one whose memories these were, did – and dropped his hand.

Lex felt a dual awareness, both him and not-him existing simultaneously. Now that he knew these weren't his memories, he felt as though he were acting out a movie, watching it unfold from inside the character's eyes. He felt every emotion, every sensation vividly, though he knew they weren't his own. It was disorienting.

*These glimpses, it's like I'm there... living what he lived. But why?* He was grateful for them, in a sense, eager to know more about his brother and hopefully learn something about himself. But he wished he could control when the glimpses came. Something poked at the back of his awareness, telling him he shouldn't be here, that there was something more important he was neglecting. He couldn't remember what, though. The sensations of the glimpse were so strong they blocked all else from his mind.

Jana turned her face to him, her eyebrows scrunched in curiosity. Their eyes locked for a minute, and he felt himself open his mouth to speak. His heart raced. Whatever he was about to say, he – *Marcus, not me,* he reminded himself again – was nervous about saying it.

The door between the kitchen and the den swung open and another boy barged through, looking about their same age but taller, and already beginning to fill out, a muscular torso where Marcus' was still scrawny. Marcus' chest swirled with a blend of familiarity and jealousy. *Steve.* His friend. And yet, at this moment, he felt distinctly unhappy to see him.

Steve was balancing plates on each arm and holding two more in his hands.

Jana laughed and jumped to her feet, dropping the instruction manual. "You're like one of those crazy waiters in the movies," she said, moving toward Steve. "Let me help you."

Lex felt Marcus sense her movement away from him like a tangible void, a coldness where her warmth had been.

Jana grabbed a plate in each of her hands, freeing Steve's arms to move. He held his two remaining plates out and smiled at her, his green eyes lighting.

Lex felt a flash of hot jealousy rush through Marcus' chest as Steve and Jana met each other's gaze. Then Steve spun his grin toward Marcus. "Pizza Rolls or Hot Pockets?" he asked, indicating the two plates he held.

Lex still swam in Marcus' pain and jealousy, a whirlpool dragging him under. He heard Steve's speech as though through a tunnel.

Lex felt Marcus sigh softly before he looked up at Steve. "I'm not hungry right now, but thanks." He turned back toward the television, reaching out to jiggle one of the cords hooked to the console. The screen flickered and then lit up in a spiral of color, and a short burst of musical notes flooded from the television as the spiral faded out into a start-up screen.

Jana let out a quick, pleased laugh, and bounced once on her heels. "You got it to work!"

Marcus turned toward her, and his breath caught in his chest. Jana's ice-blue eyes were wide and sparkling, her whole face lit up by her smile directed at him. But it was only a moment, and then the spell was broken as Jana and Steve both rushed in and dropped to their knees on either side of Marcus, transfixed by the image on the screen. The words *Press Start* danced across a black background in pixilated, white letters, while the title of the game – *Legends of Arameth* – flickered in large swirls of color at the top of the screen.

Marcus stared at the screen in shock. *Arameth.* How was that possible? But no – he knew exactly what this was. That nagging feeling when he'd seen the console. His stomach dropped. This was bad. This was very, very bad. Luther should have warned him, should have told him – but that didn't matter; it was too late for that. He needed to focus on what to do now. He glanced at Jana and Steve, but they seemed totally relaxed.

Lex rode Marcus' wave of thoughts, confused and frustrated. He had the awareness that Marcus knew something, without actually possessing the knowledge of it.

Marcus spoke, and Lex could feel his effort to hold his voice steady. "Jana... where did your dad get this game again?"

She turned to face him. "It was my grandmother's. He found it in the attic buried under a bunch of her stuff. He said she used to be some sort of game researcher or something. It only has one game, but my dad thinks it's an original, one that was never released." She grinned at him.

Lex felt a sudden panic come over Marcus with an urgent need to turn off the game. His mind raced. "Anyone want to take a quick walk before we play?" he heard Marcus say. "We've been inside for a while, now, and–"

Steve and Jana were both looking at him like he was crazy. "We've been trying to get this game to work for half an hour," Jana said. "I don't want to stop now. Maybe we can go for a walk after we check out the game. You play first; you're the one who got it working." She handed him the controller.

He – or Marcus, it was becoming harder to tell where one ended and the other began – wanted to argue, but he knew there was no way to do that without making them question him. "Okay," he said. Jana's fingers brushed his as he slipped the controller out of her hand. *What do I do?* His pulse and thoughts both raced as time around him seemed to slow down. He sent a mental plea to whatever might hear him – *please, tell me what to do!*

Jana bounced up onto her feet, one finger pointed into the air. "The drinks!" she declared. "We forgot the drinks!" She looked down at Marcus. "Wait a sec before you hit *Start*? I want to see how the game begins."

He nodded, stunned, and Jana rushed off toward the kitchen.

Steve jumped up and followed her, calling out, "I'll help you." They pushed through the swinging door and disappeared.

He dropped the controller like it was a viper and scooted back. Panic coursed through him. Steve and Jana would be back any moment. What could he possibly do? He glanced around the room. There were no exits, only curtains covering large bay windows he wasn't even sure opened. He could unplug the console and hide it, but then what would he tell them when they came back? How would he explain? Maybe he could grab the whole thing and run for it, but the only door from this room led through the kitchen, where Steve and Jana both were. He might escape, but they'd know something was up, and he'd never be able to come back. It would all be over. But if they started the console, it would be over, too. In the worst possible way.

He was trapped. *Curse Luther and my family and all of them, every one of them.* But no... he didn't mean that. He'd volunteered for this. Then he'd got caught up in it, and wasted so much time. He hadn't done what he'd been sent to do, and this was the universe punishing him. How had he thought he could ever escape it? *But Jana.*

He could hear Steve's voice murmur something in the kitchen, followed by a bright giggle from Jana. He took a breath. *Maybe I could just tell them?* No. That would risk everything. And this wasn't their fault. This was on him to fix, and he had to do it now.

He focused his thoughts on Jana – her smile, her eyes, the way that one strand of blonde hair always slipped down into her face. He thought of his family here, the ones who had taken him in and loved him with a warmth his own family had never shown, and of his tiny brother's hand clasped in his. His chest contracted. He grabbed the controller. *I love you,* he thought. This was his problem, and he would die before he brought them into any of it. It was the only way. And he had to do it quickly. He punched *Start*.

A bright light exploded through the room, and he threw his arms up over his face. Within the light a form appeared. All its features were cast in shadow and it had the shape of a man, yet not quite right, as though deformed. It made a deep sound, halfway between a chuckle and a growl, and moved toward him, reaching out with a large, dark hand.

CONFUSION SWAM OVER Lex as his awareness peeled itself apart from Marcus' once more. *What had he just seen?* He was himself again, yet still staring into the burst of light as a shadow reached toward him. The light blinded him, blocking out all else as he squinted against it.

THE WORLD TILTED AGAIN. He was standing in a dim room, the faint sound of an a cappella chorus playing from speakers somewhere in the background. His eyes strained to adjust to the dimness as he dropped to his knees, resting his head on the tiny casket. His chest felt like it was crushing inward. It was hard to even breathe.

*No guilt in life, no fear in death*, the chorus of voices swelled in the background.

Neither of those were true for him, not after what he'd done.

Someone's hand settled onto his back. "It's alright, son," a deep voice said. The man took a shaky breath from behind him. "I know this is hard for you, too. But we're here. We're still here. We'll get through this, together."

*He wouldn't say that if he knew what I've done.*

The world tilted again and he blinked, his eyes struggling to adjust in the sudden brightness. He was in a sunlit kitchen, one large window opening up to a well-tended backyard full of rich green grass, edged with rows of flowers along the fence which bordered it. A girl stood in front of the window, her back to him. The sky outside the window was a bright blue, nearly the color of–

She turned around and her eyes were red around the edges, still wet with tears.

Next to him, someone fidgeted. He glanced over – *Steve*. He was watching Jana with pain-filled eyes. *Why does Steve always have to be here?* But they'd come here together, he knew. They'd come for *her*.

She was older than in the last glimpse, maybe mid-teens. And beautiful. So beautiful. His breath caught in his chest.

"Hey," he heard himself say in a soft voice, and his heart lurched as she met his eyes. He felt desperate to help her, but knew too well he couldn't. Not this time; not with this. The realization bristled inside him, making him want to hit something.

And then came the hot wave of shame. He had seen her in the hallway after school a few days ago, not yet knowing it had been the death of her grandmother that kept her out of class that day. He had seen her eyes go wide with shock and hurt as some other girl draped on his shoulder. It hadn't been how it looked, but she had no way of knowing that. He hadn't had a chance to explain, and had unknowingly piled more hurt upon what she'd already been carrying. He stared, his throat thick and achy. Just as before, words failed him.

"Hey," she whispered back.

*"I really think she could use some friends right now."* He heard a woman's voice echo in his head, and a recognition whispered – Jana's mother; what she said to him and Steve before bringing them into the kitchen. But guilt overwhelmed him. Jana needed a *true* friend. Not him. She deserved better than him. He glanced to his side. *She deserves someone like Steve,* he thought, and it made his stomach flip but he knew it was true. Steve would bring only goodness to her life, but the best thing *he* could do for her was to stay away.

His thoughts skipped back to months earlier, kneeling in the dim room, his hand still on the casket, and Jana silently kneeling beside him, simply being there. It had been enough. But he could not do the same for her, he realized that now. The worst part was he wouldn't even be able to explain to her why.

Steve stepped toward Jana. "How are you?" he asked, his voice gentle.

*He's a good guy*, he thought. Steve was always kind to Jana, and had been a good friend to Marcus, too, despite clearly being in love with the same girl. Guilt swam through him as he glanced between them.

*Forgive me*, he thought silently.

Jana turned to look at him and her eyes widened, as though reading something on his face.

He spun and walked out the front door before she could say anything.

The world tilted once more, the slam of the door behind him morphing into a clashing of swords. He was on the ground, staring upward at the sky. Something was very wrong. His breath came in short, ragged gasps and his arms and legs felt cold – numb, though a hot spear of pain shot through his chest every time he breathed. The ground was wet beneath him. He peeled a shaky hand from its wetness and held it up to his face. *Blood.* He was lying in blood. He tried to push up with his arms but they failed him, too weak to lift his weight. *I'm dying*, he realized. *This is the end.*

Then a sharp awareness cut through him. *Jana. Where's Jana?* His mind struggled to piece things together. What had happened? He could hear shouting, people fighting nearby. He tipped his head to the side.

Blue eyes stared at him, open – empty. Her body sprawled beside him, blood pooling out around her, soaking her blonde hair. *No. No no no no no.* He reached for her, but she was just beyond the length of his arm. He pushed up, gasping as pain sliced through him, but his hand slipped in the blood and he collapsed again. Fire exploded in his abdomen and he looked down – his torso was sliced open from his collarbone to his waist. He was bleeding out.

*This can't be real*, he thought. *Not real not real not real.* But his brain drew up flashes – they had been surrounded. He'd stepped in front of Jana, shielding her with his own body. He'd fought and then collapsed, sliced from shoulder to hip by one of the enemy in one brief moment of distraction. He had felt no pain from his own wound, but her terrified scream seared him to the bone. *Jana.* He had failed her.

He turned his head back toward her. Beneath their mixing pools of blood, the ground was charred outward around them in a blackened ring. *Burnt? Why?* It made no sense – the enemy had fought with swords, not fire.

He took a ragged breath, focusing on her face, though it hurt to see her eyes so empty. But he deserved to hurt.

The world was blacking in around him from the edges of his vision.

Suddenly someone was over him, pushing a wad of cloth against his stomach. "Hey. Hey! Stay with me."

*Acarius*, his mind whispered. His face was blurry, but it was him – younger, maybe in his teens, but him. He felt a wave of regret. He must have failed Acarius in some way, too, though he couldn't remember how.

"You're going to be okay," Acarius said again. "It's all going to be okay."

*Doesn't he see that nothing is going to be okay?*

"Let me help," a female voice said, and hot pain exploded anew on his chest as another pair of hands pressed against his wound. She paused. "Did you see?"

"Yes," Acarius answered, sounding breathless.

"But how – "

"I don't know."

Lex heard himself – *Marcus, not me;* Marcus, *not me* – groan as new flames of pain burst through his chest. The rim of darkness on the edges of his vision inched inward.

"Stay with me." Acarius' voice cracked and he leaned forward, his green eyes staring directly into Marcus'.

The woman's hands moved off of him and he heard her whispering fervently, as though praying, though he could not understand the words.

Lex knew it was only a vision, but he truly felt as though he was dying. The last of his energy seeped out with his blood, leaving his thoughts heavy and fogged.

"No. Stay *with* me!" Acarius shouted.

The black edges slid inward, consuming everything.

Lex floated free in a void of nothingness, suddenly expelled from the vision. Then something yanked him backwards, slamming him into hard ground.

He blinked up, gasping.

Acarius bent over him. "Lex." He exhaled, clearly relieved. "Stay with me," he said, pressing something against the side of Lex's head. "You're going to be okay."

Fireworks of pain burst from behind his eyes as Acarius pressed his hand against the side of Lex's head again, dabbing at something. Then Acarius sat back. "It's not bad," he said. "Just a graze. The blood is already slowing. Can you sit up?"

Lex groaned as he pushed up to sitting. The world swam a bit, then righted itself. He looked around. They were on a dirt path just inside the gate, with it closed firmly behind them. Lex couldn't see much more than that, as the circle of archers surrounding him blocked the rest of their surroundings. They were all pointing their arrows at him and Acarius.

"Are you well?" Acarius asked in a low voice.

Lex nodded.

"What's wrong with him?" one of the archers spat.

Lex blinked, trying to push the lingering images of the glimpses aside and focus on the present. He must have fallen off his horse and been dragged inside. How long had he been unconscious, trapped in the vision? Clearly not long, as he could now hear loud voices approaching from outside the wooden gates. The enemy had reached them.

The archers scattered, calling out to others from the village... all except Maharan, who planted himself beside Lex, his arrow pointed at the gates.

Lex staggered his way up to standing and glanced to his sides. Acarius looked grim, paler than he'd ever seen him. Lytira fidgeted beside Acarius, her hands clasped to her chest and her head bowed as though in prayer.

"We're under attack!" A far-off voice continued the shout from the darkness behind them.

Lytira's head snapped up and she grabbed Acarius' arm. He nodded at her and she spun, running off down the dirt path into what Lex could now see was a small encampment of tents and wooden huts with leafy-branched roofs.

Acarius placed his hand on Lex's arm. "Stay here," he said, then ran after Lytira.

People – men, women, and children, none of them looking like soldiers or at all equipped to fight – stumbled out of their shelters into the small circle of light made by a fire at the center of the camp, their eyes wide and startled as the cry continued to go up in the distance. "We're under attack!"

The people ran away from Lex and the gates, disappearing into the shadows beyond the fire. Only a small portion of the camp nearest him was visible, the rest hidden by the night. Were there more people? What was beyond the darkness? Was there a way to escape?

Lex wanted to run, but... he couldn't. Acarius had told him to stay here, and though Lex couldn't guarantee he wouldn't budge from this spot once the enemy attacked, he knew he wouldn't run. This was his fight. The farmers had come for *him* and put all the rest of these people in danger. He would not run away like a coward.

He said a silent prayer that his glimpses would work in his favor this time, like they had at Acarius' ranch. Lex didn't quite trust his own fighting skills, but Marcus' were inside him, somewhere, if only he could find a way to channel them. *Don't fail me, Marcus,* he thought, but he knew his brother was long dead. Was he so helpless that his only chance for survival was to steal a dead man's skills and memories?

He would stay and fight, with or without the glimpses, even if it killed him. And it likely would. But where was Acarius? If the glimpses had shown him anything useful, it was that Acarius could be trusted. If he was going to fight, he'd feel better having someone trustworthy beside him. At least then maybe he'd have a chance.

Or maybe Acarius would die trying to protect him.

No. It was better if Acarius stayed away. Whatever Lex had done or not done, the farmers were after *him* – not Acarius. Would Acarius save Amelia after Lex was gone? He wished he'd at least had time to make him promise that. Amelia didn't deserve to be hurt because of Lex, either.

A shout went up from outside the gates and then something slammed into them, shaking the entire fence. The wood creaked.

*Is there nothing for us to do but wait for them to break it down*? Lex wondered. But maybe these people had no other defenses; maybe the gate was the only entrance or exit and there was no way for them to escape. The thought chilled him. When the gates burst they'd be trapped in here, helpless, like birds in a cage.

The archers gathered around him, all arrows aimed at the gate.

Maharan turned to Lex. "Whatever happens, this is on *you*," he growled. "You should never have come here."

Lex took a deep breath, then stepped forward. "You're right," he said. "Now move back and get your people as far from here as you can."

Maharan stared at him.

A cheer broke out from outside the fence as the wood of the gates splintered and bent inward. One more strike, and the gates would probably give way.

"Get back," Lex yelled to the archers again. Maharan and the others exchanged confused glances, then fled back into the shadows.

Lex planted himself in the center of the path from the gates to the camp. When the enemy broke in, he wanted to be the first thing they saw. He drew his sword. It felt heavy and awkward in his grasp. Fear edged in as he realized this really could be the end for him. If he didn't glimpse at the right time, he would have no clue how to fight. They'd kill him in seconds.

Footsteps thundered toward him as Acarius and Lytira rushed up, breathing heavily and followed by several others. The new strangers were dressed the same as the archers, but were all larger and more muscular than any from the first group, and they carried no bows and arrows. One of the men – the one standing nearest Lytira – was huge, almost bear-like, with a massive chest and dark, hairy arms as thick as logs. He nodded at Lex and moved up beside him, facing the gates. Acarius moved up next to Lex's other side, and Lytira stood beside Acarius. The others moved forward around the three of them and the bear-man, taking positions on both sides.

Another impact shook the fence from outside and the wood of the gates splintered yet again, just barely holding together.

Lex glanced around. Besides him and Acarius – who had drawn his own sword – no one had weapons, and Lex didn't even know how to use his. Lex turned to Acarius. "Why are you here?" he said. "You will all be killed."

Acarius shook his head. "I don't think so."

Beside him, Lytira leaned forward, as though eager to leap at the enemy the moment they broke through.

Outside, a roar of voices went up in unison, like a battle cry. How many were out there? Dozens?

"Please," Lex said, turning to Acarius. "I don't want anyone else to be hurt because of me." Suddenly he realized, *If I'm about to die...* He grabbed Acarius' arm. "Amelia," he said. "If I don't make it–"

Acarius looked at him, his eyebrows raised slightly. He opened his mouth as if to reply.

With a crash, the gates burst inward.

# CHAPTER 10

**M**en poured in through the broken gates. They were just ordinary men from Dalton and Merik'esh and maybe even some other nearby villages – except today, they were out for blood. *No, not just for blood,* Lex thought. *For me. For revenge for the people I killed and whatever else they think I've done.* Lex had only a moment to note that the men carried farming tools, rather than swords or spears, before they attacked.

One of the men from Alowen grabbed Lex and shoved him behind them. He and the others formed a line in front of Lex like a wall. The villagers cascaded into them, a giant, human mass of writhing, grunting bodies intent on murdering one another.

Lex wasn't about to let Acarius, Lytira, and Alowens he didn't even know fight his battle for him. He shoved between two of the men in the line as they fought off the attackers. Fights exploded all around Lex as Acarius, Lytira and the others engaged the charging villagers. Someone elbowed Lex in the side and shoved him, and Lex stumbled through the mob and out the other side into a pocket of stillness amid the chaos. Bodies of the enemy were dropping all around him, though Lytira and Acarius and the Alowens seemed to be faring well so far.

Lex watched them fight, awed by it. Lytira moved like a leopard on the hunt, swift and lethal, and Acarius wielded his sword like it was part of him. The Alowens who had come to help seemed sturdy as oaks, the villagers' blows glancing off them. And the man who had reminded Lex of a bear did his initial impression justice – he tore into the enemy with all the ferocity of an angered grizzly, splitting their faces with his fists.

Lex wanted to help, but how? Everyone around him was already fighting, and succeeding at it. He would just get in the way.

From the darkness beyond the tents, Lex heard a whinny. Mare and the other horses had vanished while Lex was in his glimpse. Had they been tied up somewhere? Maybe he could go and find them; he'd seen Mare in a fight and she was –

A burly villager burst out from the rest and hurled himself at Lex, his face contorted in a howl of rage. Lex threw his sword up, knowing he should swing at the man but unable to make himself do it. *How do people do this, just slaughter another human?* He braced himself to block instead and the villager tackled him, locking his arms around Lex's shoulders like a cage. Lex barely kept his footing, arms trapped against his body. The man threw his weight sideways, pulling Lex to the ground, then closed his hands across Lex's throat. Lex was still holding the sword, but it wasn't much help with both his arms pressed against his chest.

Lex's world collapsed to the small reality of himself and the man fighting him. He pushed up with his arms, relieving some of the pressure against his throat, but he could barely breathe, much less fight back. His heart raced as his head grew foggy. All this struggling, all this running and fighting and seeking... for it to end like this? *Not like this.* But any moment, more of the enemy would join in, and he'd be dead for sure.

Panic spiraled upward in Lex and he wrenched one arm loose from the man's hold on him. The sword was still in his grip but he couldn't get leverage. He struggled beneath the villager, trying to break free. *Glimpse*, he told himself. *Glimpse!*

It didn't come.

Blackness crept in from the sides of his eyes. *I'm dying*, he thought. *Like in my vision.*

The panic sank into numbness.

"Lex!" a voice shouted. *Acarius.* "Hold on!"

Lex glanced beyond his attacker, toward the sound of the voice. Acarius was fighting two men, slashing at them with his sword... but as one fell, another took his place.

"I'm coming!" Acarius yelled between strikes at the enemy.

But Lex knew it would be too late. He was beginning to float, his mind disconnecting from his body. Lex looked up at the man crushing him. His eyes were wide and wild, burning with fury. *What did I do to make him hate me this much?* Lex wondered. Inside him, the darkness stirred, whispering. He stared into the man's eyes.

The man's glare shifted from anger to hesitation and then to fear. His hands loosened from Lex's throat and Lex gasped, feeling the air rush inward and push the blackness away. Reality snapped in, the pressure on his throat and the warm sword in his hand and the pain of the man's knee in his ribs all flooding in at once. The man closed his hands around Lex's throat once more, but he seemed to have grown weak from the exertion – he was choking Lex half-heartedly.

Lex elbowed the man's arm away and shoved upward, twisting himself free. He scrambled to his feet, new energy burning in his stomach.

The man crouched in front of him, shaking, face turned up toward Lex with a look of terror.

Lex raised his sword.

The man began to beg. "Please," he gasped. "I have a daughter, a baby girl, born last week. Please, I'm sorry. Just let me go."

Flickers of a tiny hand wrapped in his own blurred across Lex's anger, dissolving it. This man had a family, a daughter waiting for him to come home. *I can't do it*, Lex thought. He lowered his sword.

The man's face shifted into a sneer as Lex saw something move beside him.

Lex spun, but the villager behind him was already swinging a sharpened shovel toward Lex's head. Lex threw up his sword to block.

The man dropped to the ground. Behind him stood Acarius, arms still upraised from striking the villager in the head with his sword hilt. He gave Lex a brief nod, then turned back toward another attacker.

Lex spun back to the villager he'd spared, ready to retract his mercy. But he had dissolved into the chaos around them.

Lex was surrounded by fighting. Acarius had two villagers on him and Lytira was holding her own against another, while the few Alowens who'd come to help were each taking two or three men on their own. They spread out in a line across the narrow dirt path, blocking the attackers from making it to the camp beyond... for now. It looked like a bizarre game, the attacking villagers crowding around, waiting to slide in and fight whenever one of their own fell. The Daltoners and Altans weren't skilled fighters but they were driven by fury... and there were dozens of them, against only a handful of the others.

Lex stared, wondering how an entire village militia could have come after him and he again managed to be the only one *not* being attacked. But it was short-lived. A cluster of men caught sight of him.

"There he is!" they shouted. They shoved toward him through the crowd, gathering any men who weren't already fighting.

Lex turned toward them and shifted his right leg back, centering his weight. He raised his sword.

The men charged toward Lex just as a feral shriek of pain cut through the air.

Lex spun toward the sound. Two large villagers had Lytira pinned against the wooden gate, a third drawing back his large shovel to strike.

"Lytira!" Acarius yelled from the other side of the path. He shoved away from the men he was fighting and raced toward her.

Lex moved toward Lytira also, the men on his heels. He was still several steps away when a large villager swung a spade at Acarius from behind.

Acarius crumpled.

Lytira snarled in rage.

Lex ran toward Acarius, but the men reached Lex first. "No!" Lex yelled. "Acarius!" He hit the ground with a thud, pain shooting through his ribs, as the weight of several men collapsed onto him.

His sword clattered to the ground, out of reach. The men pressed Lex to the ground and pulled his arms behind his back. His cheek dug into the hard ground. One of the men jabbed a knee into his back, and a bolt of pain cut through his shoulders as they pulled his arms further backward.

"Tie his wrists," someone called out, but Lex's attention was on Acarius, crumpled on the ground a few feet away. He wasn't moving.

The memory of Jana's lifeless blue eyes staring across the ground at him from the glimpse surfaced. Lex blinked it back.

Lytira let out a wordless howl of anger nearby, but her shout stopped short.

Lex couldn't see her. Had they knocked her out, too? Lex's thoughts raced. *Glimpse!* he willed himself again, but nothing happened.

Lex grunted as a knee dug into his back again, then someone yanked against Lex's hands, tightening something around his wrists. *What do I do?*

Lex thought, starting to panic. He fought against his restraints but they wouldn't budge.

The men yanked Lex upward by his shoulders and shoved him to his feet.

Something dark stirred in Lex, beckoning.

A man stepped in front of him, the man he had spared. The others circled around. The man leaned into Lex's face. "We have you now, demon," he said. His breath smelled like rotting meat.

Within Lex's chest the dark thing stretched, as though waking from a long sleep.

More men came from the sides, shoving a bleeding Lytira to her knees beside Lex.

Lytira glared at the men silently.

"Here you are, *princess*," one of the men sneered. He dumped Acarius' limp body into the center of the circle.

The dark thing in Lex yawned and rose, spreading through his veins. It was eager, ready... just waiting to be set free. A thread of fear slipped through and Lex hesitated. What was this thing inside him, begging to be unleashed? He was suddenly afraid of himself.

The dark thing collapsed inward, shrinking.

*No*, Lex thought. *Come back!* Whatever that darkness was, it was powerful. It might have been his only way out of this. He grasped for it, but it was gone.

Lex now had a man on either side of him gripping his restrained arms, and at least twenty other men standing around, watching him. He glanced down at Acarius' body and felt a swell of relief – his chest was rising and falling. He was alive.

Lex looked over at Lytira. Her eyes were alert, watching the villagers. She looked calm, so Lex forced himself to breathe. *She must have a plan.*

A group of men shoved through the circle, dragging something behind them – the large man who stood beside Lex before the gates burst open. It took four men to move him and his body sagged like a flour sack as they dragged him through the dirt. Blood ran from his head down the side of his face.

"Baram," Lytira whispered.

Lex glanced at her. For the first time since Lex had met her, she looked afraid.

More men came behind them, dragging the bodies of the other Alowens who had fought to protect Lex. They were all unconscious... or maybe worse.

Baram stirred. He didn't move from the ground, but his eyes opened and flicked around as though getting his bearings. When his gaze fell on Lytira, he stopped.

Lex watched as a silent conversation passed between them.

Lytira tensed, her muscles coiling inward as though readying for something, but Baram gave a sharp shake of his head. "No," he grunted. "Don't."

"Shut up," one of the villagers said, and kicked Baram in the ribs.

Baram grunted, but his eyes never left Lytira. She watched him for a moment then sank back, the tension slipping out of her body.

*What had she been planning to do? And why did Baram stop her?*

Lex had only a moment to wonder before someone grabbed him and shoved him to his knees. They yanked his head backward by the hair, exposing his neck.

"No!" Lytira shouted from behind him.

Lex could see only the dark sky above him and a bit of movement in his peripheral. He could feel men's hands still pressing down on his shoulders and whoever held his hair expelled harsh breaths against his neck. Lex shivered.

Behind him he heard scuffling. Was Lytira fighting to get free?

A shout. A thump.

"Leave her alone," Baram's deep voice growled.

Lex strained against the men holding him, but the firm grip on his hair still pulled his head backward and men still held both his arms. His movements only made his captors grip him tighter.

With his neck exposed and unable to see what was happening around him, he felt suddenly very vulnerable. *Glimpse*, Lex commanded himself.

Nothing happened.

The dark whisper surfaced deep within again, and Lex strained for it. It was just out of reach.

A man moved in front of Lex, holding a knife level with Lex's throat.

# THE EDGE OF NOTHING

*How many times can a person be on the brink of death in one day?* Lex thought, but still fear crept in as the knife pressed into his skin.

"What the– " the man said. The knife clanked to the ground at the same time the men let go of Lex's arms and head.

Lex dropped his head for a moment, grateful for the relief in his strained neck. He scanned for the knife, hoping to cut his wrist restraints before the men could stop him. He halted. The ground was alive, fresh green vines as thick as a man's wrist springing upward from the dirt in all directions.

Lex stumbled to his feet.

Around him, the villagers scattered back toward the gates. "Witchcraft!" they shouted. "Demons!"

"You!" one of them yelled, spinning toward Lex. "*You're* doing this."

Lex was as confused as the rest of them. The dark thing inside him had fled and the only thing Lex knew was that this wasn't him. He watched, stunned, as more vines burst up by the dozens around and between all the men. The vines grew as fast as a man could move from standing to sitting. They quickly surpassed Lex's own height and continued shooting upward, a forest of vines reaching toward the night sky.

A villager ran toward one of the vines, swinging a sword at it.

*My sword,* Lex realized.

As the man struck the vine, it curled back and wrapped itself around the man, cocooning him. Then it continued to shoot upward, carrying his screaming form with it.

Lex gaped.

"Help me!" Lytira yelled, breaking Lex's distraction. She knelt beside Acarius's body, her arms beneath his shoulders. Acarius' head bobbed like a rag doll's.

Lex rushed toward her to help, only to realize his hands were still tied. He turned, showing Lytira.

She lowered Acarius back to the ground and pulled a knife from her waist – the pocket had blended into her fitted leather tunic so that Lex hadn't even noticed it – and moved around behind Lex.

His hands popped free as a length of rope fell to the ground. Lex pulled his hands forward, rubbing his sore wrists in relief.

Lytira moved back to Acarius and slid her hands back under his armpits. Lex grabbed Acarius' feet and followed her lead as they carried Acarius down the path toward the camp.

"Here." She nodded to the side of the path, beside a tent on the outer ring of the camp. They lowered Acarius and Lytira knelt beside him, examining his head and face.

"Is he– " Lex started to say, but stopped.

A few feet away from them, in the middle of the camp, stood a little girl no more than eight years old. Her face was turned upward to the sky, her eyes closed, her arms raised. The light of the campfire behind her cast a long shadow in front of her that seemed to dance as the flames flickered. And spreading from the girl across the ground, racing outward then dipping in and out of the earth at various places, were vines. Dozens of vines. They were coming from *her*.

Lytira looked up at Lex, then followed his gaze toward the girl. She jumped to her feet. "Naya!" she shouted. "I had no idea this was– you have to get inside!"

The girl tipped her face down and blinked at Lytira. "I had to help you," she said. "Did it help?" She paused, her eyes scanning Lytira's face. Her mouth quivered. "Are you angry?" The vines shooting outward from her slowed to a crawl.

"Oh, little one, no," Lytira said, moving toward the girl. "And yes, it helped. But it's not safe. You have to hide. And you know we–"

Behind them, someone shouted. "There! It's the girl!"

Lex spun around. The villagers from Dalton and Alta were rushing toward them.

"Naya, run!" Lytira screamed. She moved into the center of the path, putting herself between the girl and the villagers.

The girl dropped her arms and took off into the camp, leaving a ring of now-motionless vines feeding up from the ground where she'd been standing.

Lex had a lot of questions, but now was the time to fight. He planted himself next to Lytira. "I don't have my sword," he said, remembering he'd last seen it in the hands of the man the vine had taken.

Lytira shook her head. "You don't need it. I've seen you kill dozens with no more than a thought."

"You– what?" Lex gaped at her.

"Just trust your instincts," she said. She glanced over at Acarius. He was still unconscious, but hidden by shadows on the side of the path.

"I don't have instincts!" Lex shouted. "I have no clue what I'm doing. I'm not even sure who I *am!*"

The men were almost upon them.

"You're a warrior," she said. "And no matter what Baram thinks, I have to be what *I* need to be."

The men crashed into them.

Lex hit the ground hard, pain bursting through his head. He lost sight of Lytira in the scuffle, but he could hear yells of alarm from the villagers just out of his range of sight. *She must be fighting*, he thought. He struggled to fight, too, but the villagers took no chances with him – he was held down by more hands than he could count, men on all sides.

"We've got you this time," someone murmured in his ear.

The dark thing in Lex awoke. It was there, right there, in the pit of his stomach, coiling like a snake prepared to strike. He squeezed his eyes shut and reached for it. His mind closed around it. He yanked.

It burst free, and Lex plunged into icy shadow.

Lex blinked and pushed himself upright. The men weren't holding him anymore. *What happened?* The last he remembered, he–

He stopped. Bodies littered the ground, shadows from the firelight flickering across them. Were they all... No. Not dead. Some were groaning now, or moving a little.

Lex jumped to his feet.

Lytira darted up, a smear of blood across her forehead. Lex wasn't sure if it was hers or someone else's. "What happened?" he asked her.

"No time," she snapped, grabbing his arm. "Run." She pushed him toward the tents.

Lex stumbled and turned. "I don't want to–"

A sound of wings cut through the darkness.

"Run!" Lytira said again. She pulled him toward the tents on the far side of the camp and shoved him into the shadows beyond the glow of the campfire. Then she spun, taking off down the dirt path again.

Lex turned, his eyes adjusting to the darkness beyond the fire's glow, and found he was not alone. A crowd of people stood staring out toward the fire, men and women and children of all ages, like silent sentries in the shadows. Just beside Lex stood Naya. "Sulanashum," she whispered, and gave him a small nod.

*Sulanashum.* The word tickled something deep in memory. Lex turned to her. "What did you–"

"Shhh!" Someone behind him hissed. "They come!"

A dark shadow appeared in the sky over the camp, hovering high above the light of the fire. The flames gushed and flickered beneath heavy gusts as rapid wing beats filled the air. *No,* Lex realized, as the rhythm of the beats shifted into clarity. The beats were slow and steady... they only sounded fast because there were more than one set of wings beating. Many more. Lex swallowed.

Dark shapes moved along the ground behind the tents. Was it more of the enemy? If so, they would soon be surrounded. Lex turned to alert the people behind him, but then the firelight flickered on metal among the shadows between the tents, and for a moment a shape was illuminated – Acarius and his sword. He slipped between the last of the tents and made his way to where the others were standing. When he spotted Lex, he moved toward him. "Ready for another fight?" he whispered, taking his spot beside Lex.

Lex felt a weight lift he hadn't known he was carrying. Acarius was okay. And if he was part of the moving shadows, then the other shapes were probably Lytira and the other Alowens.

Lex was right. Soon Lytira, Baram, and the others materialized from the shadows beyond the tents. They all looked exhausted and many of them were bloody and dirty and bruised. But they were all okay.

Lex suddenly wondered about all the villagers lying in the shadows on the other side of the camp. Were they waking now? Would they be preparing to attack? If they attacked at the same time as whatever was hovering above them, this could be bad. Very bad.

Lex turned to Acarius to ask if he knew what was above them, but there was no need. Dark shapes thudded to the ground around the fire, wings fluttering like giant locusts.

Aiacs. Five of them.

Lex's heart jolted as one of them stepped in front of the others, holding Amelia in its scaly, claw-handed arms.

She was unconscious, and the creature set her down on the dirt beside the fire, then moved back to join the rest. The Aiacs all stood just out of the glow of firelight, staring toward the shadows where Lex and the others were. They had placed Amelia in the center of the camp like an offering.

Lex glanced at Acarius but his eyes were fixed forward, watching. There was a tangible tension in the air, as though they were all waiting for something.

Lex stood as still as possible, because everyone around him was and it seemed the thing to do. But if the Aiacs attacked, what then? He had fought off an Aiac before, and with Lytira and Acarius' help he was sure they could take all five, but what about the Alowens? There were children here, babies – why weren't the parents taking them to safety?

Beside him, Lytira shifted, reminding him again of a predator tensing to leap.

One Aiac glanced at the others and then stepped forward. As it came into the firelight, it seemed to be... shrinking? Lex shook his head. It must be a trick of the lighting. But no. It *was* shrinking, its arms drawing inward, claws disappearing, lizard-body shortening and thickening and wings shriveling back toward its spine. Its scaled skin morphed into human flesh and its reptilian face contorted until it was no longer an Aiac creature, but a man.

Lex's blood turned cold. It wasn't just a man. It was *the* man – shock of black hair, pale skin, right down to the crisp white tunic which had materialized as the creature transformed – only without the pluming bloodstain from when Lex had last seen it. It was the man he'd killed at Dalton.

# CHAPTER 11

The man stepped forward. "Your demon seems to have incapacitated my farmers," he stated into the night. "I propose a trade." He stopped behind Amelia's crumpled form and nudged her with his boot. "A daughter of power for your demon. It seems more than fair."

Having that *thing* so close to Amelia made Lex's hair stand on end. He tensed, fighting the urge to run for her. He was fast; he might be able to get to her–

The pressure of a hand on his shoulder made him turn. "Not yet," Acarius whispered. "Hold."

*Hold*, Lex told himself. Acarius clearly had a plan. He wouldn't let the creatures harm Amelia... would he?

"Your demon," the man said again, "or the girl dies." He pressed his boot against Amelia's throat.

She moaned, but did not wake. Lex felt a wave of relief at the confirmation that Amelia was alive. But if they didn't do something, she might not be for long.

Lex took a step forward, but a tiny hand grabbed his arm.

"Sulanashum, don't go," Naya's plea was hushed but urgent. She tipped her wide eyes up to him. "They will kill you!"

"He's not going, little one," Lytira whispered. She cut her eyes over to Lex. "He is staying here with us."

Lex was beginning to tire of everyone telling him what he was and wasn't going to do, but he trusted Acarius and he supposed he trusted Lytira. If they said to wait, he would wait... for now. He stepped back and Naya relaxed, letting go of his arm.

The Aiac man stared toward them, and Lex had the feeling the man had no problem seeing them through the darkness. "You have five minutes to decide, or she dies," the man said. He stepped back toward the other Aiacs, slipping into shadow.

"How should we proceed, Rahmanasha Lytira?" Baram whispered.

Lytira snapped her head toward him. "I thought you had a plan," she hissed.

"I did," he said, "but this is something new. This many Aiacs would tear through our people in minutes. But so far they aren't attacking. Perhaps we can use this."

"Why don't you ask your precious clan leaders? Where are *they* in this fight?" Lytira growled.

Baram lifted his hands. "They're just trying to keep everyone safe, and so am I. You know that. You know *me*. You know I would never–"

"Never harm us? Never leave us exposed to an enemy, trapped outside the gates?" Her whisper rasped through the darkness.

Baram reached a hand toward her then seemed to think better of it, and let his hand fall. "Those were only villagers. I had no idea they'd be bringing Aiacs. And you had your horse-rancher with you," he murmured. "Is he not strong enough to protect you?"

Lex felt Acarius tense beside him.

"Hey!" Acarius growled.

"Can we focus on saving Amelia?" Lex hissed. "We're wasting time! Whatever baggage you all have to work out can wait until later."

Baram turned toward him. "You know nothing of what you've caused," he growled. "How dare you–"

"Exactly." Lex's whisper was thick. "I know *nothing*. I have absolutely *no idea* what's even going on. If someone could explain *any* of this to me, then maybe I'd stop 'causing' all these things people seem to think I'm 'causing!'"

"Easy," Acarius whispered, placing his hand on Lex's shoulder. Acarius turned to Lytira. "He's right, you know."

"We don't have time to provide Lex a full historical breakdown of the entire world of Arameth," Lytira hissed. "In case you didn't notice, we're about to be attacked!"

"Just tell me *something* that will help any of this make even a little sense. The Aiacs–" Lex nodded toward the shadows where the Aiacs stood. "You told me they were demon creatures, but you never said anything about them being shapeshifting lizard people. I mean... they're human? And I killed that *thing* back at Dalton. How is it still alive? And more importantly, how do we keep it from killing Amelia?"

Baram turned to him. "Aiacs are demon creatures," he growled, his voice quivering. "They are an abomination."

"So I've heard," Lex answered.

Acarius shook his head. "You don't fully understand what that means, Lex. The Aiacs used to be Sephram."

"Sephram?"

"My people," said Lytira. She looked to Baram. "Our people. Some of them were even family once, until Ardis stripped their souls away and turned them into *those*."

Lex stared at her. "So these Aiacs are your *family?*"

"No," she said. "Maybe. We do not know. Once they turn, they all look like the one you killed. They no longer look like the Sephram they once were. And the one before you is not the one you killed. It is simply *another*. There are many of them, and they all look the same... but they are not immortal. Nor invincible. They bleed like any other men."

*That's good news,* thought Lex. "Why do they want me?" he asked.

"Because you are Sulanashum," Naya's small voice cut in.

"Hush!" A woman placed her hand over Naya's mouth and drew her back into the crowd.

Lex looked between Acarius and Lytira. "Sulanashum?"

Acarius sighed. "Years ago, Marcus was sent to protect me, because the Ancients received a prophecy that I would be the one to save Arameth from the destruction Ardis had brought upon it." He let out a bitter laugh. "They were wrong. Marcus died and Ardis' reign holds as strong as ever. The world itself is collapsing. Your 'ground tsunami,' as you called it, is just one example." His whisper grew more urgent. "It's happening everywhere. But it wasn't until you showed up that I–"

"Make your choice!" A voice cut through the darkness. The Aiac stood beside the fire again. He leaned down and grabbed Amelia as though she were weightless, holding her limp body by the throat with one arm. He shoved her toward the fire, and her hair dangled just out of the reach of the flames. "You are out of time."

"That's enough," Lex said. He moved forward.

Lytira grabbed his arm.

"We cannot let him go," Lytira whispered to Acarius. "Perhaps if we moved–"

Lex couldn't wait for them to figure out their plans. He wrenched free of her grip and stepped forward, into the light. "I'm here," he said. "Put Amelia down, away from the fire."

The Aiac sneered. "I can feel the power wakening in her this moment," he said. "She must feel strongly for you, to stir from such a deep sleep at the sound of your voice. Interesting. Perhaps I should rescind my bargain."

Lex felt his heart speed at the Aiac's statement, but he couldn't process it right then. He pushed it aside for later. Right now, he had to figure out how to get Amelia and himself out of this without getting everyone killed.

Lex thought of Naya, of all the families standing in the shadows, of Lytira and Acarius, whom he'd come to view friends. He had brought this upon them – unknowingly, but still he had brought these creatures here. And Amelia...

He took another step forward. "Take *me*," he said.

The Aiac raised an eyebrow. He tightened his fingers around Amelia's throat.

The dark thing whispered inside Lex, shifting within his reach.

Between the tents, shadows slipped. Acarius and Lytira and the others were on the move.

"Let everyone else go," Lex called out.

"You will come willingly?" the Aiac hissed.

"No," Lex said. "I will not." He shoved his thoughts inward and grasped the darkness–

"Watch out!" a small voice yelled.

A shadow dropped from the sky, slamming into Lex and breaking his hold on the darkness within. *A sixth Aiac*, Lex realized as it wrestled him to the ground.

"Not thissss time, demonnn," it hissed.

The other Aiacs scurried forward from the shadows, ringing around Lex.

"No!" a shrill scream cut through the night as Naya rushed outward, into the firelight. She threw up her hands and vines burst from the earth in all directions.

Lex locked his arms around the Aiac atop him to keep it from reaching Naya, but the other Aiacs were there in a breath. One leapt forward, slashing the small girl's torso open with one smooth swipe of a clawed hand.

"Naya!" a woman shrieked.

Naya's small body collapsed to the dirt, blood and entrails spilling from her stomach. Her tiny mouth hung open in a soundless scream, her eyes already glassy with death.

Something inside Lex broke, and the darkness burst outward.

Time slowed.

Around him, Lex saw the Aiacs drop to the ground, mouths open in shrieks, as the now-conscious farmers rushed in from the shadows wielding shovels and spades.

He pushed himself up to standing.

All around the campfire, the ground quaked as vines and fully-formed trees burst forth from the dirt, the trees' branches swiping down whole groups of attacking villagers as the vines wrapped and strangled others.

*Naya*, Lex thought, but she still lay on the ground, her innocent face permanently trapped in a scream. He glanced around. The Alowen in the shadows stood and swayed, hands upward and eyes closed. *They can* all *do it*, Lex realized. Did that mean Lytira could, too?

From behind him, Lex heard a roar – an actual roar, as if from a bear. He turned. It *was* a bear, charging forward into the fight with a man running beside it. The man had a long, grey beard and his dark skin bore many wrinkles of age, but his body was lean and muscular and he wore the same leather fighting gear as the others. He spun among the enemy, striking adeptly with a long, wooden staff. He and his bear carved through a group of attackers, the bear swiping aside any the old man missed as though they were nothing more than bees.

Though Lex still stood in the light of the fire with the battle boiling around him, he was both there and not there. A force was pouring out of him, like a river undammed, but it seemed hardly a part of him. He felt as though he stood outside of it – outside of all of this – simply watching.

He glanced about, the scene moving in slow motion around him. The Aiacs were stumbling, as though trying to get their balance, and the villagers from Dalton and Alta were scattering, overcome by the attacking Alowen's vines and trees. But Lytira, Acarius, and Baram and the others who had fought with him were nowhere to be seen.

Suddenly, overlaid across the battle around him emerged a second scene, as though projected across the other – a forest, a small clearing among the trees. In the dirt of the vision lay an unconscious teenage boy.

Lex felt himself move toward the boy in the scene at the same time he felt himself stand still amid the battle beside the campfire. He could see both, was *in* both simultaneously and yet not fully in either one.

"Feels better, doesn't it?" he heard his vision-self say.

The teenage boy woke and jumped to his feet. The boy's left hand went up to grab his right arm, and he looked surprised.

"It was dislocated," Lex heard himself speak again. "It's good that you were unconscious when I fixed it; it would have given you quite a bit of pain."

The boy stiffened. "Uh, thank you." He fidgeted, shifting his weight from one foot to the other and uncrossing his arms, then re-crossing them.

Lex felt amusement and curiosity flood his awareness as his eyes scanned the boy. When the boy turned his face up and it came out of shadow, Lex gasped. It was unmistakenly Acarius, but no more than twelve or thirteen years old.

"I'm Acarius," the boy said, extending his hand. "Thank you for fixing my shoulder. It was hurting quite a lot, actually, and it feels much better now." His voice trailed off.

Lex felt himself turn toward the trees and say "Follow me," as he parted the branches and stepped into them.

Around Lex the camp battle still raged, enemies and Alowens passing in and out of the images of his vision as if they were only shadows.

In the glimpse, Lex made his way through the forest and out into a clearing, where several horses waited – two brown, a black... and Mare.

"My horses!" Acarius exclaimed as he emerged from the trees. "But who is this beauty?" he asked, approaching Mare. He held out a hand toward her face, letting her sniff it.

"Her name is Mare," Lex felt himself say.

152

Acarius examined the white horse. "She is well-built. Strong, and her coat is flawless. She would fetch a marvelous price in Alta, more than my three horses combined," he said, his previous discomfort seeming to vanish as he slid his hand along her coat. He turned. "Not that I'm saying you should sell her! If she were mine, no price could pry her from me." He paused. "But why 'Mare?' A horse like this should be named something more impressive."

Lex felt himself shrug. "I've found that any creature is best suited when it is called what it truly is," he said. "Mare and I appreciate the honesty." He walked toward Mare and patted her neck, then turned and offered his hand to Acarius. "My name is Marcus," he said.

The glimpse shifted.

The moon was higher now, and he and Acarius were sitting near a small fire in a clearing, the horses resting nearby.

Lex felt himself sigh and his hands fidgeted, his left fingers gently spinning a worn silver ring with a stone of deep blue he wore on his right hand. He looked up at Acarius. "We cannot remain here," he said. "We must leave immediately."

"No," Acarius said firmly. "Why should I trust you?"

Lex felt himself reach into his pocket, and his hand clasped around something hard and metallic. He removed it from his pocket and held it out toward Acarius. "This," he heard himself say, "is why you should trust me."

Acarius gasped. He reached to a cord at his own neck, lifted it over his head and held the medallion out beside the other. The two slated silver crescents shimmered side by side, their etched symbols reflecting the moonlight. "How did you...?" Acarius asked.

Lex slipped the medallion back into his pocket and then clicked to Mare, who moved over beside him. Off to the side, Acarius' horses fidgeted. "You'll ride with me. We'll leave the other horses by the road," Lex heard himself say. "Someone will soon find them. Now, let's go; we're running out of time."

The glimpse quivered and faded, and the world around Lex rushed back into full substance. He swayed, disoriented. The chaos of battle was dissipating. As one, the Aiacs screeched and leapt skyward, the wind of their wingbeats causing the campfire to gutter as they fled. The Alowens slowed to a stop as the last of the farmers they pursued fled through the open gates. There were no cheers of victory. A hush fell across the camp, then the

Alowens burst into motion, rushing to help the injured. The whole camp was a flurry of motion, except for one still figure on the ground beside the fire – Amelia.

Lex ran to Amelia and dropped to his knees beside her. He tipped her face toward him, brushing her hair back from her eyes.

She groaned, then blinked. "Lex?" she murmured, her eyes focusing on him. She pushed up and threw her arms around him, almost knocking him backward. "I knew you'd come for me."

Lex swayed under her sudden weight but steadied himself and returned her hug. Amelia pushed back suddenly and looked around. "What happened?"

Lex was still trying to figure out how to explain when Acarius strode up, his face drawn tight. "This isn't good," he said. He nodded toward the tents. Lytira stood, head bowed, as the old man with the staff waved his arms and railed at her in a rumbling tone, his cheeks puffing with each word. Lex couldn't make out what he was saying, but Acarius was right... it didn't look good. Baram stood beside Lytira, glaring at the ground while his hands pumped in and out of fists.

"What's going on?" Lex asked.

"Alowen is a sanctuary of sorts," Acarius said. "They have existed for decades by blending in. No Sephram or Alomman has shown their powers in front of humans for over a hundred years. Back then, the humans feared them and attacked them because of their natural magic. They survived by making people forget about them, by slipping from reality into legend, into stories told at bedtime. No one believed their magic even existed anymore. And now they blame Lytira for exposing them, and for putting her own people in danger. Because of the war she brought here, they were forced to show their magic, and the humans will not let this go. It may start a war all over again." He paused. "She could be banished from her clan for this."

Lex turned to him. "*I* caused this. Not her. She was only trying to help me. We have to do something."

"There's nothing we can do. Outsiders do not have a voice in clan decisions," Acarius said bitterly. "To interject would be the utmost disrespect.

It would only make things worse." He glanced at Lex. "Besides, according to their law, we have blood-guilt upon us. We will be lucky if they do not call for our deaths."

Amelia gasped, but Lex's attention was drawn across the camp to where Naya's mother knelt, face tipped upward and tears streaming from closed eyes as she rocked her daughter's small, lifeless body. A man stood behind her, head bowed, with one hand on her shoulder.

*Naya.* The blood-guilt. Why had she raced out into the light like that? She had been trying to help Lex, he knew – he *was* to blame for her death. There was no escaping it. None of this would have happened were it not for him. "It's my fault," Lex said, standing. "I'll take whatever consequence I have to, but none of you should suffer for this."

"Lex, no," Amelia said.

Acarius shook his head. "That's noble of you, but it won't matter. We are not of their clans. To them, the guilt is on Lytira for bringing you here. They wouldn't accept a deal from you, even if you offered. Only Lytira can arrange a bargain – for herself and for us."

"Then tell her to bargain me in exchange for the rest of you."

"She would never do that," Acarius said, shaking his head again. "But she'll figure something out. We must abide by their customs and let her handle it. There is no other way."

"What if she can't? What if they take it out on her?"

Acarius' hand tensed around the sword at his waist. "Believe me, they will regret it if they try to harm her."

Lex looked at Acarius, and for the first time it occurred to him there must be a history between Lytira and Acarius, a history Acarius clearly still felt strongly about. "Are you and–" He started to ask, but he was interrupted by a loud voice.

"My brothers!" The old man held up his staff above Lytira as the clanspeople gathered around. "The clan accuses Ramanasha Lytira with endangering her people."

Beside him, Lytira bowed her head.

"I have weighed her testimony and have found her offense worthy of banishment," the old man declared.

Murmurs spread across the Alowen people, except for Naya's mother, who stared at Lytira with stony eyes over the top of Naya's tiny, lifeless body.

The elder continued. "According to custom, I must allow the voice of the clan to be heard. Will any speak on her behalf?"

"I will," Baram's voice boomed. He pushed through the crowd.

"We will not accept your voice for her, Baram," the old man said firmly.

"But Elder–"

"We know your feelings for her, Baram, and we cannot accept you as a balanced voice on her behalf."

Beside him, Lex felt Acarius shift. He glanced over.

Acarius glared at Baram, his brows drawn down.

*Oh*, Lex thought.

Baram made his way to the center of the crowd and stood before Lytira and the elder. He opened his mouth as though to argue, but the elder's voice cut him off. "We expected your voicing and have already decided not to allow it. Do not pursue it further or, according to custom, you will only increase her punishment."

Baram glanced at Lytira and then at Acarius. He bowed his head and his massive hands clenched at his sides. "Yes, Elder," he said, his voice a deep growl. He stomped back through the crowd and disappeared between the tents.

"Is there another voice for the accused?" the elder called out.

The camp was silent.

The elder turned to Lytira. "Ramanasha Lytira," he declared, "You have betrayed your people and are banished from all clans within the Alliance. Leave immediately, and do not attempt to return."

The entire clan spun their backs on Lytira, except for Naya's mother, who bent herself over her child's body and sobbed.

Lytira stiffened and walked silently away, pushing her way through the hostile crowd.

Baram emerged from between the tents and stopped her. "I'm sorry," he said, reaching out a hand.

"It is not your fault," she said, but moved away, leaving his hand lingering in the air.

*It's mine*, Lex thought. He glanced at Acarius beside him; his face was grim.

Lytira reached them and Acarius moved toward her. Before Acarius could say anything she simply said, "Let's retrieve the horses and leave this place."

Acarius nodded and followed Lytira as she made her way toward the gates.

Amelia gave Lex a concerned glance as he pulled her to her feet. *No questions,* Lex thought. *Not now.* To his surprise, she simply slipped her hand into his. The familiar buzz of her energy flooded through him as they walked toward the gates.

They retrieved the horses in silence – even Mare made no sound as they untied her and the other horses from posts behind the tents and led them to the gate. Baram was waiting for them. The entrance to Alowen was littered with splintered wood from the broken gate, which had been drawn back closed, despite it bulging inward along the middle and dangling from the hinges. Baram wordlessly opened the broken gate with a pull of a cord and held it open as they and their horses passed. The last thing Lex saw as the gate swung closed behind them were Baram's dark eyes staring after Lytira.

The gate slammed shut, and Lytira sank to the ground beside her horse. Her shoulders shook with silent sobs.

Acarius let go of Mare's reins and was at Lytira's side in a moment, murmuring something as he slipped his arms around her.

Feeling as though this was a private moment, Lex led his horse a few feet away and dropped the reins to let her nibble the grass. He turned outward, away from Lytira and Acarius. He had to make this right somehow. *But how?*

The morning sun was rising, and he could finally see the terrain which had been veiled in fog and darkness the night before. The camp of Alowen was a small fortress amid a grassland valley, meadows spreading out into the distance in three directions, where the land sloped up and out of sight. But when Lex turned toward the fourth side, his breath caught. Beyond the rolling grass on that fourth side, just now visible through the dissipating fog, stood ocean – a vast expanse of blinding blue set ablaze by the rising sun.

"It's beautiful," Amelia whispered, stepping up beside him.

Lex turned toward her. Her brown hair was cinnamon under the golden light of the sun and Lex's heart jumped as her blue eyes fixed on his. She was beautiful.

"Thank you for saving me," she said.

Lex froze. What could he say to that? *You're welcome?* He should never have let her be taken in the first place, should never have gotten angry with her instead of giving her a chance to explain why she lied, should never have assumed the worst or pushed her away. If things had gone differently at Merik'esh, if *he* had done things differently, she may never have been captured, they may never have gone to Alowen – Naya might still be alive. *Naya*. Killing farmers and creatures who would have otherwise killed him was one thing, but how was he supposed to live with the death of a little girl on his conscience?

Amelia searched his face. "Lex," she said. "What is it?"

There was so much she hadn't seen... where could he even begin? One word emerged: "Naya."

"The little girl?" Amelia asked. "Lex, that wasn't your fault. You know that, right?"

He turned to her. "Not my fault? She died trying to save me from monsters *I* brought to her family's home. How is that not my fault?"

"Lex," Amelia said gently.

He shook his head. "You don't understand. There's a *darkness* in me. I felt it. I don't know what it is, but it's *me*. It's part of me. I'm not safe. I may not even be good. I could be a monster. The Aiacs called me a demon. Maybe I am one. Maybe I'm no different than them."

"No," Amelia said. "Not a chance. Darkness or not, there's no evil in you. Only good."

Lex shook his head. He had done *something* to anger the farmers at Dalton. He had killed people, maybe even more than he knew. He had felt the darkness inside himself. No, he was certain he was not *only good*. But she made him want to be. Somehow, even with all the times he had doubted and distrusted her, Amelia still trusted him completely. At that moment, staring into her eyes, he would have given anything to be what she thought he was. "Amelia, I–"

She grabbed his face and pressed her lips against his, just a soft touch. Her electricity flooded through him, setting his veins on fire. It lasted only a moment, then she pulled away. He searched her eyes and when he found no hesitation, he pulled her back toward him and kissed her again. The heat of her touch seared through him once more and he sank into it, happy to let it consume him whole.

Her hair tickled his face as she pushed away and smiled at him. "I knew you were good," she said.

It was such a strange thing to say, Lex laughed. Something about her made him feel lighter. Different. As though she burned the darkness away. "Daughter of power," he said suddenly.

"What?" Amelia asked, pulling back.

"The Aiac called you a 'daughter of power.' What did that mean?"

Amelia raised her eyebrows. "I have no idea," she said. "I've never heard that before. I'm no daughter of anything special. I'm just a regular human girl... and a pretty boring one, by the usual standards."

*If Amelia is boring by her people's usual standards,* Lex thought, *she must come from a really bizarre place.* "I've been wanting to ask," Lex said. "About you..." He trailed off, trying to find the words to capture his questions. There were so many, about her electric touch, her real hometown, her family and background.

Amelia broke the silence. "I'm sorry for lying to you before," she said. "I know I shouldn't have, but I was afraid to tell you the truth."

"Why?" Lex asked. He took her hand in his.

Amelia took a breath. "It's true that I'm an ordinary girl, where I come from." A short laugh escaped her. "Less than ordinary, really. But... I lied because I'm not supposed to be here."

Lex froze. "What do you mean?"

"I came here by accident at first, and then I did come back on purpose but I didn't know. Really, I didn't. I thought it was – but it wasn't. Then once I realized what was happening, it was too late; I was stuck."

Lex searched her face. "I don't understand," he said.

"Lex," Amelia said. "Please don't freak out..."

He was starting to worry. "What is it?" he said, trying to keep his voice steady. He trusted her, he knew that now, no matter what her past held. But still, he steeled himself for what she might be about to say. Was she with the enemy? Was she truly a spy? Was she an escaped prisoner or a stowaway or a criminal on the run?

"I'm... from another world."

Lex stared at her. "What?"

"Another–"

Her explanation cut off in a scream as her eyes fixed on something behind him. Lex turned just in time to see a shovel coming toward his face as the man he'd spared earlier swung at him.

"This is for my brother!" the man shouted. The shovel knocked Lex unconscious.

# CHAPTER 12

Lex floated in darkness. Somewhere in the distance, he heard voices. He swam toward them.

Something grabbed him and yanked him backward. Images slammed into him.

He was trapped in another glimpse, back in Jana's living room. The television screen still cast its blue glow in front of him, *Press Start* blinking across it. But now something else was in front of him, too.

"You had a mission," the Aiac hissed, its claws locked around his throat. "Mistress is not pleased."

"Let me go to her and explain," Marcus croaked.

"No," said the creature, tightening its grip. "You have failed." It dragged him across the room and held him out by one arm as it toppled a large bookcase over in front of the door.

From inside the kitchen, Marcus heard Jana squeak. "What was that?" she yelled. "Marcus?"

Someone banged on the door. "It's stuck," Steve said. "Marcus, are you okay?"

The Aiac drew Marcus back in front of him, flexing its claws into the tender skin of his throat.

"I just need more time," Marcus whispered.

The Aiac squeezed. "You've been here too long already."

Pressure built in Marcus' head from lack of air. He reached blindly next to him for a weapon, a handhold to give him leverage, anything. His fingers found the ornate brass lamp on the table against the wall behind him. He grabbed and swung.

The lamp struck the Aaic's skull with a metallic clunk. The Aiac dropped him and snarled.

Someone rattled the door-handle. "Marcus!" Steve yelled. "Open the door!"

"You will regret this," the Aiac hissed. "And so will your precious *family*." He sprung across the room and crashed out through the closed window. Glass rained to the floor.

"Marcus!" Jana's high voice shouted. "What was *that*?"

Marcus glanced toward the door. It was beginning to nudge open, the bookcase and toppled books inching forward as Steve pushed.

Marcus frantically grabbed the console and instruction manual and jumped through the broken window after the Aiac. He knew where it was headed.

Marcus slowed as he neared the house, and crept around back. His parents thought he would still be at Jana's for several hours. If the Aiac had gotten to them first, he might be too late. But if it hadn't, Marcus needed them to keep thinking he wasn't home. It was the only way to keep them safe.

He shoved the console and manual behind the hedge and pulled out his house key to unlock the back door, but it was already unlocked. He slipped inside.

The television sounded from the opposite side of the house. His parents were probably relaxing on the couch together, as they usually did in the afternoons. Unless he was too late. *Please don't let me be too late.*

A thump came from the nursery. *Gabe. Oh please, not Gabe.* Marcus slipped down the hall and into the room.

The Aiac held the infant by the throat, his tiny legs dangling over the crib. His mouth was open as if to cry, but no sound escaped.

Marcus moved toward him. "Not Gabe. Please," he whispered, meeting the Aiac's dark eyes. "Take me instead."

"You?" hissed the Aiac. "You still have a mission to complete." It lifted the infant higher.

"No! Please," Marcus whispered. "These people are helping my mission. They gave me a place to stay."

"They made you weak," the Aiac spat, its voice barely above a hiss. "I, too, have a mission. Mistress sends a message." It placed its other clawed hand across Gabe's face.

Marcus raced forward and grabbed at the creature's arm, trying to pry Gabe from its grasp. "No!" he shouted. "Let him go!"

From the living room, a voice sounded. "Marcus? Is that you? Are you home?"

The Aiac shoved Marcus back and sneered. "Go on, then," it said. "Call them in. Let them see what you truly are." It raised its arms and let go of Gabe.

Marcus lunged forward to grab the infant as he fell.

The creature pushed past him and scurried out down the hall.

Marcus tumbled to the floor, holding Gabe to his chest. "Gabe?" he rolled him over in his arms. His eyes were closed, his small form unmoving. "No!" Marcus yelled. "Gabe!" He pressed his brother to his body.

Marcus' foster parents burst into the room.

"What is–" His father stopped mid-sentence as his mother screamed.

She rushed to him and snatched Gabe from his arms. "What happened?" she shrieked. "What happened?"

"He just–he's not–I tried to help," Marcus stammered.

His mother's eyes were wild as she looked up at her husband. "He's not breathing!" she cried, placing him on the floor. She peeled back his pajamas and placed her head to his chest. "I can't hear his heart!"

Marcus' father was already in the hallway using the phone. "Yes, our baby is unconscious; he's not breathing."

Marcus sank to the floor. *I'm so sorry, Gabe. Please, please forgive me.*

The world tilted.

"Again!" the man shouted, striking Marcus across the back with his long staff. "On your feet!"

Marcus' arms shook as he pushed himself up from the hard floor. Blood trickled from his nose.

"Up!" the man shouted again.

Marcus scrambled to his feet. "I need water," he said. "It will only take a moment."

"Water breaks are for children. You are eleven years old." The man paused, his eyes narrowing. "You are a prince, are you not?"

Marcus swallowed. "Yes, Father."

"As a prince, you are a reflection of your kingdom, of your family, and of your king, are you not?"

"Yes, Father."

"And is your king weak?"

"No, Father."

His father rested the bottom of his staff on the floor, folding his hands across it. "Good. Then again."

Marcus shifted into fighting stance and braced for the staff to strike him.

The world tilted.

Marcus knelt on the hard ground of the throne room.

"You understand your duties?" his father's cold voice called out.

"Yes, Father."

"Good. We cannot accept another failure like before. Do you understand?"

*He still treats me like a child,* Marcus seethed. But now was not the time to fight that battle. There were bigger things at stake. He bowed his head. "Yes, Father."

"It is an honor to be chosen in such a way, my son," the king stated, "especially at the age of fifteen. You should be grateful for the chance to return honor to your family so soon after such an abysmal and disappointing return."

"Yes, Father."

"Say it."

Marcus clenched his teeth, then forced out the words. "It is an honor to be chosen."

"Good. Now go." His father waved his hand, dismissing him. "And do not embarrass me this time."

Marcus rose and strode from the room.

A guard stopped him in the doorway. "This time, she will kill you if you fail," he sneered.

Marcus stormed past him and down the corridor.

The world tilted.

He floated in a sea of nothingness.

Naya's small body drifted across the darkness, entrails hanging from her ruined stomach, her mouth open in a silent shriek. Her eyes snapped open. She raised one arm, pointing at him. "You," she said. "You–"

The word trailed out, morphing into a scream which became Amelia's voice.

"Lex, watch out!" the voice cried.

The world tilted.

Lex awoke to a major headache and his arms and legs tied to a chair... again. He blinked against the light. He was in a room with wooden floors, lit by a lantern hanging from the angled ceiling. Suddenly Lex he knew exactly where he was – the empty room at the Aracthea Inn, the one he'd run through between the two sets of stairs on his way to find Amelia. The small window had been covered with a black cloth, blocking any view of outside.

"You're awake!" a voice said. An old man with a scraggly beard and crooked smile missing teeth suddenly popped into Lex's line of sight, leaning upside-down over him from behind. The face disappeared for a moment as the man scurried around the chair and appeared in front of Lex, giving him a deep bow. He straightened back and gave a wide grin. "Nice to see you!"

The man was gangly, old, and looked as though neither his hair nor his long, brown tunic had been washed in some time. His whitish beard hung nearly to his knobby knees, and his spindly calves stuck out beneath the bottom of his tunic, under which he seemed to be wearing nothing. His feet were covered in makeshift sandals of flat leather and some rope.

Lex gasped. "Nigel."

Nigel's grin turned into a smirk. "Ahhh, so you *do* know me," he said. "I wondered if you would."

Lex strained against his wrist restraints. "I don't *know* you," he grunted. "But I know who you are. Now why are you holding me here? Untie me!"

"Oh!" Nigel yanked a small knife from beneath the leather strap that cinched the waist of his baggy tunic. "Sorry!" He ran around behind Lex and cut the ropes holding his wrists and ankles.

Lex pulled his hands around in front and rolled his shoulders, eyeing Nigel as he moved back in front of him.

"I'd forgotten I tied you up, you see," Nigel said with a shrug.

Lex stared at him. "No, I don't."

"Come now, no need to be upset," Nigel said, spreading his hands. "I meant no harm." He glanced off toward a blank corner of the room. "But one can never be too safe..."

Lex sighed. The man was clearly a loon, but perhaps a harmless one. "Where are we?" He asked, knowing the answer but wanting to hear the old man's explanation.

"Aracthea Inn," Nigel said.

"How did I get here?"

"You were carried," Nigel answered.

"You carried me by yourself?" Lex asked. The old man hardly seemed strong enough.

"Oh, no," Nigel said. "You were carried by *that*. I just followed." He gestured toward a dark corner of the room.

Lex turned to find a dead Aiac in the corner, still in creature form – or what was left of it. It was a mutilated mess, lacerations criss-crossing its body, its limbs twisted outward at wrong angles, and dark, black sludge oozing around from every orifice. "What did you do to it?" Lex asked, spinning to Nigel.

Nigel shrugged. "Who said it was me?"

Lex thought he caught Nigel's meaning, but he decided not to ask. He didn't know how many more revelations he could take about what he did while unaware.

"Where are my friends?" Lex asked. The last he remembered, Amelia had screamed, and – what if something had happened to her after he'd fallen unconscious? And where were Acarius and Lytira?

"On their way, I'd think," Nigel said. "When the Aiac took you they tried to follow, but Aiacs can fly, you know. In any case, I'm sure they'll find you soon. It's best we just wait for them. You know, so we don't miss them. It would be a shame to leave just as they were coming."

Lex looked at the old man. Nigel really did seem more unhinged than threatening... but Lex remembered the impression from his previous vision that there was more to the man than he let on. The glimpse had also showed him to be a friend to Marcus and Acarius, hadn't it? And Lex needed to know what was going on. He would have to risk it. "Nigel," he asked, "what do you know about me?"

Nigel stared at him. "That is a very big question with too many answers," he said.

The glimpse of the Aiac and Gabe still pressed upon Lex's consciousness. And the other vision which went with it, the one with the video game. They had to be connected, and something in him suspected Nigel would know how. "What do you know about a game called *Legends of Arameth*?" Lex asked.

Nigel's whole body went rigid.

"There's something about that game," Lex said, "and me. And my brother, Marcus. Isn't there?"

"Stop calling it a game," Nigel spat. "It's not a game; it's a myopian portal."

"A – what?"

Nigel's threw up his hands. "*Myopian*. As in you don't see the problems until..." He studied Lex's eyes then sighed, letting his arms fall. "Nevermind. You at least know what *portal* means, yes?"

Lex bristled. He hated feeling stupid, but his concept of portals was shadowy at best, more a guess pulled from some deep, foggy consciousness than an actual knowledge. And this was something on which he couldn't risk assumptions. "Why don't you explain what *you* mean by it, just in case," he said.

Nigel rolled his eyes. "It's a door between worlds, an opening. In this case, a very tenuous and dangerous one which never should have been made."

"What does that have to do with the game?" Lex asked, trying to follow.

"It's not a game!" Nigel snapped. "*Legends of Arameth* is just an overlay, a user interface, a control system for harnessing Arameth's natural electrical atmosphere and channeling it into a controlled rift, a tunnel which can carry travelers through safely from an adjacent dimension. I thought I was very clever at the time, for disguising it as a gaming system." He stopped. "In hindsight, it was a terrible idea."

He paced in a small circle, turning his back on Lex for a moment, then spun around and stuck out his hand. "I'm Nigel here, but Marcus also knew me as Luther, honorary member of The Gatekeepers, revolutionary scientist, government-sponsored technological genius, and the second traveler through from Earth via a brilliantly-engineered but terribly dangerous portal." His face pinched into a scowl. "I wish I'd never made that blasted thing."

"Then why did you?" Lex asked.

"Why does a man do any of the crazy things he does?" Nigel shrugged.

Lex stared. "I don't – "

"Love," Nigel said flatly. "I did it for love."

Lex blinked, unsure what question to even start with.

Nigel sighed again and turned, staring off toward a blank wall. "I'd just built the first console," he said. "It was unprecedented, an expansive virtual reality system which harnessed actual biological materials from the surrounding environment and used the player's genetic coding to assemble them into a physical host that could sync with the player's nervous system and interact within the bio-arena of the game, theoretically, while leaving the controlling player unharmed. It still needed tweaks, and I'd only had enough materials to test it on a very small scale, but it worked. It would have changed the entire gaming industry, not to mention the implications for medical science and robotics. But I needed funding to complete it." He took a long breath. "I put in for a grant and got it. My wife Vanessa was over the moon. She was certain I was about to make history *and* earn us a fortune. We certainly needed it. I used the grant money to finish the system, but every test I ran on it failed. I couldn't replicate my initial success. Then they came."

"Who?" Lex asked.

"The Gatekeepers. They knew about Vanessa's disease, what treatments we'd tried, how nothing had worked. And they knew why." He turned toward Lex. "Her family was in the book."

"What book?"

Nigel ran his hands over his face. "How is it possible you know so little?" He groaned. "The book. *The book.* The one that traces the lineage of the Ancient who made the first rift, crossed over to our world, got himself a human bride, and bred a bunch of half-Ancient hybrids." His voice ramped up, getting faster and louder. "The book that generations of a secret order have been entrusted with preserving in an attempt to harness the latent Aramethian energy within someone of the genetic line of dual-borns to re-open a portal to a magical world thought by all rational people to be nothing but a myth! *The book!*"

"Okay," Lex said slowly. "The book. Got it."

"I didn't believe them at first," Nigel said.

Lex wasn't sure he believed it now.

"But they had proof," Nigel said. He reached into his tunic and pulled out a leather cord. On the end hung a pendant, similar to the one Acarius had given Lex, but with different etchings.

"How does that prove anything?" Lex asked.

But Nigel slipped the pendant back under his tunic and continued talking. "The treatments weren't working because the disease wasn't in the human part of her. It was in the part tied to Arameth. And only a treatment *from* here could cure her." He paused. "They asked me to build a portal."

"But you made video games," Lex said. "Why did they think you could–"

"I did it though, didn't I?" Nigel snapped. "We're standing right here in the proof of it."

"I'm sorry," Lex said, "I didn't mean–"

Nigel sighed. "Do you know how tedious it is, telling someone things they already know? You should try it sometime. It's excruciating."

Lex bit back the words he wanted to say, and waited for Nigel to continue.

"Arameth's entire atmosphere is *electrical*," Nigel said slowly, "a reactive electrical field which acts as a protective barrier. But unlike Earth, where I come from, Arameth's atmosphere is almost like a living thing. Some even think it has consciousness. Essentially it's an intangible nervous system, pure neurons transmitting information constantly through a giant, invisible network, deciding what is allowed entry and rejecting anything it deems to be a risk to this world. Here they call it the Worldforce. It functions like a massive, ethereal computer, so once we found the place where our two worlds touched, it was only a matter of writing the right code to control it and finding a power source to supply the needed energy from our side to breach the gap. Then I simply knocked on its dimensional door, so to speak, and told it to let me in."

"That seems easy enough, I guess," Lex said.

"It wasn't," said Nigel. "It took an inordinate amount of electrical energy, risks you can't imagine, equipment I can't even explain, months and months of coding and building, and we all nearly died. But language fails to capture the true process so that explanation is the best you're going to get. Anyway, we were too late. My wife died before I even completed it."

"Oh," Lex said.

"But The Gatekeepers made me finish it anyway. They tend to be like that. Vanessa had been too weak to be our power source, even if she'd lived, so they brought me Samantha."

"Wait," Lex said. "The power source was a person?"

Nigel waved his hand. "It's not human sacrifice, if that's what you're thinking. But the portal I built was essentially an open circuit, and the only way to close it was with energy from Arameth itself."

"Samantha was a dual-born," Lex guessed.

"Exactly. The process was hard on her, but not lethal. More like running a marathon in your cells. She had to rest between attempts, and the first time we nearly drained too much from her. But in the end..." Nigel stopped.

"In the end *what*?" Lex asked.

"It worked," Nigel said gruffly. "But not as we expected." He paused. "The system malfunctioned and I had to rebuild the whole thing. Took me months. Then I came through."

"Wait," said Lex. "You said you were the second traveler. Who was the first?"

"Lily," Nigel said, his voice suddenly soft. "My granddaughter." He paused, took a shaky breath, then stared off for a moment into a dark corner of the room. Then he said, "She was the reason Marcus agreed to help me."

"To help you what?" Lex asked.

Nigel spun toward him. "To help me find her, send us home, restore the balance and close the breach!" He paused again. "Only, to do that, he had to go through back to our world himself and get her."

"Lily? But I thought you said she came through to here. Why would he have to go back to–"

"Not Lily!" Nigel interrupted. "Aren't you paying attention? When Lily came through, she was pulled in by an energy flux, completely by accident. We didn't have the correct protocols in place. The portal wasn't ready, the energy wasn't harnessed properly. It ripped her apart. Wrong place, wrong time." He paused, then continued in a calmer voice. "Her consciousness went through but her body got bounced back, and the whole system collapsed...

and not just the portal. The whole thing was affected. The Worldforce is pure energy, electricity unbridled. And Lily was a short-circuit, a live wire sparking out of control. She was trapped. No body, just consciousness, stuck in the void, unable to fully enter – do you get it now? Once I realized that, I knew we needed a dual-born, someone to straddle the worlds and pull her back."

"But if her body–"

"I can *make* her a body!" Nigel shouted. "Don't you listen? My first console would have been capable of that, especially with access to Arameth's energy to power it. But without her mind, without her soul, there's nothing to put *in* it. I needed her pulled back through, but the system was unstable. And I realized only one who carried energies from both worlds could stabilize the magic and fix what we'd done. But there were no dual-borns here; someone had to go back through and get one. I couldn't go back myself, because I'd already had to tweak the programming to get myself through after the collapse, and there were... consequences. I wasn't able. But Marcus–"

Lex felt like his head was swimming. "Marcus?"

"People from our world were never meant to cross over to this one. The portal had destabilized the Worldforce and Arameth was suffering for it. The Worldforce sees us as foreign bodies – as viruses. And with both me and Lily stuck here in Arameth, the Worldforce was reacting like an immune system on overdrive. It started small, just some bad weather and ground tremors, but the Ancients predicted it would get worse. Tsunamis, earthquakes, random bursts of electricity bolting down from the sky – they said it would be like the apocalypse. So they sent Marcus to help me fix it. He agreed to go through in my place, to find Samantha, since she was the dual-born who'd helped us open the rift. But there were complications. Samantha was dying and couldn't come. But *she* could." He paused. "Marcus was just a child when we sent him, really. We never should have put so much on him. He was only twelve, even if he was a Prince of the Ancients. But he was the one chosen to go, and we needed her."

"Who?" Lex asked.

Nigel's wild, dark eyes locked on Lex's. "Jana. Samantha's granddaughter."

"Jana was from your world, too?" Some of the glimpses were starting to click together, but Lex's understanding was like a puzzle with half the pieces missing.

"Yes," Nigel said, "but Marcus refused to bring her."

"Why?" Lex asked.

"Because his own family had sent him across dimensions with no help at all, even though he was only twelve, and he ended up lost and starving for weeks on end, and Jana found him on the streets and helped him and he spent three years living in that world and falling in love with her without telling her anything about any of it and he didn't want her to have to be a part of this. Then when he hesitated to bring her back, they sent an Aiac to kill a member of the foster family who'd taken him in, and then threatened to kill everyone else Marcus cared about if he didn't hand her over." Nigel stopped and shrugged. "Can't say I blame him for his lack of compliance. It wasn't a very inspirational form of persuasion. He came back without her."

"But I saw her. " Lex paused. "In one of my glimpses."

"Glimpses?" Nigel questioned.

"I have visions, like memories, but they aren't mine. They're from Marcus."

"Really?" Nigel asked, lifting his eyebrows. "That's interesting. How long has this been happening?"

"Since I woke up," Lex said.

"You mean here? It's only been a few minutes."

"No, I mean since I *woke up*. At Dalton. It was days ago, but... I don't remember anything before that at all."

Nigel stared at him. "That's *very* interesting," he said. "Anyway, to answer your question, if you've been seeing Marcus' memories, then certainly you saw Jana. Marcus was a bit obsessed. You may have even seen her in his memories from *here*, since the silly girl came anyway."

"What?"

"Apparently everyone back home thought Marcus had run away, after the death of his little brother. His foster family didn't blame him; officially the death was ruled as SIDS. But the police thought he might have blamed himself since he was the first to find him. Jana didn't buy it. She thought he'd been kidnapped. When she found Samantha's version of the console and realized what it did, she jumped straight through after him." He shook his head. "Stupid girl. If she hadn't been a dual-born, even with my tweaks it would have exploded her into a million pieces. In any case, we were wrong. Having her here didn't solve the problem. It made it worse."

"How?" Lex asked.

"Immune system on overdrive, remember?" Nigel said. "She wasn't strong enough to stabilize the energy."

Lex's thoughts were spinning, but one took precedence, the same question which was always present. "What about me?" he asked.

"You?" Nigel snorted, then walked toward Lex's chair and pulled something out from under it. "You were never meant to be."

"What?" Lex said, his pulse speeding.

"But don't worry; I can show you," Nigel said, standing. He shoved a dull, metallic box into Lex's lap. The console. "Now, where were those... Ah, yes," Nigel murmured. He unrolled a long cord from the back of the console and drug it toward the nearest wall, where he plugged it into an outlet.

*Outlets? Here?* Lex wondered. He'd only seen them in his glimpses. *Glimpses of the other world,* he suddenly realized. Memories from when Marcus had been there. Suddenly something occurred to him.

"Nigel, you said you had to find where the two worlds touched in order to make the breach. Where was that?"

"My attic," Nigel said, still fiddling with the outlet. "Weird, right? But they say those connected to the Worldforce are drawn toward it. My wife chose the house."

*The outlet. The Aiac bringing me here.* Something still wasn't making sense. "Why are we here, then?" Lex asked.

"Please tell me you mean that literally and not existentially. I simply do not have the time," Nigel replied. He looked up. "You mean why did the Aiac bring you *here*? Why not anywhere else in the wide, crazy world?" He shrugged. "Like I said, it's my attic. Or Arameth's version of it, anyway. On my side, it has a lot more windows." He stood. "Now, we don't have a television screen on this side of the breach, but what we need to do will work just the same, you being you." He moved back in front of Lex.

Lex looked down. The light on the console lit red.

Nigel knelt, his pointer finger hovering over a button on the front of the console. "Are you ready to know what you are?" he asked, looking up at Lex.

"Yes," Lex said, feeling something steel inside him.

"Good!" Nigel said with a grin, and pushed the button.

# CHAPTER 13

The calendar on the wall said *2002 – June.*

Lex was in a dim, wood-paneled room, motes of dust floating in slants of light from the narrow windows.

An old man knelt on the floor, hunched over something.

Lex approached, and as he reached out to the man he was pulled in, his own awareness blending with the other's. *Luther Alvari. 72. Scientist. Genius. Grandfather.*

Luther Alvari's old heart was jackhammering. He took one long, deep breath and then another, willing it to slow. *Calm, old man*, he told himself. *You can't save anyone if you die of a heart attack first.* Another deep breath. "Breathe, baby girl," he hissed. "Breathe."

Lex looked down. A girl's small body hung limp in Luther's arms.

Luther hovered his cheek over her face, his stomach twisting. *Just one soft, little breath*, he willed. *Just one puff on my cheek.* Nothing came. He lowered her to the floor and sank back onto the ground. He knew there was nothing that could help her now, not CPR or any other medical means. This was not a medical problem. This was something *other*.

Luther raised up onto his knees again, studying her. His Lily. She seemed so small now with her lifeless body sprawled on the attic floor, her wispy blonde waves spread out like a crown of feathers about her, more and more life seeping from her little frame by the moment. His eyes drifted over her slender fingers, peeking out from the sleeves of her favorite purple sweater – she always complained Luther kept the house too cold – and her bare feet protruding beneath the ends of her jeans, her stubby toes so much like her grandmother's. Her delicate, perfect face, blue eyes closed as if sleeping. He could almost believe she would open them any second, and give him her usual, goofy smile...

"She's only nine!" Luther cried out suddenly. "God, help me; she's only nine!" It was not a mindless expression; he was calling out to someone, to anyone... but there was no answer. He looked at her face – so *still*. "I'm sorry," he whispered. "I didn't know you were home." He let his face fall onto her unmoving chest. His Lily, his beloved granddaughter. Only nine, and gone.

And it was all his fault.

Lex was pulled backward.

He was kneeling on a wooden floor, frantically pulling out boxes from a pile.

"Marcus?" a voice called up. "Did you find it?"

"Almost, Mrs. Martin," he answered. He shoved the console into a large, dusty box far back in the corner and folded the top closed, then began piling the other boxes on top of it. *They'll never think to look for it in their own house, right?* he thought. Or this could be a huge mistake. But he didn't have many options. "Got it! Coming down!" He placed the last box on the pile then grabbed the dust-layered catcher's mitt he'd found in the first box and headed back down the attic ladder.

Jana's mom was waiting for him below. "Always makes me nervous when you kids go up there," she said.

Marcus paused, one foot still on the ladder. "I didn't know anyone went up there."

She waved a hand. "Oh, not very often. Jana does now and then when she needs to pull out something from storage."

Marcus stepped down and folded the ladder back up. It was too late, now. He'd try to sneak back in later and move it somewhere safer.

"I always worry about spiders," Jana's mom continued. "Anyway, what were you looking for up there, anyway? You said it was something for a school project, but Jana didn't mention anything."

Marcus held out the mitt. "It's for history," he said, knowing Jana had a different history teacher. "A presentation on the history of my favorite sport. I thought an old mitt would be a good way of showing how the sport has continued through multiple generations. Jana said her grandfather had one stored up there."

"What an interesting idea," she smiled. "Though I'm surprised your dad didn't have one. Didn't he play baseball in college?"

"I wanted more than one," Marcus said, "to show the widespread impact."

Mrs. Martin nodded. "I like your creativity," she said, then winked. "I hope you get an *A*."

"Thanks," he said, giving her a smile. "I'd better get home."

"I'll tell Jana you stopped by," she said.

"No need," Marcus replied, holding his smile in place. "I'll see her at school tomorrow." The pain of that lie clenched his chest.

Mrs. Martin looked up at the attic door. "It's a shame about that old video game," she said. "Jana was so excited when her father found it." She turned back to Marcus. "But of course that doesn't matter; we're all just so glad you're safe. Being in the room when those thugs broke in must have been terrifying. No one blames you for running home–" She paused. "Oh, I'm so sorry. I nearly forgot that was the same day that Gabe–" She reached out and stroked his hair. "You know we think of you as family, too, right? If you ever need–"

Marcus felt the walls closing in on him. "Thanks," he said. "I need to go."

He rushed out of the house.

Lex was pulled backward.

Jana sat on the edge of her bed, the tulle of her prom dress pluming up around her, staring at a box on her bedroom floor. Her therapist had said prom would be good for her, doing a normal teenage thing.

She was starting to think *normal* just didn't work for her.

She leaned over and pulled back the top of the box. There it was – the console. She still didn't understand how it had ended up in a box in the attic. Hadn't it been stolen *that* day? The thieves, Marcus' brother, her grandmother's dead, then Marcus disappearing... it all seemed so long ago, a lifetime rather than just a couple years. When she'd found the console while looking for her grandmother's old dance heels, she'd been stunned. For some reason she'd brought it down to her room without even mentioning it to her parents. Just looking at it brought back a flood of memories: Hot Pockets. Steve. *Marcus*.

But then *everything* reminded her of Marcus. That was the problem.

She reached inside the box and pulled out the console. Something stirred inside her, a sharp flutter like razor-edged wings. She gasped and leapt to her feet, the console under one arm, and rushed to the small television in the corner of her bedroom. She crouched in a panic to attach the wires and cords of the video game. It was like a primal urge, a *must* felt deep within. She clicked the last cable into place, grabbed the controller, and reached toward the console's power button.

The doorbell rang. "Jana!" Her mom's voice called out.

Jana jumped up, dropping the controller on the floor. Steve was here, and they'd be late if she didn't get down there. She hated being late; it only made people stare more. But at least she was going with Steve. She would never have even considered going without him, even if she had once imagined her prom date being someone else.

She grabbed up her small purse, sliding a lipstick into it, and glanced into the mirror. "Marcus gone," she told her reflection. "He isn't coming back." She smoothed back some stray hairs with one hand, and gave herself a stiff smile. "You are going to have a *magical* time. The best night of your life." She nodded once, then strode toward the door.

Lex was pulled backward.

Marcus knelt on a hard floor in a dark room. An Aiac stood on either side of him. In front of him, out of sight in the shadows, stood something else.

"Tell me again!" snapped a cold voice.

"I'm to kill him," Marcus said.

"Before…?"

"Before he fulfills the conditions of the prophecy."

"And if you don't?" the voice asked.

"You will kill me," Marcus answered.

"And?"

"And anyone in this world or the other I care about."

"It's good to see you were listening." The voice let out a laugh, then cut off suddenly. "Now get out of my sight."

Marcus bowed his head, then stood. "Yes, Mistress."

Lex was pulled backward.

Marcus stood in the shadows of the trees, just out of the shaft of moonlight slipping down through the canopy, watching Acarius sleep.

*Do it now*, he told himself. *It's already been too long.*

He took a breath and lifted the knife, watching the moonlight ricochet off it. Light, redirected, bounced from tree to tree as he turned it. He lowered the knife.

*Jana. Mom. Dad. Mrs. Martin. Mr. Martin. Steve.* The names he recited to remember why he was doing this, why he even cared. *Steve. Mom. Dad. Mrs. Martin. Mr. Martin. Jana. Jana. Jana.*

Jana would hate him if she knew what he was about to do.

He took a step.

After tonight, he would hate himself.

*He's my friend.*

He lowered the knife.

*This isn't who I am.*

The knife fell from his fingers into the dirt.

He kicked it toward the trees. *Curse Ardis, the prophecy, the Ancients, all of it.* They didn't own him. They couldn't control him.

*She'll kill them all.*

He wouldn't let that happen.

He would find another way.

A blinding light split the night sky.

In the clearing, Acarius startled up to his feet in an instant. "What's happening?" he shouted. "Marcus?"

Marcus ran toward him, squinting against the sudden brightness. "I don't know," he said. "Let's go; hurry!"

He turned toward the trees.

The light slid inward, vanishing into a sliver just as a shape stepped out of it.

Marcus stared and blinked. Was it really–

"Jana?"

Lex was pulled backward.

"What's happening to her?" Marcus shouted. He knelt over Jana's body as it shook, her eyes rolled up in her head.

"A seizure," Nigel said. "It should stop in a moment."

Marcus cradled his arm behind Jana's skull, protecting it. Jana's body relaxed, her breathing evening out. She was asleep now, like before. He slipped his arm from behind her head. "I *know* it was a seizure," Marcus said. "She had one yesterday. What I'm asking is *why*."

"I told you before; she's destabilizing. Travel affects dual-borns differently, since the portal uses their energy to power itself. We had no way of knowing quite *how* much, since Jana was the first dual-born to actually come through. I had hoped for a different outcome."

Marcus turned to Nigel with a cold stare. "Fix it," he said.

Nigel's mouth dropped open. "Marcus," he said after a moment. "Don't you think I would if I could?"

Marcus knelt down beside Jana again, turning his back on Nigel. "Leave," he said. "Please."

Nigel slipped out through the tent door.

Lex was pulled backward.

Nigel paced in an empty tent. "The lips the teeth the tip of the tongue the lips the teeth the tip of the tongue the lips the teeth the–"

"Can you stop that?" Marcus snapped, pushing open the flap.

"Sorry," Nigel said, turning toward him. "It helps me focus."

Marcus peered in at him and sighed. "I'm sorry. I just–"

"I know," Nigel said softly.

Marcus let the flap drop closed and moved away from the tent.

*Focus,* Nigel told himself. *Focus.* "The lips the teeth the – LEX Protocol!" he shouted.

Hurried footsteps neared the tent and Marcus stuck his head back through. "What?"

Nigel threw up his arms. "LEX Protocol!" he yelled again. He spun toward the tent door. "The console, where is it?"

"Right where you–"

"Bring it. Hurry!"

Marcus ran off.

Nigel bounced on his heels and clapped, then went still. "You're getting rusty, old man," he told himself. "You should have thought of this long ago."

"Now, now," he answered himself. "You are seventy-eight years old, not to mention the stress on your mental capacities from traveling through a portal into another dimension. Go easy on yourself."

"Easy? Never!" he called out. "That would make me soft!"

Marcus stepped in, holding out the console and another small box.

"Thank you," Nigel said, grabbing it from him. "Now get out and let me work."

Marcus let the flap swing closed behind him, leaving Nigel alone.

Nigel dropped to the floor and set down the console, then opened the box and pulled out a keyboard, a portable monitor, and a small, plastic cube. "Battery backup still charged. Good, good. Attach the cables. Powering up, why is it so slow, oh there it goes, command screen, yes, yes, everything's here." His fingers flew across the keyboard.

__*Access: core*
__*Core: Program LEX*
__*Program LEX: Override*
__*Override: All*

He peered at the monitor, waiting while the system processed the language he had created to control it. The cursor at the end of "*All*" blinked once. Twice. The screen flickered.

He took a breath.

*Initiating Override* The words appeared on the monitor.

The screen flickered.

A bright light flashed.

Nigel's victorious laugh rang out in the tent.

Lex was pulled backward.

Marcus lay on the ground, staring up at the sky. His body felt like lead. Every breath was a struggle. He looked to the side. Jana's blue eyes gaped at him. *No,* he told himself. *No. Not like this.* He reached inside, found that familiar whisper of darkness, and ripped it wide open.

Lex was pulled backward.

He floated in a void of nothingness, of blackness and silence and the great empty chasm of not-being. He was in Marcus' mind again – except Marcus' mind was a thing dispersed, just barely holding substance. Lex strained to pull the bits together, to focus.

"Is he – " he heard a voice say. *Lytira.*

"No. No!" *Acarius.*

"Move aside!" *Nigel.*

Scuffling. Movement.

"Let's hope this works." *Nigel.* "I reset the protocol a couple years ago, but channeling this much will fry the– "

"What are you saying?" *Acarius.*

"We only have one shot." *Nigel.*

"Do it." *Acarius.*

A beep.

"What is it– " *Acarius.*

"Is it supposed to– " *Lytira.*

"Everybody get back!" *Nigel.*

A deafening boom shook the void, followed by static.

Then silence.

*Marcusssss.* A voice hissed, a sound of ice and danger.

"No," Lex heard Marcus say. "Leave me alone. No!"

*Calm.* Another voice spoke, flooding the void with warmth.

The first voice fled.

*Safe now,* spoke the second voice.

"Safe," Marcus echoed.

*Safe,* the voice replied.

Marcus sank into silence.

Lex was pulled backward.

He was still in nothingness.

*Sulanashum.* The word hissed by, like a snake in passing.

Silence.

*Speak the prophecy,* a warm voice prompted.

Lex spoke. "I – I can't remember."

*Sulanashum.* A chorus of voices.

"What is that? I don't–"

*It is time. You are ready.*

Lex was pulled backward.

He was falling through nothingness again, only this time he *knew* he had done this before. Something flashed bright to the right of him. He glanced over.

*Amelia.* She blinked into being just beside him, then was gone.

In the darkness, Lex felt something approaching, like a surface flying up to meet him. He braced himself for impact.

His world burst apart.

There were screams, and feet running, then a man's voice. "Is that–"

"Grab him!" a gravelly voice commanded.

The pinch of fingers digging into his arms surprised Lex – he was back in a body. Why couldn't he see anything? He tried to force his eyes open, but they wouldn't move.

"What about the girl?" another man asked.

"She's not important. Let her go," said the gravelly voice.

Lex's body felt limp, out of his control. The air around him smelled like smoke.

"We've got you, demon," someone growled against his ear. He felt himself being dragged, then a second set of hands grabbed his ankles.

"Tie him up in the shed," the gravelly voice said. "And you – fetch Earl. Quickly!"

He felt his mind sink away, falling into blackness.

He was pulled backward.

Lex blinked his eyes open. He was back in the chair in the Aracthea Inn, with Nigel still in front of him.

Nigel smiled. "Welcome back."

Lex shook his head, trying to make sense of what he'd just been through. He felt as if part of him were still moving while the rest was stationary. "How did I–"

"The Worldforce carries residual consciousness from those who have passed through it," Nigel said, crouching in front of him. "They're like emotional imprints. They fade over time, but the strongest ones stay longest." As he talked, he lifted Lex's eyelids one by one, examining his eyes, then peered into each of Lex's ears. "Not everyone can see them; our brains simply can't function on the right wavelengths to process them. For most, the travel feels like being sucked through a dark tunnel. We can't see what's really around us." He moved back to stand in front of Lex. "But you – well, you have Worldforce *in* you, now, so – I'm guessing you're able to see them when you make contact with it. And you spent so long there after your death, I imagine you left behind quite the catalog of your own imprints, too."

"Worldforce *in* me?" Lex asked. "I don't–"

"Yes, well, it's part of the process. The console meshes its programming with the Worldforce's energy to create the portal. Ordinarily, whoever's passing through is moving too quickly for any of the Worldforce to soak into them. But you were practically swimming in it for quite some time. You were bound to take some of it in. At least, that was the theory." He paused, and leaned in toward Lex's face. "Was I right? Did you see what you needed to see?"

Lex stared at him. "I don't know." What *had* he seen? What did it mean? He took a shaky breath. "I mean, yes, I saw things. But I– I mean– I think–" He paused. There were so many pieces, but he felt a certainty, a knowing he had lacked before.

Nigel leaned even closer. "Who are you?" he asked.

"Marcus." The word escaped before Lex could even process it.

Nigel clapped his hands. "Yes!" he shouted. "I knew you'd see! It's so much better to realize for yourself who you are than to have someone else force it on you, isn't it?" He leaned forward. "Officially, you're Prince Marculian, firstborn son of the former king of Arameth and the only heir of the last living family of Ancients," he stated. "Or at least you were. Now you're the 'son of prophecy,' best I can figure, so I guess none of the other stuff matters much anymore. Took me long enough to puzzle that out, though."

"Wait... *former* king? Son of prophecy?" Lex asked.

"Yes," nodded Nigel. "The monarchy was dismantled in the Great Wars over a century ago, but your father refuses to acknowledge that. He's carrying on the family line of royalty as if anyone cares." He laughed. "I suppose some do. The rest of the world, of course, doesn't care that the Ancients were endowed as the rulers of Arameth because they don't even know Ancients exist. It was part of the peace-arrangement – to wipe all memory of magic from the peoples' minds so they would stop attacking anyone magic-born. It worked, mostly... at least until you showed up. Things have gone a bit crazy since then. People seem to think you're a demon in service to Ardis, which is a bit of a sign their memories are returning, since Ardis is a goddess worshipped by Ancients exclusively... not that her power isn't far-reaching. Oh, and yes, your sudden rebirth *clearly* makes you the son of prophecy – *Sulanashum*. It's not like just any one can come back from the dead."

*Sulanashum.* A flurry of half-knowings swirled in Lex's mind, like an old song he knew but couldn't quite remember the words to. They teased at him, but eluded his grasp.

Nigel watched Lex with interest.

The knowings continued to bounce around in Lex's head, almost making sense, like a sentence cut up into words then blown about by a breeze.

"Come to think of it," Nigel continued, "after your display at Alowen, the Aiacs must know who you are, *and* that you fulfilled the prophecy you'd been sent to destroy. Ardis had sworn to kill you for not slaying Acarius, only you died before she could, so... I'd guess she'll be coming for you. Anyway, I've been holding this for you." He reached in his tunic and pulled out a silver ring, topped with a dark blue stone.

Lex took it with shaky hands and slipped it onto his right ring finger. It fit perfectly.

"You're the son of prophecy now," Nigel said, "but I suppose part of you is still the prince." He looked up at the ceiling. "You know, maybe you always *were* the son of prophecy, and just had to become not-yourself in order to become what you truly are. Huh. It's so hard to tell with prophecies." He looked back at Lex and shrugged. "Do *you* know?"

Lex shook his head. "I remember more now, but it doesn't feel like *me*. It's like I'm still seeing Marcus' memories, but I'm someone else. Someone separate."

"Him and not him, yes, of course," Nigel nodded. "You are who you were before but also someone new. Fascinating! You would be a scientific marvel, if science could explain this. Actually, I suppose it can, since I created the technology which caused it. I just haven't figured out the terminology yet. Who knew that technology could alter prophecy? Or is it the other way around?"

"But how?" Lex asked.

"LEX Protocol," said Nigel. "Didn't you see?"

"Some," Lex answered. "But what was it?"

Nigel's face turned serious. "A failsafe, and quite a clever one, though not without its flaws. It was a backup, so to speak – an agreement between my code and the Worldforce."

Lex stared.

"You still don't– Ah, I know. Yes. Think of it this way. If the portal was me knocking on the Worldforce's door, the LEX Protocol was my offer to jump out a window... as long as it would catch me. See?"

Lex shook his head slowly.

Nigel sighed. "I told you that when I came through the portal, there were consequences, an impact on me, yes?"

"Yes."

"One of those impacts was that the Worldforce and I are... let's say *linked*. It is more clear that way. Yes, *linked*."

"What does that mean?"

"It talks to me," Nigel said. "And I to it. When Jana destabilized and the Worldforce started going berserk, I sent it a request: 'Spare me, if ever I come to you. Make me part of yourself.' Though in much more numeric words, of course."

"I don't understand," Lex said.

"LEX Protocol was only ever meant to work once," Nigel said. "*Lex* means 'law,' you see, in Latin. Well, 'rule,' actually, but it amounts to the same in this case. It was the law of our agreement. And it was meant to work on *me*. I thought, if the worst happened, at least I could spend my final years there in the Worldforce – with Lily. It was my retirement plan, if you will. Only, in the end, we had to send you instead."

"But why?" Lex whispered.

"Because you are *Sulanashum*, clearly, though at the time we were attempting something else entirely. Fate is a backwards thing, it seems. In any case, you are who you were but you are also who you were not, and the *who* you are now is not quite the *who* you were before. Think of yourself as Marcus 2.0, a caterpillar turned butterfly... or moth, if you prefer the fuzzy back and feathery antennae; I rather do. You are a metamorphic being, a new creation, a–"

"Lex?" Lex offered.

"Yes, exactly." He smiled. "A Lex. It's a good name, isn't it? Lucky I didn't name the protocol something clunkier. Anyway, you'd best get used to it. There's no going back now, though I suppose you could change your name if you really wanted to. I do have to say, you look remarkably good for someone who's been dead for seven years... not to mention that you aged backwards."

"What?" Lex asked.

"You were missing for seven years, didn't you know? We all thought you'd just died and then exploded into bits so small they evaporated, which given the circumstances didn't seem all that unreasonable. We hoped at least part of you had made it through, but then nothing happened, so we reasoned probably not."

Lex stared. *Seven years.* Seven years since since Marcus – no, *he*, himself – had experienced any of the things he'd seen. Seven years between death and waking up at Dalton. Had he really just been floating in the void that long? He had no memory of it.

Nigel peered at him. "The age reversion is really astonishing. I mean, the science of it is one thing, but to actually see it in person..." He grabbed Lex's chin and tipped his face to the side, examining it. "You were nineteen when you died, but now I'm guessing what, seventeen?"

Lex pulled out of Nigel's grasp and nodded, remembering the certainty he'd had about his age when he'd first awoken in Dalton.

"Thought so," said Nigel, backing up a step. "After all, that's when the anomaly occurred which forced me to reset the protocol. I tweaked it later to include a separate algorithm for you and each of the others, just in case, but you were nearby when I did the initial reset. It must have locked in your bio-data for that moment in time then pieced you back together when you exploded, which is fascinating, actually, because I never expected the protocol to result in any kind of corporcal–"

"Wait," Lex interrupted. "When I exploded?"

"Yes, didn't I already say that? As you died, you sent out a burst of dark energy for who-knows-what-reason, then you exploded. I'd only just activated the LEX Protocol, so I'd say you survived by about a nanosecond or so. How's that for good timing?"

Lex thought about the battle at Alowen, the dark whisper he'd felt. "Dark energy?" he asked.

"Your birthright power," Nigel answered. "Every Ancient has one. Yours was dark energy, power over death."

Lex blinked. "What?"

"Death-powers," Nigel said. "That's what you had. Have? Had. I mean... unless you still have them. Do you?"

Lex ignored the question, because he had one of his own. "If I had power over death, then... why did I die?"

Nigel laughed. "It wasn't like that. You couldn't *stop* death. You could cause it. To others. Or maybe to yourself, though I'm fairly sure you never tried. It was more a transfer of energy. You could drain others to charge yourself up. I never did figure out quite what you were charging up *for*, but draining your enemies turned out to be excruciatingly painful to them and usually resulted in them collapsing unconscious or dying, so that was fairly useful. But you could only target a few at a time. Fortunately, you had palace battle training, so you always just killed the rest the ordinary way."

"Oh," Lex said, his mind swimming.

"Anyway," Nigel said, "when Jana began to completely destabilize, we—"

"Wait," Lex said. Something startling had just occurred to him. "You said she destabilized from passing through the Worldforce when she used the portal, right?"

"Yes," Nigel said, stretching the word into three syllables.

"What if someone *else* came through, like a normal human? What would it do to them?"

"What it did to me, of course," Nigel said. He shuddered. "I do not recommend it."

*Oh no*, Lex thought.

Nigel studied Lex's face, then said slowly. "Why do you ask? Has another come through?"

"Yes," Lex said, his heart sinking. "I think so."

Nigel jumped up and began to pace. "This is not good, not good at all," he said. "The Worldforce here in Arameth is already unstable from the last breach, and another Earthborn coming through could be disastrous. Not to mention the impact it could have on the person. Did this person seem to be in pain at all? Unhinged? Suffering?"

"No," Lex said. "Well, not mostly. But she was... electric. I mean, there was an energy about her, like touching a frayed wire."

"That's... odd," said Nigel. "But probably also terrible. Why did she come here? Did she reveal her purposes to you?"

"She said she came here by accident."

Nigel shook his head. "Impossible. She would have to be working with The Gatekeepers. It takes one who possesses the power of the Ancients to even activate the console, and they monitor the full lineage."

"Daughter of power," Lex murmured. He turned to Nigel. "It's what the Aiacs called her."

Nigel went still. "What is her name?" he asked.

"Amelia," Lex said.

Nigel stared. "Are you certain?"

"Yes," Lex said. "At least, I think so. She's lied to me before, but I think she was honest about that."

"Huh," Nigel said, shrugging. "There goes that theory. In any case, she could be in great danger. We must find her immediately."

The door to the room burst open.

Acarius barreled in, glanced around, and stopped on Nigel. His eyes went wide. "You!" he shouted.

Nigel leaned toward Lex and raised one hand in front of his mouth, as though to keep Acarius from reading his lips. "We had a bit of a misunderstanding a few years ago," he whispered loudly to Lex.

"You tried to kill me!" Acarius yelled. He stormed toward them.

Nigel straightened and dropped his hand, meeting Acarius' glare. "The prophecy said the one to save Arameth would have to die and be reborn. How was I to know you weren't the right one? If I recall, *you're* the one who said you were to be the 'prophesied son,' or whatever nonsense."

"'Son of prophecy,' and I *know* you know what it's called. But don't try to distract me. You tried to *kill* me!"

Nigel shrugged. "In my defense, I thought you'd come back to life. Besides, you aren't dead. Look, here you are!"

Acarius glared at him, then his eyes fell on the console in Lex's lap. "Wait. What did you do?"

Nigel held up his hands. "Don't ask me," he said, nodding toward Lex. "*He's* the one who came back from the dead."

Acarius narrowed his eyes.

Lex looked between them, then set the console down on the floor and stood. His mind felt claustrophobic, too many thoughts crowding in on him. "Acarius, I... did you know?"

Acarius' stern face melted into something like remorse. "Yes. I'm sorry, Lex. I wasn't sure at first, and then once you told me about the glimpses, I realized... but I thought it best to wait until you were ready to know. I didn't want to overwhelm you."

Lex glanced at Nigel. *He* clearly hadn't shared that concern. Lex's head spun with all the memories suddenly poured into it, his own past and the pasts of others. He had a whole previous life, and somehow it all led to *this*, to him being brought back as Lex... how was he supposed to process that? What did it even mean?

Acarius moved toward him. "Listen, I–" He paused. "I really am sorry. Marcus and I... *you* and I... we were best friends. I would never do anything to harm you. I know I lied, but I was trying to protect you. I'm sorry."

Lex wanted to be mad, but... *would* he have been able to handle the truth sooner? He wasn't sure. Maybe it really had been for the best. He looked at Acarius. "Please don't lie to me again."

"Never again," Acarius answered. "I promise. I hope you can still trust me."

Lex didn't know Acarius well, but somewhere deep in him, Marcus did. He nodded, and Acarius' concerned face relaxed into a smile.

"I know you must have a lot of questions," Acarius said. "Maybe we could–"

Lex cut him off. "Thanks. I definitely want to talk about some things later. But right now, please, tell me what happened after I was taken. Where's Amelia?" He had plenty of questions, and hopefully he could sort through them later, but what Nigel said about Amelia was making him anxious.

Acarius looked surprised, but didn't argue. "She's with Lytira. After you got knocked out, we rushed over just in time to see an Aiac swoop down and grab you. I jumped on Mare to go after you, but Amelia was acting strangely, muttering about monsters. She started shaking. We thought the Aiac taking you had pushed her over the edge. Lytira put her on a horse and took her down to Alta, where our friends from Merik'esh headed after things there went south. I came here, after you." He put his hand on Lex's shoulder. "Don't worry, Lex, I'm sure she's fine. It's probably just shock. Those who aren't used to battle seem to get it the worst. But Zenora is in Alta – the healer from Merik'esh. She'll be able to help her."

"I don't think it's shock," Nigel said.

"Why not?" Acarius asked.

Lex turned to him. "She's–"

The door burst open again and Lytira skidded into the room, panting. Her eyes took in everything at once, then she turned to Lex. "It's Amelia," she said. "Hurry." She ran back out through the door.

Lex spun to follow her, but Nigel grabbed his arm. "Wait, Lex," he said. "In the void, did you see Lily? Was she there?"

Lex's heart squeezed at the desperation in Nigel's eyes. "No," he said. "I'm sorry."

"Right," Nigel said. "No matter. Now come on, we need to help Amelia!" He gestured toward the door.

"Lex," Acarius called warily from out in the stairwell, dragging his name out, "you may want to hurry..."

Lex ran through the doorway.

# CHAPTER 14

L ex raced down the stairs behind Acarius and out into the inn's dining area. It was empty of patrons. Lytira knelt on the floor between the tables, her hand propping up Amelia's head.

Amelia was on the floor, seizing.

Lex rushed toward Amelia, but before he could reach her she took one heaving breath, then went still. Lex dropped to his knees beside her. "Is she–" He placed his fingers on her face beneath her nose. She was breathing. She was also fire-hot. He yanked his fingers away and turned to Acarius. "What does she need? What do we do?"

Acarius shook his head. "I don't know."

Lytira turned toward Acarius. "This isn't like Jana," she said. "When Amelia seized, it threw both of us off the horse. I mean, *threw* us, like we'd been struck by lightning. It was a full minute before I could even push myself off the ground to get to her, and by then she was like this. She goes still, then every few minutes there's another attack. We didn't even make it to Alta, but I don't think Zenora would have been able to help with this, anyway."

"There has to be *something* we can do," Lex shouted. "Anything!"

Acarius clenched his jaw. "Lyt," he said, turning to Lytira, "I think–"

"No," she said firmly. "No. Absolutely not."

She and Acarius stared at each other for a moment, then Lytira's shoulders slumped. "Ugh," she groaned, throwing her head back. "You're right. It's the best chance we've got."

Lex looked between them. "What is?" he asked.

"Zeriphath," Lytira said, "the home of my people. They have the best healers in the land for... this sort of thing. Not that there's ever been one quite like this, but still, they may know what to do to help her."

"I thought your people were at Alowen," Lex said.

Lytira shook her head. "That was my clan of *choice*, the one I joined when I came of age. But Zeriphath is my birth-clan." She sighed. "Father will not be pleased to see me."

Lex bit down on his question, feeling it was not the right time.

"Let's go then," Acarius said. "I have a feeling Amelia's only going to get worse if we wait, and Zeriphath is not close by." He knelt down and reached for Amelia, to help Lex lift her.

"I've got her," Lex said. He slid his arms beneath Amelia's neck and knees and stood. She was heavier than she looked, but not too much for him to carry.

"Mare's outside, and Lytira's horse should be, too," Acarius said. "Let's go."

"Wait," said Lytira, reaching out to him. "On my way to Alta, I passed a group from Merik'esh, some of ours. They'd heard something about your sisters."

Acarius stilled. "What was it?"

"They all made it to the agreed place, but there were problems getting there. Someone was hurt. Not badly, but they sent a message for you to come as soon as you could."

Acarius' eyes fell closed. "Did they say if Liz was still with them?" he asked.

Lytira nodded. "She is."

He sighed and opened his eyes. "Then they'll be alright for another few days. I'll go to them after we get Lex and Amelia to Zeriphath."

"Are you sure?" Lytira asked. "I could take Lex and Amelia by myself."

Acarius gave her a sad smile. "I know you could," he said. "But I would never ask you to. Let's go."

He pushed open the inn door and strode out, with Lytira right behind him.

Lex followed, holding Amelia in his arms.

"I'll meet you at the stable," Lytira said once outside. "I'm going to grab some supplies."

When they reached the stable behind the inn, Lex glanced around. "Wait, where's Nigel?"

Acarius shrugged. "He tends to come and go whenever it's most convenient for *him*. Anyway, he can take care of himself, but we don't have time to hunt all over the city for him. We need to go."

Lex nodded and let Acarius help him lift Amelia onto one of the horses. Lex mounted behind her, and Acarius climbed onto Mare.

Lytira appeared in the stable door, two huge bundles in tied-up tablecloths slung over her back. She handed one to Acarius, which he balanced in front of him on Mare. Lytira strode to a nearby horse and secured her load to the back of its saddle. "I sure hope they don't mind me borrowing you," she cooed to the horse. "You're a beauty. Perhaps I won't return you."

Lex glanced at her.

She met his gaze. "I didn't mean that, of course," she said, "though we probably won't return *these*." She patted the bulging tablecloth and then swung herself up into the saddle just in front of it. "After all, we are going through The Fallows. We'll need all the supplies we can carry. But I left payment for them."

*The Fallows*. Memories from Marcus surged through him. "Why?" he asked.

Lytira blinked at him. "Because it's the only way to get there." She shrugged. "Let's hope we survive it." She clicked her horse into motion and headed toward the stable doors.

They rode through the hills and stopped by nightfall where the meadow met the desert. The Fallows spread out before them, a barren stretch of moonlit sand which seemed endless in every direction but the way they'd come. The night sky hung over The Fallows like a dark curtain, stars pricking through it like tiny, backlit holes. Nothing was visible on the other side of The Fallows – the other side was too far away.

Lytira moved her horse next to Lex's and pointed to the sky in the distance. "See the purple star?" she asked.

Lex squinted. One star did look almost violet rather than pure white like the others. He nodded.

"That's the gain-star. It's directly above Zeriphath. If we get separated, ride toward that star as quickly as you can. Understand?"

"Why would we get separated?" Lex asked.

She shrugged. "Just a precaution." She turned to Acarius. "Ready?"

"No," he said. "I hate The Fallows."

Mare tossed her mane and whinnied.

"Who doesn't?" Lytira said. "But the only way through is... through. Let's go." She urged her horse onto the sand.

Lex felt the night close down around him. He remembered The Fallows from Marcus' ride – his own ride, he now realized. It hadn't been pleasant. "I've been here before," he muttered. "I remember."

Acarius brought Mare up beside him. "Yes," he said. "You were saving my life."

The memory flashed back – Mare kicking up sand as the two of them raced across The Fallows, dehydrated, exhausted, and moments from collapse. Yes – there was something on Mare's withers in front of him, strapped against her then held by Marcus' own weight as they galloped. A hunched shape. A body. He had not remembered that part before.

Lex looked down at Amelia, secured to his horse in front of him in the same way. Her brown hair spilled down over her face. Lex pushed it back, checking her breathing, which was still shallow but steady. As Lex remembered, riding with an unconscious body had been hard on both Marcus *and* Mare. Had it been hard on Acarius, too?

He asked.

"I had a few bruises, but I lived," Acarius smiled at him. "This time we'll go at as comfortable a pace as we can, but it's best not to linger in The Fallows longer than we have to. Ready?"

*Here we go again,* Lex thought. He nodded.

Acarius led Mare out onto the sand, where Lytira waited. Lex followed.

It seemed like they'd been riding at a steady gait for hours, yet the sun showed no sign of rising. Darkness spread in all directions, and Lex found himself checking often for the purple star to be sure they hadn't veered off course.

After an hour or two more, they slowed down to give the horses a reprieve, but Lytira and Acarius thought it best not to stop completely. They kept their horses at a walk for a while, the horses' hooves struggling as they sank into the sand with each step.

Lex glanced up to check the gain-star again. It was steady in the distance, far out across the sand. Lex blinked. The sand seemed to be shifting, bulging up in places then sinking back down again. *Is it just my eyes playing tricks on me?* he wondered. He focused ahead, only to have his eyes drawn back to the sand around him. The sand was definitely shifting; several bulges rose up then lowered just a few feet from him, as if the sand were beginning to boil. He stopped his horse.

Acarius and Lytira rode ahead, not seeming to notice.

"Guys," Lex called out, his voice ringing through the hollow night. "Something's weird."

The others halted and turned back toward him.

Following Lex's gaze, Acarius tipped his face down toward the sand. His eyes went wide. "*Lytira*!" he yelled.

Lytira snapped her face down toward the ground, then looked back at Lex and Acarius with wild eyes. "Go," she said. "Go. Go!" She turned her horse in the direction of the purple star and kicked it into a gallop.

Lex glanced down again, too curious not to, and realized the sand wasn't bubbling up after all... something was rising from beneath it. All around them.

Acarius looked back over his shoulder. "Lex!" he shouted. "Come on!"

Lex shifted Amelia against his horse's neck and leaned forward over her, kicking his horse into motion.

They had barely gone ten steps before the bulging shapes emerged around them, dark pillars rising from the sand like living statues. The horses reared and halted, suddenly surrounded by columns of black leather which, Lex realized, were actually creatures, their dark wings wrapped tight around them. They emerged in a scattered ring around the three riders, blocking them in, then let out a hideous, unified screech, their wings snapping outward to reveal black, batlike bodies. Lex cried out as the edge of a dark wing swiped his face, slicing it open.

The creatures were large as cows but with furry, two-legged bodies and long, leathery wings tipped with small, clawed hands. They surrounded the riders and their horses, long wings outspread and blocking them in. The one that had sliced Lex leaned toward him. Its face was that of a giant bat but with dark, almost-human eyes. Its thin lips peeled back into a grimace as it eyed him, revealing yellow, needle-like fangs. Lex had the distinct feeling the creature was sneering at him.

Suddenly the creature nearest Lex let out a haunting hoot and shot upward toward the sky. The others followed it upward and the night echoed with their answers to its call as the creatures all circled above the riders.

They screeched again and Lex's horse bolted. He struggled to get control of it while also protecting Amelia from slipping, but the horse was too panicked to slow down. Acarius and Lytira pulled up beside him and his horse calmed slightly, falling into stride with the others. Overhead the creatures followed, continuing to circle above them.

Lex shivered and leaned forward, pressing Amelia tight to his horse and urging the horse to go faster. "What are they?" Lex yelled to Acarius over the sound of the horses' hooves and the creatures' hollow howls above them.

"Wrasseks," Acarius yelled back, then turned to Lytira and called out, "Where do you want to stop?"

The creatures were taking turns diving down at them, as if it were a game.

"Here!" Lytira yelled. Her horse reared as she tugged its reins.

"Why are we stopping?" Lex yelled.

"We could never outrun them," Acarius answered, turning his horse. "We have to fight."

Lytira hopped off her horse into the sand as Acarius and Lex circled back toward her. The creatures were upon Lytira before the others reached her.

Lytira fought the wrasseks with swift grace, the blades of her daggers flashing in the moonlight as though extensions of her arms. One creature crashed to the sand as her dagger struck between its ribs and another dropped as she sliced its throat, but the rest swarmed above her in a raging flock, another swooping down to replace each one that fell.

Acarius paused only a moment before plunging straight into the middle of the swarm. The creatures covered him but he fought from Mare's back, his sword like a glinting blur amid the dark mob, as Lytira stabbed at the creatures from below. They were killing many of the wrasseks but getting battered in the process, and more kept swooping down from the night sky to join the fray. There were just too many of them.

*I have to do something to help*, Lex thought, but he didn't dare leave Amelia unprotected – the creatures could shift their attention to her at any moment – plus he still wasn't fully confident in his sword-craft. Instead, he closed his eyes and went still, reaching for the darkness.

# THE EDGE OF NOTHING

It was there, a small thread hiding in his chest. He gripped it and then opened his eyes, focusing on the wrasseks as he drew it gently outward.

An ear-splitting shriek sliced through the night. Lex almost lost his grip on the dark thread.

Acarius turned to him. "No!" he yelled. "Don't stop!"

Lex re-focused his vision on the creatures as his mind probed inward, adjusting its grip on the darkness. He tightened his mind around it and drew it steadily outward again.

The wrasseks dropped to the ground, their bat-like wings thrashing as their bodies writhed in the sand. Lytira jumped back, and Acarius eased Mare out of the middle of them and dismounted. The wrasseks continued to screech in pain as their bodies flailed in the sand.

Then the creatures fell silent and Lex's vision immediately began to go dark. He swayed, and his arms slipped away from Amelia against his will.

"I've got you," he heard Acarius say as firm hands pushed against his side, steadying him on the horse.

Lex closed his eyes and breathed deeply. "I feel weird," he said.

"It's the dark energy," Lytira said. "It needs release. Bring him down to the ground."

Lex felt himself dragged from the horse and placed in the sand. His head throbbed and his eyelids felt too heavy to open. The darkness was pulsing with him, crushing his lungs. "What's happening to me?" he wheezed.

He felt soft fingers press against his forehead. "You can absorb dark energy, but you are not meant to hold it indefinitely," Lytira said. "If you absorb too much and do not release it, it will destroy you." She paused. "As it did last time."

"To be more specific," Acarius said, "you will explode."

"Acarius!" Lytira chided.

Memories of his time as Marcus flooded in. Those final moments – was that what happened? Had he absorbed so much darkness it ripped him apart from the inside? But no; in those final moments he had pushed it outward purposefully; he remembered that. He had grabbed whatever had been holding it back and intentionally torn it wide open. He had exploded himself *on purpose*. But... why?

Lex felt the darkness inside him receding suddenly. He let it drain away, feeling it all funnel into a condensed space, like a small box within him, upon which he quickly shut the lid. The pain in his head vanished and the weight on his chest lifted. "Actually," Lex said, opening his eyes, "I knew I exploded. Nigel told me that part." He blinked a few times. "I think I'm okay now."

Lytira removed her fingers from his head and stared down at him. "Are you sure?"

Lex pushed himself up to sitting. "Yes, it's gone. I feel fine."

Acarius and Lytira exchanged a look.

"What?" Lex asked.

"That doesn't make sense," Acarius said to Lex. "Marcus – *you* – always had to do something to release the energy when you absorbed too much. Some of it you channeled out while fighting – I never was sure how – but the rest... well, I was too close one time and it felt like being in a small blast. My chin hair didn't grow back for a week." His voice grew thoughtful. "You said it was only a fraction of what you could hold. You called it spill-over." He paused. "Are you sure you feel okay now?"

Lex rolled his shoulders then stood. "Yeah," he said. "I feel fine." He could still feel the small cube of darkness inside him, but it was cold and still, no longer stirring.

Lytira stood too, and peered at him. "Well, you do look better," she said, though her expression was still uncertain. She moved toward her horse. "We should continue our journey. The wrasseks are a bad sign. We still have at least two more days in The Fallows at the pace we've been riding, and more trouble could be coming."

Lex glanced around. The cow-size bodies of batlike creatures littered the ground. "Why are they a bad sign?" he asked. "I mean, they're bad enough by themselves, but... does it mean something?"

"The wrasseks do not live in this part of the world," she said. "If they are here, it means the Aiacs have partnered with Galgor."

"And Galgor is...?"

"A place you should hope never to go." She turned her horse toward the gain-star. "I'm going to ride on a ways and make sure things are clear. I'll wait for you up ahead."

"Lex, are you sure you're okay to ride with Amelia?" Acarius asked as he mounted Mare. "Mare and I could carry her for a bit."

Lex mounted his horse behind Amelia's slumped form and brushed the hair from her face. She looked peaceful, her chest moving in slow breaths as though sleeping. "No, I'm good," he answered.

He and Acarius eased their horses into a steady gait, following the trail Lytira's horse had left in the sand.

They caught up to Lytira and the next few hours were calm riding, though with nothing but sand and darkness for scenery, Lex began to grow bored. No one seemed in the mood for talking. As the night went on – far too long, it seemed – the silence and Lex's concern for Amelia turned his boredom into anxiety. When the morning sun finally broke above the horizon and Acarius announced they should stop to share a small breakfast, Lex sighed in relief.

"We should also get some rest while we can," Lytira said as they dismounted. She handed out small, pressed cakes from the bags that seemed not quite the right consistency to be bread. "The day grows hot quickly, so the morning hours are the best chance we'll have for sleep with any level of comfort. By noon we must be moving again. It is not good to linger too long in any one place in The Fallows."

*They keep saying that,* Lex thought, but he shared their desire to be out of this place. "Okay," he said. The idea of rest seemed prudent, but he was wide awake. "I'll take the first watch while you two get some sleep." He moved Amelia gently to a blanket on the ground and found a water-skin and a pail in one of the bundles. He poured some water onto a cloth and squeezed a few drops into Amelia's mouth, then poured some liquid into the pail and watered his horse and settled down into the sand beside Amelia. He ate his pressed cake while Lytira and Acarius watered their horses then spread blankets on the sand to sleep.

Lex stared out across the desert while his friends slept, his eyes sliding toward Amelia often. As the sun rose higher, the glare across the mustard-colored sand became almost painful and the air seemed to grow twenty degrees hotter. The horses began to shuffle their legs, and their coats were moist with sweat. Lex grabbed a now-warm water-skin from Lytira's bundle and refilled the pail. There were dozens of water-skins inside her bundle. It seemed excessive, but if the rapid warming of the morning was any indication, they'd probably need all of them to make it across The Fallows. But the horses were doing most of the work, and he felt for them. He emptied two whole water-skins into the pail and allowed his horse to drink until the pail was empty before refilling it and moving to the next horse.

Mare was the last horse to drink, and she was gulping up the last of her water when she stiffened and her eyes went wide.

Lex fell still – he could feel it, too, a slight static charge in the air. He set down the pail and looked around. His eyes stopped on Amelia. Her back was arched and she was breathing rapidly, small tremors running through her body in waves.

"Acarius! Lytira!" Lex yelled as he rushed over to Amelia and crouched down beside her.

Acarius was on his feet, sword drawn, too fast for Lex to see how it happened. "What?" he said, his eyes darting around. "Is there–" He stopped as he saw Amelia. "Oh." He moved toward her.

Lytira appeared beside him, tucking her dagger back into its sheath at her belt. "This does not look good," she said, kneeling beside Lex. "It's starting again."

Amelia suddenly fell still. Her body relaxed and her breathing turned slow and steady again.

Lytira stood. "We should be on our way soon. I'm not sure how much time Amelia has."

"Until what?" Lex asked.

Lytira turned to him. "That is the problem. I do not know. Her energy is unique; I haven't seen one like it before."

Acarius placed his hand on Lex's shoulder. "You didn't sleep, and you won't do anyone any good if you're falling off your horse from exhaustion," he said. "Lie down and rest for a bit, and then we'll go. I'll watch over Amelia for you and wake you if anything happens."

Lex could feel weariness coming from the deepest part of his bones, but he couldn't imagine sleeping with Amelia's condition so uncertain. "No, that's alright," he said. "You both need more rest, too, and I don't think I could fall asleep right now. You two lie back down, and I'll wake you when the sun's all the way up so we can go."

After a moment of hesitation, Acarius nodded, and he and Lytira moved back toward their separate blankets.

The next thing Lex knew, Acarius was shaking him awake. Lex sat up, brushing away the sand which crusted his sweaty face. Amelia still slept peacefully on the blanket next to him, though her breathing was a bit more rapid than when he'd last checked.

"It's almost noon," Acarius said, gesturing to the sun above them. "We need to get going." He moved back toward Mare, packing his folded blanket into his bundle. Beside him, Lytira did the same.

Lex turned back toward Amelia, preparing to lift her back onto his horse. Was it his imagination, or was her breathing getting even quicker? He leaned down and brushed her hair back from her face. Her eyes darted side-to-side beneath her closed eyelids. A worm of anxiety worked its way through his chest as he knelt beside her and studied her more closely. Her lips parted, as though she were trying to speak. "Amelia?" Lex whispered.

Mare let out a shrill whinny.

Lex spun around to see a small sinkhole opening up beside the horses. He jumped to his feet. The horses scrambled away from the hole, only to have the new sand beneath their hooves start to crumble, too. The hole was the size of a large washbasin, and was spreading outward.

"Lex!" Acarius shouted, running toward him with Mare at his heels. "We have to go!" He helped Lex lift Amelia onto the horse and secure her, then pulled himself up onto Mare.

Lytira's horse pranced nervously on the other side of the expanding chasm as Lytira mounted it.

Sand poured over the edges of the hole as it grew steadily larger.

"Let's go. Let's go!" Lytira called.

Lex mounted quickly and followed Acarius and Mare in a wide berth around the hole.

Just as they reached Lytira, the ground beneath all of them began to give way. Lytira screamed as her horse's back legs slid into the chasm. Acarius grabbed for its reins, but too much of its weight had already tipped into the gaping hole. The horse's reins slipped out of his reach as it scrambled against the sand with its front legs, but the crumbling ground gave no support. Acarius gripped Mare with his knees and lunged his body sideways, grabbing

Lytira's arm just as her horse lost the last of its footing and toppled backward, disappearing into the abyss. The hole stopped its movement for a moment, as though digesting its prey.

Mare trotted backward away from the edge as Acarius pulled Lytira up onto Mare behind him.

Lex stared at the sinkhole, his heart squeezing at imagining the animal's fate. It had not deserved that.

Lytira shivered, her eyes still watching the chasm. "Be at peace, gentle one," she whispered, touching one finger to her forehead.

Acarius looked back at her, his expression sad. "We need to move," he said.

More sand tumbled down over the edge of the hole as it grew a bit larger.

"Ready when you are," Lex said.

"Ride, Mare," Acarius said as Lytira tightened her arms around his waist. Mare took off, this time at a gallop.

Lex adjusted Amelia in front of him and kicked his horse into motion behind them.

They galloped for several minutes before Acarius deemed it safe to slow down. Lex was relieved to be moving at a pace less jarring for Amelia. When they galloped, her unconscious body had bobbed in front of him like a rag doll; he had worried about every jolt she took.

"Let's stop just for a moment," Acarius said. "I think we could all use the breather." He slid off Mare and Lytira followed, sinking down to the sand. She patted it with one hand as though checking it was solid.

Lex's pulse was still racing from what happened before, but he was beginning to realize that things like this just *happened* in Arameth, mostly when he least expected them. He slid off his horse and checked Amelia. She was breathing calmly, no signs of her earlier distress, though Lex couldn't help but wonder if she had any injuries from the riding. It was hard to tell, without her ability to express pain or discomfort.

Acarius walked over and handed Lex a water-skin as Lytira stood, seeming to have regained her composure, and began watering the horses.

Lex watched her, noting the edge of anxiety beneath her movements. The sinkhole had really shaken her. Or maybe it was the fate of that poor horse.

Then he noticed Acarius standing behind Lytira, looking as though he was fighting back a smile. *What's going on?* Lex wondered.

After a moment, Lytira noticed as well, and turned to Acarius. "What?" she asked flatly.

His face split open into a wide grin. "You screamed," he said.

Lytira's mouth dropped open. "I did not," she insisted. "I never scream."

Acarius shook his head, still smiling. "You did. Right before I saved your life – which of course you don't have to thank me for – you most definitely screamed."

Lytira narrowed her eyes. "No," she said simply.

Acarius turned to Lex. "Help me out," he said. "She screamed. You heard it, right?"

Lex glanced between the two of them. "I'm staying out of this," he said.

"Because I didn't scream," Lytira said.

"You did and you know it," answered Acarius.

They stared at each other for a moment, Lytira's gaze sharp as a blade and Acarius' filled with amusement.

Then Lytira sighed. "Thank you for saving me," she said.

"You're welcome," Acarius replied. Then, in a serious tone, he said, "I really am sorry about the horse. He was far too kind a creature for such a fate."

"I only hope he is at peace now and that his death was swift." Lytira said. "I know you tried to save him. I saw you grab for his reins. It was good of you." She turned back to watering Lex's horse.

"If it had been Mare, I'd be devastated," Acarius replied. "I know you didn't know the horse for long, but I also know how you feel about animals. I'm sorry I wasn't able to save both of you."

"You did what you could," Lytira said softly, still looking away from him. "Thank you."

"You're welcome," Acarius said again. He stood for a moment in silence behind her. Then he muttered, "But you did scream," and walked quickly back over to Mare.

Lytira tensed. "We should go," she said, but from the side Lex could see her mouth twist up into a smirk.

Lex turned back to Amelia. She seemed fine, but there was no way of knowing how bad things were with her, at least not until something happened again. He pulled himself up into the saddle behind her. "How much longer until we reach Zeriphath?" he asked.

"If we ride slowly but steadily through the afternoon and most of the night, we should be there by morning," Lytira answered.

She mounted Mare and Acarius pulled himself up in front of her and eased Mare into a slow gait. Lex followed.

They rode in silence, their eyes scanning the ground and sky for any more surprises. When night began to fall, Lytira leaned up and murmured something to Acarius. He nodded, and she turned to Lex. "Let's camp here for a few hours and eat and get some rest," she said. "I'll take first watch."

Lex didn't realize how exhausted he was until he dismounted and found his legs would barely hold him. He eased Amelia off the horse and down to the sand. When he had made her as comfortable as possible and was sure she was still breathing evenly, he squeezed some more water into her mouth from a wet cloth. He tipped her head up to be sure she wouldn't choke. He wasn't sure if she was actually swallowing any of the water, but it made him feel better to at least try. He spread out his own blanket next to hers and sank down onto it.

Acarius came and sat beside him while Lytira busied herself checking the supplies and dividing up some food for their evening meal.

After a few moments, Acarius leaned toward Lex. "She did scream. You heard it, right?"

Lytira whipped her head around and glared at them, and Acarius snapped his mouth shut.

Lytira moved to the far side of Mare and went back to digging in the bundle, though a bit more aggressively.

Lex fought back a chuckle. "What was all that about?" he asked.

Acarius turned his head toward Lex. "Lytira likes to insist nothing ever startles her." He leaned in conspiratorially. "She's as calm as stone during most battles. But that hole surprised her; you heard it as well as I did. She screamed." He looked pleased with himself.

"People get startled all the time," Lex said. "Why should it matter?"

Acarius shook his head. "Not her people, and certainly not *Rahmanasha* Lytira. Sephram of her status pride themselves on two things: skill in battle, and nerves of steel. You may see them howl in pain or anger, but in fear or surprise? Never." He shrugged. "Well, almost never. Lytira finds it embarrassing to show raw emotion, but I rather like seeing those glimpses of what's going on in her mind. They're rare but I've seen more of them lately." He chuckled. "Maybe being around humans has started to rub off on her."

"Wait," Lex said. "Lytira isn't... human?"

Acarius turned to him. "I keep forgetting how little you remember," he said. "In the normal sense, no, she's not human, though technically neither are you."

"I'm not?" Lex asked, feeling he should be more shocked than he was.

"No. You're an Ancient, one of the magical races of Arameth along with Sephram and Alomman, though each race has a different ability. Humans are non-magic. In fact, they don't even remember magic exists, at least until recently. But it hasn't always been that way. The Ancients caused that."

Lex remembered Nigel saying the same thing. "The Ancients could wipe memories from a whole world's worth of humans?" he asked.

Acarius nodded. "The Ancients can do lots of things. They possess the ability to wield the elements with a word, bending them to their will."

"You mean like doing spells?" Lex asked, remembering things he'd seen on Earth television.

"Something like that. They have to learn the right wording to coerce the elements and how to harness the energy, but once they've learned it they can manipulate the elements around them. They're strongest with air and water, but they can do some other things, too." Acarius answered.

"Wow," Lex said. "Can I...?" He didn't even finish the question. He truly couldn't imagine himself bending elements with a word. It was like something from a movie.

Acarius shrugged. "Maybe? I don't know. I never saw you use any magic other than your dark energy power. Marcus was obsessed with figuring out how to use his birthright magic. He thought it would be the key to winning, if he could just understand it better. I think he was just starting to get a handle on it when he– I mean, you– well..."

"Died?"

"Yes," Acarius answered. "I'm never quite sure how sensitive of a subject that may be for you."

"I'm getting used to it," Lex replied.

"Huh," Acarius said. "Anyway, the Ancients are extremely powerful... though less now than before. Since the Worldforce went crazy, the magical peoples have been weakening. No one's sure exactly why, but we think it's tied to the Core."

"The Core?" Lex asked.

"It's where the Ancients live," Acarius answered. "They moved there just before the Great War, and it somehow made them even more powerful. But now, whatever it did for them seems to have fizzled. The Sephram and Alomman have suffered since the Worldforce destabilized, too, but the Ancients seem to have grown far weaker than the rest, as if it's draining them somehow. Not that they aren't still powerful... *I* wouldn't want to go near them, that's for sure. But they're weaker than they used to be. The terrors the Ancients' magic caused during the Great War were the reason magic had to be wiped from human memory."

"You've mentioned that war more than once. What was it about?" Lex asked.

Acarius took a breath.

"Oh, here we go again," Lytira muttered from near the horses.

Acarius turned to her. "What?"

She ignored him, looking instead at Lex. "He loves telling this story," she said.

Acarius shrugged. "My dad used to gather us around the fireplace at night and tell us stories about the past," he said, his voice going soft. "It reminds me of him."

Lytira blinked, as though his response had surprised her. "You tell it well," she said after a moment. "Like a true historian."

Acarius leaned toward Lex. "In her world, that's a compliment... I think," he murmured.

Lytira smiled at Acarius, then turned back to the horses.

Lex had a feeling his people's history wouldn't be pleasant, but he needed to know. "Tell me," he said. "I'd like to hear it."

Acarius winked. "It's a long story. Maybe some other time."

Lex was a little disappointed, but something about Acarius' face made him not press the issue. But he still needed to understand more about his past. "Acarius, when I was Marcus, what was I like?"

Acarius fell silent for a moment, then answered quietly. "You were the best fighter I'd ever seen, and also the smartest. You somehow knew the perfect strategy for any fight. You were fast and strong." He paused. "You could also be a bit of a jerk sometimes, especially when people didn't want to do things your way." He laughed. "But you meant well. You were one of the bravest people I've ever met."

Lex listened in silence, processing all this. Somehow, he was this person he knew so little about, and yet... he was also *not,* thanks to whatever Nigel had done. "The LEX Protocol," he said suddenly. "What exactly did it do?"

Acarius shook his head. "I don't know. Nigel explained it some, but I think it didn't even really do what *he* expected it to. He said it would transport the target somewhere safe, for a while, until they could return... but that we could only use it once. It was our last resort." He paused. "You know, I think he meant to use it on himself, but when he saw your energy destabilizing, he used it on you. He knew how important you were."

"Why?" Lex asked. "Why me?"

Acarius gave a sad laugh. "I asked the same thing, when you said I was the prophesied one. I don't know for sure, but ... I think maybe Nigel always knew it was you. At least, until afterwards. Then none of us knew what to think. After the damage cleared and we were safe, Nigel reset the device. Then we all waited. Nigel said it might take a few minutes, but – you never came back. I waited there a full day and night before he finally pulled me away. 'We failed,' he told me. 'He's gone.' We really thought you were dead."

"Oh," Lex said. *Seven years*, Nigel had said, from the time Marcus died to when Lex appeared. Nigel said things hadn't gone as he expected, but... what exactly *had* happened? Where had Marcus – Lex – he, himself – been all that time?

Acarius watched him, a sympathetic look passing over his face. "I wish I could tell you more," he said. "But none of us really understand what happened. I'm just glad you're back." He gave him a small smile.

"Me too," Lex said, though part of him wondered whether he'd have ever had the consciousness to realize he was stuck somewhere else if he *hadn't* come back. And he still had so many questions. About himself, and about his past. "The Ancients... I mean, my family... were they..." He thought of the harshness of his father in the visions, but was unsure what exactly he wanted to ask.

Acarius watched him for a moment, then said, "You did everything you could to please them, for a while. You said it was never enough." He paused. "I believe you were stronger without them. But I know it hurt you when they turned on you, and I was sorry for that."

"The Ancients sound terrible," Lex said.

"They are a force to be feared, when they want to be," Acarius answered. "Ancients individually aren't all that powerful – their magic takes a lot of energy and they tire easily – but together they can wreak havoc. Then of course there's the birthright magic, like your dark energy ability," Acarius said. "Those didn't exist before the Ancients moved to the Core. Now, every Ancient is born with one. Of course, since the Worldforce went crazy and the magical races weakened, most birthright abilities aren't that powerful. Except for yours."

Lex turned to look at him.

"Your birthright magic is more powerful than any I've seen an Ancient wield," Acarius continued. "You told me the tutors at the palace assigned to train you weren't even sure what to call your ability. You always called it 'the darkness,' but that was a little macabre for their tastes. What you can do, Lex... it's unique. No one's even quite sure how it works."

*Not even me*, Lex thought. How much had he figured out about his ability, as Marcus, that he hadn't yet remembered?

"What about Ardis?" Lex asked, thinking of his visions. "Did anyone figure out how she's involved in all this?"

Acarius looked up at the sky. "No one had heard of Ardis before the war, but the stirring of dark creatures from Galgor, the fracturing of this world... it all began with her. Most believe her to be a force of evil – a demon – rather than the goddess emissary the Ancients claim she is. But the Ancients serve her unflinchingly. She only shows herself to the Ancient royals and their appointed priests, in the temple they built for her in the palace at Arameth Core. No one else has ever seen her." He paused. "It was her prophecy to the Ancients which made them send you to find me."

Lex's mind was in chaos, his Marcus-memories blurring over into his Lex ones. All these memories, yet there was so much about his past he still didn't understand.

Lytira moved to the other side of the horses, and Acarius turned his gaze to follow her.

Lex watched him, marveling how Acarius' whole face seemed to change when he looked at her. After a moment, Lex asked quietly, "Earlier, about Lytira, you said 'Sephram of her status.' Exactly what status *is* she?"

"She's a princess," Acarius said, glancing at him. "Or the equivalent of it for her people. *Rahmanasha* means 'daughter of Rahman,' and Rahman is their current, elected king. They have sort of a democratic monarchy. They choose a family line, and all future royals come from that line, unless the family is denounced by the Alliance or the biological line is disrupted, in which case, a new royal line would be elected. Lytira is Rahman's only child. She would have been next in line for the throne."

"Oh," Lex said. His mind raced back to Alowen, to the respect shown her at the gates, and her later banishment. "Then, at Alowen..."

"Their decision holds," Acarius said sadly. "Princess or not, she violated clan rules. The clans are all ruled separately by elders, but banishment by one clan results in banishment by all. The king's rule is technically above that of the elders, but he can only reverse a clan punishment if it is proven unfairly given. In this case, I doubt that will happen."

"She was only trying to help me," Lex protested.

"The clan always comes before outsiders," Acarius shrugged. "When it comes to letting an outsider die or risking their own, the rules are clear, and she broke them." He looked at Lex. "I don't think she regrets it. She believes it was the right choice."

*But do I?* Lex wondered.

Just then, Lytira walked toward them. "You two should rest while you have time," she said gently. "We still have a long ride ahead." She handed them each some food.

Lex ate quickly, checked on Amelia, then straightened his blanket out on the sand and stretched out on top of it. A few feet over, Acarius did the same.

Something occurred to Lex. He turned toward Acarius. "You said the Ancients, Sephram, and Alomman each have a different ability. Ancients can do spells. Is that not the same with the others?"

"No," Acarius answered. "The Ancients are versatile but limited by knowledge of spells... except for their birthright magic, of course. But with the weakening over the past few decades, most birthright abilities are barely more than parlor tricks. Except, as I said, for yours. There is no known spell that can do... whatever it is you do."

Lex was still trying to figure out what exactly it was he did, too.

Acarius continued. "The Sephram and Alomman, however, cannot wield spells. Their magic is intrinsic, a connection to an aspect of our world. They need no word or language to harness it, they simply will it and it *becomes*. All Sephram and Alomman are born with the magic specific to their people, and they are limited to this innate magic. Because the Ancients can wield spells, there are many things the Ancients can do which the Sephram and Alomman cannot. But what they *can* do, they do better than the Ancients ever could."

"So, the Alomman... they do... plants?" Lex asked, unsure how to phrase it.

"Alomman have the magic to call out to living things within the earth, for lack of a better explanation. They can bend the very soil to their will, and any plant within it," Acarius answered.

"Oh," Lex replied. "And what about the Sephram?"

Acarius smiled. "You'll have to wait and see," he said, then rolled over.

Lex turned onto his back, staring up at the steady stars above him. He was asleep within moments, without even realizing he'd closed his eyes.

# CHAPTER 15

Acarius woke Lex a few hours later to tell him he'd already taken a watch to let Lytira sleep, and it was time to go. They rose, ate a quick breakfast of the strange pressed cakes again, then loaded up and started toward the gain-star. When the sun rose a few hours later, Lex's only guide for whether they were still on course was Lytira's total confidence. "We've veered a bit. Head this way," she would say occasionally, pointing a finger at an angle in front of them, and Acarius would adjust Mare's direction. Lex simply followed.

As they rode, a question occurred to Lex, sparked by something Nigel had said. He moved his horse closer to Mare. "The humans at Dalton called me *demon*," he said to Acarius, "and you told me they think I'm working with Ardis. How could they, if Ardis is a goddess worshipped by the Ancients, and all humans have forgotten about magic?"

"That's been bothering me since the moment I heard you appeared at Dalton," Acarius answered. "The humans have their own religions, of course, but none of them include Ardis. When I heard rumors Ardis sent a demon to Dalton bearing the face of the dead hero, Marcus, I didn't believe it could really be you – how could I, when I'd watched you die? I thought it was some sort of a trick... or worse, a trap. But with the uncertainty about the prophecy, I had to be sure. I was just on my way to Dalton to figure out what was going on when you stumbled into me."

"Uncertainty about the prophecy?" Lex asked.

"Apparently it's not worded all that clearly," Acarius responded.

"What exactly *does* the prophecy say?"

Acarius turned to him and shrugged. "You would never tell me; you said it was bad luck to know your own fate. You just gave me a basic summary... which turned out to be wrong, because we all thought *I* was the one destined to save our people." He paused. "Since you're the one back from the dead, I'm pretty sure it's you."

*Great*, Lex thought. *I'm the only one of us who knows the prophecy, and I don't even remember it.* "Does anyone know what it actually said?"

"The Ancients do, I believe. It was a prophecy given to their seers by Ardis, after all. And maybe a few others. There are some, even in other places, who had... visions. They weren't the same as the prophecy, exactly, but they agreed with it."

They were both quiet for a moment, then Acarius spoke again. "We did *not* know, when I headed out to look for you, that an Aiac was living in Dalton. If we had, I may have handled some things differently." He rode in silence a few moments before continuing. "Anyway, to the humans, someone returning from the dead is unnatural and demonic, and Ardis is believed to be the source of demonic energy, including what created the Aiacs. At first we thought the humans heard of Ardis as a religious figure, without realizing her ties to the Ancients or her relation to magic. But that was before we knew about the Aiacs living in Dalton and other villages. Now we know the Aiacs have been appearing among some of the humans and awakening their awareness of magic. So we know *what* they're doing. It's the *why* that continues to bother us."

Lex let this idea roll around in his mind as they rode.

The heat in The Fallows seemed to increase by the moment as the day wore on. They took frequent, short breaks to pass around the water-skins and offer a drink to the horses, but before the sun had even reached its peak, they had consumed the last of the water. Things grew bleaker when they stopped for an early lunch and Lytira handed out now-stale bits of the pressed cakes, announcing it was the last of their food.

"How is that possible?" Lex asked. "The bundles were full of supplies!"

She dumped the bundles out into the sand. There were several more cloth-wrapped packages of the pressed loaves, but they were all either hard as rocks or covered with a thick, grey mold.

"It happens in The Fallows," Lytira said. "Food spoils in a matter of days, especially once the horses begin sweating. The heat from the air dries some of the food out, while the moisture from the horses' perspiration rots the rest of it. Travelers have long-since tried rotating the food within bundles or other methods of preservation, but it never works. It is one of the curses of The Fallows ... nothing survives long traveling through here, including food."

Lex was already feeling uncomfortly thirsty, and he knew the hunger wouldn't be far behind. "How much farther do we have?" he asked.

"Far enough that we dare not stop again," she said. "Spending any longer than necessary in this heat could be deadly without food and water. We'll have to ride through, even if we get tired."

*Get tired?* Lex thought. He was still tired from the previous day, even after the few hours of sleep he'd gotten.

They continued on, and with the heat from the sky above reflecting back up from the sand, Lex felt as though he were baking in a kiln. They rode on for hours, too hot and exhausted to talk.

Lex's horse began to stumble, and again Acarius offered to carry Amelia. "Lytira could ride with you for a bit instead," he suggested.

Lytira looked as uncomfortable about that idea as Lex felt. "No, thanks," Lex said. "We'll be okay. Let's just keep moving."

The sun was long past the noon point in the sky when a dark sliver appeared on the distant horizon, a lumpy shadow rising like a shoreline across what Lex had begun to think was an endless sea of sand. Lex wondered if it was a mirage signaling the beginning of the end for him.

But Acarius saw it, too. "Zeriphath," he said, turning to Lex. "We're almost there."

Lex straightened up, consolidating all his willpower. *Almost there.* They were going to make it.

"I'm a bit surprised we haven't seen any lagaroths or pippits," Lytira said suddenly. "At least one of them has usually smelled us by now."

Lex flicked his head toward her. "What?"

Acarius looked back at Lytira behind him. "What have I said about bad luck? You always do this."

Lytira shrugged. "I was just saying it's unusual."

"What are lagaroths and pippits?" Lex asked, his voice coming out more panicked than he'd intended.

"The pippits are kind of endearing, actually," Lytira said. "They were a common pet in Arcalon near the shore areas, though no one knows where they originally came from. Arcalonians would let them roam outside the villages in communal herds, and the children would often bring some back to run around in their homes. Pippits nest in forested areas during breeding season, but they spend the rest of their time in sandy areas, where they dig burrows and feed off insects and whatever plants they can find. Of course, when they got loose in Alleanza during an attempted trade arrangement and made their way into The Fallows, the unusual environment here...changed them a bit."

"How, exactly?" Lex asked.

Acarius gave Lex a wide smile. "Instead of being pocket-sized, herbivorous fluffballs, they are now wolf-sized, *carnivorous* fluffballs with a slight tendency for territorial aggression." His smile looked a little forced.

Lex stared. Were they serious? But then something occurred to him. "Wait, wolf-sized? You have wolves here?" A memory had surfaced of a wolf he'd seen once on a television show. "I thought those were Earth animals."

"Of course we have them," Acarius said. "Not here in The Fallows, but other places. You said once that you were shocked to see so many of *our* animals on Earth while you were there. I don't quite understand it, but it seems Arameth and Earth have similar species and climates, just as we both have humans. Though there are also some differences, of course."

"Like pippits," Lytira interrupted.

*And like magical people,* Lex thought. He was fairly certain Marcus hadn't found any of those on Earth. But then again, the humans of Arameth hadn't known magic existed in their world for the past few hundred years, so who could be certain? There had been at least one Ancient on Earth at some point, that much was clear.

Lex noted with a distant sort of curiosity that he still thought of Marcus as not himself, in some ways. Some memories had returned to him completely, in which he *knew* he'd been Marcus, but others still felt like retold stories, like watching a movie in his mind rather than having acted in it. This whole coming-back-from-the-dead thing was strange.

"By the way," Lytira said, looking at Acarius, "Pippits aren't carnivorous. They still eat insects and plants as well as meat. I believe that makes them *om*nivorous." She turned to Lex. "They seem to prefer insects and only attack people as defense when startled, though they have been known to eat one on occasion."

*Of course*, Lex thought. "And the lagaroths? I'm almost afraid to ask."

"Highly intelligent, man-eating lizard creatures roughly the size of horses," Lytira said. "They are shorter though, of course; they run low to the ground. They usually feed on pippits, but they prefer the taste of people. I think people may have been their natural diet, before the pippits arrived."

"People, like... humans?" Lex asked, feeling his voice climb again. "Because, we're" – he gestured between himself and the others – "not like *regular* people, so they won't want to eat us, because we're not human. Right?"

Lytira shrugged. "I meant 'people' in the more generic sense. Lagaroths seem to enjoy eating Sephram, humans, Ancients, and Alommans equally. I'm not certain there's much taste difference between us, or maybe they just get tired of eating pippits. In any case, both the pippits and the lagaroths live near the Northern edge of The Fallows, these days." She pointed forward, in the direction they were headed. "The pippits like having access to the northern woods for building their nests, and the lagaroths, though they prefer to stay in The Fallows, frequent the edges to feed on the pippits."

*Great*, Lex thought. *Of course they live exactly where we're headed.* "But we're almost to Zeriphath, right?" he asked. "I mean... how likely is it that we'll run into either of those before getting out of The Fallows? And do they ever stray out, toward Zeriphath?"

"Oh, Zeriphath isn't *out* of The Fallows," Lytira said. "It's on the edge. That line of trees you see up there" – she gestured to the dark blur ahead of them – "is where Zeriphath stands, right where the forest meets the sand. The woods around it are the pippits' favorite breeding grounds, though they usually stay back from the gates. Our guards shoot them with arrows if they get too close."

Lex was relieved to hear that last part, but the idea of nearing Zeriphath was definitely less comforting than it had been.

A sound cut through the dry air. "Is that... hoofbeats?" Lex asked.

He and Acarius turned their horses around to look. From the distance, a dark shape sped toward them. It seemed to be someone riding an animal, though it looked too short to be a horse. The beast and its rider were partially concealed by the cloud of sand the animal kicked up around them as it galloped.

"Who is it?" Lex asked, his mind racing through all the possibilities for who – or what – might be coming for them.

The rider grew closer. Acarius and Lytira drew their weapons, and Lex leaned instinctively over Amelia, shielding her.

The horse and rider barreled straight at them – then shot past them in a blur, just avoiding plowing into Acarius. "Sorry, can't stop!" a voice yelled. "I'm late and there's a lizard chasing me!"

*Nigel.*

Acarius, Lex and Lytira exchanged a brief, shocked glance before turning their gaze back toward the cloud of whipped sand Nigel left in his wake. Racing toward them from the sand-cloud was the largest reptile Lex had ever seen. *Lizard* didn't adequately describe it. It called up memories from something he'd seen in a zoo in his time living Earthside as Marcus... but while those predators were most at home in the water, this one ran at incredible speed across the sand, its short, muscular legs flicking grains of yellow in all directions as it sped toward them.

Lytira and Acarius still weren't moving, and the lizard thing was getting closer by the second. "Guys?" Lex called out, starting to panic.

His horse shuffled its legs nervously, then looked toward Mare – who was completely calm – and fell still.

"Don't...move," Acarius grunted through his teeth. "Movement makes lagaroths more aggressive."

Lex fought a powerful urge to run, barely managing to hold his ground. The creature was almost on them when Lex realized the lagaroth's eyes were focused past them... on Nigel, who was still riding. Lex turned his head to see how far Nigel had gotten, and at his movement the creature flicked its gaze toward Lex, as though trying to decide whether he was worth stopping for. Lex froze. The lagaroth refocused on Nigel and ran right past Lex and the others.

About a hundred paces beyond them, Nigel seemed to forget he was being chased. He yanked his animal's reins, causing it to rear. "Wait!" he shouted, his face breaking into a smile as he looked backward. "I just realized – it's you guys! Why didn't you say something?" He circled his animal back around, directly into the path of the lagaroth. The tip of its long tail slipped past the others in the sand, its eyes locked on Nigel as it sped toward him.

Nigel rode toward the others waving happily, apparently oblivious he was riding right into a murderous lagaroth.

"No!" Lex shouted. He reached for the lagaroth's tail as it slipped past. He was too high atop the horse and missed, but Lytira was already in mid-leap.

Lytira landed on the surprised lagaroth and drove a dagger straight into the back of its neck. The creature thrashed for only a moment before going still, and a trickle of black liquid oozed from its wound as Lytira removed the dagger. She wiped the dagger clean with a cloth she pulled from a pocket, then slid the dagger back into its sheath on her belt and calmly climbed back onto Mare behind Acarius.

"Well done, as usual, my girl," Nigel called out as he neared them.

As he got closer, Lex realized the animal Nigel rode was a donkey, with large buckteeth sticking out past its lips and a strange patch of yellow hair poking up from its head.

"Why aren't you there yet?" Nigel called as his donkey ambled toward them. "You left ages ago! Here I was, all in a rush, thinking I was late... and you haven't even reached Zeriphath yet! This isn't a vacation, you know."

The donkey glared at the horses as it approached, as though annoyed by their presence.

Lex quickly explained the need to ride at a slower pace for Amelia's sake. "But I am anxious to get there," he added. "She's been having strange attacks, and I don't know how much longer she can hold out."

"Well, that's inconvenient of her," Nigel said, raising his eyebrows. "She'd have gotten help much more quickly if she hadn't been unconscious." His voice brightened. "But I suppose she can't help it. Anyway, didn't you just say she's in urgent need of care from Zeriphath? Why are we all standing here? Let's go!"

The others exchanged glances then simply followed Nigel, who was already riding toward the dark blur ahead.

As they neared the end of The Fallows, the dark blur refined itself into a spread of rich green forest. The forest spanned as far as they could see in both directions, forming an abrupt line where the sand ended. Directly in front of them, a pair of large, wooden gates towered like a doorway to the forest itself, rimmed by branches above and trees on either side – the gates of Zeriphath.

Lex had been expecting a camp, like Alowen, but this was far too large and elaborate for that. Its presence loomed behind the trees in both directions, dissolving into the shadows of the forest. The tops of Zeriphath's dark stone walls vanished in the thick treetops. The walls were finely constructed, smooth and with no footholds for climbing, but they were also tiered – the front part of the wall formed a wide ledge about double the height of Lex atop his horse, with a tall lip around it. The bottoms of the tree branches hung just above that lip, concealing most of the ledge. *What do they use that for?* Lex wondered. Through the branches, he could just barely make out that the ledge formed a sort of recessed platform, and that behind the ledge the walls shot steeply upward again. Beneath the draping branches, the dark stone of the city almost blended into the shadows between the tree trunks, save the one clear area in front of the gates. The trees' camouflage made it difficult to tell how far the walls spanned.

"How big is this place?" Lex asked as he stopped his horse in the sand.

"Big," Acarius shrugged, pulling Mare up beside him.

"Still your horses!" a voice shouted from above.

"Ack!" Nigel screamed, throwing up his hands.

Lex looked up to find himself under the aim of multiple arrows yet again, now by a group of dark-skinned, shirtless, and extremely muscular men with headfulls of long, beaded braids – only this time, the arrows were on Acarius and Lytira, too.

Archers had materialized upon the platform on either side of the gates, their lower halves concealed by the ledge around the wall as they stepped outward from the branches like shadows taking form. *Of course*, Lex sighed inwardly. He dropped his horse's reins, just to be certain they didn't think him about to go anywhere. The archers had probably been there the whole time, watching unnoticed. At least they hadn't loosed their arrows on anyone yet.

"Rahmanasha," one of the archers nodded to Lytira. Some of the other archers glanced at him, then focused back on the intruders below.

"I would like to speak with my father," Lytira stated in the regal voice she had used at Alowen.

"Your *father* is under obligation to bar your entry, due to your sentence of banishment," a voice boomed in response.

The archers pulled back and knelt atop the high wall, their bowed heads just visible over the lip of the ledge, as a man stepped forward. He was larger than the others and somehow gave the impression of also being more solid, his arms and legs resembling chunks of stone that had fallen from the mountain of his body. The lines of his muscles cut sharp edges beneath his flesh. He was shirtless with braided hair like the others, but tall enough that the leather wrapping which covered his waist and part of his legs was partially visible above the wall's ledge. The surface of the wrapping was etched with pictures, as though burnt onto it – symbols and images that appeared to be lions circling a man with his arms upraised. The man stepped forward, peering down at them over the ledge, and crossed his bulky arms in front of his chest. "Well?" he said, staring directly at Lytira.

Looking up at him, Lex felt the distinct impression that this man was a walking avalanche and they were all about to be crushed.

"Hello, Father," Lytira said, looking up. The expression in her eyes was as flat as her tone. "I see you've missed me."

A man to the right of the wall shot to his feet. "You will address our king with respect, fallen daughter!" he shouted.

*So this is Rahman, the Alomman-Sephram king,* Lex thought. The man was certainly impressive enough to be a king.

Beside Lex, Nigel dropped his hands and bowed forward, resting against his donkey's neck in an attempt at a posture of respect that looked more like he'd just fallen asleep. Then again, maybe he had.

Rahman gestured downward with his hand, and the man who had stood knelt back down, bowing his head again.

"Am I 'fallen,' then, Father?" Lytira asked. "Is that the decree you've settled on?"

"I have not settled on anything," Rahman's low voice rumbled. "Though, as always, you make nothing easy for me." He paused. "You have been banished, child. You know as well as I what that means. You have betrayed our people. You should not be here." His voice softened slightly on the last statement, a crack in his mountainous presence.

"I have betrayed no one, Father," Lytira answered, her voice still cool as stone. "I admit I caused loss and pain to our people, and for that I can make no excuse, save this – I did only what I believed to be right, for our people as well as others."

The king's arms relaxed slightly. "Then you have an explanation for what you have done?"

"Yes," Lytira answered.

The king sighed and turned to his left. "Aral," he called, and a man stood up. "You will be my Ear on this matter."

Aral tipped his head forward. "Recording what has been heard," he answered.

"You will do this *here*, Father?" Lytira asked, her voice rising slightly. "Outside the gates?"

"You are banished," the king responded. "Unless you prove reason for us to make an exception, *outside the gates* is where you must stay."

Lytira grunted. "You know there are pippits out here," she muttered. "And I killed a lagaroth not a hundred paces back."

The king paused, looking down on her. "Then if another interrupts us, I trust you can dispatch it." He turned to his right. "Tala?"

To Lex's surprise, a woman stood – he hadn't noticed her among the archers. Her torso, unlike the men's, was covered in a fitted leather top nearly the same tone as her skin. "Yes, my king?" she asked.

"You will be my Heart," the king answered.

"Ensuring what you have heard is truth," she replied.

Acarius leaned over to Lex. "The hearing ceremony," he whispered. "The king can make an exception for extenuating circumstances, and allow temporary asylum to one who has been banished, but only if he has two elders among his clan who agree with his decision. In this case, their role will be to ensure his decision is unbiased, since the matter involves family. As I said, it's sort of a democratic monarchy. He's the king, but there are procedures for this sort of thing. Even if they side in her favor, it won't reverse what's been done. It will only initiate the process." He paused. "But it's still a good sign. I half expected him to turn us away, especially with me here."

"Why? Did you do something, too?" Lex asked.

"Oh. Well, I *may* have been the reason Lytira ran off from her clan as a teenager," Acarius said. "I don't think her father likes me much."

"What?" Lex asked.

Lytira silenced them both with a glare before Acarius could answer.

"We aren't supposed to talk during the ceremony," Nigel sat up and whisper-yelled.

One of the archers turned his arrow on Nigel, who threw his hands back up in the air and draped himself over his donkey's neck again.

In front of Lex, Amelia's head suddenly shot upright.

The archers leapt to their feet, all arrows turning on Amelia.

"What– where am–" Amelia stuttered. She looked around in panic, still tied to the horse and unable to move much more than her head.

Lex reached gently toward her shoulder, and she jumped as he touched her. "It's okay," he said. "It's me."

She visibly calmed, though her voice cracked as she asked, "What's happening?"

"Just be still," Lex murmured, very aware of the arrows trained on her. "Can I cut her free?" he asked, looking up and raising his hands away from where his replacement sword hung against his saddle – his other one had been left at Alowen.

The archers turned their gaze to the king, who hesitated a moment. "Who is she?" he asked. "Why is she tied up?"

There was a rustle in the branches, and one of the archers wordlessly turned and loosed an arrow into the forest. There was a shriek, and something thumped to the ground. The archer calmly replaced his arrow with one from his quiver and aimed it back at Amelia.

Lytira slid off Mare's back and moved toward Lex and Amelia's horse. Some of the archers turned their arrows on her, while the others stayed fixed on Amelia.

Without waiting for permission, Lytira slid the dagger from her belt and sliced the ropes which held Amelia to the horse.

Amelia pushed upright, moaning as she moved.

"Are you alright?" Lex asked.

Amelia nodded, then went stiff as she finally looked upward and saw the arrows aimed at her.

"She's a daughter of power, Father," Lytira said. "She needs help. That's why we're here."

# THE EDGE OF NOTHING

The king's dark skin suddenly seemed a few shades paler. He glanced to the man and woman who had been appointed to help with the ceremony, and they looked as pale as he did. The woman gave a quick nod.

The king turned away. "Open the gates," his voice boomed as he strode away, disappearing into the shadows beyond the ledge. The archers lowered their bows and followed him into the branches.

A moment later the gates swept open, and a group of guards led Lex and the others into Zeriphath.

Lex noticed all the guards were dressed like the king – shirtless and with leather coverings around their waist which hung to their knees. Each guard's leather was decorated with seared images, and though each was unique, they all featured some kind of animal. The guards were barefoot, as were all the other people in the city, who were now emerging from doorways all around to watch them pass. The people were dressed the same as the guards, the men shirtless and the women wearing dark leather tops above their waist-coverings, which also had etched symbols and animals on them, every one different. The children, who peeked out from behind the adults all around the clearing, wore leather tops and waist coverings as well, but theirs were empty of etchings. Lex felt eyes on him from every direction as the guards led them further into the city and shut the gates behind them.

Zeriphath gave the impression of a giant forest clearing turned into a small city. It sprawled out in a massive circle, following the curve of the outer walls, but despite its size there were no streets or sidewalks or any of the typical elements Lex would have expected from a city. The ground was the bare dirt of a forest floor with sprigs of grass growing up in places, and the dwellings the people came out of were essentially multi-story tree-houses, wooden structures built right around the existing trees of the forest, which stood in concentric rings inside the wall of the city. The only clear area was a circular courtyard of packed dirt just inside the gates, which interrupted the ring of trees and created a wide, round community area, wherein stood a large wooden barn, a cloth-tented market space where townspeople seemed to be trading goods across wooden tables, and a towering wooden structure toward the back of the courtyard that reached nearly as high as the treetops around it and seemed to have been carved entirely out of one massive tree. It had a large, open doorway cut into it near the base, and from the rows of glassless windows carved into its height, it appeared to extend several stories before giving up on being a building and becoming a tree again. A natural canopy of overhead branches covered the city in shade, making it noticeably cooler than it had been outside the gates and blocking out much of the sky. Lex looked around in awe, feeling as though he'd just been swallowed by the forest. After so much time on the searing, wide-open sand, it was rather jarring.

Archers were still climbing down wooden ladders built against the city walls, returning to the clearing now that the unexpected visitors were inside the walls. On this side, the stone walls spread upward to the heights of the tree tops, uninterrupted save for door-size openings on either side of the gates, which apparently were how the archers – and the king – had accessed the ledge outside. The archers took up positions around the clearing, though their weapons were lowered.

The guards led Lex and the others through the clearing and toward the towering building in the back. As they moved inward, Lex felt more and more eyes on him as people continued to emerge from their dwellings. They appeared in doorways and railed porches on all levels of the tree houses, and as Lex looked around, he noticed some of the houses had signs outside, marked in a language he didn't recognize. Were they names, to identify who lived there? Or did it mean something else? The people stared silently as the group passed, and each face Lex's gaze landed on seemed either curious, shocked, or upset. *I guess they don't get many visitors*, Lex thought. Or maybe it was *who* the visitors were which had the people on edge. That was an uncomfortable thought, given that Lex and his friends were now literally surrounded by people who didn't seem to want them there, and with no escape except back into The Fallows.

In front of him, Lex saw Amelia's posture tense as she glanced around. He could feel the warm buzz of energy around her again. He leaned forward. "Are you okay?" he whispered.

She glanced back at him and gave a quick nod, but her face was pinched and nervous. She turned back around, her hands fidgeting with the horse's mane.

The guards approached. "Dismount," one of them said.

None of the group moved, and Lex saw Acarius glance at Lytira, clearly unhappy with the thought of leaving Mare.

After a moment, Lytira slid off Mare's back, and Acarius sighed but followed.

"Can you stand?" Lex asked Amelia.

She nodded, and Lex dismounted then reached up to help Amelia down. Her legs buckled a moment but she caught herself, and gave Lex a shaky smile.

Guards approached, taking hold of both horses, though Acarius still didn't look comfortable with the idea. Mare glanced uncertainly at him, but he patted her and she seemed to calm a bit.

Nigel looked around, then hopped off his donkey and held out the reins. A guard took them, and all three animals were led away toward the massive barn, then around to the back of it rather than through the closed doors on its front.

Acarius shifted his feet, and Lytira leaned over. "They will not harm her," she said.

"I know," Acarius answered, though his expression didn't seem quite so certain.

The guards backed away toward the edges of the clearing and the few people who had been milling in the market area grabbed their things and hurried off into the ring of houses, leaving the five visitors standing alone in the courtyard just in front of the tall tree building.

The people continued to stare at them from every direction.

Lex was just beginning to wonder if they were expected to do something when the king appeared in the carved doorway.

"Come inside," his voice boomed. He turned and disappeared back into the building.

The others followed.

Lex found himself in a large lobby area of a surprisingly-fancy palace, if you could call it that when it was all made from a hollowed-out tree. The floors were laid with smooth, dark stone the same color as the outer walls of the city, and the inside of the tree had been buffed and polished until its wooden walls shone. An ornate, padded throne stood in the center of the lobby, the only thing in the room except for two carved doors revealing staircases winding upward into the tree. The ceiling above them was tall, and also made of wood.

Acarius leaned over. "This is where the king hears petitions from the people," he whispered. "Those doors lead up to the other levels. The second floor has dwellings for the king's advisors and officials, and the third has rooms for honored guests of the king – not that they often get visitors. Everyone else, even the archers and guards, live out among the people. It's their custom for the warriors to stay out among their families, where they can enjoy normal lives but be ready at a moment's notice if their protection is needed. The royal family lives in here, though, on the fourth floor... or they did. It's only the king himself up there, now. But he stays there so he has a clear view of everything within the city and anything approaching outside the wall."

"So he saw us coming?" Lex asked, also in a whisper.

"That would be why all the archers were already up on the wall," Acarius answered. "They don't normally have so many out there."

The king made his way to the throne and sat upon it, crossing his arms as he faced them. "So," he said, his eyes on Lytira.

Lytira opened her mouth to speak, but before she could say anything the king cut his eyes to Acarius, then back to Lytira. "I thought you and the half-blood were through," he said flatly.

"We're not together, Father," Lytira answered. "Not in that way. But our paths have merged once more in service of a larger purpose."

Lex saw Acarius shift his feet. *Poor guy*, Lex thought. He didn't know the history between Acarius and Lytira, but it was clear Acarius still felt something for her.

The king sighed, then said, "Fine. You said you could explain why you acted as you did at Alowen. So, *explain*."

As he spoke, the man and woman he'd appointed as Ear and Heart appeared through one of the doorways and took their places on either side of the king.

Now it was Lytira's turn to fidget. "I'd have thought that was clear now, Father," she said. She gestured toward Lex and Amelia. "Do you not understand who they are? Or what's at stake?"

The king leaned back in his throne and sighed, closing his eyes and pinching the bridge of his nose with his thumb and forefinger. "Daughter, must you make everything difficult? You *know* the ceremony. You must declare the intent behind your violation of our laws, and plead for mercy from the elders and your clanspeople."

"Your laws are antiquated, Father, and is not ceremony for the sake of ceremony meaningless? You see them standing here before you, a son of prophecy and a daughter of power. I know you can sense what they are; do not attempt to deny it. You know how long we have waited for them, how hard we fought to save Marcus and Jana, believing them our answer, and how devastated the people were when we failed. Now here he stands before you again, and beside him another daughter of power. It is a miracle, Father, and the very words of prophecy come true! Yes, I put our people at risk... to protect *him*. To save the one meant to save us all. What explanation beyond that do you need?"

The room fell silent.

Lex could feel Amelia's energy humming beside him; she was nervous – he had come to recognize the shift in the frequency of her power, if power was in fact what the hum was. *Daughter of power* and all the fuss about her seemed to indicate she could do...something. What, exactly, he wasn't sure. So far it had only seemed to cause her seizures and illness. He glanced over at her, but her eyes were locked on the king and his advisors. Lex turned his gaze back forward as well, feeling as though he were waiting for a sentence to be passed on himself, rather than just Lytira.

After a moment, the king spoke. "We of the Alliance have never acknowledged such a prophecy, nor do we bend our laws for it."

"That's a lie!" Lytira yelled. "You know mother–"

"Do not speak to me of your mother!" The king cut her off, his loud voice reverberating off the polished-wood walls. "She spent her dying days filling her head with stories of prophecies, believing they finally gave meaning to her so-called visions! What good did that do *any* of us?" He paused, and when he continued his voice was softer. "She was ill, Lytira, you know that. She was too apt to cling to the hope that all her visions and the illnesses which struck her night and day without warning or control actually *meant* something. But you and I, we have always been practical. Now you stand before me, with a story of fulfilled prophecy and heroes reborn, and back together with that half-blood yet denying it to my face. There are many in this world with *power*." He nearly spat the word as he glanced at Lex and Amelia. "What I sense in them could mean little... or nothing at all." His voice grew firmer as he turned back to Lytira. "You broke the customs of our people and exposed your own clan to danger for the sake of an outsider. Because of your actions, a child died, and several of the Alowen clan were injured. And now you have come here, knowing danger may well follow you to this place also. Do you have no further answer for this?"

Lex glanced over at Lytira, and was shocked to see her stone face had melted into the devastated expression of a rejected child. "No, Father," she said softly, looking down. "I do not."

The advisors on either side of the king leaned in, whispering something, then straightened back up and fixed their gazes forward again.

The king sighed. "The Heart declares your statements to be truthful, and the Ear has recorded your testimony. But I, the *king*, am not in agreement. According to the laws of the ceremony, you and your companions are granted sanctuary within our walls until this matter is taken to the clan and decided." He rose from his throne. "Remain here, and guards will show you to your quarters." He turned and exited through one of the far doors, the Ear and Heart following behind him.

Lex dropped his shoulders and let go of the stiff posture he'd been holding. "Whew," he breathed. "That was... intense." He turned toward Lytira. "Are you–"

He stopped. Nigel was already in front of Lytira with her hands in his own wrinkled ones. He whispered something to her, soft enough that Lex couldn't make it out. Lytira's face was still devastated, but she nodded at whatever Nigel had said.

Acarius stood nearby, watching the exchange and looking more helpless than Lex had ever seen him.

Lex turned to Amelia. Her face had gone pale, and something about her energy felt strange, a change in the texture of the hum. "Are you okay?" he asked, leaning toward her.

"What? Oh, yeah, I'm fine." Amelia gave her head a small shake, then smiled – not very convincingly. "I'm just tired."

Lex felt a surge of worry. "Are you sure?" he asked.

"Yeah, of course," she said, and this time her smile was a little more genuine.

Footsteps sounded outside and the group turned to see four guards entering the building from the courtyard.

"You will follow us to your quarters," one of them said.

Two of the guards moved toward one of the doors which held the stairways, then turned back, clearly waiting for them to follow.

"Not you," a third guard said, placing his hand on Amelia's shoulder. As soon as he touched her, he jerked his hand away and took a full step backward, looking cautious not to get too close again.

"Wait, why?" Lex asked, stepping toward Amelia.

"Did the fallen princess not say this one needed help? I have been instructed to take her to see our healers," the guard answered.

"Stop calling me that," Lytira said, looking over. "But yes, she needs help."

Lex spun toward Lytira. "Are you sure that's a good idea?"

Lytira turned to him. "Do not let my father's actions discolor your view of our people. Our healers are good and honorable, and the best in the land. They are sworn to only heal, not harm. They will help her."

"Really, I'm fine," said Amelia. "I'll stay with the rest of you."

Lex wanted to agree with her, to say she was better off with the group, but one look at her pale face – which was now covered in a sheen of sweat – forced him to think otherwise. He leaned in toward Amelia. "I trust Lytira. She saved your life, when you had your first attack. She's protected both of us, for some reason, even when it cost her all of this. If she says they'll help you, I think maybe you should go. At least let them take a look at you."

Amelia's face changed, suddenly vulnerable. "Attack? I don't remember anything, or even how I got here. I'm scared, Lex," she whispered. "I don't know what's happening to me."

Lex reached toward her face, tucking that one piece of hair which always swung down in front of her eyes back behind her ear. "I don't know either," he said. "But maybe they can help." He turned to the guard. "I'll go with her," he said.

"That is not permitted," the guard answered.

Amelia grasped Lex's hand and moved it away from her face. "I'll be okay," she said. "You go, and I'll just see the healer, then come back. Right?" She directed this last part to the guard.

The guard nodded. "Assuming our healers determine you are healthy, you will be brought back here, to our guest lodgings. However, the female guests must reside in separate quarters from the males," he said, narrowing his eyes at Lex.

"Right, okay," Amelia said, her voice bright. "Then let's go." She smiled at Lex. "I'll see you soon?"

"Soon," Lex answered. He watched the guard lead her away, and the room felt suddenly far more empty.

One of the two guards near the doorway cleared his throat. "We will lead the rest of you to your quarters now," he said. "Except for Rahamanash–" He stopped himself. "Except for Lytira."

Acarius tensed. "Why not Lytira?" he asked.

The fourth guard stepped up behind them. "The princess is requested in the king's quarters," he said. "Though I suppose I'm expected to call you a *former* princess, at least for now."

Lytira turned toward him, and her rigid posture softened. "Saro," she said, relief clear in her voice.

Lex looked questioningly at Acarius, who leaned toward him and whispered, "He was the queen's personal guard before she died. He used to care for Lytira when the queen was too ill to do so."

"It is good to see you, child," Saro smiled. "Now come, quickly. Your father is waiting."

Lytira nodded and followed him toward the far door and up the stairs.

"Well," Nigel said, "I guess that leaves just us... The Three Musketeers!"

"What are musketeers?" Acarius asked.

Nigel's mouth dropped open. "What do you *mean*, what are Muske–"

"We will take you to your quarters now," one of the guards near the other door declared.

Nigel shrugged. "Off we go, then," he said, and walked toward the guards.

"I hope the quality of the guest beds has improved more than their hospitality," Acarius said, moving behind Nigel.

Lex hurried after them, no choice but to follow.

The guards led them up a winding staircase of polished wood. As it curved upward, sunlight spilled through small, open windows carved into the outer walls. The staircase was narrow and they moved single-file, Nigel following the first guard, Acarius behind him, then Lex with the second guard taking up the rear. *Probably to prevent any attempt to escape,* Lex thought.

A sudden sound from outside made Lex stumble, one foot halfway to the next step. A deafening rumble shook the air. "What was *that?*" he asked.

"The lions," the guard behind him answered calmly. "It is their feeding time."

"The *what?*" Lex asked, but he didn't really need to. He had just reached a window which gave a clear view of the grassy area below. Just behind the barn he'd seen earlier a pride of lions roamed, uncontained by any walls or barriers, between the barn and the other buildings. "You have *lions* in the city?" he asked, his voice rising in panic. He thought of the horses being led behind the barn, right where the lions were now pacing. *Feeding time?* His heart sank. "The horses..."

Acarius looked back. "The lions do not harm the people...or the horses," he said. "Right?" He turned to the guard.

"Of course, Master Acarius," the guard replied. "You are our guests. We would never allow them to harm your animals."

"Master? You still call me that? I'm impressed," Acarius smirked.

"You may have upset our king, but your status remains unchanged," the guard answered.

"I see," Acarius said thoughtfully. "But my friend is worried about our horses, so..."

"As I said, we would never allow the lions to harm them," the guard responded.

Acarius nodded, then turned back to Lex. "See? All good."

Lex blinked. "But... *lions.* They eat– in the– they're roaming free!" He had trouble even forming the words to express the danger everyone else clearly didn't understand.

Acarius shrugged. "Trust me; it's not the weirdest thing you'll see here." He turned back toward the stairs, heading up to catch Nigel and the other guard.

"They are the king's personal animals," the guard behind Lex supplied. "They do not harm his people or his guests. He would not allow it."

"Oh, right," Lex said, "Of course! He won't *allow* it. Well, that just makes it all make sense, because lions seem like the sensible type that would, you know, follow those sort of rules."

Another roar shook the air outside the window.

"Oooh, I love that sound!" Lex heard Nigel's voice drift down from the stairs above him.

The guard shrugged. "We feed them well. Why would they disobey? Now, may I *please* show you to your quarters?"

Lex squeezed his eyes shut. He suddenly felt like the most reasonable person in this place, which was pretty bad since he was an amnesiac hero raised from the dead by prophetic science-magic channeled through an energy-harnessing device disguised as a video game console. "Sure," he said, tossing his hands upward. "Why not? Point the way!"

The guard pointed up the stairs with raised eyebrows.

Lex sighed and trudged upward toward the others.

# THE EDGE OF NOTHING

# CHAPTER 16

The guards showed them into their quarters, then shut the door and left. Lex looked around. It was a comfortable enough room with polished wood floors, walls, and ceiling and small, open windows carved in the outer walls. There were two narrow beds in the room – *I am* not *sharing a bed with Nigel*, Lex thought – a dresser, and a small corner area separated by a wooden partition which, from the washbasin and strange, squat contraption he could see behind it, Lex guessed was probably the washroom and toilet area. He immediately wondered how plumbing worked inside a tree. Maybe it didn't. He made a mental note to ask later, before it came time he needed it.

The room was positioned on the third floor on the front side of the towering tree-palace, and the windows provided a view of the courtyard area and even part of The Fallows just outside the front gates, visible through a gap in the branches above the city wall. However, The Fallows apparently sloped up from there – Lex hadn't noticed it from ground level – and the room wasn't high enough in the palace for him to see very far beyond the slope.

Nigel walked to one of the beds and climbed into it, then curled up and pulled the covers over his head.

*How can he go to sleep after all that?* Lex thought. But it was Nigel.

Lex walked to the far side of the room and leaned out of one of the windows, which was just large enough for his head but not big enough for his body to fit through, and looked up. To both sides, a few feet above window-level, hung the lower branches of the trees which formed that part of the city's canopy. The tree building rose straight above them, carrying on into the canopy and then up above it. It suddenly occurred to Lex that the king's quarters were probably camouflaged along the treetops, removed from the city as though his house was simply part of the forest.

Lex pulled his head back inside. "How does the king keep a watch on the city if his level is up above the canopy?" he asked Acarius.

"It's both above and in it," Acarius answered. "The king's level is more like a two-story house, with some rooms just below the treeline and then a private office quarter for him with viewing windows above the canopy. They call it the fourth floor, because that's where the entrance is, but much of it actually hangs down into the third floor, just above us. Some of the windows on the other side of his quarters are beneath the canopy, and the rest are above. It's actually a pretty cool setup." Acarius flopped down on the empty bed. "Ah," he said. "A good upgrade. Masha must have gotten better at making mattresses."

Lex narrowed his eyes. "How are you so calm, and how do you know so much about this place?"

Acarius pushed up onto his elbows. "I used to live here," he said. "In Zeriphath, I mean. Not in this exact room. I was on the fourth floor, with the royal family."

Lex stared. "What?"

Acarius swept his legs over the edge of the bed and leaned his elbows onto his knees. He stared at the floor as he spoke. "My mother – my biological mother – died when I was a baby. I was found and sent back to my clan, but they rejected me. The Frosts found out, and took me in. They raised me, and they were the only family I knew, until the prophecy happened and you – I mean you as Marcus – came for me. Things were getting bad and the neighbors around the ranch, when they found out I wasn't... normal... came after me. At first we thought things would be fine, and you began training me at the ranch, but after I was attacked one night, you and my father decided I'd be safer here, in Zeriphath. That ride you remember through The Fallows? That was you bringing me here. The healers here saved my life, and the queen insisted the king take me in. She'd seen me in her visions. The king agreed and I spent my teen years here, with them. They became my family, in a way, though I missed my parents and sisters back at the ranch. And the king never particularly liked me. But they were nice enough, for a while at least."

Lex had so many questions. He decided to start at the beginning. "So, you're... I mean, I know they call you half-blood, but you said *clan*, like the Sephram and Alomman. Are you one of them?"

"Yes and no," he said. "My mother was Sephram, yes, but my father was human. I still don't know who he was, but it was clear my clan viewed me as something which should never have been. After centuries of keeping the bloodlines pure, a half-blood was an abomination." He shrugged. "I can't blame them, I guess. My human side weakens my abilities, so I can't do any of the things they can do. I'm really more human than I am one of them – but not human enough for the neighbors to accept me, apparently. When they found out I had magic in me, they wanted me dead."

"But not the Frosts. Are they... like you?"

"No. The Frosts are human. Well, most of them anyway. One is adopted like me, but from Arcalon. Hers is a different story. But the others are all ordinary humans, though the Frost family is nothing like most humans. My dad was one of the bravest men I've ever known. He risked his life to keep peace between humans and the magical races, and the neighbors never even knew. They thought he travelled so much because he sold and transported horses." He let out a short laugh.

Acarius' answers were only giving Lex more questions, but he tried to focus. "So did I... I mean, did Marcus... stay here with you?" Lex had no memories of this place, not that he could recall.

"No," Acarius said. "They don't usually allow outsiders. They made an exception for me because I had some of the bloodline in me, and because the queen wouldn't take *no* for an answer. She could be quite persuasive when she believed in something." He smiled sadly. "She was a good woman."

Something struck Lex. "So then you and Lytira grew up together?"

"In a sense," Acarius answered. "I was already a teenager when I came here, and so was she. But for a while, we were sort of like family. Officially I was considered her adopted brother, though I never thought of her parents as my parents. I already had parents."

*Oh*, Lex thought. "Is that why the king was so upset when you and Lytira..." He trailed off.

"When Lytira and I *what*?" Acarius asked, smirking. "What exactly do you think happened between us?"

Lex felt himself blush. "I don't know," he said. "But you said–"

Acarius laughed, then fell silent. After a moment, he said, "We fell in love... if you can call it that when you're only sixteen."

From the look on his face, Lex guessed that was exactly the thing to call it.

"But then the world outside went crazy and, well, when you think you're the prophesied one, things get complicated," Acarius continued. "You and I had to leave, you know, to fulfill our destiny and all sorts of glamorous things which eventually resulted in us all nearly getting killed. *More* than nearly for some of us." He looked at Lex. "Lytira insisted on coming with us. You can imagine how her father felt about that."

"Yeah, wow," Lex said. "If today was any indication, he probably threw a fit."

"The world's most epic one," Acarius said. "He threatened to ban Lytira from the clan if she didn't stay. Of course, the queen convinced him not to, and though Lytira hesitated for a while, in the end, she came anyway." He paused. "It would have been better, I think, if she'd stayed."

"What happened between you?" Lex asked, not sure he should but unable to stop his curiosity.

"We grew apart," Acarius answered softly. "We failed at our mission, her mother died while she was away, I returned to the ranch to be with my family, and Lytira decided to join the Alowen clan rather than returning home."

"Why didn't she—"

"Stay with me?" Acarius asked. He sighed. "I already explained how the neighbors reacted to *me* being not-quite-human; how do you think they would have reacted to her? After we failed, we had someone from Arcalon adjust the humans' memories of what happened, but Lytira didn't deserve to live a life hiding who she was, not with what she can do. She deserved to be with her own people."

"And you?"

"I'm a half-breed. They don't want me. I didn't belong there. Besides, Lytira is a princess of her people. She is – was – in line to be queen one day. She needed to be with someone her people would accept, someone who could match her in power."

*Like Baram?* Lex wondered, thinking of the large man at Alowen who had helped Lytira. But he didn't dare ask it, not after how Acarius had acted when he saw the two of them together. A lot of things were starting to make more sense.

"But now?" Lex asked. "I mean, now you're travelling together again, right? So maybe–"

"You heard what she said to her father," Acarius answered. "She's with us because it serves a greater purpose. That's all. Besides, *now* we may have cost her her throne, her clan, everything. I wouldn't blame her if she never wanted to see any of us again once this is all through."

"I'm sorry," Lex said. There seemed to be nothing else to say.

"Anyway," Acarius said, exhaling, "we have other things we need to discuss. You do realize the attack by the wrasseks on our way here means someone is still after us, right? Wrasseks do not live in The Fallows, or anywhere near it. If they were there, they were *sent* there. Someone must have known we'd be heading this way."

"Which means they know we're here," Lex stated.

"Exactly."

Lex groaned. Could they never catch a break? "Who do you think it is? The Aiacs? I thought we'd killed them all."

Acarius ran his hand over his eyes. "It could be more Aiacs, but I think it's probably something worse." He paused.

Lex could feel his anxiety mounting as he waited for Acarius to continue. Something *worse* than Aiacs?

"Lex, there's something about the prophecy you should know," Acarius said finally. "When the prophecy was given that I would be the one to restore stability to the Worldforce – or at least we thought that's what it meant – the Ancients weren't the only ones to send someone after me. While the Ancients were sending you, we later found out that another, a dark king from Galgor, was also after 'the son of prophecy.' Galgor had been uninhabited for centuries, or so we all thought. It was said to be a rocky, barren place home to only huge, dangerous beasts and creatures like wrasseks. No one knew who this sudden 'king' was or where he came from, we only knew he controlled the monsters of Galgor, and his name – Malleck Dross."

At this, Nigel sprang up from under the covers. "Malleck Dross!" he shouted, his eyes wide. Then he fell back, apparently talking in his sleep.

"What in the–" Lex said.

Acarius turned back to him. "I'll explain that in a minute," he said. "As for what this supposed king was after, we didn't know for sure. He seemed to want to prevent the Worldforce from being stabilized, since he focused all his energy on trying to find and kill me. *You* got to me first, and by the time we realized someone else was after me, there was so much going on with my neighbors and other things that we couldn't tell who might be working with him or whom to trust. The Ancients wanted you to bring me back to the Core, but you didn't trust them. Instead, you and my father reached out to Zeriphath and arranged for me to come here. I lived here while you traveled between here and the villages being a typical hero... but after a year with no signs of anyone still after me, everyone assumed Malleck Dross had died or disappeared or maybe just given up. By that time, I was sixteen and trained well enough that you and my father felt I could return to my family's farm... as long as you were with me, of course. We continued to train there."

"Train in what?" Lex asked.

"Sword-fighting, mostly," Acarius said. "I don't have magical abilities, so it's pretty much all I can do, but I at least wanted to be good at it. And with your palace training, you were one of the best. Everything I know about fighting, I learned from you. Before you came, I was just a horse-rancher, although the Sephram part of me does give me slight advantages, like enhanced reflexes and superior hearing."

Lex shook his head, unsure whether to be proud of having trained one of the best fighters he'd ever seen, or embarrassed that his own skills had atrophied so greatly.

"Anyway," Acarius continued, "word spread among the magical peoples about 'the son of prophecy' being trained by the prince of the Ancients." He smiled. "For a while, we were quite the celebrities. But then the Worldforce spun into chaos again once Jana came through, and the humans couldn't be kept in the dark anymore. When ground-tsunamis, earthquakes, and random sinkholes are happening all across the land and lightning rains down randomly from the sky, it's hard to pretend everything is fine. That was around the time Lytira came to find us. She believed in the prophecy, and her mother's visions of me, and wanted to help save the world. We all did – it was our noble quest." He laughed again, but not happily. "You see how that turned out. Anyway, as word spread people began calling for us, asking us to come rescue their cows from sinkholes, or to settle disputes between magical clans and their human neighbors. We went. How could we not? We were *heroes*." His voice bit down on the last word. "But word spread too far. The forces in Galgor heard, too."

"Oh," Lex said, not liking where this was going.

"At first it was just wrasseks showing up – a sure sign Galgor was after us," Acarius continued. "But then the Aiacs came. That was the first we'd ever seen them." He gave a small shiver. "After watching a few of our friends be taken as Aiacs, we learned they were tied to Ardis and the Ancients. Only a demon-goddess like Ardis could do something like that. It seemed your people and Galgor had teamed up to ensure the prophecy didn't get fulfilled."

"Why Galgor?" Lex asked. "What do they want from all of this?"

Acarius shook his head. "We don't know. Not much is known about Galgor, but the stories say it is a place of darkness, of dark magic and monsters and demons – perhaps even where Ardis first emerged; many of us never believed the story that she emerged from the Worldforce. The Worldforce is good and balanced – or it used to be – and Ardis is anything but. I still don't know the exact wording of the prophecy the Ancients received, but during that time you did tell me two things about it: that it involved a son of prophecy and a daughter of power... and that the son of prophecy was meant to survive whatever happened; he would not die. You meant it to reassure me, that I would be okay. But a few weeks after the Aiacs and wrasseks came after us, so did Malleck."

"I don't understand," Lex said. "He's just a king, right? How could he be worse than Aiacs and wrasseks?"

"He was powerful, more powerful than any Ancient, but with a dark magic unlike anything I've ever seen, except for in you. Malleck's abilities are different, but it's the same dark energy. We knew they were trying to stop the prophecy, but when they finally came in full force and trapped us, they didn't target me and Jana, they targeted *you* and Jana... and suddenly I realized the prophecy never had been about me. It was about you all along. I didn't have a chance to figure out why the Ancients sent you for me if it had always been about you. Things went horribly wrong, and even your magic was no match for Malleck. When you and Jana died, the Worldforce spiraled out of control, the whole land was thrown into chaos, and I knew we had failed. The Aiacs and wrasseks disappeared – their job was done. The ground tsunamis, sinkholes, the things you've seen – those have been happening all over Arameth and getting worse for the past seven years, ever since you died. People live in terror of the very ground they stand on. Nowhere feels safe. But the Aiac and the wrasseks had all but vanished until you reappeared. They're here for *you* – the son of prophecy, the one who survived after all – and the daughter of power with you. And if the wrasseks are involved, that means Malleck Dross is, too; I'm certain of it."

Nigel sprang up again. "Stop saying that name!" he shouted.

"Gah!" Lex cried, startled. "Why does he keep doing that?"

Acarius sighed. "Oh yeah, that," he said. "Nigel was attacked by Malleck personally, during the battle that killed you and Jana. He only just escaped with his life by sending out an energy blast from the device he'd brought to do the emergency LEX protocol – like a channeled portal which turned the energy into a laser. It knocked Malleck back and injured him enough for Nigel to escape in the chaos and find his way back to us. Since you exploded soon after, everyone believed Malleck to have been destroyed in the blast that killed all the Aiacs and wrasseks. But given what we're seeing now, I'd guess he survived."

"I need more blankets," Nigel said, throwing himself back under the covers.

Lex wasn't sure he'd ever quite get used to people talking about him exploding. But he had to ask. "What happened, exactly, when I... exploded? I only remember bits of it."

Nigel piped up, just his head emerging from the covers this time. "It was like what you usually do, only in explosion form. It would have killed *everyone*, except I had just initiated the LEX protocol, which – as a safety precaution from the last time when I blew up half my lab – included an opposite energy push which put a bunch of us in a sort of safety bubble. When things dissipated, the ground around us was like a crater, and you and Jana and everyone else around us had been blown to pieces... but all the other Sephram around us were already dead or taken as Aiacs anyway, and Jana had already died, too, so I guess that was fine. And we know now that *you* didn't completely explode, because part of you got caught by my LEX protocol and sent into the Worldforce for safe-keeping. That LEX protocol had been meant for me, you know, but I used it on you because you were supposedly important. It saved your life, I'm pretty sure. You're welcome." He slid back under the blankets.

Acarius turned to Lex. "Now Malleck, it seems, has come back to finish the job. Lex, if he had wrasseks in The Fallows, he definitely knew we would come here. It's only a matter of time until he realizes we've killed the wrasseks he's sent and sends more... or something worse. We have to get you and Amelia somewhere safer, before you or anyone else here get hurt."

Lex knew Acarius was right, but– "Amelia is still too weak. We can't leave until they figure out how to help her. Besides, where else would we go?"

"I have a place," Nigel's voice muttered from under the covers.

Acarius turned toward Nigel's bed. "You still have it?"

"Of course," Nigel's voice answered. "Where do you think I keep my spare socks?"

"What place?" Lex asked. "What's he talking about?"

"Nigel has a hidden place in the woods where he lived after we faked his death," Acarius answered.

Lex blinked. "What?"

Nigel pushed the covers back and sighed. "Of course. I mean, didn't you figure that out from the fact that I no longer go by Luther?"

"Um, no," Lex said. "I didn't. Could someone please explain why Nigel is pretending to be dead?"

"*I'm* not pretending to be dead," Nigel answered, sitting up. "Luther is."

Lex looked to Acarius, who shrugged.

"It started before the prophecy which sent you to me," Acarius said, "when you'd just come back from being sent to Earth but had returned without a daughter of power to help seal the breach. That was a good thing, by the way. You later realized the Ancients probably just wanted to destroy Jana and prevent the prophecy, on Ardis' command, since you'd been ordered by Ardis to kill me, too."

"Wait, you knew that?" Lex asked. "I mean, I saw it in my memories, but..."

"Of course," Acarius said. "You told me. We may have started as a kid prophesied to save the world and his guardian/trainer/designated-assassin, but we became best friends. There isn't much you kept from me... I think."

"Oh," Lex said.

"Anyway, the Ancients were rather upset that you had come back without a daughter of power, but they were even *more* upset that you had betrayed them in order to save an Earthborn girl, then continued to stay and assist this crazy Earthborn man" – Acarius gestured to Nigel – "and help him try to find his granddaughter. When they sent you after me and you failed to kill me as instructed, they turned sour on the whole thing and decided we *all* had to go. They were hesitant to kill you or me right away – you are the prince, after all, and I was a prophesied savior, so I think they wanted to be subtle about it – but they didn't have those qualms about Luther. They kept sending assassins, and eventually we all got tired of fighting them and just decided to fake Luther's death."

"I died very tragically," Nigel said, standing up. "Fortunately, I was already half-mad from the Worldforce constantly blabbering on in my head, so afterward all I did was stop trying to act normal. I ditched my earth clothes for these fine digs"– he spun, displaying his dirty, old tunic – "and embraced my inner crazy to become the amazing Nigel, an eccentric but brilliant old man and mentor figure to the great Acarius, once-prophesied-savior-turned-horse-rancher."

"Wow, that's very... self-aware of you," Lex said.

"Thank you," Nigel said, nodding. "We told everyone I was a former scholar with a slight case of addle-brain his parents hired to be his tutor after he returned home from Zeriphath. I had to live in his family's barn for a while, but I liked horses anyway, and eventually I got upgraded to my swanky hut in the woods."

*That was an upgrade*? Lex thought.

"Anyway, no one's thought of me as anything but Nigel for years now. We were already a year or so into the mentor act when the battle with Malleck and the others went down. I'd been at the ranch the whole time you were training Acarius, although I suppose no one guessed you and Acarius had also been teaching me to fight. I'm spryer than I look, you know." He winked.

"Nigel's hut might be just the place for us to stay while we figure things out," Acarius said. "No one but Nigel even knows where it is."

"And it was meant to stay that way," Nigel said, narrowing his eyes. He sighed. "But I suppose plans change."

"What good will it do to hide out in the woods?" Lex asked. "Isn't there something we should be doing to stop all this?"

"It won't be hiding out," Acarius said. "We just need time to contact our allies in other places and figure out what's really going on so we can form a plan. But it'd be best to do that somewhere isolated, where others won't be put in danger by our presence."

"Right," Lex said. "Okay."

Acarius clapped him on the shoulder. "It's set, then. As soon as the healers clear Amelia, we'll head to Nigel's hut. I'm sure the king will be glad to be rid of us."

It didn't escape Lex's notice that Acarius said nothing about Lytira. Lex wondered if she would join them, and how her talk with her father might be going.

Nigel suddenly got a thoughtful look very unlike himself. "Arcalon," he said, turning to Acarius. "They've got to be involved in this somehow."

Acarius nodded. "I agree."

"What *is* Arcalon?" Lex asked.

"They're a nation down to the south beyond the mountain range known as Batherol's Stand," Acarius answered. "They are a fringe faction of the Ancients who broke off from the rule of the Core during the Great War. However, Batherol's Stand is also home to the human fortress of Raith, an isolated city of eccentric, superstitious people who for whatever reason avoid all contact with the outside world. Arcalon is the only nation in communication with Raith these days."

"I thought no humans remembered magic," Lex said. "Does Arcalon pretend to be... normal?"

Acarius shook his head. "Raith was the only remaining human city – at least to our knowledge – who remembered the existence of magic. The spell which wiped everyone else's memory somehow missed them, and the knowledge of what lived outside their walls drove them to lock themselves inside. But eventually they needed supplies, so they established trade with Arcalon. The Ancients of Arcalon bred with some of the humans of Raith, creating their own mixed race. Over time, the Ancient blood was diluted to the point that the Arcalon people don't really do magic anymore, except for producing some of the most talented seers the world has ever seen. The

Ancients nearly destroyed them after the Great War for breeding 'abominations,' but part of the peace treaty required that the half-Ancients of Arcalon would not be harmed, so long as they stayed walled off beyond Batherol's Stand, in their own small part of the world."

"So they just stay trapped there?" Lex asked.

"They don't seem to mind," Acarius answered. "They have a whole region of the land to themselves which many of the humans don't even know exists since the mountains above them are so impassable. They have a beautiful lake-city, Elar'eludan, which feeds out to the sea. Many suspect they actually do travel beyond their restricted boundaries by water, but if it's true, they do so carefully. They've never been caught. None of the magical clans have anything against Arcalon, except for the Ancients themselves, but *they* have something against pretty much everyone. The Sephram-Alomman Alliance has a port where Batherol's Stand and the Sea of Aram meet, which their merchants use for trade with Arcalon." He paused. "That's how the pippits got loose, actually. But other than the Port of the Alliance and occasional trade with Raith, Arcalon pretty much keeps to itself."

Lex attempted to process all this information. "You said they have seers?" he asked. "Like the ones at the Core? And like Lytira's mother?"

"Yes and no," Acarius said. "Seers can be from any clan or race – except full-blood humans of course – and no one quite knows how they get their abilities. But for some reason, seers born of the half-human-Ancients of Arcalon are far more powerful than other seers. They have more clarity to their visions, more detail. They can predict things quite accurately, whereas most visions are more abstract. My sister, Liz, the adopted one – she is a seer. She has visions frequently. They seem a lot like your glimpses, which is why I thought you were having a vision when I first saw you collapse on the hill. She was found as a baby outside the border of Arcalon by my father on one of his trips and when he tried to return her, her aunt and uncle insisted there was a family dispute happening which had killed her parents, and that she'd be safer with humans. So my parents adopted her."

*Liz*, Lex thought. *The blonde one.* The one he'd momentarily mistaken for Jana. No wonder she looked different than the rest of the family. But that raised another question. "If you're also adopted," Lex asked, "then why do all the rest of your sisters look so much like you?"

Acarius shrugged. "It's not that uncommon for adopted children to end up resembling their families in some way."

All three men jumped as the door to their room burst open. The king rushed in. "Have you seen Lytira?" he asked, his voice strained. "Is she here?"

"No," Acarius said, shaking his head. "We haven't seen her since she left to meet with you."

"Curse the very air and ground and every bit of earth that—" The king's shouted curses trailed off as he rushed out and back down the hallway.

Lex glanced at Acarius, who was suddenly like a spring compressed tight with anxiety.

"If she– I– I need to go," he said, rushing for the door.

A guard blocked his path. "You must stay here," the guard said, filling the doorway. "We will deal with the king's daughter." He pushed the door shut.

Acarius pulled against it and shook the handle, but it wouldn't budge. "They've locked us in," he said, sinking to sit against the door.

Suddenly there was a knock. Acarius jumped up in surprise and pulled the handle, and this time the door opened.

A Sephram woman stood in the doorway, covered in a full-length leather dress which touched the floor. Etchings of animals and symbols swirled across the surface of the leather, featuring mostly some sort of heron.

"Healer," Acarius said, bowing his head. "Please, come in."

Lex saw Acarius' eyes glance past her, as though assessing whether he could make a break for it, but the guard stood close behind her.

"I am not staying," the healer said. "I have a message for the son of prophecy."

Lex hesitated a moment before realizing she was talking about him. He moved toward the door.

Acarius stepped back, moving out of the way as Lex came forward.

"Sulanashum," the healer said, nodding to Lex. "I have word on the daughter of power."

"Amelia?" Lex asked. "How is she? Is she coming back here now?"

The healer met his gaze. "No," she said, "she is not."

Lex felt panic climbing up his throat. "Where is she, then? Can I see her?"

"No," the healer said again. "The daughter of power is unwell. She has gotten worse."

Lex clenched his teeth, swallowing the panic. "What happened?" he asked, almost a whisper.

"We have her stabilized now," the healer answered, "but she is weak, and there is still much to do. Many things to check. For now, she must rest. When she wakes, you may see her. We will call for you."

Lex breathed out, feeling some relief. "Okay," he said. "Thank you."

The healer nodded and turned to leave.

Suddenly Acarius let out a wordless shout. Lex spun, just in time to see Acarius jumping back from the window. "Move!" Acarius yelled, spinning toward him. "Let me through!"

Lex rushed to the window as Acarius pushed past him, trying to spot what Acarius had seen. The courtyard looked fine, everything was normal, except – there, outside the wall. A large man lumbered toward them through The Fallows, carrying a dark bundle in his arms.

Lex raced after Acarius, who had already burst out into the hall. The guard shouted after them but decided to follow rather than stopping them, clearly alarmed by Acarius' behavior.

Lex followed the rushing Acarius down the winding staircase, through the lobby of the palace, and out into the courtyard.

"Open the gates!" Acarius screamed, a panic in his voice Lex had never heard before. "Open the gates!"

The guards turned to him in shock but seeing the urgency on his face, chose to obey rather than questioning, something which impressed Lex at the same time it surprised him. They pulled large ropes on either side of the gates, and the heavy doors swung open.

Standing outside the gates was Baram, holding a large black panther in his arms. The creature was unconscious and wrapped in a thin blanket, which was already soaked through with blood. "It happened so fast," Baram blurted as he gently lowered the animal to the ground. "An Aiac got her in The Fallows. She only barely survived."

Acarius rushed over and knelt beside the animal.

"Call the healer!" someone yelled, and the guards inside the gates burst into motion.

"They're coming," Baram said, looking up at Acarius. "Aiacs, wrasseks, all of them. They're almost here. And if the rumors in the villages we passed on the way here have any truth to them, Malleck himself is with them."

Lex was still trying to process what was happening when the panther began shifting beneath the blanket. He focused on its face, afraid it would awaken startled and attack someone... but it was still unconscious. The movement wasn't from it waking, it was from it *changing*. The creature shrank and morphed right before his eyes, the dark, fierce face of the panther suddenly becoming the unusually pale, very *non*-panther face of Lytira.

"What the–" Lex whispered. So *that* was what Lytira could do. His mind raced back, remembering the panther in the forest. Had it been her? Could *all* her people do that, or only Lytira?

Lex sank to his knees beside Acarius, the seriousness of the situation suddenly hitting him. That was *Lytira's* blood covering the blanket... lots of it.

"The healers are on their way," a guard said, placing his hand on Acarius' shoulder. "We should not move her until they assess her injuries."

Acarius pushed Lytira's matted hair back from face tenderly, his face desperate and helpless. His fingers came away streaked with blood, and he stared at them wordlessly.

Baram stood. "Tell King Rahman my people are near. We will fight with you, if he wills it." He turned, his clothes shredding as his large body morphed into a giant bear before racing off along the treeline into the distance.

Lex stood in shock, trying to process what he'd just seen and filled with concern for Lytira.

The king burst through the crowd at the gates, shoving aside anyone who didn't move quickly enough. "What happened?" he shouted, seeing Lytira on the ground. "Who did this?"

A group of healers ran up and dropped to their knees around her, touching her face, lifting her eyelids. One of them lifted the edge of the blanket and peered under. "We must get her inside," he said, standing.

The guards lifted her at once and rushed her into the gates, the healers right behind them.

Acarius stood to follow.

"No," the king growled. "You will stay here. You have brought enough trouble on my people." He spun toward the gates.

"My lord," Acarius called out, his voice hollow.

The king stopped and turned back. "What?" he spat.

"Baram had a message. The forces of Galgor are coming. The Alowens will fight with us, if you wish. But you should alert the people. Get everyone to safety."

"To *safety?*" the king spat. "And where would you have us go? This is on *you*, half-blood, you and your 'son of prophecy.' If Lytira survives this, if any of us do, I will ensure you never see her again. Tell Baram we do not need his help; we will be remaining inside our walls. This is your battle, not ours. Let him help *you* if he desires." He stormed inside the city. "Close the gates!" he called. "Prepare the defenses!"

Lex and Acarius watched as the gates slammed shut in front of them.

# CHAPTER 17

L ex and Acarius stared at each other.

"What do we do now?" Lex asked.

Suddenly shouting was heard from inside the city. "Get her away from my daughter!" the king's voice boomed.

Lex and Acarius moved toward the gates. What was going on inside the city? A moment later, one of the gates inched open and Nigel's head poked out.

"Hurry!" he whispered, waving them toward him. "Come inside!"

Lex and Acarius slid in through the gap in the gate. Hardly anyone noticed their entrance, as all the attention was on the scene the king was creating in the courtyard.

"I want that *daughter of power* out of my city," he snarled. "I will not stand by and watch any of my people die because of her!"

"But, my king," pleaded one of the healers, "she is still too weak. We cannot move her."

"I do not care how weak she is!" the king yelled. "Put her outside the gates!"

"Apologies, my king," said another healer, giving a small bow, "but we cannot. We are sworn to heal and not harm. Putting her outside the city would undoubtedly harm her."

The king roared in frustration. "Then at least move my daughter to another house! I don't want her anywhere near that *thing*." He stormed off toward the tower.

The healers rushed back toward the ring of houses and ducked into one with a sign hanging above the second story. It occurred to Lex suddenly that the signs probably indicated where different tradespeople lived; rather than having a business district, the tradesman and healers of Zeriphath simply took up shop in their homes among the people.

As the king stormed past the crowd, his eyes caught on Lex and Acarius. "How did *you* get back in here?" he yelled. He rounded on Acarius, backing him up against the gate. "This is your fault somehow," he snarled. "What was she doing out of the city? Was this *your* idea?"

"No. I didn't even know she had gone," Acarius answered, meeting the king's eyes.

"Why would she go?" the king bellowed, leaning right into Acarius' face.

Acarius stared back, his face blank. "I have no idea," he said. "Perhaps you should ask Baram."

The king growled and spun away, stomping back toward his palace. "Throw them out of the city! *All* of them!" he yelled without looking back.

Lex glanced around at the guards then at Acarius, unsure whether the plan was to go willingly or put up a fight.

But the guards weren't moving. They shifted uncomfortably, glancing at one another as though uncertain whether to obey the king's orders. After a moment one of them stepped forward.

"I'm sorry, Master Acarius," he said, "but we must obey the king." He pulled the cord to open the gates. "Call to us if anyone approaches. We will not leave you to fight alone."

Lex, Acarius, and Nigel were just stepping through the open gate and back out into The Fallows when the elders who had served as Heart and Ear rushed toward them. "Shut the gates," they said to the guards. "These men will remain inside." To the guards' questioning glances, the Heart replied, "The king is unwell. He will be remaining in his quarters for a while. You will tend to the needs of these men and equip them with whatever they require for battle." With that they turned away and headed back toward the palace.

As soon as they were gone, Acarius rushed toward the house where the healers had disappeared. Lex followed. The house they entered was set up like a normal dwelling, with a small kitchen area and a place for sitting. The healers were still on the bottom floor, preparing something in a bowl in the kitchen, but Amelia and Lytira were nowhere in sight.

Acarius hurried toward one of the healers. "Please, can I see her?" he asked.

"I am sorry, Master Acarius, but I do not think that is a good idea," one of them answered. "She is hurt very badly, and we are in the middle of treating her."

"How is she?" Acarius asked. "Will she be alright?"

"It is too soon to tell," the healer answered.

Acarius turned and walked out of the building.

The healer moved toward the stairs in the back.

"Wait," Lex said. "What about Amelia? Can I see her now?"

"I do not think that is a good idea either," the healer said. "She is still very fragile, and it is best if she rests." She placed her hand on his arm. "Do not worry. As soon as we have word on either one of them, we will let you know." She gave him a small smile and went back up the stairs.

Lex moved outside and found Acarius pacing in front of the house. Lex hesitated a moment, but his curiosity was too much for him. He just needed something in his life to make a little bit of sense for once. "Hey, Acarius," he said gently, "I know this might not be the best time, but... what just happened... outside the gates?"

Acarius didn't answer; he just sank to the ground and dropped his head between his knees.

"Oh, you mean the panther thing?" Nigel asked, moving toward them. "Yeah, they all do that. Well, not that *exactly*, I mean, they don't all turn into panthers. Each has his or her own animal."

Lex stared. "What?"

"Yeah, it's the Sephram thing," Nigel said with a shrug. "They turn into animals. I thought that was pretty obvious by now."

Lex shook his head. "Yeah...I get that part...I just... They *all* do it? You mean they're, like, born turning into animals? Do the children do it, too? How does it work? Don't they ever hurt each other?"

"No, no, no," Nigel said, "It's way more complicated than that. These people don't know how to do anything simply." He sighed. "Children can't turn. It happens at puberty, and there's a whole process for it, like a rite-of-passage ceremony. They send them into the woods to figure out which animal they are each naturally attuned to, and approach it in the wild. Supposing a Sephram doesn't die by choosing the wrong animal and getting mauled to death, a bonding occurs and gives the Sephram the ability to turn into that animal at will for the rest of their life."

"So..." Lex said, still confused.

Nigel stared at him and spoke slowly. "A Sephram only gets one animal form for life. Lytira's is a black panther. All the other people have different animals. Of course there is some overlap – some of them turn into the same animal – but it's not like it goes by family or anything like that. It's a very individual sort of thing."

A startling thought suddenly occurred to Lex. "So then the lions behind the barn, are they..."

Nigel laughed. "No, no, those are lions. Just regular, plain old lions."

"Then why are they here?" Lex asked.

"It's the second part of the bond," Nigel answered. "Once the bond is sealed, a Sephram also has the ability to communicate with and call on animals of his bonded type. Sometimes, when a Sephram spends a lot of time in the wild in his animal form for whatever reason, he becomes part of a natural animal group, just like a regular animal would in the wild, except in this case one of those animals is a Sephram. You follow me?"

Lex thought he did. He nodded.

Nigel looked pleased, and continued. "The Sephram aren't always the leaders of their animal groups, but in this case, being as honking big as he is in his Sephram form, the king had no trouble winning the leadership of the pride, if you see what I mean."

Lex was still trying to process everything. "So they can all do this?" he asked.

"Except the children, yes," Nigel answered. "Why do you think Ardis uses them to make Aiacs? She needs their shifting ability. Of course she turns it all demonic, which is a different kind of thing, but it's still the same ability at its core."

*Oh*, Lex thought. Despite being one of the coolest things he'd ever seen, the Sephrams' ability was still a lot to take in.

"Now, if you don't mind," Nigel said, "I am going to go hide. I didn't much like getting nearly killed the last time, and I'd like to avoid it. I'll just wait in the house with Amelia and Lytira – I know you'll be protecting that." He winked at Lex and went inside.

Acarius stood, seeming to wake from his stupor. "Don't be fooled," he said. "He pretends to be a coward, but he'll be out fighting with the rest of us."

Unsure what to say, Lex simply nodded. The two of them stood for a moment in silence.

A few breaths later, Nigel appeared beside them, holding a sword. "Alright, you got me," he said, shrugging. "I'm a sucker for a fight. I did have to swipe a sword from one of Amelia's guards, though. Did you know Sephram carried swords? I thought they all used arrows. But it's a good thing, because I'm a lousy aim with a bow." He turned to Lex. "Oh, Amelia says *hi*, by the way."

Lex felt a jolt shoot through his chest. "What? She's awake?"

But before Nigel had a chance to answer, an ear-splitting siren sounded throughout the city.

"The alarm!" Acarius shouted as they all threw their hands over their ears. "The city is under attack!"

"Aiacs and wrasseks approaching!" a guard yelled. "Everyone inside! Guards, to the walls!"

Lex turned to Acarius and Nigel, who stared back at him. It was happening.

"Master Acarius," one of the guards called, running up to them. "One of my men believes he spotted Malleck Dross among the Aiacs. He is here."

Lex looked between Acarius and the guard in surprise. Was Acarius calling the shots now? What had happened to the king and the elders?

Acarius simply nodded once. "Send a runner to Baram," he said. "He and the Alowens are waiting in the western edge of the forest. And tell the archers to–"

"Son of prophecy!" A deep voice boomed through the air, seeming to come from the sky itself.

Lex cut his eyes to Acarius. "What is that?" he asked, feeling an edge of panic mounting in his chest.

"Malleck Dross," Acarius sighed. "Nigel, will you–" He started to ask, but Nigel was already running back for the healer's house. "Okay, so maybe he's a *bit* of a coward," Acarius said, turning back to Lex. "But can you blame him? He's a crazy, bird-boned old man."

"Son of prophecy!" the voice boomed again. "Show yourself!"

"I'm pretty sure he means you," Acarius said, raising one eyebrow at Lex.

"Yeah, got it, thanks," Lex said. "But what do we *do*?"

"Nothing," Acarius said. "I mean, eventually he'll attack, and we'll fight back. Beyond that, I've got no plan."

"Great," Lex said.

"Hey," Acarius responded, sounding a little offended. "I'm not usually the strategist, you are. And besides, it's not like I had a ton of time to plan."

"Perhaps I am not being *clear*," the voice echoed. "*Prince Marculian* – he who called himself Marcus and was destroyed then reborn as Lex – the *son of prophecy*. Show yourself!"

"At least he knows his history," Acarius said.

"This isn't funny," Lex said. "What should I do?"

"Sorry," Acarius sighed. "You and I always used to joke in battle. I forget sometimes that – nevermind, it doesn't matter. Anyway, like I said, *you* should do nothing. It's not like you're just going to walk up on the wall and turn yourself over to him. That would be insane."

The deep voice called out again, this time sounding a bit amused. "Are you a *coward*, son of prophecy, one meant to heal the entire Worldforce?" He paused. "Do the people know whose dark power truly killed the masses that day? Or have you blamed that all on me?"

The archers were still stationed on the wall, but townspeople began to peer out of their houses, eyeing Lex.

"What's he getting at?" Lex whispered.

"He's just messing with you," Acarius answered. "He means what happened when you exploded, but everyone already knows that. He's trying to get in your head."

"Where is he?" Acarius called up to one of the guards in a hushed voice.

"We don't know," the guard answered. "We cannot spot him. But there must be at least a hundred wrasseks and Aiacs down there, just staring up at us." The fear on the guard's face was plain.

"Just hold and wait," Acarius told the guard, then turned back to Lex. "Why are they not attacking?" he whispered to himself.

"People of Zeriphath," the voice boomed, changing tactics. "You are harboring the son of prophecy and the daughter of power. They, and they

THE EDGE OF NOTHING

alone, are what I seek. Release them to my army within the hour, and your people will be spared. Refuse to do so, and you will all be slaughtered. You have one hour."

The sky went eerily silent.

Inside the city, chaos broke loose.

"I say we turn them over!" a woman yelled, emerging from her house. "They aren't part of us, and I will not allow my family to be slaughtered for their sake!"

There was a murmur of assent around the courtyard as more townspeople joined the conversation.

"He's lying," a man said. "They will attack us, no matter what we do! I say we barricade the children inside the barn, then shift and fight!"

"There aren't enough of us," another man responded. "And the only grouping within miles are the king's lions. Who knows, in his state, if he'll even command them to fight! The king's gone mad, you all saw it! I say we turn them over and be done with it."

One of the guards stepped forward. "He is *Sulanashum*," he said. "We cannot betray him."

"Who believes in that Ardis-cursed prophecy anyway?" a woman spat. "I trust *nothing* from her *or* the Ancients. Turn them over!"

"Silence!" a voice roared through the courtyard.

A hush fell across the people as everyone turned toward the sound.

The king stood in the courtyard just in front of his palace, lions flanking him on either side. He towered between them, every bit as intimidating as they were, even in his Sephram form. "We. Are. Sephram," he bellowed, punching each word. "We do not betray our guests to an enemy, no matter how *unwelcome* those guests may be. In my pain over my daughter's injury, I nearly forgot that. But I am your king, and I will not allow you to betray your honor simply because you are afraid. Sephram are often afraid. But we never bow to it. These people are here under the decree of asylum as part of the ceremony, and we will honor it. We will offer our guests our protection, come what may. The children will be placed with a force of guards in the barn. Every able-bodied adult will shift. We will fight like Sephram, with ferocity and honor. And when this is over, if any of our *guests* are still alive, they will *leave*." He directed these last words at Lex and Acarius, then turned and

261

strode past the crowd into the healers' building, where his deep voice could be heard asking to see Lytira.

There was a brief silence, then the people broke out in hushed conversation.

"Children, to me," he heard someone say, and a group of guards stepped into the center around the man who had spoken. All around the courtyard, parents hugged and comforted their children before urging them off toward the guards.

"What do *we* do?" Lex asked Acarius.

"First, I'm checking on Lytira, I don't care what the healers say. And then–"

A bone-chilling scream from the far ring of houses interrupted his statement. The whole courtyard of people turned toward the sound, everyone suddenly silent.

Then a woman dashed out from between two houses. "Aiacs!" she screamed, her face wild. "They're in the city!"

The people burst into motion, some of them rushing the children toward the barn while others shifted right in the middle of the courtyard. Wildcats, wolves, large cats of several kinds, some deer, birds of prey nearly as large as the wolves, and some smaller creatures Lex couldn't name – Sephram shifted in every direction and the courtyard filled with animals and shreds of former clothing. The pride of lions moved into the courtyard, a huge, thick-maned male taking up the center. He moved to the middle of the clearing and let out a roar which shook the buildings. The other animals responded, their primal battle calls filling the air.

Mare darted around the back of the barn straight for Acarius, who swung up onto her back in one smooth motion.

"Now what do we do?" Lex called up to him.

"We fight," Acarius answered, lowering his hand to Lex.

Lex mounted behind him and glanced around as Acarius turned Mare in a slow circle among the other animals. The Sephram in their animal forms were tense and glancing around, uncertain from which direction the first attack would come.

"Maybe it was a false alarm?" Lex whispered.

"I don't think so," Acarius answered, "though I don't know how an Aiac made it into the camp without the guards seeing it fly in. There are archers covering every inch of the wall, and if something crashed in through the canopy, one of the guards would certainly have heard it."

Another scream cut the air and one of the deer in the courtyard shifted back into Sephram form, then stumbled. She screamed again, seemingly oblivious she was standing naked in the middle of everyone as she scrambled backwards. All around her others backed away, too, some still in animal form and others shifting back to Sephram. Sephram and animals scattered in all directions, though a few in the center of the chaos seemed to be trying to fight something.

Acarius shoved Mare through the other animals to see what was happening. There in the center of the crowd was an Aiac, pinned to the ground by a dark wolf who held fragments of the Aiac's bleeding throat in its jowls. On the ground next to it, its face shredded and pinned by a large bobcat, was another Aiac. And another Aiac lay beside that one, its throat crushed in the grip of a hawk nearly the size of a man.

Lex looked around, stunned. Where had they all come from? None of those Aiacs had been there moments ago.

Another scream broke out and Acarius spun Mare toward it. One of the Sephram – a large heron – seemed to be struggling to maintain her form. Her beak shrank some, then shot out long, then faded back toward her face yet again as her wings slid inward to the length of normal arms. She dropped to the ground on hands and knees, then tipped her face up to them, her eyes filled with terror.

Lex gasped. It was the healer who'd come to see them in their guest quarters, the one with herons on her dress.

"Help me," she pleaded, then her face shifted again, her long braids shrinking up toward her head and morphing into dark, close-cropped hair, her feminine nose widening and lengthening a bit,and the rich color of her skin melting away into a pale, grayish tone. The face blinked up at them, its dark eyes now completely familiar, and gave Lex a grin that made his blood run cold. It was the face of the man Lex had killed, of the man from Dalton, the man who'd taken Amelia, the same face they all had – the face of an Aiac.

The Aiacs weren't coming into the city – they were appearing from the Sephram within it.

# CHAPTER 18

Sephram began shifting into Aiacs around the courtyard.

"What do we do?" Lex asked.

"I don't know," Acarius said, looking around. "I don't know."

The Sephram who remained turned toward the Aiacs, forced to fight off their former clanspeople. They were holding their own, but more could turn Aiac any moment.

"These people cared for me for years," Acarius said, looking in shock. "They were my friends. I know once they turn they're not anymore, but I–"

Lex glanced to Acarius. "What about you?" he said. "You're half Sephram. Will you–"

"No." Acarius shook his head. "I can't shift, remember? I'm safe. Besides" – he pulled a pendant from beneath his tunic, just like the one he'd given Lex – "even if I could, this would prevent it."

"The pendant?" Lex asked.

"It prevents the shift, among other useful things," Acarius said, then his eyes went wide. "Oh crap!" He leapt off Mare and raced toward the healers' house.

Lex had never heard Acarius say *oh crap*, and the phrase immediately drew up memories of Earth and Steve and Jana. Lex ran after Acarius, wondering if *oh crap* was a phrase Nigel had taught him, or if Marcus had taught it to Acarius himself.

By the time Lex caught up to him in the house, Acarius was already running back down the stairs. The leather cord he wore around his neck to hold the pendant was missing. "She'll be safe now," he said, his eyes falling closed with relief. Then he opened them and took a deep breath. "She looks okay," he said. "She's asleep but she's not as pale. What they're doing must be working." He turned to Lex. "Amelia looks fine, too. They're both still sleeping."

Lex desperately wanted to see Amelia, but knew it wasn't the right time – they needed to do something to help the Sephram. "What now?" he asked Acarius.

Acarius glanced outside. "I have no idea. I know we should do something, but– I just– these people were my friends, Lex. I can't... Wait, where's Mare?"

Acarius rushed all the way out, glancing around the clearing. Lex followed him, and his heart sank – the clearing was a bloodbath, bodies of fallen Aiacs everywhere, sprinkled with some of fallen Sephram. And still Sephram continued to turn, more Aiacs springing up every few minutes. If it didn't stop soon, there'd be no Sephram left.

"There!" Acarius pointed, his voice sounding relieved.

Lex followed his hand and saw Mare gallop across the clearing, headed for the barn.

At that moment, the king let out an air-shaking roar in his lion form, then ran for the barn. His pride followed, taking up a guard in front of the barn doors. *They're protecting the children*, Lex thought, his heart squeezing. The remaining Sephram followed the king's lead, joining him against the doors as the Aiacs grouped up and moved toward them. The Aiacs had the Sephram cornered against the barn doors, and as fierce as the king and his people were in their animal forms, they were outnumbered.

Acarius pulled Lex back inside the healers' house. "They haven't seen us," he whispered. "Maybe there's something we can do."

"But what?" Lex asked.

"I don't know," Acarius said, squeezing his eyes shut. "I don't know, I don't know, I don't know."

Malleck's voice boomed outside again. "It would be a shame to keep turning you until there are none of you left; After all, Aiacs are a dime a dozen but each of you have families, lives – it really seems a tragedy. Perhaps you should just surrender."

"It's Malleck changing them?"Acarius hissed. "How is he doing that? Only Ardis has the power to create Aiacs."

*He has dark energy*, Lex thought, *the same as I have, right? Maybe I can do it, too*. But he had no idea where to begin even trying, and even if he could, how would it help? Even if it meant he could control the Aiacs he turned, it would only be taking more Sephram's lives.

A chorus of screams sliced through the air – high-pitched screams, like those of children. Lex and Acarius raced outside.

The roof of the barn was being lifted off by a horde of airborne wrasseks, gripping it from all directions. The wood holding the roof to the barn creaked and splintered, and the children inside screamed again.

"No," Acarius moaned. "No, no, no!" He stood in the doorway, clearly wanting to rush toward the barn but knowing it would be foolish.

Lex looked around wildly. They couldn't just charge in, there were far too many Aiacs. But there had to be *something* they could do.

*The dark energy.* Lex reached inward and found the thread of it, slipping it outward from the cube he'd formed it into. He felt it mold to his grasp, surrendering to his touch. He opened his eyes, focused on the wrasseks, and pulled the darkness slowly outward.

The wrasseks gave a small chorus of shrieks and spun their heads toward the house where Lex stood. Lex pulled harder, but his head was beginning to swim. He hadn't accounted for the sheer force of the darkness among them, all together. He could feel it everywhere – from the wrasseks over the barn, the Aiacs in front of it, even from up in the sky and outside the gates. The city seemed to be drowning in it. If he pulled that much energy in, it would crush him – or worse, explode him, and everyone around him, including Lytira and Amelia, injured and asleep above them. How far would the explosion reach? To the Sephram outside? To the children? The wrasseks hissed and turned their focus back to the barn as Lex released his hold on the darkness. He would have to think of something else.

The roof of the barn gave way and the wrasseks tossed it aside. The children were exposed, caged prey for the taking. The king spun and barreled through the barn doors, leading the Sephram inside to protect the children. The Aiacs moved in front of the barn doors, blocking the king and the other Sephram inside.

But the wrasseks did nothing. They simply hovered above the barn, staring down into it.

Lex and Acarius could see the adult Sephram cornered just inside the doorway, making a final stand between the Aiacs outside and the children within, with the sky above them completely open to the wrasseks' attack.

Then the screaming started again, this time with a different tone.

Lex expected to see the Sephram leap into action to fight off whatever it was – another Aiac turned among them? A wrassek dropped down unseen? Something else entirely? – but none of them moved. They were staring inward at something, in shock.

"What's happening?" Lex asked.

"I don't know," Acarius answered, shaking his head wildly. "I don't know."

"The children," a voice behind them gasped. "They're – turning. I saw it from the window."

Lex and Acarius spun around.

"Lytira!" Acarius shouted. He reached to embrace her, then noticed the pain she seemed to be in and pulled back. "Are you okay? You should be resting!"

"The children – are – turning!" she gasped again. "We have to help them."

She moved for the door.

"What?" Acarius said. "No, that's impossible. They can't even shift yet, they – wait. Unless the Aiacs don't feed off of the shift. Maybe it's something in the blood. But... oh, Worldforce rescue us, we cannot slaughter *children*," he said. "No wonder the others aren't moving."

"Only a couple of the children turned so far," Lytira said, "and my father's lions pinned them to the ground but did not harm them. But they cannot hold them indefinitely, and if some can turn, so can the rest. They will have to kill them. The children will slaughter them all, if they don't. Though perhaps their parents would prefer that, to killing their own offspring." She leaned against the doorframe, breathing heavily from her brief speech. She seemed resolved, but her voice had betrayed her sadness.

It was a devastating situation, but Lex was focused on something else at the moment. "They took the roof off," he said, staring at the barn.

"Yes, we all saw that," Acarius said, turning to him with a confused look.

"No, I mean – I thought it was to get the children, but... they're not attacking. What if it was for a different reason?"

"I don't follow," Lytira said.

"What if Malleck has to *see* them to turn them? It would make sense, right? Don't magicians – people of power, whatever you call it here – don't they usually have to see their target to use magic on them?"

"Not always," Lytira said, "but... you could be right. It would explain why the wrasseks are just hovering there. They're ensuring a clear line of sight for him."

"And why no one was able to spot him in the attacking forces," Acarius said, his eyes going wide. "He's not down there. He's up in the trees."

Lytira raced outside, wincing from pain, and planted herself in the middle of the courtyard.

Acarius gaped for a moment before racing to her side. "Are you crazy?" he hissed. "We're completely exposed!"

"I think that's her point," Lex said, moving to Lytira's other side.

Lytira took a shaky breath, then stretched her spine tall and assumed the regal posture Lex was used to seeing her carry. "Sephram!" she called out. "To me!"

The Aiacs spun toward her, seeming surprised, then part of them broke off in her direction. From inside the barn, the king's large lion eyes peered outward, studying the scene. Then something in them seemed to sharpen, as though understanding Lytira was trying to work a plan. He let out a low rumble and his lions backed off the Aiac-children they'd pinned, letting them up.

He turned back toward the courtyard, watching Lytira.

Lytira flicked one hand to the left, so quickly Lex wouldn't have noticed it had he not been standing on that side of her.

Whatever the signal meant, the king had seen it. He shifted toward the doorway, and his pride fell in behind him. The Aiacs still facing the barn tensed, preparing to fight.

The few guards who were still in Sephram form inside the barn huddled all the children together in a group, protecting them.

Above the barn the wrasseks fidgeted in the air, as though uncertain what to do.

Lytira gave a small nod, and at her signal, the king and his pride leapt forward, tearing apart the Aiacs in front of them, a smaller group now that some had moved toward Lytira. The Aiacs which had moved toward Lytira spun back toward the barn.

"Run for the houses!" Lytira screamed. "Get inside!"

Sephram-animals sped in all directions through the courtyard, forming a protective circle around the guards and children as they dashed for cover. The animals abandoned all attempt to fight the Aiacs in favor of their princess's command and getting the children to safety. The Aiacs, slow to realize what was happening, were a few steps behind but when they began to catch up to the children, the king's lions peeled off from the group to take the Aiacs down.

There were still too many Aiacs, but the houses were within a few paces of the barn and with a quick dash outward, soon all the children were inside the nearest couple of houses, with the Sephram animals shielding the doors. "Get inside, too!" Lytira yelled, and the adults shifted backward, melting into their Sephram forms as they huddled into the houses alongside the children.

Only the king remained, standing in lion form like a sentry under an overhang between the two houses which hid his remaining people.

Now that the courtyard was clear of all but Aiacs – other than Lytira and her friends – the archers still atop the wall let loose their arrows, picking off as many Aiacs as they could. But not for long. Wrasseks from beyond the walls swooped up, pulling the archers over the ledge and down into the waiting army outside. At the same time, the remaining Aiacs in the courtyard suddenly took flight, disappearing over the walls of the city. The haunting yell of the last archer to fall hung in the air as the rest of the city fell silent.

Then the king began to shift.

Lex watched in awe as the massive lion shrank back into a still-massive but slightly smaller man, and a guard from inside the house rushed out, handing the king a blanket to wrap around himself before darting back inside.

"My brave Lytira," the king said, moving toward the courtyard... and out of the cover of the houses.

"Father, no!" Lytira yelled.

It was too late. The king began to shift before them yet again, his dark skin lightening to a pallid grey. "I – am – so sorry," he moaned, then let out an inhuman howl as the change took him, leaving the smirking face of an Aiac in its place.

"*No!*" Lytira yelled. She started to leap toward the creature, but Acarius grabbed her arm.

"No, Lyt, please, you're still hurt," he said, pulling her back.

The Aiac moved toward them, grinning, its human form shifting into creature form as it neared them, wings outspread.

"No, let me," Lex said. He closed his eyes and reached inside to the small thread of darkness which had called to him since the fighting began, and eased it from its prison again.

The darkness whispered through him, cool and smooth. He tightened his mind around it and opened his eyes, focusing on the Aiac. He could do it. He wanted to. With just one Aiac, he could focus it and control how much darkness he took in. But – this was their king. What if the people saw this as a betrayal, for him to kill it? What if Lytira did? Lex pulled at the darkness and the creature howled and stopped, turning its cold eyes on him. Lex had it – it would only take a tug... He hesitated, ready but uncertain.

Lytira shoved past him, dagger in hand, and drove the blade right into the creature's eye.

Lex dropped the darkness and felt it slip back into its box within him as he gaped at Lytira.

"That was not my father," she said. "There was no need to hesitate." She turned and walked toward the houses which held her people.

Lex stared after her, the courtyard suddenly quiet again.

Acarius came up behind him, patting him on the shoulder. "You did well," he said. "I would have hesitated, too. He was their king. And your realization saved all those people." He nodded toward the houses, where the Sephram still took cover.

"Stay inside," he heard Lytira say to the people. "We don't know yet why he pulled his forces, but he has to see you to change you. No one leaves the houses until we have a plan."

Suddenly a child pushed out through the doorway, evading the grasp of the adults. "Mother!" she yelled, rushing toward the body of a fallen Sephram in the courtyard.

"No!" Lytira yelled, reaching for her.

# THE EDGE OF NOTHING

The child screamed and dropped to her knees, already starting to change.

Lytira's eyes filled with tears as she slid a dagger from her belt. "Gods forgive me," she whispered.

"Wait!" Lex yelled. If it was dark energy that changed them, and he could absorb dark energy – and if she wasn't all the way turned yet, there would be some of her normal energy left, so draining her might not kill her – yes, he could do this. He had to try. He closed his eyes, feeling out for the energy, not just within him but outwardly, too. Yes, he could feel it – the same dark presence he'd felt with the wrasseks and Aiacs outside the barn. Inside of him, his own thread of darkness shifted, as though drawn to the darkness outside. Why hadn't he noticed this before? That dark thread inside him was like a magnet, both pulling and being pulled by the dark energy outside him. He felt for the threads of darkness coming from the girl and within him and forced his mind to grab both ends, slowly drawing them together.

The outward darkness resisted, like a line with a heavy fish on the end. He pulled it gently but steadily, careful not to break the connection, and after a moment it gave, sliding toward him.

Lytira gasped. "It's working!" she said. "It's working!"

Lex didn't dare break his concentration to open his eyes. He clamped even tighter, continuing to pull.

The tension went slack and a stream of darkness tumbled in on him, detached from whatever had held it on the other side. Lex stumbled beneath the weight of it, staggering as the cool trickle of darkness turned hot inside him, beginning to churn.

He opened his eyes. Lytira crouched on the ground in front of him, her arms around the little girl... who was still a little girl, and crying into Lytira's shoulder. "Shh," Lytira soothed. "Hush, little one." Lytira looked up at Lex, her face a mask of awe. "You reversed the change," she said. "Sulanashum," she whispered, her eyes filling with tears. "Just like my mother said."

Lex still felt the darkness churning inside him but he tried to ignore it, hoping it would subside as it had before. "I only wish I knew sooner I could do that," he said, "Maybe I could have saved more."

"We know not what we do not know," Lytira said, still gazing up at him. "But when we know, we act. You did what you could. Thank you."

"You did well," Acarius agreed, joining them. "You did *really* well."

A laugh rang out through the air, causing them all to look up. Nothing was visible in the canopy, but the voice boomed nonetheless. "That was impressive," it echoed. "Now let's see what you do about this."

A group of wrasseks swept up onto the outer wall of the city, and Lex *felt* the change before he saw it. It was like someone had opened the floodgate on a river of dark energy, its cold surge rushing through the air above the city in all directions. The wrasseks on the wall began to tremble and change, their dark wings spreading, their round bodies growing, their fur dropping off, replaced by scales. Their batlike faces contorted and grew outward into toothed maws until what stood atop the wall was no longer a group of wrasseks, but crouching, grotesque dragons with wingspans as large as the houses.

"Go," the voice commanded, and the creatures dove inward on the city, avoiding Lex and the others in the courtyard and instead tearing into the houses where the Sephram hid. The houses broke apart like kindling beneath their powerful, clawed feet, whole sections of roof coming off in one swipe. The creatures moved downward, smashing the houses floor by floor from the top toward the bottom.

"Out!" Lytira yelled, and the people obeyed, shifting back into their animal forms as they rushed out into the courtyard.

"Can you stop it if he turns them?" Acarius asked, seeing the people once again exposed.

"I'm not sure," Lex said. "I'll try."

The Sephram huddled the children together, taking up formation around them.

"Where are the king's lions?" Lex asked, suddenly realizing their absence. He hadn't seen them since the people had rushed to the houses.

Acarius glanced around. "I don't know," he said. "For that matter, where's Mare? I haven't seen her in a while." He looked suddenly worried.

But then Lytira cried out and doubled over, and Acarius had something entirely new to worry about. He rushed toward her. "What is it?" he asked.

Lex clamped on the darkness inside him, ready to use it if Lytira was beginning to change.

"Ah!" Lytira cried out again, and when she looked up at Acarius, her face was pale. She pulled her hand away from her stomach and it was covered in blood. "I–" she said, then collapsed to the ground.

Some of the animals shifted back to Sephram form, rushing toward her.

"Take her inside!" Acarius commanded. He looked around. "Where are the healers?"

A wolf rushed forward, shifting into an old woman as it ran. "I think I'm the only one left," she said as someone grabbed the blanket off the dead king and handed it to her to cover herself.

"Help her," Acarius said. "Please."

The woman nodded once and rushed inside.

Lex glanced up at the sky. The dragons had vanished. The wrasseks were gone. No more Aiacs were appearing. What was Malleck up to? Lex looked back toward Acarius and froze as something on the ground caught his eye. It was a dark fog, almost like black smoke, creeping inward from the walls in all directions. It was moving toward the clearing. "Acarius," Lex called out, his voice trembling, "what is that?"

Acarius looked down. "I don't know," he said, a phrase he'd said more times in the past hour than Lex had heard him say the entire time he'd known him.

Lex closed his eyes and probed outward toward the fog. His eyes sprang open. "It's dark energy," he said. "It feels like an entire ocean of it." And it was moving in on them.

As the fog moved inward it began to take shape, sloping upward into upright, almost human-shaped forms, like dark-cloaked sorcerers floating toward them. Lex probed again. There was no life to them; they weren't creatures – they were pure, dark energy personified.

The energy within him throbbed in response, aching to burst outward. He clamped down on it but it thrashed and boiled, as though the fog were calling to it.

"Acarius?" Lex called. "Something is" – he had to stop for a breath as the rush of darkness surged up inside him, forcing him to clamp down on it even harder – "wrong."

The Sephram in the courtyard pressed in against the children, shielding them as the shapes moved inward, but then the fog turned, all the cloaked forms spinning in unison and heading directly for the nearest house – the one where the guards had taken Lytira.

"Protect your queen!" Acarius yelled, and for a moment no one moved.

*Do the people not recognize Lytira as queen, even though her father is dead?* Lex wondered. Did they still consider her banished?

But then the Sephram shifted into motion, half of the animals herding the children toward a house on the other side of the courtyard while the other half raced to defend their queen from the fog.

It proved futile. The fog split, part of it cutting off the group with the children before they even reached the houses. As the other group leapt into attack toward the other part of the fog, they simply crashed right through it. The fog dissipated, then reformed a few feet over.

*Maybe it's just an illusion*, Lex thought, but his guess was quickly shattered as the Sephram who had leapt through the fog dropped to the ground, convulsing. Dark liquid spilled from their eyes as they thrashed, then fell still... dead.

The other group rushed the children away from the fog and back into the center of the courtyard, regrouping their now-much-smaller force around them. The children's eyes darted wildly around the clearing, terrified, as they huddled within their protective circle of animals.

The fog shifted again and crept toward the house which held Lytira – and also Acarius, who now stood like a lone soldier in the doorway, holding his drawn sword.

Lex reached inward for the darkness, but he didn't have to reach far. It was right there, on the surface, pushing to burst out of him. He wrapped his mind tight around it, holding it in place as he sent part of his attention outward, seeking a hold on the dark fog.

The dark fog responded to his touch, warming the darkness within him and tugging at it, enticing it outward. Lex clamped down on the darkness inside him again, despite it starting to feel like a boiling pool of lava within him, its pressure building, and reached outward further. He could feel the edges of the fog, could grasp them if he could reach just far enough to shift his grip on it, but – what would happen if he did? He was full to the brim with darkness already, and the sea of dark energy that formed the fog was massive. There was no way he could contain it.

He forced his eyes open, the darkness in him still raging and lurching outward, trying to break free. The fog was almost to Acarius.

"Lex?" Acarius asked, looking down at the fog and then back up at him. "What do I do?" His eyes betrayed his fear, and Lex wanted to tell him to run, but knew he'd never leave Lytira.

Lex clamped his eyes shut, wrapped his mind around the fog, and yanked inward as hard as he could.

# CHAPTER 19

The darkness rushed in at him.

Lex suddenly felt like he was drowning, pressed beneath the weight of the dark sea.

He opened his mouth to cry for help, but no sound would come. He couldn't breathe. He forced his eyes open, and saw that his efforts were working – the dark fog was retreating from Acarius...from everywhere, actually. But despite that victory, Lex's heart raced with fear. The fog was retreating, yes, but it was all funneling straight into *him*. He would never be able to hold it all.

He shifted his grip on the darkness inside him, loosening it a bit. The churning mass within him poured out through the gap he'd given it, colliding with the dark sea pushing inward.

Lex felt a small release of pressure. That little shift had done something to the way the darkness moved, taking some of the weight off him. He could breathe again. The darkness continued to press inward but now it felt propped up a bit, as if held by an invisible tentpole. He was in a small pocket within the darkness, safe... for now.

The dark fog was already a few feet back from Acarius, and was slipping away from the Sephram and the children, all rushing toward Lex. *I can do this*, he thought. *I can take it.* He continued to pull the darkness inward, watching it slide toward him across the courtyard like an inky ocean in which someone had just pulled a drainplug.

*Leeeexxxxxxxxxxx*, a voice hissed in his mind.

He jumped, nearly losing his grip on the darkness. His heart raced. *What was that?* He shook his head and refocused.

*Lexxxxxx*, the voice hissed again, and Lex went suddenly cold.

He knew that voice. His mind flew back to a dark, cavernous room where he knelt, head bent, knees aching from the cold stone floor. *Mistress*. His mind said it, almost against his will.

The voice responded, carrying the sound of a smile. *There you are, my pet*, it cooed. *I've missed you.*

Lex's heart lurched, trying to escape his chest. He knew that voice. He knew that person. He finally remembered who Mistress was. *Ardis*. And somehow, when he used the darkness, she could see him.

The voice let out a cold laugh.

Lex lost his hold on the darkness.

It collapsed inward, crushing him. He couldn't breathe. He couldn't move. In his panic he glanced around the courtyard, expecting the darkness to be escaping his grip, but it wasn't – it was only pouring in on him more quickly.

Acarius stared at him with wide eyes. "No. No! Not again!" he yelled, rushing toward Lex.

*Stop stop stop please stop*, Lex tried to cry out, not wanting Acarius anywhere near him when it happened, but he couldn't form the words.

And then one, simple thought overwhelmed all others: *Amelia*. Lex's gaze flicked toward the house in which she probably still slept, unconscious, unaware of any of this... and completely vulnerable. Malleck Dross had wanted Amelia, too. Lex wished he could go to her, to make sure she was okay. He felt like a dam holding back the rush of darkness. When he finally gave way, would Acarius make sure Amelia was safe? Would any of them even survive it? The world swam, inky ocean spilling into the corners of Lex's vision.

This was it. This was the end of it. *Help me!* Lex pleaded to whatever being, whatever god or goddess, whatever force existed which had chosen him, sent him, selected him for this. *I've failed again.* He squeezed his eyes shut as the last of the darkness outside him rushed inward, coalesced with the darkness within him – and exploded.

But just as Lex felt himself fragmenting outward, something caught him, and pressed him back in.

Lex felt the darkness retreating inside him, quivering almost as though it were in pain. A warm, bright presence spread through Lex's chest, and

Lex realized the dark sea within him was shrinking, evaporating in the heat. Gradually the weight of darkness lessened enough that Lex could breathe again, and the inky pressure eased back from his head. He could still feel the dark lake churning inside him, but it was manageable now, and getting lighter by the moment.

Lex opened his eyes and looked around, trying to figure out what was happening. Amelia stood on the balcony of the second floor of the healers' house, arms reached toward him, body shaking, blazing like a torch. Even her eyes were on fire. Her gaze was focused intently on Lex, the air between them crackling with a stream of white-hot light like a solid tube of lightning. Lex looked down and gasped as he saw he was aflame, too, the lightning pouring into his chest and through his body, turning him into a living beam of light.

Lex turned his arm in front of his face in awe. He could feel the warmth of Amelia's power on him, but it didn't burn. It wasn't painful. It felt like standing in a warm shaft of sunlight, and the cool, dark pool inside him continued to evaporate until was just a thread again, content to lie in wait within him until he called it. All the extra darkness he'd taken in was gone.

Amelia's light surged, a blinding pulse which filled the city with its searing hum.

A piercing howl cut through the sky above them for one long moment, the sound of something dying. It carried Malleck's voice.

Then the light snapped back into itself like a flash of lightning, and vanished. The courtyard went quiet.

Amelia dropped her arms and sagged against the balcony rail.

Lex rushed toward the house, looking up at her. The relief inside him was overwhelming, the freedom of no longer being crushed by the dark sea. "How did you...?" he asked, his voice filled with awe. But he stopped, suddenly slapped by a memory – himself, standing amid the enemy, drowning in darkness; and Jana, sending out light toward him but it fizzling, weak. She had tried to save him, too, to save Marcus, but her powers had been different. She hadn't carried Amelia's energy.

Amelia had succeeded where Jana had failed.

This time, they had survived.

Acarius rushed toward Lex. "What did you – that was – how did you – are you okay?" He shouted, peering into Lex's face. His eyes were wide, and his body was trembling – with fear or excitement, Lex couldn't tell.

Suddenly Acarius threw his arms around Lex. "You lived," he whispered, crushing Lex in a tight hug before pulling backward. "Thank the heavens alive, you lived. The last time I saw you do that, you–" He stopped, but he didn't need to finish. The look on his face made it clear.

The gates of the city burst open, and Baram and a group of others tumbled in. Baram was in Sephram form, a pendant around his neck like Acarius' but with different symbols. Lex noted this to ask about later. Behind Baram stood an assortment of Sephram and Alomman in various states of dress – or undress, in the Sephram's sake – battered, dirty, and some bleeding.

"Are they gone from here, too?" Baram asked, his eyes still wild from battle. "We've been trying to fight our way through to the gate for the past hour, then they all just vanished."

"What?" Lex asked, turning toward him.

"They all vanished," Baram said again. "Aiacs, wrasseks, even the dark fog. Something in the sky let out a howl, there was a bright flash of light, then the whole army just dissolved right in front of us. We were in the middle of fighting, and suddenly we were the only ones there."

Acarius moved toward him. "You were unharmed by the blast? How is that possible?" he said. "A blast like that should have destroyed everything in its wake." He paused. "Shouldn't it?"

Baram shook his head. "I don't know. It was different this time. I had just gotten my people over the hills the last time we fought Malleck, so I can't be sure, but from where we stood last time it looked like the blast was dark energy. This time it was bright, like being in the sun itself."

*Baram was there*, Lex realized. He had been part of the battle the last time this happened.

Acarius looked up at Amelia with a shocked expression. "It was her," he said, sounding surprised. He moved toward her. "You did it. It was different this time, because of *you*."

Amelia blinked down at them. "I did...what?" she asked. "I just–" She swayed a bit.

Nigel rushed out onto the balcony behind her, steadying her with his arms. "Easy," he said. He lowered her to sit on the balcony floor. "You still need rest."

Amelia sat, but scooted toward the edge of the balcony, looking down at them. "I don't know what happened," she said. "I just felt... I felt Lex. I knew he needed me. And the heat inside me, it was – I couldn't hold it. When I came outside to see what was happening, it just burst out of me. I couldn't stop it."

"Thank the heavens you didn't, child," Nigel said, stroking her hair, "or we'd probably all be dead."

The Sephram had shifted back to their normal forms and now emerged from the houses covered in whatever blankets or hastily-donned clothes had been nearby. The children followed close behind them, staring at Lex and Amelia.

Lex glanced at the Sephram children, realizing too many of them now hovered behind adults who were not their parents, those who had taken over protecting them when no one else was left. They had won the battle here, but the cost had been high.

The Sephram gathered in the courtyard, glancing between Lex and Amelia.

The healer who had been tending Lytira rushed out from the house. "You can see her now," she said to Acarius, before hurrying into the door below Amelia's balcony.

Acarius raced toward the other house, disappearing inside it.

In a moment the healer was on the balcony with Amelia, peering into her face. "Come, child," she said. "Let's get you downstairs. You need something to drink and eat."

She pulled Amelia to her feet, supporting her weight as Nigel moved to Amelia's other side. The courtyard fell silent, and the sound of them helping Amelia slowly down the stairs echoed from inside the house.

After a moment Amelia emerged, still supported by Nigel and the healer, but looking less pale than Lex had seen her in a long time. She was clearly still weak, but something about her had changed. She thanked the healer and Nigel and moved away from them, insisting she felt strong enough to stand on her own. She walked toward Lex and stopped in front of him.

They stared at each other for a moment. Lex wasn't sure what to say.

The Sephram moved in around them. "Daughter of power," one of the Sephram stated. All around Lex and Amelia, Sephram and Alomman men, women, and children dropped to their knees and bowed. Even Baram bowed, his deep voice murmuring "Daughter of power," as he dipped his face toward the ground.

Lex glanced at Amelia, who looked suddenly very uncomfortable. "I'm not – I mean, I guess I am, but I don't even know what I did. You don't have to do that," she said to the people. "Really. I'm just... me."

The Sephram rose to their feet, and Baram turned toward Amelia and Lex. "Thank you, Sulanashum. Daughter of power." He nodded to each of them in turn. "Malleck Dross is finally destroyed. Perhaps now the balance will be restored to the land and our people can once again live in peace." He walked toward the back of the crowd to join the other Alowens.

What *did* this mean? Lex wondered. Yes, they had defeated Malleck, but... was that it? Was it done? Would the Worldforce now suddenly snap back into place and everything go back to normal? Even with everything it had cost them, it seemed too easy.

The Sephram parted, heading off into houses or busying themselves checking on the damage left from the battle. The courtyard was littered with bodies, and the air still hung thick with the smell of fire and blood. Lex thought again, the cost had been high. Perhaps this *was* the end of it. But something pulled at the back of Lex's mind, more instinct than memory. This was bigger than just Malleck, he was certain of it. And somehow his family, the Ancients – and *Ardis* – were at the center of it.

Nigel emerged from one of the houses, having some kind of animated conversation with the healer, judging by the ferocity of his arm gestures.

Lex turned to Amelia. "*Now* he shows up," he said, giving a small laugh. He didn't fault Nigel for hiding, not really, but of course it was like him to appear only when all danger had passed.

Amelia looked confused. "What do you mean?" she asked. "Didn't you send him?"

Now it was Lex's turn to be confused. "Send him where?" he asked.

"To guard me," Amelia said. "When I awoke, I was still weak and shaky, but I could hear the battle outside, and I was so scared. Then I looked up and there he was, standing guard at the foot of my bed with a giant sword, like he was ready to murder anyone who came into the room."

Oh," Lex said, his concept of Nigel suddenly shifting.

A cheer went up from the people still in the courtyard, and Lex turned to see Acarius and Lytira emerging from the other house.

"You're okay!" Lex said, moving toward them.

Lytira nodded. "I reopened a wound and had already lost too much blood," she said. "That was all. I'm fine."

The healer rushed over. "She just needed the wound reclosed and a bit of medicine, but *now* what she needs is rest. Magical healing can only do so much, you know," she said, narrowing her eyes at Lytira. "Sometimes what a patient really needs is sleep."

"I'll rest soon," Lytira said.

The healer raised her eyebrows.

"No, really, I will," Lytira assured her.

The healer smiled. "That's right. You will." Then she turned and walked toward another of the houses.

"Hey, Acarius," Baram's deep voice rang out from over near the barn. "You may want to come here."

Acarius glanced at Lex, and Lex knew at once from his face what he was thinking. When had they last seen Mare? *Please let Mare be okay*, Lex silently pleaded. He raced after Acarius toward the barn.

Acarius stopped so suddenly that Lex actually bumped into him. In front of them stood Baram, and behind him stood Mare, teeth bared. Behind her, sheltered in a corner where two buildings joined, were the donkey, the other horse... and the lions.

At the sight of Acarius, Mare closed her lips and lowered her head, and Acarius moved forward. "It's alright," he said, stroking her. He turned to Baram. "What..."

Baram shrugged. "I do not know," he said. "I found them back here, and she seemed to be... *guarding* them."

Acarius pressed his forehead to Mare's face. "You crazy horse," he murmured warmly.

Mare stepped to the side, and the horse and donkey moved past her and out into the courtyard. Behind her, the lions still crouched, their backs against the wood of the buildings.

"She was guarding *lions*?" Lex asked.

"It's true, then. The king is dead?" Baram asked Acarius.

Acarius nodded.

"The severing of the bond disorients the animals," Baram explained to Lex. "When a Sephram bonded to a group dies, the whole group suffers. It leaves them weak and disoriented for a while, like recovering from a – what did you call them?" He looked to Acarius but then seemed to remember. "A seizure. But they will be okay, after a bit of rest. They would have been very vulnerable for a time, and with so much commotion to startle them, they may have even attacked some of the people in their confusion. Had that happened, the people would have been forced to slay them. Mare may have saved their lives."

"What do we do with them now?" Lex asked. "Will they stay here?"

Baram shook his head. "I will alert one of the Zeriphathians. They will care for them until they are stronger, then they will be set free. We do not keep captive those who are meant to run wild." He nodded to Lex, then turned and walked back into the courtyard.

Lex stared at Mare in awe, who suddenly turned one large eye toward him and stared right back. The aggression she had held toward him seemed to be gone; now she seemed more curious.

Acarius stepped back and Mare moved toward Lex, then lowered her head and nosed his shoulder. Surprised, Lex reached up and stroked her face.

"See?" Acarius said. "She does like you."

"Took her long enough," Lex replied.

The healer approached, leading Amelia by the hand with Lytira and Nigel in their wake. "I must speak with all of you," she said.

Lex turned toward her, eyeing Amelia to see if something was wrong, but Amelia looked okay.

The healer turned toward him. "Amelia says she feels much better now, and I agree her energy has shifted. It is no longer volatile. But..."

"But?" Lex asked.

"What she is, what she can do, it does not lie dormant. There is still an undercurrent, a pressure building. Without understanding what it is, I cannot help her any further. She may soon begin to have attacks again. Her energy is unstable."

Amelia shook her head. "No, I'm better. I am. Something about connecting with Lex like I did... it fixed me. I don't feel the pressure building anymore. I think I'm okay."

The healer glanced between them, and apparently giving up on convincing them, turned to Acarius. "I do not understand what's happening with her powers," she said. "I have not seen this type of ability before, not even with the other daughter of power. I am bound by duty to be honest about her care, and I do not believe her healed. She will destabilize again. Without help, she will regress. She may become dangerous, and not only to herself."

"What do you suggest we do?" Acarius asked.

"I do not have the answers," the healer said, "but the Ancients will. This sort of power... they will know its source, and what to do about it. They will know how to help her."

"We can't go to the Ancients," Acarius said. He turned to Lex. "They've wanted you dead for years. If you walk in there, they'll kill you on sight, and probably Amelia, too."

"Wouldn't it be different, now?" Lytira asked, moving toward them. "He has both proven himself Sulanashum and discovered a daughter of power. He is their prince. Would they not be pleased?"

Lex looked to Acarius, uncertain why Lytira seemed not to know that the Ancients never wanted the prophecy fulfilled. Behind Lytira, Acarius gave a quick shake of his head.

Lex turned back to Lytira. "I don't remember much," he said, "so I can't be sure. They may still be angry, and it would be too risky." *Amnesia*, Lex thought. *Always the perfect cover story.*

Lytira nodded. "You are right. Caution is probably wise," she said. "Your father has never been reasonable, much like–" She stopped.

They were all silent for a moment, uncertain what to say. Then Acarius spoke. "I'm sorry about your father, Lyt."

She took a deep breath. "I am, too. Despite his flaws, I loved him."

"And he loved you," a woman said, approaching.

It was the Sephram who had served as Heart in the ceremony. That seemed to Lex to have been years ago. Had it only been hours?

"Rahmanasha," the woman said to Lytira, "the remaining elders have gathered, and are calling for you."

"Now?" Lytira asked.

"Now," the woman nodded.

Lytira gave Acarius a glance, then followed the woman back toward the palace tower.

The others looked at each other for a moment, then hurried to catch up. The Heart looked back at them, noticing they were following, but did not turn them away.

The throne stood empty in the center of the room when they entered, a fact which made Lex's chest contract. He could have saved the king, if only he had known soon enough what he could do. That was a guilt he would have to carry; he could add it to the growing list. His lack of awareness about himself and his past continued to put others in danger, even now that he knew so much more. How many other things did he still not know?

A small group of elders, all of them dirty and bruised from battle and clearly having seen better days, stood on either side of the throne. They turned to face the doorway as the group entered, and the Heart squeezed Lytira's hand before taking her place among the other elders.

Lytira stepped forward.

Lex felt suddenly anxious. Was this the final stage of the ceremony? Surely they would reverse Lytira's banishment, after all that had happened... wouldn't they?

He glanced at Acarius, who also looked nervous. That couldn't be a good sign.

"Rahmanasha Lytira," a tall Elder stated, his voice echoing off the wooden walls. "The elders have reached a decision on your ceremony."

Lytira bowed her head, seeming ready to accept whatever they had decided.

"You have yet again endangered our people by bringing enemies to our doorstep, and your actions have resulted in the death of our king."

Lytira's head sank lower.

"But you have also shown steadfast loyalty to your friends, a fierce faith in the strength of our people, uncommon courage in battle, and a willingness to risk your own life for ours."

Lytira looked up. "Then...?" she asked softly.

"Our people need a new leader, Rahmanasha, and we find no reason to open the ceremony of election to select a new ruling family when we have one of our people's bravest warriors right here. It is your right to rule, daughter of Rahman. Of course, with your father..." He paused. "Without the king to reverse your banishment first, we will need an accord. Elders from at least one other clan must assent to our decision before it can be final."

"We are present," a voice called from outside the door.

Lex and Acarius moved back to allow room for a new group of people to enter – Baram and those who had come with him. An old man moved toward them, the very one who had banished Lytira at Alowen. He stepped forward, along with two other men and a woman.

The Zeriphathian elder who had spoken earlier nodded to him. "Welcome, brothers and sister," he said.

The man spoke again. "The elders of Alowen beg forgiveness for overhearing your ceremony."

The other elder bowed his head, accepting their apology.

The elder from Alowen continued. "We assent to the repeal of Ramanasha Lytira's banishment," he said, turning toward Lytira. "And to her appointment as Queen of the Sephram- Alomman Alliance."

Lytira stared at him. "You do?"

He nodded. "I am an old man, but I can still admit when I am wrong. You broke our laws, child, and you caused our people much pain. But if the reports I heard from within the city are true, you have also done everything in your power to protect them, in your own way. The spirit of our people is ferocity and honor, and you have demonstrated both." He turned back to the elders around the throne. "We offer our accord with your decision."

Beside him, Lex saw Acarius break into a smile.

"Lytira, daughter of King Rahman and Aliara the Seer," the Zeriphathian elder said, "the throne is yours."

The Heart moved toward Lytira. "Come, my queen," she said. "We must conduct the ascension rituals."

Lytira glanced back at Acarius, her eyes wide, and he gave her an encouraging smile.

The Heart led Lytira out through one of the back doors.

The people dispersed, filtering back out into the courtyard. Lex and Acarius followed, and Nigel approached and pulled Amelia off to the side, talking to her about something.

"What now?" Lex asked, turning to Acarius.

Acarius shrugged. "Nothing. The ascension ceremony is private; no one is allowed to witness it." He stopped. "I'm not even sure what they do. Anyway, that's it. She's queen."

Something in his voice sounded strange, and Lex turned toward him. "Why don't you sound happy?" he asked.

"What do you mean?" Acarius said, forcing a smile.

"I mean *that*," Lex said, pointing at Acarius' face. "It's the worst fake smile I've ever seen. Did you not want her to be–" He stopped, the truth suddenly hitting him. Lytira being queen meant she would be fully into the world of the Sephram and Alomman, a world in which Acarius had said he didn't belong. Lex shook his head. "She's the queen now," he said. "And you just risked your life for her and for these people. Surely they'll let you stay here. You did once before, right?"

Acarius sighed. "It's not about that," he said. "Of course I could stay. Lytira's father was the only one who never wanted me here. But..."

"But?"

"But I won't," Acarius said.

Lex blinked. "Why not?"

"Because she deserves better. She deserves someone who can really protect her, who would make her stronger instead of–" He took a breath. "Instead of a half-blood, like me. The royal line has to be pure, and me being here would only be a complication." He glanced at Baram, who was talking to a group of the other Sephram, then back to Lex. "I can't do it, Lex. I can't stay here and watch."

Lex's heart sank.

Nigel and Amelia walked toward them. "Why the grumpy faces?" Nigel asked. "Didn't we just defeat a lord of darkness and his minions and save a whole city?"

Acarius stared at Nigel for a moment, then sighed. "Yeah, we did." He gave Nigel a small smile. "I'm glad you survived, you nut. How was it cowering in fear while the rest of us fought the battle?"

Nigel grinned. "It was quite restful! Besides, I had lovely company." He winked at Amelia.

Amelia gaped. "I wasn't cowering, I was unconscious!"

"No one said you were, dear," Nigel said, patting her on the head like a child.

Amelia's mouth dropped open.

A group of Sephram emerged from the tower. "The queen requests you," one of them said.

"Me?" Acarius asked.

"All of you," the Sephram responded.

"Oh," Acarius said. He turned toward the tower, the others following.

They entered the lobby to find Lytira seated on the elaborate throne, shifting awkwardly. "Why is this thing so uncomfortable?" she muttered. She looked up. "Oh!" She stood. "You're here."

"You don't have to do that," Acarius said, gesturing to her. "Stand, I mean. You're queen now."

Lytira narrowed her eyes at him. "So?"

The others glanced around nervously.

"Anyway," Lytira said, moving toward them. "What's the plan?"

"What plan?" Lex asked.

"The plan for how to help Amelia, find out who Malleck was working with – he certainly didn't amass such power on his own without anyone noticing, right? – and take care of Ardis and the Ancients. We can't just have them roaming around wanting to kill our Sulanashum, can we?"

"Oh," Lex said, "I mean, we haven't really gotten that far."

"I was thinking we could head to Arcalon," Lytira said, starting to pace. "They may be weak in magic but they keep the best historical records in all of Arameth. They might have something that could help us."

"Wait..." Acarius said. "We?"

Lytira raised an eyebrow. "Of course. You all wouldn't survive a week without me." She smirked. "And as the queen, it's not only my duty to protect my people here locally, but to ensure the safety of our clans *everywhere*. I can't do that if I don't even know what's happening. Besides... don't we still need to check on your sisters?"

Acarius gasped. "My sisters!" His face went pale.

Lex really couldn't blame Acarius for having forgotten temporarily; they had been a bit busy.

Lex turned to Lytira. "Aren't you needed here, though?"

She shrugged. "My father occasionally traveled, when the need was strong enough. He simply appointed a trusted warrior and an elder to watch over the people in his absence. I can do the same. We have elders here, and as for the warrior, Baram would stay and do it, I'm sure."

"Right," Acarius said. "Baram."

Lex glanced at Amelia. She looked stable enough at the moment, but the healer had said that might not last. "How far is it to Arcalon?" he asked Lytira.

"It is far," Lytira answered.

Acarius sighed. "It's on the far southern edge of the continent, and we're currently on the northern end. I'd say a couple weeks of riding, at least, if we went by land. But I'm not sure that's the best idea. The Port of Lanian is a couple days south of here, and we could take a boat down the coast to the Port of the Alliance, right on the border to Arcalon. We'd probably attract less notice that way."

"I agree," Lytira said. "I'll send word to Lanian and arrange a boat for us."

"Wait," Lex said, a memory surfacing. "I think I... do I get seasick?"

"Yes," Acarius shrugged. "But you'll survive it."

*Great*, Lex thought. "How many days will the boat trip take?"

"A week or so," Lytira answered. "But that's not the worst of it. First we have to pass back through The Fallows to get to Lanian."

*Of course we do,* Lex thought.

"What's The Fallows?" Amelia asked.

They all stared at her.

"It's just a bit of sand, dear," Nigel said, patting her hand. "Nothing to worry about."

Lex turned to Amelia. "Are you okay to travel?"

"I think so," she shrugged. "I feel fine right now. And anyway, being near you, with your... powers... makes me better, I think. If I start to feel sick again, maybe you can help me."

Lex wasn't so sure. He hoped he could. "I'll try," he said. He turned to Acarius. "But what about your sisters?"

"They're at Arcalon, too," he said. "That's where they went to wait for me. I can check on them there, then we can search the Hall of Records to see what we can find out about you and Amelia."

"And if that turns up little," Lytira said, "we can always go to Harthgil."

Acarius stared at her. "Harthgil is a myth," he said.

"It certainly isn't," Lytira responded. "My mother spent her early childhood there, before coming here. Besides, don't you know by now that plenty of myths are founded in reality? A place can lie hidden beyond the mountains farther than most people care to travel, without that place ceasing to exist."

Acarius shook his head. "How did I not know? Your mother never mentioned it."

"Living with us for a year doesn't mean you know all our family secrets." Lytira smiled slyly. "There is plenty more you don't know, as well."

Acarius looked surprised. "What else haven't you told me?"

Lytira ignored him and turned to Lex. "Harthgil has access to a different sort of magic entirely. If the answer to what's happening to you and Amelia doesn't lie with the historians in Arcalon, then we'll find it in Harthgil."

"Sounds like a plan," Nigel said. "When do we leave?"

"In the *morning* at the earliest," the healer spoke up. She moved toward them from the door of the tower. "The queen needs her rest."

The healer approached Lex, and pulled him aside. The others glanced over but then turned and moved a few feet away, seeing the healer clearly wanted privacy.

"What is it?" Lex asked.

"It's about the daughter of power," she said. "I can see you care for her. You must know the truth. Yes, her energy is quieter now. But it will build again. And every time, it takes its toll. While you may help to stabilize her, if she continues this way eventually the attacks will destroy her. Though she has both human and Ancient blood in her, the power in her is something other.

It is pure Worldforce energy. We cannot explain why she has it, but we do know her human body can only take so much. It is not meant to withstand such power."

"What can we do?" Lex asked.

"Get her to the Ancients," she said. "It is the only way." She squeezed his arm, then left him.

The others came back over.

"What did she say?" Acarius asked.

Lex saw no reason to lie to his friends. "She said Amelia needs to go to the Ancients."

Acarius gave him a blank stare. "We can't; you know that, right?"

Lex shook his head. "What if it's the only way?"

"I'm okay for now, really," Amelia said. "I don't like what I've heard of the Ancients, and besides, I don't want anyone to be in danger because of me. Let's try Arcalon first, and if that doesn't work, then we can decide. Okay? I really think I'll be fine, as long as I stay near you."

Lex sighed, realizing they didn't really have a better option, at least not until they fully understood what the Ancients and Ardis were up to. Hopefully they'd be able to figure that out at Arcalon. "Okay," he said.

"Okay. Bedtime!" Nigel called out.

Lex couldn't argue. Not only was he exhausted, but the sun filtering through the canopy had faded – it was clearly almost night.

They trudged up the stairs to the guest level, where two guards waited in the hallway. "Your room is here, Daughter of Power," one of them said, gesturing to a door on his left. He nodded to Lex, Acarius, and Nigel. "You three may stay in the room you occupied earlier. Queen Lytira, I will escort you to the royal quarters."

Lytira turned to Acarius. "I guess I'll see you in the morning." She followed the guard up the stairs.

Acarius stared after her, then sighed and walked toward his room. Nigel followed.

Lex turned to Amelia. "Well, goodnight then," he said.

"Lex, wait," Amelia said. "Please come in. Just for a minute. I'm just... not quite ready to be alone."

Lex glanced at the other guard, who was staring at them from the far side of the hall.

"I don't think that's a good idea," he said.

"Please, Lex," Amelia said. "It's been a long day, and I just need someone to talk to. I won't keep you long."

Lex glanced at the guard again, but the guard made no objection. "Okay," Lex said. He followed Amelia into her room.

# CHAPTER 20

A melia entered the room and sat down on the bed. Lex followed her inside, and shut the door behind them. He glanced around. Amelia's room was much the same as his own but smaller, and with only one bed. He moved toward it, stopping in front of Amelia.

"So," he said, very aware of how alone they were. "How are you feeling?"

"Okay, I guess," Amelia sighed, leaning back onto her hands. "I'm just so..."

"Tired?" Lex offered.

"Confused," Amelia replied. "I don't even understand what in the world I just did. I'm not like these people, Lex. I'm not like any of you. I don't have *magic*. I'm just a normal person."

Lex sat down on the bed beside her. "I'm pretty sure you're not," he said, turning to her.

Amelia sighed again. "No, I guess I'm not. I see that now. But I still don't understand it."

"Amelia, what you can do is amazing," Lex said.

Amelia let out a short laugh. "I know," she said. "Usual me would be completely ecstatic. I'm suddenly a comic-book superhero! But that's the problem. Stuff like this isn't *real*. Not in my world. It's like I fell through a portal into Wonderland and now I can't get back. It's amazing, don't get me wrong, but... I'm so overwhelmed. I don't even know how to process it."

Lex sat in silence beside her, wanting to reassure her but uncertain what to say.

She turned to him. "Do you know I thought this was a game, at first?" She laughed.

Lex shifted to face her. His heart sped at finally hearing something about who she really was, how she got here.

"I never thought it would be my 'inner strength' that nearly killed me," she said. "That's ironic."

"What?" Lex asked.

"It's just something my dad used to say, that I had a lot of inner strength. But I never imagined it turning into something like this. Ever since I first came through the portal, it's been like something is burning me from the inside out. Well, until what happened earlier. Now it's finally eased off. I can still feel the warmth, but it's calm, like just a small candle here." She tapped her chest.

"Amelia," Lex said, sensing his chance. "How did you get here? Where were you before?"

"Earth." She shrugged. "The same as Nigel, or so he said."

Lex watched her quietly. After a moment, she seemed to realize that hadn't been enough to appease him. She looked away and her posture sank a bit. "My mom died when I was little," she said softly. "My adoptive mom, I mean. My first set of parents were killed in a car accident when I was a baby."

"I'm sorry," Lex said.

"It's okay. I don't remember them, or my mom. For most of my life, it was just me and my dad. But when they adopted me, he'd never expected to have to raise me alone. He loved me, I know, but – it was hard on him. I could see it. And I didn't make it easier."

"What do you mean?" Lex asked, wanting to know more, to know everything about her he could.

She sighed. "I wasn't the best kid. I got in trouble a lot. I acted out. I skipped school, stole packs of gum, you know, stupid rebellious teenager stuff."

Lex didn't know, but he nodded anyway.

"But then my boyfriend – at the time, the one I told you about when we first met – he wanted to do something more exciting." She paused. "We broke into a house."

"Oh," Lex said.

Amelia shook her head. "It was stupid, I know. And we got caught. My dad flipped out. The owners decided not to press charges, but my dad was furious. My boyfriend told everyone it had been my idea, and dumped me.

I was heartbroken." She paused. "I thought he loved me." She slid her hands down her face.

Lex's heart ached for her.

"My dad grounded me but I didn't care by that point. I refused to leave my room for days," she said. "And then the dreams started."

"Dreams?"

"Just one, really. Always the same one, of this one particular house. I would walk in, see a light on up in the attic, and move toward it." She took a shaky breath. "Anyway, after a few nights I felt like I'd go crazy if I didn't leave my room, so I snuck out. I didn't pay attention to where I was going, I just walked... and then I was there. At the house."

"The same house from your dream?" Lex asked.

Amelia nodded. "I knew it was wrong, but... I broke in. I went toward the attic, and there it was, just like in my dreams, though the light wasn't on. I pulled the ladder down and climbed up, and there was this video game console, sitting there in the floor. It was like it was calling to me. There was nowhere to plug it in up there, and no TV to attach it to, so I brought it downstairs. I just needed to see what it did. I couldn't very well turn on lights and television in some other person's house in the middle of the night, but I also didn't want to steal it. It felt wrong. I was still standing there, trying to decide what to do, when the homeowners woke up and saw me. I knew if I got caught breaking in again, I'd be done for, so... I ran."

She paused again and Lex waited, hoping she would continue.

After a moment, she did.

"I was halfway down the block before I realized I still had the console. I hadn't meant to steal it. But at that point, what else could I do? I ran home with it and hid it under my bed. I spent the whole night terrified they'd track me down, and by morning I decided I didn't want the stress. I was going to return it. But before I did, I thought after all that time seeing this house in my dreams, being drawn to the thing, it would be a shame not to at least see what it was." She sighed again. "I turned it on, and *poof*, here I was. In Arameth."

"Really?" Lex asked. "Just like that?" He thought back to what Nigel said about the danger of using the console, but Amelia made it seem like nothing.

"Yeah," Amelia shrugged. "Of course, I was freaking out. I had no idea what happened or where I was. But then I thought of my room, and *poof*, I was home again. At that point, I was excited. I thought I'd stumbled across a high-tech virtual reality game that could read brainwaves or something. But then I got scared. People with technology like that wouldn't just let it slide that someone took it. This was tech that didn't even exist yet, as far as the public knew. It could have been a top-secret government experiment or a new product still in testing, but either way I knew I'd be punished for taking it. I decided I'd have to put it back without them seeing me, instead of just returning it and apologizing. But they had already seen me in their house. They would figure out who I was and come after me. I was terrified. I hid it back under my bed, and suddenly felt totally exhausted. I knew I wouldn't be able to do anything until night came, so I thought the best idea was to lie low. I hadn't planned to go to sleep, but I did, and when I woke up... I was back in Arameth. Somehow I'd come through in my sleep."

"Wow," Lex said.

"Yeah," Amelia replied. "After that I just kept coming through again and again, after school or when I knew my dad wouldn't be home. Every time I came through, I was in a different place. I knew I should get rid of the console, but I couldn't bring myself to do it – I was having fun exploring. Going through and coming back made me feel weird, though, like really tired. I'd have to rest, but then by the next day I'd feel fine so I'd go again. I'd gone through maybe five or six times before I ended up in Dalton. That was the day I ran into you, and you saved me from that Aiac. After I saw you, I felt this... it's weird to say it, but I felt a connection. So I followed you into the woods."

"The day we saw the panther and then you asked me to hold you when it got cold," Lex said, connecting the dots.

Amelia blushed. "Yeah. It was cold, but... it may have been a little more than that. I'm so sorry. I mean, I thought you were some advanced A.I. hot guy who was part of the game. I didn't know you were real. I was just trying to have some fun."

Lex didn't understand what A.I. was or half of what she'd said so far, but that last part was clear. "You thought I was hot?" he asked, feeling as though he should focus on more important details but unable to stop himself.

"Yes," Amelia said, blushing again.

Lex felt a little thrill at seeing that he'd unsettled her.

"Anyway," she said, "I popped back out while you slept to check on things. All the injuries I'd gotten, the clothes I'd stolen from Dalton just for kicks... they were all gone; I was back to normal. I figured it must be virtual reality then, but by that point I couldn't resist. I came back again and spent the day with you and Acarius, even though every time I went through and came back, I felt... not quite right. Achy, weak – like when you're coming down with the flu. I shrugged it off as stress, or maybe the *actual* flu. Anyway, I stayed here until the attack at Acarius' ranch, but I was starting to feel very strange, like a buzzing in my head and all around me. I popped back home – I'm so sorry, I know I left right in the middle of the fight but I didn't think any of it was real; I thought it was all a game! And I was enjoying being with your character, then feeling foolish that I – but I didn't know. I'm so sorry. I must seem terrible to you."

"Not at all," Lex said, still trying to piece together some of the gaps in what she was saying.

"Anyway, that time when I went back through, I felt the drain even more. And when I looked down, the injuries I'd gotten were still there. I panicked and almost didn't come back, but then I thought of you in the middle of a battle, and if there was any chance it was real, then I couldn't just leave you. Nigel explained to me earlier that with my destabilization, travelling is very dangerous. I realize now that I must have caused that explosion when I left, but I had no idea at the time. I came back to chaos. When you and Acarius sent me off with Mare to hide behind the hills, I decided I was done. This world, whatever it was, was too much for me. I tried to get back home, but I couldn't. I was stuck here."

"Oh," Lex said. "Why didn't you ask for help? I'm sure if you told us..." He didn't know how to finish that statement, so he changed direction. "Maybe Nigel could have done something."

"I was afraid to tell you," Amelia said. "I knew what I would have thought if someone told me they stumbled into my world thinking it wasn't real, flirted with them thinking they were a pretend character, blew up their friend's house accidentally, abandoned them in the middle of a fight, then came back and still tried to run away from all of it. You'd always looked at me like I was... I don't know, special. And I didn't want you to see me the other way."

"What other way?" Lex asked, leaning toward her.

"As a thief," she said. "A coward. As what I really am."

Her eyes turned wet but she kept her gaze on his, waiting to hear Lex's judgment of her.

What *did* he think of her? She wasn't perfect, but... thinking of his own past, of the second chance he'd gotten, of all the pain he'd caused people in both his past life and this one, her mistakes seemed small in comparison. He could finally see beneath the shield she usually held around herself, to the warm, vibrant heart she kept behind it. Lex understood what it felt like not to belong, to be confused and alone and always doing the wrong thing. He never really belonged anywhere, in either of his lives, and he was beginning to see that not knowing who he was extended back beyond his memory loss. He had *always* felt lost, except with Jana when he was Marcus... and a few times with Amelia, especially today in the battle. But Jana was gone, a fragment of his past, and he was here now with Amelia. Somehow, it seemed this was how it was always meant to be. Marcus had loved Jana, he knew. But he wasn't entirely Marcus anymore. He had felt Amelia's presence consume him for a few moments in the courtyard, and it felt... right. Like he was finally home. There was something tying him and Amelia together, he was sure of it, even if he didn't exactly understand what.

Amelia was still watching him, waiting for him to say something. She didn't have the benefit of a fresh start like he did, a chance to leave the pain behind. She was still carrying the weight of her mistakes.

Lex brushed away a tear on the brink of slipping from her eye. "That's not what you are," he said. "People make mistakes. Sometimes innocently, and sometimes because, in the moment, we're afraid or hurting. People make poor choices. I know I have. But it takes courage to be honest about them. That is who I think you are. Courageous. You saved my life today."

Amelia gave him a small smile. "Thanks for saying that, but I still feel terrible. I feel like such a fraud. Everyone here thinks I'm some 'daughter of power,' but I'm not. I'm just a screwed-up girl from Earth who stole somebody's portal thing and got stuck in a world of magic. I'm not anything special. And I've been lying to everyone from the start. When they all find out, they're going to hate me. They'll never be able to trust me."

"I think they know," Lex said. "At least some of it. But Amelia, what you can do, it's not... normal. People who come through from Earth can't all do what you can do."

"Really?" Amelia said. "I heard them talk about Jana having some sort of powers, and Nigel is crazy, but he's brilliant, and so I thought... I don't know, I thought it was a Superman thing, like I come here and the environment just makes me able to do things."

Lex squinted at her. "What?"

Her tears had vanished, and she was staring at him. "Could the others who came through really not do this?"

"No," Lex said. "They couldn't. I mean, it's not like there have been a whole lot of you, it's pretty much just Nigel and Jana, but no. They couldn't do what you can do. You're special, Amelia. I think there's a reason you're here."

Her face sank. "Please stop saying that," she said, her eyes filling with tears again. "I'm not special, Lex. I've lied and stolen and pretended to be from Arameth, and – oh, the clothes I stole from Dalton, those people were poor, you know, and it might have been their only spare clothes – and because of me, the Aiacs have killed so many people, and... I'm not worth it, Lex. I'm not. I don't deserve this. I don't deserve–" She stopped.

"You don't deserve what?" Lex asked.

"I don't deserve you. You say I saved your life, and I know we're connected, I can feel it, but I'm not the right person for this. You're so pure and good, and I'm not, and you've been so kind to me, and I've just been..."

Lex leaned forward and kissed her.

Her heat surged through him, warming him all over. He leaned in, deepening the kiss.

Amelia kissed him back, and at first it was gentle, but then it grew more intense. Lex felt her presence pulling at every inch of him, begging him to move closer.

He placed his hand on her face and pulled back from the kiss, leaning his forehead against hers. "I should go," he said.

Amelia blinked at him. "Now?"

"Yes. Now," Lex said, standing.

"Stay," Amelia said. She grabbed his hand. "Nothing has to happen," she said hurriedly, "I just... I'd rather not be alone. You could sleep on the floor. Or the bed, and I'll take the floor."

"I can't," Lex said, sliding his hand away. "They don't allow it." *And I can't trust myself.* He leaned down, placing a gentle kiss on her cheek, then turned for the door.

"Lex, wait," she said. "I know you can't stay, but I really am scared. Everything is so different here. I'm different. This thing inside me... I just feel so overwhelmed."

Lex wanted nothing more than to move back toward her, but he held himself still. "I'll be right outside the door, then," he said. "Don't worry. If anything happens, or you get afraid, just call for me. I'll be there."

"You're going to be in the hall all night?" Amelia asked.

"All night," Lex said. "Don't worry, I'll get some pillows and a blanket, and I'll be comfortable enough. Goodnight, Amelia."

She looked relieved. "Goodnight," she said.

Lex slipped out and shut the door behind him.

When he walked into his own room, Acarius and Nigel were already asleep in separate beds. Lex slipped a pillow and a spare blanket off one of them and went back out into the hallway. The guard eyed him as he set up a makeshift bed outside Amelia's door.

"Do you need assistance?" the guard asked.

"Just staying nearby, you know, in case she needs me."

"I see," the guard said, staring blankly at him.

Lex pulled the blanket up over himself and sank down onto the pillow. Despite the hard floor beneath him, he was asleep within moments.

He awoke as the canopy-filtered sun began to peek through the carved windows at the end of the hall, which was still mostly dark. He sat up, his whole body feeling stiff, and stretched his arms above his head. The guard was still eyeing him... or maybe it was a different guard; Lex had been too tired the night before to really pay attention.

"Did you sleep well, Sulanashum?" the guard asked.

Lex nodded, and stood to gather up his pillow and blanket. Should he check on Amelia? Maybe it was better to let her sleep.

A sharp light filled the hall.

"What was that?" the guard said.

It flashed again. Lex turned toward Amelia's room, but the sliver under her door was still dark. The light had come from Nigel and Acarius' room.

Lex and the guard raced toward the other door just as Amelia threw her door open. "What happened?" she said, her face panicked. "I thought I felt–"

The guard yanked the door to Nigel and Acarius' room open, pushing Lex and Amelia back with one arm. "Wait," he said. "There could be danger."

Lex could hear a woman's voice inside the room. "He has your sisters," the voice was saying. "You have to come!"

Lex tried to look around the guard, but between the guard's arm and Nigel and Acarius, who stood between them and the woman, he couldn't see anything. "Let me through," he said, shoving the guard's arm aside.

Acarius and Nigel turned toward him as he barged into the room, both of their faces stiff with shock. Their movement parted the obstruction like an opening curtain, revealing the woman behind them.

Lex froze, staring at her.

Behind him, Lex heard Amelia gasp.

The woman's mouth dropped open. "Marcus!" she shouted. She flung herself at him, throwing her arms around his neck. "You're alive!"

*Jana.*

End of Book 1

# Find out what happens next!

Get your copy of The Lex Chronicles, Book 2 – *The Path to Paradox* now!

[https://books2read.com/pathtoparadox](https://books2read.com/pathtoparadox)

**Or grab the whole rest of the trilogy at once in the Lex Chronicles Trilogy Collection! https://books2read.com/lexchroncollection**

# Come Find Me Online!

If you enjoyed this book, **please take a moment to leave a review on the book retailer where you purchased it.** These reviews are a *huge* help to indie authors like me... they help persuade new readers to give my books a try!

Want to be an insider with weekly updates, exclusive bonus content, and more? **Join my Patreon!** Find all the perks and details at https://www.patreon.com/ccrawfordwriting.

If you love **clean young adult fiction** and want a portal where you can read a bunch of clean YA books, interact with the authors and other readers, and help us build a community around clean YA fiction, **check out Pirate Cat Publishing**, a joint project between myself and another indie author, M.J. Padgett! **http://piratecatpub.com**

If you'd like to receive updates on future releases, behind-the-scenes info on my writing, and personal updates about my life (and my kids... and my cat), please subscribe to my monthly newsletter at http://ccrawfordwriting.com/subscribe.

You'll even get free downloads for subscribing!

You can also find me at:

Website: http://ccrawfordwriting.com.

Blog: https://www.ccrawfordwriting.com/blog.

Facebook: https://www.facebook.com/ccrawfordwriting/

Instagram: https://www.instagram.com/ccrawfordwriting/

YouTube: https://www.youtube.com/ccrawfordwriting

Discord: https://www.ccrawfordwriting.com/join-my-discord-server.

Or contact me directly at **ccrawford@ccrawfordwriting.com.** I'd love to see your comments and respond to any questions you might have. Thank you so much for reading!

# ACKNOWLEDGMENTS

This series is the hardest – and most fulfilling – thing I have written to date. I believed in this story from the beginning, but it took me over a decade to finally be ready to write it, and what you just read is the result of a combination of sheer stubborn refusal to give up, lots of coffee, doubt, prayer... and help. There were so many moments when I felt as lost in this story as Lex himself, when I doubted the whole project, buried it for a while, and then pulled it out again and agonized over it, still at a complete loss as to how best to tell the story. This story that began as a spark of an idea over ten years ago is *finally* written. It has been through so many versions, and has grown and changed... the map and its world are still the same I hand-drew in pencil on a folded piece of paper over a decade ago, but the story it holds is simultaneously so much more than I ever imagined it could become, and yet somehow exactly what I believed it could be. For that, I have no explanation except that I had help... from flashes of inspiration, and from a whole slew of friends and family and support people.

It takes a writer to write a book, and in my case, it takes a village to keep that writer from going crazy in the process. *Special thanks to*:

My husband, Jason, for protecting my writing time like it was a real job (even when it wasn't yet making money!), and for listening to all my ideas but never trying to read over my shoulder while I wrote. And to my kids, for the head bumps and encouragement and understanding that my writing time is important to me... and for your absolute, pure belief in me that makes me belief in myself again.

To my alpha readers, Christy Freeman, Beth Burnett, MJ Padgett, and Kimberly McCauley: Thank you for joining me on this crazy train *while it was still in motion!* You trusted me not to make us all crash and burn. At times, that was probably unfounded, but I love you for it. Your feedback gave me the encouragement to keep going and helped me hone my direction whenever the story began to drift. Thank you, thank you, thank you!

To my beta readers, Christy Freeman, Beth Burnett, MJ Padgett (you three were crazy enough to read parts of it more than once; thank you!), Kate Bryant, Emily Fertic, Marita Crozier, Sara Ramos, my sister Shelley Linder, my aunt Janet Hall, Jenna McCann Reynolds, and Noel Harris ... Thank you *so much* for your input and feedback on this book. You helped me catch errors, you made some stellar suggestions that improved the book so much, and you gave me such incredible, encouraging feedback. Thank you all!

And to my amazing editor, Christy Freeman, who – as you can tell from the multiple mentions – has read this book more than any one person should have to... *thank you* for listening to me ramble, for getting excited about my work, and for giving me your time and energy to ensure my book goes out into the world with its shirt buttoned and shoes tied. Your support has been such a blessing to me, I don't even really know how to express it. Thank you again and again and again!

# Don't miss out!

Visit the website below and you can sign up to receive emails whenever Crystal Crawford publishes a new book. There's no charge and no obligation.

https://books2read.com/r/B-A-HVEK-DQSEB

BOOKS 2 READ

Connecting independent readers to independent writers.

# Also by Crystal Crawford

**Legends of Arameth**
The Edge of Nothing
The Path to Paradox
The Ends of Exile
The Rise of Ardis
The Lex Chronicles Trilogy E-book Collection

**The Stalker Mystery Set**
I'm Not a Stalker
The Five Suspects
The Choice

Watch for more at ccrawfordwriting.com.

# About the Author

Crystal Crawford is a homeschooling mom of four, part-time writing teacher and non-profit Director, author, former animal trainer, and full-time introvert. Her imagination is her happy place! (But a deserted beach is nice, too.) She writes fantasy and YA, with a smattering of other genres as well, and she believes in meticulous creativity -- carefully crafted stories that impact and entertain readers. She strives to provide quality, clean fiction with strong values, and books that take readers on an exciting ride and deliver all the feels.

Read more at ccrawfordwriting.com.

Made in the USA
Monee, IL
18 May 2025

17713710R00194